THE GIRLFRIEND ZONE

LAUREN BLAKELY

Lauren Blakely Books
powered by dogs

COPYRIGHT

ABOUT THE BOOK

In my defense, I had no idea the tattooed, glasses-wearing, soulful hottie I spent one perfect day—and one unforgettable night—with was a hockey star on my father's team.

And Miles didn't know I was the coach's daughter.

That's the point of a "no-work-talk" date.

But now? He's as forbidden to me as I am to him.

When I land a new gig as the team photographer, we vow to keep it professional. We mostly succeed...except for that time after a game when he couldn't keep his talented hands off me. And, okay, maybe that other time before a road trip. But I swear, it won't happen again.

Too much is at stake—I can't risk my heart or my father's team.

But when I'm asked to dog-sit Miles's pack of rescue pups for a few weeks, I discover there's more to him than I ever imagined—a man who's genuine, thoughtful, and irresistibly real.

He looks at me like he can't believe his luck. Touches me like he never wants to let go. And listens to my hopes and fears.

My heart's getting dangerously attached. But if I follow it... am I putting everyone's dreams on the line?

Tropes: coach's daughter, the one who got away, starts with a bang, second chance vibes, age gap, forbidden hockey romance, forced proximity, workplace romance.

DID YOU KNOW?

To be the first to find out when all of my upcoming books go live click here!

PRO TIP: Add lauren@laurenblakely.com to your contacts before signing up to make sure the emails go to your inbox!

Did you know this book is also available in audio and paperback on all major retailers? Go to my website for links!

For content warnings for this title, go to my site or email me laurenblakelybooks@gmail.com.

TRIGGER WARNINGS: - parental abandonment - negative treatment/ableism related to hearing loss - explicit sexual themes, including rough sex

THE GIRLFRIEND ZONE

By Lauren Blakely
Love and Hockey #4

PRELUDE: WHEN WE MET

Last summer

1

MY FUTURE WIFE

Miles

I didn't expect to meet my future wife today.

I had other plans. But as she heads toward me in the coffee shop's doorway, I know that's who she is.

Maybe the ink on her arms does it—the stenciled flowers cascading down them—or possibly the mesmerizing sea-blue shade of her eyes. But honestly? It's probably the cute-as-all-get-out smirk she sends my way.

I'd smirk at me, too, considering the spangled and sequined mannequin I'm lugging down Fillmore Street. The full-size feathered headdress is wider than the door, and the espresso cup glued into the dummy's stiff fingers seems a little weird. No way is my future wife going to realize I'm her future husband with this level of awkward.

But I'm not the kind of guy to let a six-foot-tall faux showgirl get in the way of Fate.

The inked beauty holds open the door to the shop, and I step up to prove that chivalry isn't dead.

"I've got this." I manage to grab the door with my free hand, opening it wider so she can exit first. Inside the café, Birdie—AKA Grandma—has caught sight of the byplay and watches, eagle-eyed, from behind the counter.

The brunette with the flower tattoos sweeps her gaze over my cargo. "I hope your date appreciates what a gentleman you are," she teases as she slips past to the street.

"Actually," I lean in and stage-whisper, "she doesn't have much to say." I glance at the mannequin Birdie asked me to bring to her. Well, insisted, really. *Be a dear and grab Dolly from the foyer, will you? I need a greeter for the shop.*

"Occupational hazard, maybe," the woman deadpans. "She's trained to keep smiling no matter what."

"She does have a hell of a poker face," I agree, furrowing my brow at Dolly, then meeting the brunette's eyes again. "I can't say I know her opinions on anything, really."

"But maybe that's what you want in a date?"

"Nope. A good date needs opinions."

"Oh? Are you a fan of opinions?" She sounds doubtful as she adjusts the sweater she carries. It's September in San Francisco, which means you never know if it'll be warm or breezy—or both.

"Love them," I say definitively, matching her raised brow. "The more the merrier."

"Noted." Her tone is playful, the kind of playful that says *keep talking.*

"In fact, here's one for you," I say, leaning in just slightly as I lay the groundwork for asking her out. "The espresso here is excellent."

"You're gallant, *and* you give free hot beverage advice too? Is it my lucky day or what?"

"It's mine. That is if you want to share some of your opinions with me."

She takes a beat, likely assessing me with those curious eyes. Then she nods toward the neon menu behind the counter and gives a sly smile. "Here's one. Coffee drinks are vile."

"That's a bold statement to make in a coffee bar."

She rolls her beautiful blue eyes. "A '*bold*' statement? Really?"

I grin, delighted that the future Mrs. Falcon has the quick wits and sense of humor to catch that. "What? You don't like coffee or coffee puns?"

"I like good puns." Her lips twitch in a sly, bewitching smile.

With my free hand, I clutch my chest melodramatically. "You wound me."

"I'm made of pure marshmallow fluff when it comes to helping out my grandmother."

Her brow arches in a playful challenge. "Did you really just drop that helping out a grandma bit to let me know you're the kind of guy who helps out his grandmother?"

Taking my arm from Dolly's shoulder I gesture to the inside of the café—a perfect place for a date. It's preseason but there's no hockey practice tomorrow, so why not lock in the chance right now? "Maybe I did. I'd be happy to explain more over a not-coffee beverage of your choice."

She taps her to-go cup with polished black nails. "I'm a green tea girl."

"This is great. You think coffee is vile and prefer to drink something that smells like a just-mown lawn. Look at all the opinions we have."

"So many more to learn, I'm sure," she says and we're this close to a date, but then she dips her face and checks her phone screen.

It's in her hand, and from the looks of it, someone's calling, but I didn't hear it ring.

Odd. I'd think it was a *save me* tactic, but her phone flashes with the word *Dad*.

She raises her face, her smile fading, and the playful atmosphere shifts. Before she answers though, she looks my way once more. "I hope you get to enjoy your next not-coffee date," she says. Then, with maybe some reluctance in her expression, she turns away and answers her phone in a warm voice, "Hi, Dad."

She walks up the street. Away from me.

I stand there for a second, weighing what just happened. Did she actually turn me down or did she leave the door open? I'd like to think that was a bread-crumb—*not-coffee date*—but she could just be phenomenally smooth. I'm not sure. But then, I remind myself this wasn't going to be as easy as asking her out right here, right now. Nothing good comes easily. I watch her go, admiring her attitude, her sass, her banter, and, well, let's be blunt—her ass.

But what gets me most is when she reaches the corner. It's almost imperceptible—just a quick glance over her shoulder—but I see it. She steals a final glance at me.

Yes. Fuck yes.

It was a breadcrumb, and I will take it. Follow it. And devise a plan.

I pump a mental fist, then haul Dolly inside High Kick Coffee, past chattering customers camped out at tables and a handful of people waiting to place their orders. Birdie has plenty of employees here to tend to them, but she opened a coffee shop because she likes people as much as she likes bling. In typical Birdie fashion, everything in High Kick Coffee sparkles, from the countertops to the mirrors on the walls to the clock with a woman's leg kicking back and forth to keep time.

I prop Dolly out of the way behind the counter as my grandmother starts an espresso for me. "Tell me the brunette with the flower tattoos is a regular," I say, thoughts still centered on the woman who's gotten away for now.

"Why? Are you in love already?" Birdie teases with a knowing grin.

"More like insta-infatuation," I admit, leaning on the counter. "But sure, call it love."

Birdie's smile widens. "The woman with the flower tattoos is a photographer. We're working together soon." She gestures to her old showgirl photos hanging behind the counter—pictures of her kicking her leg high while wearing spangled bikinis and feathered headdresses. "Time to update the pics, don't you think?"

I try to imagine Grandma dusting off her sequins and feathers to recreate her glory days on the Vegas stage. Is she serious about the photo shoot? She did insist I drag Dolly all the way from her home to her coffee shop after this morning's practice. When my grandmother has a vision, I wouldn't put anything past her.

"New photos sound great." I lean my elbows on the counter in an oh-so-casual way. "Especially if you let me know when you're doing them."

"We haven't picked a date yet."

"But you will," I predict.

"I will," she says with a sly smile. "Eager much?"

I shrug. "I know what I like. What's her name?"

"Leighton," Birdie says. "She comes in about once a week."

"Leighton," I echo, enjoying the sound of it. "Perfect. I'd hate to miss her, so I guess I'll be stopping by every day till I ask her out."

Birdie laughs, shaking her head. "You were always my most determined grandchild. Now, be a dear and put Dolly by the door. She has a job to do."

"Right." I carry the mannequin to the front where she can welcome customers to High Kick Coffee—where the caffeine comes with an extra kick.

Before I duck back into the shop, I sneak one last look up the street.

You'll be back, Leighton, and so will I.

I return to the counter as Birdie steps around the counter to the stool I always sit in.

"How was practice?" she asks, eyeing me over the steaming espresso she slides my way.

"Great," I say, pride surging through me. "Playing better than ever."

"You've worked so hard. I'm not surprised," Birdie says.

"I think it's more that I have the best coach." I owe Coach everything. I'm still grateful for the chance he gave me when my career was circling the drain a couple years ago. My last team let me go, and for a while there, I was sure my hockey days were done.

Now, everything's looking up—and has been for my last couple of seasons with the Sea Dogs.

Especially with my future wife coming back next week.

So I can buy her a cup of tea and hear more of her opinions.

2

VERITABLE STUD

Leighton

Does High Kick Coffee grow hot guys? There are at least six seriously attractive men in this bustling coffee shop, with its retro vibe and mid-century sophisticated playlist of Cole Porter tunes and Ella Fitzgerald jazz standards. Something my dad would listen to when he's alone in his office. He has such Dad taste.

And let's not forget that gorgeous guy with the opinions and the showgirl mannequin. His heated eyes and cocky smile have been living rent-free in my head for three days.

Okay, where is the guy I'm meeting? None of the cuties here match the photo of the model I hired to pose with my new client, Katrina, this afternoon. His name is Crash and he fit the bill for the client—young, sexy, and confident—a veritable stud. He even sent me a video saying, "I'll make Katrina feel like a queen."

Sold.

I hired him for her first boudoir shoot since she divorced her lying, cheating, conniving scumbag of a husband who banged the babysitter.

Her words.

Mine were *Thank you for trusting me with your pics*.

I also promised her I'd meet with the model before I photograph them together later today. Just to make sure he's not a dick.

I whip out my phone, scrolling through Crash's photos as I shuffle into the line to grab a tea and figure out which guy I'll be paying today. That's when my phone rings—directly in my ears of course.

Veritable Stud flashes on the screen, and I smile, relieved Crash is calling. I swipe to answer, then peer around to see which of these guys is on his phone.

Not a one.

With a foreboding feeling, I say, "Hey, Crash. Are you almost here?"

"Yeah, about that..." His apologetic tone is not a good sign. "I totally messed up the days. My bad."

No kidding, it's your bad. But this is the other reason I wanted to meet him early.

"It's okay," I say. It's not, but I can make this work. "When do you think you'll be here?"

There's a mix of apology and excitement in his tone. "Yeah, I'm in line for *The Undead Infected Brainmeat Part Six*, and if I leave, I'll lose my place."

Classic. Men are such clown cars of excuses. You never know which excuse is coming, but they never fail to surprise you with a new one popping up.

"But this is the date you agreed to," I point out diplomatically, clinging to faint hope. "We were depending on you."

Katrina deserves to feel beautiful today, dammit.

I've been working my butt off building my photography business—from boudoir to fashion and even to sports—since I graduated from college last year. I just returned to San Francisco a few months ago, and this shoot is a big chance for me to build my own boudoir business. I pride myself on making my clients feel like the beautiful, empowered goddesses they are.

GODDESSES DO NOT GET STOOD UP FOR ZOMBIE GAMES!

"Where are you in line?" I ask. "I could push the shoot to later today."

"Yeah, about that..." But he doesn't mean yeah. He means nah. "After I get it, I'm gonna play it."

Crash is a trainwreck. "Fine," I say before hanging up. "Have fun with that."

I don't have time for *I can't believe this is happening*. I need a backup plan.

I open my contacts list for online agencies that might deliver in a hurry, then realize I've reached the counter. There, I'm greeted by none other than Birdie LaShay, the owner of High Kick Coffee, rocking a pink feather boa like she's still on stage.

"What's wrong, sweetie? Did someone disappoint you?"

"Is it that obvious?" I sigh.

She nods. "You have that look. The 'he's not showing up' look." She lowers her voice. "App guy? Those apps are trouble."

I drop my head into my hands. "I only wish it were a date letting me down."

She arches a brow, humming. "So, you're single?"

I nod. "Very, very single."

Her lips twitch into a smile before she schools her expression. "Is it your father? Sometimes they let you down too."

But my dad wouldn't. "It's work. Crash ditched me for virtual zombies." I glance at the café clock. "I have a boudoir shoot and an hour and a half to find a replacement hunk."

Her smile brightens. "Don't worry, darling. You'll have plenty of time to prepare because I've already solved your problem. Just like that." She snaps her fingers and tosses her boa over her shoulder with dramatic flair.

"Do you have a hot barista stashed behind the counter?" I ask.

She leans in conspiratorially to whisper, "Even better. My grandson—handsome as they come—has a rest day today."

"A rest day from what?"

Her eyes dart sideways for a second, and she talks faster. "Cooking. It's very intense. Have you seen that show *The Cub*? The one about the chef in Seattle? He looks like that. Inked too."

Okay, *okay*. I'm officially interested. I've only gotten to know Birdie a little over the last few weeks, and I had no idea what her grandson did. But a chef could work for my photographic needs. A good chef is used to the spotlight. A good chef has posed for a few pics. A good chef also knows how to focus his attention elsewhere—on the food. "Is he a good chef?"

"Oh, yes. And he looks just like the guy from that show," she adds with a proud grin. "But with darker hair. Dark eyes. Will that work for your photos?"

Yes, chef. I know the popular show she means. "If he's even close, I'll be in your debt."

Her grin widens. "Trust me, honey. I know exactly what I'm doing here."

As she whips out her phone, something tugs at my brain. A connection. I turn my gaze to the doorway, where the fabulously dressed mannequin welcomes customers. The coffee-loving guy from the other day *did* say he was helping his grandmother, but that doesn't mean he's the same guy. Does it?

But I dismiss the thought and the little burst of excitement that comes with it too, focusing instead on Birdie. She's a lifesaver and her fingers fly faster than a teenager's across the screen before she sets it down. "I texted him. Now, give me your digits," she says, trying to sound trendy, and it's adorable.

I comply, happily handing over my number. She beckons me to hand over the to-go cup I always carry. "Now, let me get you your green tea, sweetie pie. You're going to need your energy for this photo shoot. I know it's going to be amazing."

Quickly, she pours me a tea.

I pay and thank her, but before I can head back out onto Fillmore Street, she says, "Oh, and Leighton?"

"Yes?"

She beckons me closer and whispers, "Best not to ask about work. He's a little shy about that."

I smile. "That's sweet."

"Yes, isn't it? He's so talented *and* so humble."

"Winning combo," I say.

She simply smiles, looking pleased to have solved my dilemma.

Leaving the café, I text Katrina with an update. As I turn toward the studio space I rent when I can, I glimpse a familiar looking guy on the other side of the street. Except for his glasses, he *does* remind me of the man with the mannequin the other day. First dates can be complicated and romance even more so, but I've been hoping I'd run into him again.

Just not right now.

When I have no time to entertain so much as the idea of a good-looking man.

Not even the ridiculously handsome man I might have dreamed about since I met him.

I need to prep the studio. Take the pictures for my client. Do an amazing job.

And I really need Birdie's grandson to be my hero today, whether he's the guy from the other day or not.

3

THE UNDERGROUND GRANDMA
MATCHMAKING SOCIETY

Miles

We're going to have words, Birdie and me.

I stride into High Kick after just missing Leighton. I'd spotted her hustling up the block in the opposite direction, but I didn't stop her or call out because, one, that's creepy. And two, that's really fucking creepy.

But Birdie is in big trouble with me. I march to the counter and park my hands on it.

"Why didn't you text me that my wife was here?" I ask, narrowing my eyes in displeasure. "I planned to be here sooner, but after practice, Coach called us into the video room to review some things."

Birdie tugs on her pink feather boa like it's the source of her many grandmotherly superpowers. "Do you think I don't have anything better to do than text you?" she asks breezily.

"Name a better use of your time than giving me the chance to ask her out." I sigh and shake my head in disappointment. But really, I'm shocked. Birdie has been dying to set me up since Joanne and I split a few years ago. The world assumed our relationship petered out when I moved to San Francisco to join the Sea Dogs. In reality, she'd had enough of an injured boyfriend who'd spent the better part of a year in a low-level funk. And, I get that. I had enough of myself too.

But that's the past, as Birdie likes to remind me. So why would my grandmother miss a golden romance opportunity?

"Well..." Birdie draws out the word with a sly smile. "Leighton and I talked about her job. That was very important."

"So, while you discussed your headshots and whatnot, you didn't once think, 'My favorite grandchild in the universe would jump at this opportunity to meet her properly'?"

She straightens, chin up as if offended. "I was helping her with an emergency. She was stood up for a photo shoot."

I bristle, my mood shifting. Lip curled, I hiss, "Who would do that to her?"

Birdie looks devilishly delighted. "I knew you'd feel that way. That's why I told her you'd pose for her."

I blink, speechless, trying to come up with a reasonable explanation—like Birdie wants to join some secret underground grandma matchmaking society and this is part of her initiation.

Fine by me. But I don't want to seem too eager, so I say, "Just to clarify—you volunteered me as tribute...for a photo shoot?"

She takes off her feather boa and wraps it around my neck, holding the ends like a glittery lasso. "You heard me,

Miles Falcon. If I rely on fate to put you both here at the same time, you'll never get the chance to ask her out. So I made things happen."

"Forgive me for ever doubting you," I say.

"You're forgiven," she says haughtily, releasing her grip on the feathered noose.

"Good," I lean in like we're going for a pre-game briefing on the opposing team, "Give me the details. Does she know who I am?"

"I only said you're my grandson." Her brown eyes shift away from mine. "But take some grandmotherly advice. Don't talk about hockey."

I frown. "Why would I? The photo shoot isn't on the ice, is it?"

"Nothing like that." She puts her hands on her hips as if I'm a kid again. "My point is that women don't want to hear a man blather on and on about his job. Talk about other things. Hobbies, pets, the city, the last great movie you saw, your favorite song." Her face brightens with an idea. "You could take her geocaching. You love to do that, and solving all those treasure hunt clues is a fun way to get to know each other."

None of this is bad advice, but I'm baffled about why she thinks I need it. Does she think I'm that hopeless in the romance department?

"Got it. But, so you know, I wasn't planning to discuss hockey."

"Of course you weren't, dear." She smiles and pats my arm. "I just have to look out for you, you know."

"Yes, I'm sure it's all part of your work in The Underground Grandma Matchmaking Society."

"That's brilliant! If no such group exists, I'm going to start one."

"No one would be better." I steer the convo back to more relevant intel. "So, does she know I'm the guy who ran into her outside the shop the other day? The one with the mannequin and the opinions?" Fuck it, those details don't matter. I wave them away. "I'll take care of all that. Where do I need to go? And when is it? Please say 'today,' because we're leaving tomorrow for away games."

Birdie tuts at my concerns. "Oh, sweetheart. You speak as if I don't know your schedule by heart. The appointment is in about an hour." She glances pointedly at the ticking clock then back at me.

Tick-tock, get moving. She doesn't need to tell me twice.

If I leave for the final pre-season road trip without at least getting something started with Leighton, I know in my gut that I'll regret it.

"I'm there." I wheel around to take off, but then spin back. "Where is 'there,' exactly? And what kind of photo shoot?" I'm not going to miss this opportunity, but I also don't want to show up unprepared.

Mischief flicks across Birdie's eyes. "The kind where all you have to do is take off your pants."

I freeze, not sure I heard that right. Yes, I'm shocked—shocked at how perfect that sounds. I head to the door, stop, and then remove the feathered boa.

"You don't like the accessory?" Birdie asks innocently as I return to the counter.

"Love it." I place it in her hand with a grin. "But I'll just have to take it off anyway, right?"

"You were always my smart one."

And a smart guy doesn't miss chances.

* * *

Walking down the Hayes Valley street, I check my reflection in the window of a record shop up the block from Leighton's studio. Dark button-down, sleeves rolled up. Jeans, motorcycle boots, black glasses. I can't wear glasses on the ice, but I swapped out my contacts after practice.

I've got none of the telltale signs of an athlete. No hoodie, no sneakers—Birdie doesn't want me to talk hockey? That's easy enough. I didn't get two bachelor's degrees for nothing.

I drag a hand through my messy hair, which has been wild my whole life, and continue down the block. The guy in my reflection looks composed. But inside, I ping with excitement, and the focused awareness I get before I step onto the ice. When my world narrows to the game, nothing but the game, I block out everything else.

Turning at Elodie's Chocolates, I count the street numbers, and just past Risqué Business, I spot a white door tucked between storefronts. On the list of businesses labeling the buzzer panel, I find Hush Hush Photography.

I press the button.

A few seconds later, a pretty voice asks through the speaker, "Hi! Is that Miles?"

"That's me."

I don't mention I'm the guy about to ask her out on a date.

"I'm on the second floor. Come on up."

She buzzes me in, and I bound up the narrow stairway. There are a couple of businesses on the second floor, but the red door is unmissable. A vintage sign with lovely feminine lettering reads *Hush Hush*.

I raise my hand to knock, and the door swings open.

Fuck me, she's gorgeous. A black shirt slopes down her

shoulder, exposing creamy flesh I want to kiss. Long jeans dust the floor, and I bet they'd look great *on* the floor too. The silver bracelets jangling on her wrists draw attention to the fine black lines of the flower patterns crawling up her forearms. But my eyes keep returning to her face. Chestnut waves frame her high cheekbones while long silver teardrops dangle from her ears. Her pink lips are slick with gloss. Her eyes are big, beautiful pools of blue. They flicker in surprise, but also with something like intrigue.

She tilts her head, her long earrings dangling. Her smile takes its sweet time forming as she looks me up and down slowly, like she's savoring a scotch, taking a bite of decadent chocolate, watching a sunrise. "It's you."

"It's me."

"Did you bring your opinions?" she asks.

"Only if you brought yours."

"I guess we'll see." She lifts her index finger, gesturing to my face. Her nails are polished in shiny black. "You didn't have on glasses the other day."

"You noticed."

"I'm a photographer. It's my job to notice things."

"Are the glasses a problem? I can manage without them for the shoot."

She studies me like she enjoys the question, or maybe making me wait for her answer. Finally, she gives a flirty shrug. "There might be a glare but I can edit it out. They're too sexy to take off."

I don't smile nearly as broadly as I want to. "I knew I'd appreciate your opinions."

"Well, then." She holds the door open. "Come in and stay a while."

"I think I will."

I step inside and look around.

Wow.

This isn't a date, but it's the perfect setting for one. From the bed at the center with its satiny duvet to the sapphire blue chaise longue to the ruby red chair and white, fluffy rug, the studio oozes sensual vibes.

And if there were ever a better wingman than this studio—or wingwoman—I wouldn't believe it.

4
————

STOP THINKING OF ARTICHOKES
AND HOT MEN

Leighton

I have the feeling that Birdie is up to something. It couldn't be that she sent her ridiculously hot grandson to be an underwear stand-in. Not a random grandson, either, but the guy who was *this close* to asking me out the last time we crossed paths.

As someone who adores her own Grams, I have mad respect for this level of matchmaking puppetry.

Only I don't have time for it right now. Katrina will be here in twenty minutes, and this shoot is too important for me to get lost in the flirting zone with this hot chef with his hot, thigh-hugging jeans, and the shirt sleeves that can't hide the breadth of his biceps or the strength of his shoulders. The rolled cuffs reveal a leather bracelet and a tattoo of an arrow on the fair skin of his muscular forearm. He looks strong for a chef. Must be all those cast-iron skillets he lifts. Yes, this man can cook me artichokes anytime.

Stop thinking of artichokes and hot men.

I shake off thoughts of two of my favorite things and get down to brass tacks.

"Birdie told you about the shoot?" I'd bet she didn't disclose much.

"She said you're a boudoir photographer," Miles says, gesturing to the studio space, with its bed and plush furniture meant to showcase sensuality and luxury. "But I can pick up the context clues too."

I toss him a look. Hush Hush studio is run by a more seasoned photographer who is, of course, not here at the moment because I've booked it for the rest of the day. But he doesn't need the details of just how new I am to the job. I've got a few gigs under my belt as well as my assistant work. And, really, I *am* a boudoir photographer, though it's not all I shoot.

I gesture to the emerald velvet curtains, then the red satin sheets. "Did something give it away?" I ask innocently, looking at him when I talk. I find that often *trains* people to do the same for me, before I know them well enough to ask them to look my way. It's a tricky balance since some men misread prolonged eye contact. But if I don't look at him, I might miss something he says. My hearing loss is only moderate, so I can hear well enough but it's still helpful to see someone's facial expressions and their lips moving as they talk. Those details can fill in the gaps with softer sounds that are harder to hear.

There's nothing soft about Miles though. Not his body, or his words as he tips his forehead toward the obvious centerpiece of the room—the ruby red velvet chair. "Hard to say. Probably just a vibe," he says, coolly, casually, but with that undercurrent of sex in his voice.

And loss or no loss, I can hear and read his tone perfectly.

Come to think of it, there's always been a hint of sex in his voice. And it's dangerous—the gravel in his tone sends a charge through me. He doesn't talk like a guy my age. Like a twenty-three-year-old dude bro who sends thirst traps of himself in gray sweatpants with pecs that move on their own. Miles talks like a man, with a little mileage on him, and the knowledge that comes with experience.

I turn away from him so I don't get swept up in this lust. "I should finish setting up."

"Can I help?" he asks, and he's close enough that I can still hear him.

"I'm good, but walk with me, and I'll give you the details." I tell him a little about my boudoir style— empowering and focused on making *her* feel beautiful— as I adjust the lighting, then head to the dressing room where I've set up a wardrobe. Katrina's bringing her own outfits, but I always keep options on hand—silky robes, lace, stockings, dress shirts. I have plenty of those, along with a dozen pairs of black heels in every size.

"So, here's the plan for today," I say as I wrap up the tour.

"I know nothing about boudoir, but I'm a fast learner. Tell me what you need me to do," he says, his voice steady, a ballplayer ready to step up to the plate.

"Katrina isn't doing a typical couples shoot—she's not part of a couple anymore. Most of her shots will be solo, traditional boudoir shots, focusing on the woman, so we won't need you the whole time. But since the whole point of the shoot is empowerment, when we bring you in, we want you to focus on her. *Only her*. Even if she's not inter-acting with you. Or looking at you."

My goal is to make her an object of desire rather than to show the interplay of desire.

"Got it," he says with a nod, like he's recording these details. "Where do you want me?"

I take a beat to let the double meaning roll over me. "For a few, we want her sitting in this chair." I gesture to the plush red chair that screams luxury. "And you'll be on the bed, shirtless and in jeans. The bed is just a few feet away, and most of the time, she won't be entirely in focus. The shot will be about..." I stop, collecting my thoughts, before I give him the specific direction, "It'll be about your desire *for her*. The way you look *at her*. Like she's beautiful. Like you can't look away. Like you want her desperately. Okay?"

He nods, his eyes never leaving mine. "Like I want her desperately," he repeats.

The air crackles and it's so clear he's not talking about another woman.

But I stick to the plan. "You're comfortable with that?" I ask. It's important that he understands the type of photography I do—the consent and trust involved. It's not pornographic; no one will be having sex, of course. But he needs to be comfortable with the heightened sexuality in the shoot.

"One hundred percent," he says. "What else do you need?"

For you to stop turning me on with the way you listen.

"I want some shots where..." I pause then explain, "you're getting up, like you're prowling toward her. Same idea. You need to have her."

His dark brown eyes lock onto mine, deep and mesmerizing, flecked with gold at the edges. There's a line between his thick eyebrows. I bet he's ten years older than

I am. I wish I didn't find it so sexy, the age difference. But I do, especially his intensity now here in the studio, even though it's unnerving too. I know I can use it in the photos if he can channel it, and that's what matters. "And I want to *feel* that in the photos. Can you do that?" My voice sounds breathy as I ask it. Too breathy.

A slow smile shifts the corners of his lips. "I think I can, Leighton," he says, low and raspy, but still deliciously deep. "Should I just think about something I really want?"

The fucker. He knows what he's doing to me. His gaze doesn't waver, and there's something about the way he looks at me from behind those glasses that seems like he knows things a man should know. I feel like my panties are slipping off from the way he's looking at me.

"Yes," I manage to say, trying to hide the way I feel since I don't know what to expect from him.

Maybe that's why I walked away from him the other day. I wasn't sure if he meant it when he asked me out on a date. First dates are their own kind of hell. I don't love to spend an hour with a stranger—let alone share with him the things I don't love sharing. That's why I don't jump at the chance to have tea with strangers, even ones as tempting as Miles. Getting to know someone takes trust. I trust my family, my sister, and my friends. Above all, I trust myself. But anyone else? Not so much.

I snap back to the present and continue. "The goal with this shoot is for Katrina to feel like she's the star of the show, and you're here to shine a light on her."

"I think I can do that," Miles says, his voice as steady as ever. "I can definitely get the hang of that."

I wasn't entirely sure if the sparks between us were real the other day. But they're so real now, shimmying down my spine, heat pooling low in my belly.

This is bad. I can't start a boudoir session feeling turned on. I can't be thinking about a model while I'm shooting Katrina. I push the lust away, praying he can't sense it. But the fact that he's so focused on me—it's unraveling me. And I can't afford to unravel.

I tug at my neckline, adjusting it, looking for something tactile so I can stay rooted in the moment. "I hope you wore your best underwear. If not, I've got black boxer briefs in all sizes," I say, as clinical as possible. Yet discussing what he'll wear—when he soon takes off other clothes—feels anything but professional. "I'll go grab them," I add quickly, turning to the wardrobe, hoping he didn't notice the way my skin heated just being near him.

"Leighton," he calls out.

I spin around. "Yes?" My voice sounds squeaky.

"I already wear black boxer briefs. I can show them to you if you want," he says with a tease on his mouth. His lush, sexy, flirty mouth that belongs to a man, not a boy.

Never have I wanted a man to strip so badly. That's why I say, "You know what? I'm just going to trust you on that."

"Fair enough. And I'll trust you to help me focus on the client. I can tell this is important to you," he says, his tone serious. All the flirting has been stripped away now. "I want it to go well."

Holy shit. He's not flirting—he actually cares about my job.

And that only makes me like him more. "Thank you. That means a lot to me—that opinion."

"Good," he says with a smile that's too disarming.

I turn around for real, vowing to take several deep breaths and focus entirely on the client who's about to arrive. I steady my breathing as I check my Nikon's settings. I have the lens perfectly adjusted, when my phone buzzes with an incoming text and I scan it.

Dad: Still on for breakfast tomorrow at the usual?

I told Birdie he'd never disappoint me. He's the most dependable person I know. Just like how he's never missed a game coaching the Sea Dogs in five years, he'd never miss a breakfast with his daughter.

I write back that I can't wait, then tuck my phone away to focus on the guy who's with me. Briefly, I imagine introducing Miles to my dad at some point. After a few dates.

And...that's a risky thought. One best ignored for now. Good thing my phone rings— in my ears—shifting my focus. It's probably Katrina looking for parking. That's a state of life in San Francisco.

I hit answer. "Hey, Katrina, are you here? The lot can be hard to find, but I can tell you where it is."

"I'm so sorry. My youngest is sick. The school just called, and I need to go pick him up. His dad's out of town, and my mom's at work. I know I paid a nonrefundable retainer, but I just can't make it today."

My shoulders sag. I pinch the bridge of my nose. "I'm so sorry he's sick. Of course we can reschedule."

She promises to get back to me soon, and when I hang up, I turn to find Miles sitting on the edge of the bed, looking at me expectantly. "She's not coming?"

"Did you hear that? Our conversation?" I ask, surprised. The phone connects with my hearing aids, so any noise or sound from my phone goes directly into my ears.

He shakes his head. "No, but I could see the disappointment in your eyes."

Oh. He's good with facial expressions too. That's... interesting. Unusual too. He pauses, his gaze thoughtful. "You really wanted this to happen today, didn't you? Not just for her—for yourself too?"

I swallow. He's been flirty, direct, and clever, but this...this understanding side of him? The way he reads me? It's all new to me. And because it is, I choose honesty. "I was really looking forward to it," I admit. "I had some great ideas. Some new poses I wanted to capture."

The studio goes quiet. I can almost see the gears turning in his mind. Then he stands, strides over to me, and offers me a hand. "Use me. Show me what you wanted to do." He steps even closer—dangerously so. "Practice with me."

5

JUST LIKE THAT

Leighton

I have steady hands. No one wants a photographer with shaky fingers, so I have half a mind to reprimand myself as I set the Nikon on the tripod carefully, fighting against my own nerves.

Am I really doing this? Filling in for my client with the sick kid? And doing it with the guy who's standing in for a zombie hunter—Birdie's grandson, no less?

I could change my mind. I could say, *you know what? There's no need for this, but I appreciate the offer.* Except, one glance around the studio I share with other boudoir photographers—the studio I booked *and* paid for today—and I'm not sure I can find a reasonable excuse to back out.

It's not against a photographer's code of conduct.

I'm not stealing time from someone else.

The only issue is me, and the attraction I feel for this man. I don't want it to get in the way of my judgment.

So yeah, I can do this but with some rules. I need control over this shoot, over myself. It's not that I don't trust him—I don't trust how easily he could make me drop my guard. I've spent too long building my walls to let them crumble in one afternoon.

"Why don't we try with clothes on?" I say, because that feels a little safer.

He nods easily. "Whatever you want."

It feels like he means that—on a deep and real level. Like this man wants to give me my wishes and dreams.

But really, it's best I focus those on photography so I don't get carried away.

I mentally cycle through the poses I had planned for Katrina. I know exactly which ones I want to start with. I've been dying to try these out.

First, I turn on a playlist from my phone, letting it pipe into a portable speaker. I don't mind the quiet, but music helps nearly everyone relax during a shoot, mostly so they aren't simply hearing the echo of their own thoughts. Plus, I'm used to the faint background tunes as I work. Once a soft, sultry tune drifts around the studio, I point to the bed, nerves buzzing through me even as I take control.

"Lie down. Unbutton your shirt." That's exactly what I'd say to him if Katrina were here posing too. But she's not here, so the command feels entirely personal.

Like it's me giving it to the man I flirted with at the coffee shop, rather than the photographer to the model.

I'm not sure if that's good or bad.

Or just...reality today.

I expect him to strip as he walks over to the bed a few feet away, but instead, he watches me, tilting his head to the side, then slowly undoes his buttons, one by one, until his shirt falls open, revealing strong pecs that taper into stronger abs. A smattering of dark chest hair draws my eyes, especially as it trails down his abs and disappears into his jeans.

I've photographed countless bodies before. I know how to admire form without letting it get to me. But this feels different—it feels personal. His casual confidence makes me want to drop my defenses, and that scares me. It's not just his body—it's the way he carries himself. It's like he's daring me to trust him.

Pretty sure he's also daring me to look at him, so I indulge in the offered view. I'm tempted to comment on his six-pack—heck, it's even an eight-pack. To say, *"Who knew carting a few dozen heads of cabbage could shape abs like that?"*

But Birdie said not to mention what he does for a living. So I don't. He's probably an Internet chef or something. I don't even ask his last name.

All I know is Miles The Hot Chef is a man unfazed by partial nudity. A man who knows what he brings to the table. "Will this do?" he asks with confidence and certainty. I'm not used to men who speak like this. The guys I dated in college and since I graduated last year always seem like they're either trying too hard or running away when they learn I'm, well, *complicated*.

He seems so comfortable, as if he's done this a hundred times. But there's something in the way his eyes follow me, like he knows exactly what I'm thinking. Like he's offering himself up but also watching me closely to see if I'll accept.

"That'll do," I say, trying to stay composed even as heat races through me.

He undoes his boots and takes off his socks, then his watch too, setting it down on a table. He heads to the bed and there, he stretches out on it, not needing instructions. It's like he knows exactly how I want him to look. He parks his hands behind his head, stretches out his long legs. He's relaxed but poised. "You said I should look like I want her, right?"

I swallow roughly, my mouth suddenly dry. "Yes. Please. That would be great."

"Good, because I should really look that way right now," he says, in a faint voice, but still I can make it out.

My heart is beating so fast, I swear he can hear it.

I really need to concentrate on the task at hand, not on the way he makes me feel. The way he watches me too. While I know guys my age can and do wear glasses, there's something about them that makes a man seem...more mature. Like, he's settled into who he is. Or maybe that's how Miles comes across.

Tearing my gaze away from him, I ensure the composition is just how I want it, with both of us in the frame even though we won't be touching. I adjust the focus so the camera will follow him if he moves, then grab the tiny remote I can use to trigger the shutter. With that in my hand and everything ready, I move to the plush red chair and sit down, drawing a deep, steadying breath.

"Just watch me," I tell him, but that feels redundant since he's done nothing else since he started taking his clothes off.

"Easy enough," he says.

I lean back, letting my hair fall down my spine, pushing my chest up, my legs stretched out in front of me —a classic pose that any good dancer knows how to use. The kind that comes in quite handy in boudoir.

But this pose doesn't feel like it has before when I've snapped self-portraits. Nor does it feel like it has the times when I've shot couples where he's mere inches from her, about to touch her. The small space between us makes me feel watched in a whole new way. I feel admired. Out of the corner of my eye, I can tell Miles is staring like he can't look away. I trigger the shutter, and then there's a click, then the flash.

I slide my hand into my hair on the right side—the side he can't see right now.

Another press. Another click.

I move my hand down my chest.

Then a few more clicks.

I break the pose and glance over at him, and he speaks first. "Did that work for you?"

Not *How'd I do?*

His concern is only me. On giving me what I want. Or really, what I need.

Normally, I'd check the back of the camera myself, but nothing about this shoot is normal anymore, least of all the charge in the air, the ions crackling between us, the heat shimmering in this space. "Do you want to see?" I offer as I rise.

He's up in no time, standing next to me as we peer at the viewfinder together. He's close enough that I can smell him. Clean and soapy, with a hint of sandalwood or something darker—something earthy and warm. The scent wraps around me like a slow, steady pulse and it goes straight to my head, fogging up everything else.

I'd like to say I'm affected by scent as much as the next girl, but I think I'm more affected. What I've lost in one sense, I more than compensate for with others. My eyes rival an eagle's. My nose is nearly as good as a dog's. Sometimes that's annoying. Today, it's intoxicating and heady as I breathe in that hint of cologne or aftershave while I scroll through the pictures.

In every picture, I'm soft, a little out of focus, but he's not. Miles is looking only at me, like he doesn't want to miss a single small shift I make from shot to shot, my fingers in my hair, my hand sliding down my chest.

Yes. This is exactly what I wanted to capture—the moment when desire ignites. The moment before it turns into touch. The anticipation of what's to come.

"It's good," I say softly but what I really mean is *you're good.*

And that's hard to say. I'm wary of getting too personal, even though everything with him feels very, *very* personal.

"Yeah, I think your model's delivering exactly what you're looking for," Miles says, his deep voice sending a fresh wave of heat through me. He turns, his eyes locking on mine. "What do you think? It's like I want her, right?"

He's so steady, so sure, and that certainty in his tone both excites me and knocks me off-kilter. He's waiting for me to take my turn. Wanting me to keep going.

I really shouldn't do this. I really shouldn't flirt with him. I'm crossing a line here—my own line of trust on a first date. I don't like to get this close. And yet...

"Yes. You look like you want her. You seem to be nailing it on the first try," I reply, throwing the flirt right back.

His grin deepens. "Do you want me to look like I'm about to get up and prowl toward you next? Like I need to have you?"

I swallow again, the tension rising between us. He's remembering everything I told him. And he's taking control. "I do."

He moves to the edge of the bed, sitting down, elbows

on his knees, hands clasped just under his chin. A strong, masculine pose. Full of energy, even though he's not moving. "Will this work?"

God, he looks like a sinful portrait already. I'll call it *A Man on Edge*.

Actually, this wasn't on the shot list—him solo. But I want it anyway. Improvising, I grab the camera from the tripod, moving closer to him, snapping a couple of shots of him up close and personal. His face is so interesting, from the scruff lining his jaw, to the nose that's nearly straight, but not quite, to the darkest of brown eyes that crinkle slightly at the corners behind those glasses. He's not perfect, but those imperfections are doing it for me. I inch even closer, needing to capture him from every angle, wanting to record everything he's giving right now.

I stop. "Just feeling inspired," I say, explaining myself.

"Want to show them to me?"

It's dripping with invitation. I narrow the distance, sitting next to him on the bed. He leans in, his shoulder bumping mine as we look at the camera together. I can barely concentrate on the images on the back of the device. He's even closer to me than last time we checked out the shots. So close that if I turn my face, he might capture my lips in a kiss.

I blink off the thought as I pull away so I can set up the camera again on the tripod.

"So, now you want me to stalk over to you?" he asks, reminding me of the pics I want to get.

The reason we're doing this.

To test my skills. To try new things. To capture a man in motion, a man who can't stand to be away from his woman. It's an action shot of sorts, and there should be just enough room to capture him moving toward me.

Well, here goes. "I do, but it'll be a little different this time," I say.

"How?"

Am I doing this? Yes. I'm doing it. I look at those dark brown eyes, so soulful, so heated. "Sit down and find out."

I'm going off script. I take a breath, check the settings once more on the back of the camera, then move to the chair a few feet from him. Close enough that he could stretch out an arm and touch me.

The remote in my hand feels like a timer, so I reach for the hem of my shirt, then stop thinking and just act. In one swift move, the shirt is gone, leaving me in my jeans and black lace bra. The cool air hits my skin, but it's nothing compared to the heat in his eyes.

This time, I do hear him clearly—a quiet sound, almost imperceptible, but unmistakable because it can only be one thing.

A low, reverent *holy shit.*

And now, I don't feel nerves washing over me. It's power. I'm the photographer, I'm the subject, and I'm the object of his desire.

I smile, feeling like a queen—exactly how I wanted my client to feel. How Miles is making me feel.

He stands, closing the short distance between us with each trigger of the remote and *click, click, click* of the camera.

We didn't script what will come next. But he's moving next to me now, straddling the chair, sinking down behind me, his hands sliding down my arms.

"Like this?" he murmurs.

I shudder, closing my eyes, giving in as the camera clicks. "Just like that."

6

THE NEXT BEST THING

Miles

I run a hand down her arm, letting my fingers glide across her skin before setting my palm on top of hers—the hand not holding the remote. Her breath hitches—it's the most gorgeous sound I've ever heard.

I slow my movements, running my left hand over hers, curling our fingers together, drawing out the moment. As she clasps my hand in return, she sighs softly, leaning her head back. Her thick, silky hair brushes against my nose. I don't even bother pretending not to inhale it. I make a show of it, running my nose along the soft, chestnut waves.

"You smell like vanilla and brown sugar," I murmur as I drift closer to her earlobe so I can kiss her there.

She tenses though, and I'm not sure what to make of that reaction. Maybe I've gone too far. Too fast. But then she turns her head back to glance at me, pulling her body away slightly. Like there's a play I didn't expect on the ice,

I try to read her body language. But it's hard because there's a quirk in her lips now, like she's amused. "And I bet you like that—vanilla and brown sugar."

Ah, that's better. Her sass. I fucking love her confidence. I tighten my fingers around hers. "What gave it away?"

"I don't know. It's hard to say," she teases, still twisting to look at me, even as she wriggles her ass against my hard-on. And I do know how to read *that*.

"Some things are more obvious than others."

"This one seems fairly obvious," she replies, her voice a little dreamy, a little lost in the moment. But then she takes a deep breath, like she's snapping herself out of it.

Hmm.

Maybe I've been missing her cues all along? "Do you want me to stop?"

She's quiet for a beat before she says, "No."

I pause in case she says more, but she doesn't. I take her word at face value as I let go of her hands and slide mine up her arms, tracing the flowers inked into her skin. I watch the fine hairs rise under my touch while listening to her quiet gasps and the soft murmur of her breath. She melts into me, and I feel her relax, little by little. I want to kiss her right now. But I hold myself back, resisting the urge. I want to make her wait for it, but I also want to be dead sure she wants *this*.

I lift a hand to sweep her hair to the side so I can kiss the back of her neck, but the second my fingers make contact, she jerks away. "I need to...check the settings," she says.

Oh. Okay. I'm a little lost. "Sure. Go ahead," I say since I'm not really sure what she wants anymore.

She nibbles on the corner of her lips, then, like it costs

her something, she asks, "Can I take more pictures? I have a pose in mind."

Best to go with the flow. I'll chalk the earlier awkwardness up to, well, the fact that we're half-dressed in a photo studio and we hardly know each other. Intimacy is going to be awkward sometimes. It's best to talk it out though, and at least she's trying. "Take as many as you want. You're the star of the show."

She pops up to adjust the camera. Her fingers move quickly over the settings, and after a few seconds, she comes back to me. This time though, she doesn't sink onto my lap, with her back to my chest again. Instead, she straddles my thighs, so she's facing me.

Well, then. That's clear.

"This is a better pose," she says, like she needs to explain herself, when I'm so good with it.

"Whatever you want," I reply.

One hand is still curled around the remote trigger. With the other, she drags her shiny black nail down her chest, toward the swell of her breasts. "Kiss me here. For the camera."

That's all the invitation I need. I dip my head, pressing a soft kiss to her skin, instantly lost in the taste of her. Her warmth. The beat of her pulse beneath my lips. The scent of brown sugar and vanilla lingering in her hair while the camera captures the way I touch her.

I kiss my way up her chest, to her throat, flicking my tongue lightly against the hollow there. My brain short-circuits. Everything I've been holding back starts to crumble. I want to grab her face and kiss her deeply, but when I reach up to cup her cheeks and haul her close, her eyes widen—just for a second.

Fear flickers across them.

Something's wrong. "You okay?" I ask, pulling away.

"Yes, I'm great. It's fine. It's just—" She cuts herself off, not finishing her sentence.

"Do I make you uncomfortable?" I ask again, my brow furrowing.

She shakes her head adamantly. "No. I swear. I just..." She shifts a few inches back, wincing. "I don't usually kiss this fast."

Oh, fuck. I don't want her to think I'm *only* trying to get her naked, even though I'd very much like that. "I'm sorry. I shouldn't have pushed."

"You didn't," she whispers. Then she sighs heavily, closing her eyes, like something pains her. She lets go of the grip on the remote.

I feel like a total piece of shit. Except, she's not moving off me. She's still straddling me. So I wait for her to go next. When she opens her eyes a few seconds later, she sets a hand on my chest, grabbing the fabric of my shirt, twisting it in her fingers. She parts her lips, breathes out heavily again, clearly at war with herself.

I have no clue what's going on, but I do not want to make her feel uncomfortable.

"Should I leave?" I ask, trying to fix the mess I've made. "I should leave."

"Don't."

So I don't.

Another big breath, then she straightens her shoulders, gripping my shirt tighter. "I don't like to talk about this so soon," she says with a frustrated groan I didn't expect, then she finishes in a strong voice with, "I wear hearing aids. And I don't want you to touch my ears when you kiss me."

I blink. I didn't see that coming. Only because...I had

no idea. Her hair is so long, and it covers her ears, and I haven't gotten any sense that she hasn't heard me when I've spoken.

But as I roll the tape on the last few minutes, all her reactions make perfect sense—the way she tensed when I got too close to her hair, the way she moved away when I ventured near her earlobe. So many questions ping through my mind, but when I look at her eyes again, there's a barrier in those blues.

Her guard is all the way up.

Like she thinks...

Ah fuck.

She thinks I'm going to leave.

She thinks this turns me off.

She thinks I'm like some asshole who must have done that to her—left when he learned. And I immediately want to find him and kill him.

I do the next best thing. I lift my hand to run my knuckles down her cheek. "Thank you for telling me. And I have one opinion on that right now and it's this—I'd really like to take you on a date."

She relaxes, slowly but surely, her lips curving into a soft smile, like that's what she needed more than a kiss. "You do?" She sounds enchanted. Maybe amazed.

I don't waste a single second. "I really do." I glance at the clock on the wall. "What are you doing right now?"

Her smile deepens. My chest tightens with excitement as she says, "Going on a date with you."

I slide my hand down her chest once more, my fingers tracing her soft skin, sensing her comfort with each touch returning. "That's right, you are."

We untangle from each other, moving off the chair. "I

just have one question," I say since her honesty was seriously brave. I'm not about to tell her this out loud—it would sound patronizing—but I'm even more drawn to her for it.

"Sure, what is it?" she asks, sounding hesitant as she pulls her top back on.

"Is there anything you need from me? So you can hear me better?" I ask, buttoning up my shirt.

Her smile is warm, maybe even a little grateful, and it does something funny to my chest. "With them in, I can hear you about eighty-one percent of the time," she says with a smirk.

I tilt my head, curious. "That's specific."

"So are the hearing tests these days." Her tone turns more serious as she adds, "It's like I tell my friends: I just prefer to see your face when we talk—it helps a lot to fill in any gaps. So maybe don't wear a mask?" Her delivery is deadpan.

"And to think I was going to grab my zombie mask."

She raises her hand like a stop sign. "Wait, are you into zombies?" Her look tells me she'd show me the door if I said yes.

"No. Are you?"

"The guy who was supposed to do the shoot today canceled because of a zombie video game launch he just *had* to be at. Apparently, it's a thing."

"Well, then I'll change my answer. I love zombie games because they gave me this chance for our first date." Emphasis on *first*. I want Leighton to know I'd like to see her again. I need this to be a great date for her. Something fun, since she could probably use that after her shoot fell through *twice*, and after opening up the way she did. "How do you feel about geocaching?"

She tilts her head, her brow furrowed. "Never been. Is it fun?"

"Would I take you on a bad date?"

"I don't know. Would you?" she teases.

"Try me."

"We've already established I'm saying yes. Now, you'll really have to impress me with this treasure hunt."

"Challenge accepted." I grab my socks and boots, tug them on, and we head out of the studio onto the streets of Hayes Valley. I open my geocache app, scrolling through nearby options. "There are some cool ones around here, but some of the best are in the Presidio. How do you feel about heading there?"

"I feel pretty good about it, Miles," she says, and I notice her mood seems lighter now, more upbeat. That's everything I could want. This date has barely started, and already, I don't want it to end.

* * *

The Presidio is a national park with great views of the Pacific Ocean and the Golden Gate Bridge. It boasts some terrific nature trails, towering trees and a handful of redwood groves. But it's also home to some seriously fun caches.

Like the sixth one we've been hunting this afternoon. "It's over there," she says, pointing toward a green park bench with absolute certainty.

I gape at her. "Seriously? You already found it? And you said you'd never been geocaching."

She gives me a saucy look. "Yes, I kept my secret geocaching skills hidden from you, Miles."

"You totally did," I reply as we trek along Tennessee

Hollow Trail. She found the first cache in under five minutes—a trolley car keychain tucked above a stone in a low wall. Now, she's hunting under a bench and pulls out a small toy car from a baggie.

"Look! I've always wanted a red sports car," she quips, holding it up, victorious and deservedly so.

"You're cramping my style," I say, shaking my head in mock defeat.

She bumps her hip into mine. "Can't help it if I'm better at this than you."

I loop an arm around her waist and pull her close. She tilts her chin up, her lips inches from mine, waiting for a kiss.

But I stop short. "Not yet," I say, savoring the moment.

"Why not?" she asks, her lips teasingly close, a playful challenge in her voice.

"I want to make you wait for it," I say, enjoying the game.

She pouts. "You're a tease."

"I'm only a tease if I don't follow through...later," I add, brushing a finger along her jawline.

She sighs softly, her eyes flickering with desire. It takes all my willpower not to lean in. But discipline's my middle name. I pull away, nodding toward the trail. "Next cache?"

"If you can handle more of my geocaching excellence," she says.

"And I thought we were a team."

"I guess I'm competitive," she says with no remorse. But she has no idea how competitive I can be.

"I can handle it."

Her eyes sparkle with the thrill of the challenge as we continue down a narrow path.

We've been out for a couple hours, and somehow, we

haven't talked about my job. Maybe because there's so much else to talk about—the trails, the park, where we should look. "So, you're doing Birdie's photos?" I ask, breaking the comfortable silence.

"I am. She wants them at the coffee shop, high-kicking on the counter. I think I love her," Leighton says, laughing as we walk along a small creek.

"That's Birdie's style for sure."

"I can't wait. It's exciting to shoot different types of photos."

"You do more than boudoir?" I ask.

She nods. "Well, I've only just started out. I graduated from college last year," she says. "But I apprenticed while I studied, and over the past year, but I just returned to San Francisco a few months ago. I've done a few boudoir shoots and want to do more, but I do some sports, lifestyle, fashion, headshots—whatever feels right. And honestly, whatever pays the bills."

It hits me—she's a whole decade younger than my thirty-three. I sort of guessed that, but didn't know it till now.

There's no point in pretending we're the same age. "I graduated more than a decade ago. A decade and a year."

She laughs. "That's specific."

But that's all she says, so I suppose she'd already figured out there are some years between us. "And you do sports photography too?" I ask, returning to that. Sure, Birdie said not to discuss my job, and that's fine by me. But I don't want to leave out details that might matter to her.

"I do," she says. "I did that in college for the school paper—online of course—which is where I really learned to shoot." Then she pauses, giving me a serious look. "But we don't have to talk about work, Miles."

And that's clear—she doesn't want to. "Fair enough," I say, and I guess Birdie really does know best, so I'll keep following her advice. And I should give credit where it's due. "Confession time," I say, glancing at Leighton who's walking next to me.

"Oh, is it now?" she asks, clearly intrigued.

"Birdie said I should take you geocaching. I'm pretty sure she engineered this whole date. Wouldn't surprise me if she'd called that model and asked him to cancel."

Leighton smiles knowingly. "She asked me if I was single."

I crack up. "She's about as subtle as an anvil. And I'm going to seriously owe her."

Her eyes lock with mine, glimmering with mischief. "You are."

There's that confidence that hooked me the other day —that flirty, bold side of Leighton. It pairs beautifully with her more vulnerable side. I reach for her hand, tug on it, and pull her close to me again, stopping her on the trail as trees canopy us, and birds flicker from branch to branch. She lifts her chin, her gaze challenging. I slide a finger along her bottom lip, and she bites the pad of it, just enough to send a charge through me.

"Soon, soon," I whisper. "I swear I'll kiss you soon."

"So you say," she says.

I graze my thumb along her jawline. "I will. I'm the guy who was going to keep coming back to the shop just to run into you."

"So you're about as subtle as an anvil too."

Damn, she can keep me on my toes. "I like to think of it as determined. I had a plan to ask you out."

"What was your plan?"

"I didn't ask you that first day because you got a call."

"My dad. I was having lunch with him that day."

I smile. It's nice that she's close to her family. "I figured I'd keep showing up till I saw you again. Hell, I was going to show up the day of Birdie's photo shoot if I had to."

"Fine, fine. You're determined."

I take that as the compliment that it is. Determination has brought me to where I am in life. Grit, too, has powered me through a nearly career-ending ACL tear when I was with Vancouver, and given me a second chance with a new team after Vancouver said *see you later*. So, yeah, determination is my strong suit. "I'm not afraid to go after what I want," I tell her, then nod to the path. "Now, we'd better get moving because *someone* very much wants to be kissed."

She narrows her eyes at me as we resume our pace. "Tease."

"And you like it."

"You're the worst," she says.

"You like that too."

"You're not at all subtle."

"Also, you like that," I say.

She rolls her eyes. "Oh my god, do you have to win every conversation?"

I smile smugly. "Says the woman who turned geocaching as a team into a competition."

"Your fault. You took me geocaching."

"For someone who wants to be kissed so badly, you're taking an awfully long time finding the next cache."

"You and your opinions."

"You like them too. Almost as much as I like yours."

"Fine, you win."

We continue on the path, wandering across a footbridge, then walking along the small stream it arches over.

Leighton spots our quarry, a small, metal lockbox hidden next to a rock near the water. "There's a lock on it," she says, crouching down.

I join her. "Smart. They don't want just anyone picking it up," I say, checking the app for the code. I punch in the combination, and the padlock clicks open.

Leighton's breath hitches as she pulls out a silver chain with a vintage heart locket, holding it up so the heart's swinging back and forth. "It's beautiful," she says softly, wonder in her voice. "Can I open it?"

"Go for it."

She flicks the locket open, and a folded piece of paper falls out. I catch it before it hits the ground.

"Fast reflexes," she says, impressed.

"Yup." I don't mention they've been honed over a lifetime of sports, including a decade in the pros. I unfold the note and read it out loud. *"A treasure for a treasure."*

Her blue eyes widen. "They want us to take it?"

"Looks like it," I say, looking for a proper trade. I run my thumb along the faded vegan leather bracelet I wear on my right wrist. "We should leave something in its place. All I have is this. My brother gave it to me when I moved here."

And on the inside is an inscription—*You've got this*. I needed that reminder when I moved to San Francisco. Tyler knows better than anyone how tough the sport can be—he plays hockey, too, in Los Angeles. But I keep those details to myself.

"Too special to leave behind?" she asks gently.

"Kind of," I admit. "But we can come back and trade again for it."

She touches my wrist lightly. "That sounds like it means a lot to you, and it might not be here then." She lifts her hand to her right ear, where one of the long teardrop earrings hangs, but now I can see she wears more earrings. Little silver studs of stars and a skull climb up her ear. She must think the better of leaving those, though, since she lifts her wrist and shows me a slim silver bracelet instead. "This is from a flea market I went to with friends. I could leave this."

"You don't have to," I say softly, meeting her eyes, not wanting her to leave anything behind.

She smiles, running her fingers over the locket in her hand. "It's part of the game. You give something up but get something in return. And I want to."

"If you insist," I say.

"I do."

I kneel before her, taking the locket in my hand, and dusting it off with the cuff of my shirt. "Let me put it on you."

She lifts her hair, her expression briefly nervous, as though she's expecting me to notice her hearing aids. But I didn't when she touched her earring, and now I'm focused on her face, like I suspect she prefers. My fingers graze her skin as I loop the chain around her neck then fasten the clasp. Being this close, the urge to kiss her is almost overwhelming, but I hold back, letting the anticipation build even more as I touch her once again. The scent of her hair drifts past my nose, mingling with the warm, September air, and the late summer scent of the forest.

"Beautiful," I whisper, but my gaze isn't on the locket or the trees.

She doesn't look away from me as she touches the necklace at her throat. "I'll return it soon."

I see an opening, like a breakaway on the ice, and I go

for it. "Sounds like we need a second date to give it back then," I say.

Her eyes sparkle. "We do."

Then she slips off her bracelet, leaving it in the box with the note it came with—a promise, and a plan for us to see each other again. When she closes the lockbox, she turns back to me. Her eyes have darkened. "You've made me wait long enough. Are you going to kiss me now?"

I reach for her hair, careful to touch her just past her temples, letting my fingers slide slowly through her soft strands. "Yes, but I'm going to need something from you."

"What is it?" She sounds breathless.

"I want you to take a picture of it, like I can't look away from you. Like I have to have you. Like you're all I've been thinking about all fucking day." I pause as her cheeks flush with color. "Because you are."

She swallows, then grabs my face, shakes her head, and says, "Now."

Fucking love her desire. But I *think* I want to edge her just a little more. I like her need far too much. "I left my watch at your studio," I point out, covering her hands with mine, holding her tight.

Her lips part in surprise, maybe delight. "You did that on purpose."

I nod in admission. "I did."

7

A LITTLE INTO YOU

Leighton

The drive back to the studio takes forever and no time at all. But we're here now as dusk falls over the city. We leave the twilight behind, heading up the steps. With each foot-fall, anticipation winds tighter in me, higher.

I'm the only one using the studio today, so when I unlock the door, I'm confident it'll just be us. Still, I look around the space, reassured to find it empty, just like we left it. I head over to the chaise this time to set up the camera in front of it—I've been low-key vibrating the whole way here, imagining capturing our first kiss on film —when Miles grabs my hand, jerking me back toward him, pulling me against his body.

I can feel how much he wants me.

"You're going to send me that picture." It's a demand, rough and intense, matching the need in his dark brown eyes.

My head is swimming with desire and surprise. I've

never met a man like him, one who's actually interested in the artistic side of me. One who wants a picture of us. I have a feeling he's going to want pictures of so much more, and I'll probably give him what he wants because I want that too.

I want to see how we look coming together. But right now, I'm not sure I remember how to adjust a setting on the camera. I'm not sure I can hold a single thought in my head that doesn't revolve around the heat curling through every cell in my body, the need pulsing through my veins.

Still, I'm determined to give him what he wants, and to give it to myself too.

"Yes," I say, quickly crossing over to the camera on the tripod and grabbing the remote trigger. I'm so used to the remote that it's no big deal to hold it while I do things—I learned how to shoot boudoir both with others and through self-portraits.

"Good, Shutterbug. Because I want *us* to see it," he says, and that word thrums through me—*us*.

A promise, once more, of another time.

When I spin around, he's right there, eyes on me. And I'm nothing but raw need. "You've been driving me wild all day," I tell him. "Do something about it."

I'm almost shocked to hear my own words. It's so strange to say exactly what I want. To know he wants to hear it.

To know he can handle it.

His smile is devilish. "I'll do whatever you want, Leighton."

But when he closes the distance to me, I tense for a few seconds, expecting him to forget what I told him earlier, since most guys just do. They get caught up. They don't listen. They don't care. I half expect him to drag his fingers through my hair and over my ears.

If he did, there'd be loud ringing in my ears.

But Miles has proven different all day.

He's an incredible listener, so when he takes off his glasses, sets them down on a low table, then lifts a hand slowly, I choose to trust.

And he curls that hand around my throat, gentle yet entirely possessive. And setting my heart to flames.

He inches closer, licks his lips, and drops his lush mouth to mine.

There's never been a kiss like this. It's soulful and filthy at the same time. His hand stays firm on my throat, his fingers holding me tight, the locket resting against my chest. His lips are soft as they coast over mine, his stubble scraping my face deliciously. His tongue slips past my eager lips.

And I ache everywhere as I help the camera capture our first kiss with a push of the remote.

The sounds he makes are hungry, carnal, and I swear I not only hear every single thing but feel it too, everywhere, all at once.

The kiss feels like the type of photos I try to capture. Sensual, moody, and most of all, a prelude.

It's not a first kiss at a picnic, or in a park, or under the sun. It's a first kiss where the lights are low, night is calling, and the doors are locked.

I'm so glad that the woman I rent the studio from is out of town today because I'm pretty sure I'm one minute away from doing something risky.

As Miles kisses me slowly, seductively, making my head swim with longing, his thumb and forefinger circle a little tighter around my throat. His touch there is possessive, but full of restraint, like he won't cross lines until he gets the go-ahead. I want to give him all the go-aheads. Sparks rush down my body, and I ache for so much more. I inch closer, pressing my body to his. He makes a noise low in his throat, a dirty rumble. His other hand ropes around my waist, traveling to my back. He slips it under my shirt, laying it flat against my skin.

I make some kind of incredibly uncivilized noise. I wish I could say it was a deep, throaty purr, but it's more like a needy plea.

Miles breaks the kiss to look at me, a smirk on his lips, fire in his eyes. But coiled restraint too. This man is a portrait of caged lust. "Tell me what you want," he says in a rasp, letting go of my throat and running the back of his fingers down my cheeks. "So I can give it to you."

My chest flips.

Who is this man?

Is this what I've been missing? Is this what I never experienced when I dated guys my age in college? This kind of focused attention. These direct questions.

I honestly don't know how to start answering him, but I give it my best shot because honesty has gotten me this far today. Into the arms of a man who's not afraid to manhandle me—the way I want. And I want it...a little rough.

Here I am—doing something risky. Asking him to fuck me in the studio. "You," I begin, taking that small step.

He fiddles with my bra strap. "In case it's not clear, you've got me. You've got all my attention, Leighton." He pauses and licks his lips. "I'm just a *little* into you."

He drags out that word, tone dry, making his meaning clear.

He's *a lot* into me.

"Show me," I say.

Tilting his head, he studies my face, then says, "If you insist."

His fingers travel to the hollow of my throat tracing it, drawing a circle over it, before he brushes them along my jawline, dragging them there. My breath hitches from the firm touch. From the sheer different-ness of it. Has anyone ever touched me like this before? I don't think so. It's so specific, so purposeful. It's like he's finding ways to touch me that are *only* for me.

Like his hands are telling me how he doesn't need to thread his fingers through my hair to turn me on. He'll find other ways to arouse me, and since I'm ludicrously wet, he has. But I know, too, that he's holding back. I can see his restraint in the tension in his shoulders, the tightness in his jaw.

I'm going to have to take the next step. Say the next thing.

"When I said *you*, I meant I want *all* of you," I add. That's clear enough, but just in case it wasn't, I press my body even closer so I'm rubbing against the outline of his erection. Making my intentions crystal clear.

For a hot second, his eyes go glassy. His breath stutters. But then he gains control again.

"All of me?" he asks like it's a question, even though it's an amused *me*, as if he's having too much fun with my words as he keeps one hand looped firmly around my waist. "How exactly do you want all of me?"

Oh my god. He's toying with me.

I groan in mock frustration. "You want me to spell it out?"

"I do, Leighton," he rasps out. "I really, really do."

I roll my eyes, but it's doing little to mask how turned

on I am. "Fine—then here's an opinion for you." I pause, letting him hang there on my every word as I run a hand down his chest, over the buttons on his shirt. I lift my chin, look him in the eyes. "I want you to fuck me hard. And a little rough."

Something in his eyes seems to snap, a tight wire breaking as he scoops me up without warning. "I'm going to fuck you exactly the way you want, Shutterbug."

"Oh," I say, blinking as he grabs my ass nice and tight and sets me down on the chaise behind us. He lays me on it, climbs over me. Grabbing my wrists, he pins them over my head and lowers his body to mine. This time it's just us. No record of the moment as I let the remote fall from my hand.

The weight of him is extraordinary. He grinds against me and I pant. I thread my fingers through his messy hair while I drag my other hand down his arm. He's so outrageously fit, I can't stand it. The strength of his arms, the size of his chest, the way he covers me.

I seriously can't wait to take off his clothes. I'm vibrating with desire.

I wrap my legs around him, hooking them at his ass— the muscles in it tell me he doesn't miss glutes day. I want to send a thank you note to his gym membership.

"Seems like you're more than a *little* into me," I say dryly.

"Yeah, a fucking lot," he says, then kisses me till I'm clawing at his shirt, trying to take it off.

He wrenches away, sits up, then undoes the buttons in no time. I tug off my top. I'm just in my black bra again, and like that I stare at this thoughtful, considerate, passionate man in a whole new way. He's no longer the subject of my photographs. I'm not looking at him through a lens. I'm free to gaze at him in a fresh new way. I lift a hand, stroke his face, memorizing the whiskery scratch of his stubble before I say, "Fuck me now, Miles."

He offers me his hand and tugs me up. "Go on a second date with me."

A laugh bursts from me. "You already asked me out for a second date. Did you forget?"

"I'm making sure."

"Are you worried you won't be any good in bed, so you need to secure that second date now?" I tease.

His eyes darken. "For that, you're getting multiple orgasms."

"Lucky me," I say.

"No. Lucky me."

We both make quick work of shoes, then he unzips my jeans and slides them down my thighs, but he's careful when he takes them off, making sure they don't land inside out in a pile on the floor.

And I think...I could fall in love with him.

Then, I'm nearly sure I could when he folds them. Fine, he folds them over once. But still, he fucking folds them before setting them on the table next to the chaise. He cares about everything.

He turns back to me, his gaze eating me up from head to toe, his eyes lingering on the flowers inked all over my arms before returning to my face. "You're fucking gorgeous, Leighton," he says, locking eyes with me. It's intense the way he looks at me, how he talks to me, but most of all how he listens. How he shifts between Leighton and *Shutterbug*, how sometimes he's serious and sometimes he's playful.

He advances toward me again, then sinks to his knees.

My throat tightens, my heart slamming against my

rib cage at the sight of this big man on the floor, hooking his thumbs in the black lacy waistband of my panties. Reverence flickers in his stare, but he's not slow and sweet when he pulls them off. He yanks them down, and when I step out, his eyes glimmer with flames. He stares at me half-naked—no, mostly naked—in front of him.

A big, needy breath escapes his lips. Then he dips his face toward me, and gives a tease of a kiss to my clit. "After you come on my cock, I'll spend a good long time eating you. But first, you need to get fucked hard like you asked for."

Holy fuck.

I asked for it. I did. But he's giving it. Oh, how he's fucking giving it good with his words.

He rises, fishes into his pocket and pulls out his wallet, then hands it to me.

With eager fingers, I reach for the condom, not caring about anything else. Like I'm going to scour his ID anyway. With the protection in hand, I set down his wallet as he sheds his jeans, then his briefs. His thick, hard cock points at me. Standing at full attention.

And with a bead of liquid arousal just waiting at the tip. My mouth waters. Then I can't help it—I smile. "I like that opinion very much," I say, reaching out and gripping his shaft.

He's hot and hard, the skin smooth and velvety to the touch. I glide my hand up and down his length. He shudders, like the feel of my hand on him is too much. But it's a *too much* he seems to crave, since he covers my fingers, guiding me along as he throbs in my hand.

His eyes float closed.

He groans, so low I can barely hear the sound. But I'm

not sure I need to *hear* it. I can *feel* his groan. I can see his throat move.

Then, he opens his eyes and blows out a breath, like he's shaking off the momentary lapse in his focus. He bats my hand away, and takes the condom. "Now show me how pretty you look when you're riding my cock."

He sits on the chaise, covers his cock, and pulls me down onto his lap. "And get rid of this fucking bra right now," he says, nodding to the lace still covering me. "But leave the locket on."

Yes, sir.

I unhook my bra as he grips the base of his dick and offers it to me. I take the offered prize and rub the head against my wetness. His breath hisses, and the sound and vibration from it thrums through me, turning me on even more. I sink down. An inch at first.

I moan. He groans.

I sink more till he's filling me all the way, stretching me deliciously, and he's cupping my tits too. It's a sensory overload, and so is how he stares too. Like he can't believe his luck.

He plays with my nipples for a few seconds, then sweeps his hands down my sides. I shiver as he goes, watching his arms, the strength in them, the way his muscles flex, how the arrow tattoo melts right into an inked tree, bursting with bright leaves.

They're as beautiful as he is. I tear my gaze away from them, looking at his face.

For a moment, the world blurs at the edges, going a little soft and sweet. It's just us, here in the studio in the early evening, no one knowing where we are, what we're doing, or that we're both having the best date ever.

"Hi," he whispers.

"Hi," I say.

And the best dates end...like this.

He grips my waist, fingers digging into my flesh, and he takes the reins, taking over. I'm hardly riding him. It's more like he's fucking up into me.

With hard, deep thrusts that have nothing in common with the soft way his hands just grazed my flesh. No, now he's rough, like I asked. Controlling, like I want. Powerful, like I need.

My hands curl tightly over his muscular shoulders, and Miles locks eyes with me as he drives up into me. Everything about this feels raw and necessary. The deep kind of fucking that's a little merciless.

A little ruthless too.

I see that in his eyes, in the tension lining his jaw and the power in his body. He's fucking up, but he's also moving me on his dick, using me, but letting me use him too.

He seems to catalog my every reaction. When he hits a spot deep inside me that makes me shudder from my head to my toes, he smiles wickedly and chases that spot again. And he hits it.

I gasp.

"You like that? When I fuck you hard?"

"Yes," I answer, in a desperate pant.

His hand travels up my chest, and he squeezes my right breast. "And this?"

"Yes." I grow hotter, and he has to feel that, because his eyebrows shoot up.

"Oh, you really fucking do," he says, seeming so damn pleased.

"I do," I gasp.

He brushes his lips against mine. "I can feel your sweet pussy gripping me harder."

Another gasp. Another crank of the temperature inside. But I can't answer him. I don't even know what I'd say if I could. My body has all the answers though as he twists my nipple, and I throw my head back. "Yesssss," I moan, unbidden.

He kisses my throat then pulls back, grabbing my face. "Look at me when you come."

I gasp but nod, my eyes focused on him. His dark eyes are on fire. His mouth is a demanding line. His need is etched in his face. "I will," I say.

"Look at me because I want you to see what you fucking do to me," he says, almost like an accusation.

And I love being accused like this. "What do I do to you?"

"You drive me fucking wild," he says, the words harsh, so harsh they send a jolt of lust through me.

"How wild?"

"I'm so fucking into you," he says, a feral sort of promise that's way over the top for a first date.

And yet...it feels wholly true.

Or maybe it's just that everything feels true with him. True and raw and electric as he drops a hand between my thighs. His thumb strokes my clit, his cock fills me up, and his words grip my dirty soul.

My vision blurs, sparks shooting behind my eyelids as lust grips me so deeply, and I come in seconds.

A long needy series of *oh god, yes, oh god yes, oh my fucking god.*

And when I'm done, this man I'm sitting on is smiling at me. Smiling as I nearly collapse in his arms.

"I'm not done with you, Shutterbug," he says, tsking

me as he maneuvers me easily on the chaise. In no time, he's pulled out, flipped me to my back, and is pushing my legs up my chest. With the condom still in place, he notches the head of his cock against me once more, staring down at me so our gazes are locked. "Now I want another one, Leighton."

"If you think you can," I tease.

"I can and you fucking will," he says, and it's a little scary how he says it, but a lot thrilling.

"Give me one then," I toss out, challenging him right back.

"I don't back down," he says, then braces himself on those strong, sinewy arms. He shoves into me, and I scream from the blunt way he takes me, pushing my knees up to my chest and driving into me.

Miles is doing everything I asked. He's not fucking me delicately.

He's a little rough. A little demanding. A little angry. And I've never been more turned on than I am when this thoughtful, kind man goes wild on me.

It's exactly the kind of sex I think I've always wanted but have never known to ask for. Till I met a stranger who seemed...enchanted by me.

Oh, god. My heart beats so fast. My pulse surges. The awareness that this is happening pulls me under—there's some kind of fierce chemistry between the two of us.

It's not just the rough sex. It's the real connection. The way he's treated me all day. Most of all, it's the knowledge that I'm as into him as he's into me.

My mind spins and I grab his ass, pulling him deeper till I'm falling apart again too. Several mind-bending seconds later, he groans, then jerks. "Fuuuuuck," he grunts, his whole body slamming hard into me once more, pushing me up the chaise longue farther as the aftershocks radiate through me.

He drops his face into the crook of my neck, collapsing onto me. Sighing long and hard, moaning, lost in the moment.

Which is, admittedly, a nice compliment.

Except, I've no choice but to shift around to accommodate his face in my neck, and with my right ear nearly pressed against the cushion, the top of my hearing aid is knocked loose.

Oh, shit.

The custom mold is still inside my ear—that's not likely to come loose on its own ever—but the behind-the-ear part? That little silver bitch has jumped off my ear and burrowed into my hair. That usually only happens when something gets caught in my hair, like the string from a face mask at the doctor's office, or corded headphones.

And now, a hot, strapping man fucking me hard into the cushions has done the job.

Subtly, or as subtly as I can, I sneak a hand into my hair, hunting for it in my strands. But Miles rises up, looking down at me curiously.

Awkward.

Never have I ever searched for a hearing aid post-sex. Because never have I ever had one dislodge during sex.

"Is everything okay?" he asks with genuine concern.

"Yes, fine."

"Do you need—"

"Nope," I say brightly, cutting that idea off at the knees. I don't need help freeing my hearing aid from my own hair, but I also don't want anyone else touching it. They're expensive and necessary. They're for my hands only.

In a few seconds, I free the piece from my hair without having to pull the whole thing out of my ear, thank god. But still, I scoot up on the chaise and turn away from him, quickly tucking the small silver piece back where it belongs.

It's not that I can't hear without it. I can manage. But it's that—none of this is sexy. And it's kind of embarrassing. Like some asshole once said to me after a couple dates last year when he learned I wore them. Nick's words? *"Well, that's embarrassing. Especially at your age."*

Yup. I'm twenty-three and wear something most people associate with the elderly and have since I was sixteen.

Fun times.

Best to move on. "I should get dressed," I say evenly since I don't want him to think this bothers me. I don't want him to feel sorry for me. Or to tell me I'm beautiful right now, because if he does that, it will feel like he means *you're beautiful even with your hearing aids.*

I don't want that kind of response, and I don't need that kind of reassurance. But before I can slide out from under him, Miles wraps a hand gently around my arm, and says, "I'm sorry. Did I knock it out?"

I pause, absorbing the words. The question. The intent. He's not trying to make me feel like I'm *oh so inspiring* for being able to have sex with hearing aids in. He's just acknowledging that they're part of it and that he's, well, cool with it.

And that's a much better response. "Yes, but it's fine now," I say. "They survived the great fucking."

He laughs, then turns sober quickly. "Do you need anything?"

For you to stop being so fantastic because I'm going to start expecting a unicorn to arrive on my doorstep tomorrow.

And since I'm too much of a realist to believe in good fortune that I don't make happen with hard work, I say, "I'm good."

I should get dressed. Say goodnight. Head home to my roommates. Go out on a high note, so to speak.

But before I can grab my shirt, he slips an arm around my waist and pulls me back to him, forcing me to look at his too handsome face. "Can you hand me my glasses?"

My heart stutters from the simplicity of the request. They're not the same—glasses and hearing aids—but neither one of us has perfect senses and I know that was a purposeful reminder. I hand them to him, and he slides them on, pushes them up, then says, like it's a goddamn order, "Let's have that second date now."

"Now?" I repeat in case I didn't hear him right. Because who does this? What man puts himself out there this way? This can't be real. I'm not sure I feel ready for a man like Miles, who seems so certain of who he is and what he wants. I've never dated anyone like him before.

"Yes," he says. "I want to see you again. I have to go out of town tomorrow, but come over tonight, Leighton. Let me cook dinner for you. Are you hungry?"

This isn't how dating works. This isn't how men work. This isn't how *I* usually work...but I don't want tonight to end either.

"I guess we'd better find your watch and get out of here then," I say, and after we clean up the studio we're closing the door behind us a few minutes later.

8

YOU COULD SAY I'M A FAN

Miles

I don't believe in wasting time. I've lost enough of it, from an injury that sidelined me for half a season a few years ago, to the dark place I went in my head from all that downtime, to the long hours on the bench when I first started out. Proving myself, earning my spot—none of that came easily. I know how fast time can slip away, especially in this life, where focus and luck matter as much as talent.

When I meet someone I actually like, I'm not about to let that chance slip by—especially with the season starting in a couple weeks, when life will only get busier. Sure, relationships don't always work out. Hell, they rarely do, something I learned the hard way with Joanne, but something else I've been learning since I was a kid? Life is short. You need to grab your chances because they might not come around again.

So why not see her again now? This way, I can explain

to her why I can't go on a second date for the next few days while I'm away with the team. I played along with Birdie's "rules" for our first date, but this is our second, and it's time to come clean. As we drive back toward my home in the Marina District, though, there's something I don't want to forget. Something that I'll probably enjoy on the road trip. "I want those pictures," I say with a half-smile. "Guess that means I'll need your number."

She waggles her phone. "What's yours?"

I rattle off the digits and she enters them on her phone. Mine buzzes on the console seconds later.

"See? I didn't give you a fake one," she teases.

I laugh. "Didn't think you would."

"I'll send the pictures tomorrow, after I touch them up," she says.

I raise an eyebrow. "Oh, you think I need photo-shopping?"

"Trust me, everyone needs a little."

I grin, trying to keep it light. "What will you do about Katrina? Any chance she might want another shoot?"

"Why? Are you considering a career change?" she quips, giving me an amused sidelong glance.

This could be a good opening to the what-do-you-do convo, but first, I want to make sure I don't need to swing by a grocery store. "You know, maybe I am. But more importantly—any food restrictions? Anything you're in the mood for?"

She taps her chin, her eyes narrowing thoughtfully. "Hmm...do you have artichokes?"

I chuckle, pulling up to my block across from Marina Green where Richardson Bay sparkles under the moonlight. The Golden Gate Bridge stands watch over the water. "That's a very specific craving."

"I know what I like," she says, shooting me that confident look she sent my way when she walked past me in High Kick the other day. The smile that caught my eye. "Lots of veggies. So, do you, Miles?"

There's that challenge in her tone again. It's the kind that says she'll keep me on my toes and she wants me there. Fine by me. "Guess it's your lucky day. I've got artichokes, red peppers, mushrooms…how about mushroom and artichoke pasta with a little olive oil and salt?"

Her smile turns mischievous. "So the chef is going to make me pasta."

"Chef, huh?" My brow quirks as I pull into the garage. *Does she actually believe that, or is this some inside joke I'm missing?*

"Well, that sounds gourmet to me," she says.

Okay, she's just teasing. Fair enough. "Watch it, Shutterbug. You'll be begging for my artichoke pasta in no time."

She laughs lightly as we get out of the car. "We'll see."

"I'm sure we will." I grab the door to my home, holding it open for her, then flicking on the interior lights. Once inside, her gaze lingers on the hoodies hanging on the mudroom hooks, and she raises her brows slightly. "Sea Dogs fan?"

"You could say that," I say.

"Same," she replies.

That's a relief. Maybe she's known I play all along but hasn't wanted to make a thing of it. Fine by me. I untie my boots, and she slips off her shoes, following me into the living room, her eyes widening just a bit as she looks around at the open-floor plan, with the kitchen spilling into the living room. The open layout, eco-friendly furniture, and minimalist decor make it feel simple but modern, and the view overlooking the water doesn't hurt.

Here comes that awkward moment when someone realizes that I make enough money to afford a sweet place. When they become more interested in the status than the person.

But instead she says, "This is...nice. Very you."

And that's it. That's all.

"Thank you. I like it here. Make yourself at home," I say, heading to the kitchen. "Want some wine? Or beer?"

"White if you have it," she says.

"I do," I say, spinning around to grab a bottle from the wine fridge as she drifts over to the couch and picks up a few framed photos on the end table.

I uncork the bottle, mentally rehearsing how I'm going to bring up my career. My place doesn't scream "hockey player"—no pucks or jerseys on display. Just doesn't feel necessary. But dropping the intel in casual convo can get awkward and it has in the past. I've seen the switch flip before—someone interested in "Miles" becomes starry-eyed over "Miles the hockey player," talking about the money or asking for tickets. And that's the last thing I want with her.

She picks up a framed photo. "Is this your sister with the *Give Plants a Chance* bumper sticker on the beer tap?"

I can't see the pic from here, but I'm sure which one it is. "Yes. That's Charlie. She owns a punk rock vegan bar in Darling Springs."

"And I love her already," Leighton says, then sets it down.

"So, I'm heading out of town tomorrow," I say, hoping to steer things that way as I bring her the glass.

She takes it with a *thank you* then picks up a photo of

my mom and Harvey with their four Chihuahuas. And that could be a good entry. "They're cute."

"My mom and stepdad. They have four rescue Chihuahuas. They like to travel, and sometimes I dog-sit when I'm in town," I say, then return to the kitchen, pulling out ingredients from the fridge. "I travel a lot for my job."

After she takes a sip, she tilts her head thoughtfully. "Huh. That's not typical for your line of work, is it?"

So, she doesn't know what I do—or maybe she knows something and just doesn't care. Kind of refreshing, really.

"Actually, it's pretty normal," I say, grabbing a jar of marinated artichokes and a pepper. She's studying another photo now, the one of my brother and me at a Supernova game. Tyler's in his game gear; I wasn't playing that night, so I'm just in a Sea Dogs hoodie in the picture.

Her eyes flick to me, widening with recognition as she holds up a photo. "Is this you and...a Supernova?"

I smile, setting down the knife. This is the perfect moment to explain things since she seems to be a hockey fan. "Yeah, my brother's on the Los Angeles team. I, uh... play hockey too." I try to read her expression as she processes this.

Her face goes pale, and her gaze shifts down to the food I'm chopping on the cutting board. "You're...not a chef?"

I frown. So there was something to her chef comment earlier. I pick up the jar of artichokes, loosening the top. "No. You called me a chef earlier. Why did you think that?"

She stares at me, her voice almost a whisper. "Birdie told me you were one—a chef." Her voice is heavy, full of dread. "You're not just a Sea Dogs fan," she says, absently waving her hand to where the hoodies hang. "You play for Noah McBride?"

I blink. I didn't expect her to jump straight to the coach. "Yes. Are you a big fan of his?"

Only that hardly adds up. He played more than a decade ago.

"You could say that," she says, her voice tight. "He's my dad."

The jar of artichokes slips from my hand, hitting the floor with a clatter. For the first time all day, I have no words.

9

HOW TO CUT A DATE SHORT

Leighton

"But...but Birdie said you're a chef!" I point out, my voice shooting toward the sky, as if somehow repeating Birdie's words could erase the absolute horror of what Miles has just admitted.

And horror is on his face too. "I wish I were a chef! No, I'm not. What the fuck would make her say that?"

I point wildly in the direction of Fillmore Street, as if pointing to his grandmother. "She told me you were. She said not to bring up your job—that's why I didn't say anything. I was trying to be respectful."

His eyes flash with frustration, but I catch a flicker of realization in them, too, as he stares at the ceiling for a beat, like he can't believe this is actually happening. He looks back at me, finally. "And she told me not to discuss my job with you. She said nobody wants to hear about that on a first date. She said to talk about other things. Holy fuck—I should have told you what I did sooner."

He drags a hand across his brow, looking like he's received the worst news of his life. And honestly, it kind of is.

"You're...Miles Falcon," I say, since I need to voice it out loud, and as I do, the truth hits me with full force. I didn't put Miles the chef together with Miles Falcon the Sea Dog, because why would I? I legit thought he was a chef; I don't study the pictures of the players on my dad's team. I haven't been to a game in a while, since I studied abroad the year I think he joined, and, well, I've been pretty busy in the last year too. "You don't look like a hockey player. You look like..." I flap my hands at him, still adding up how the hell this misunderstanding has happened. "Well, you look like a chef. With the boots and the black and the glasses."

He sighs heavily. "Yeah, well, I only cook for fun. I play hockey for work. And I thought you knew."

"How would I know?" I'm nearly shouting. "I don't memorize pictures of the players."

Also, hello! He plays hockey. He's not a movie star. But that's rude to point out.

Miles holds up his hands in surrender, clearly frustrated with himself now. "I don't know what I thought. I guess I thought maybe you knew I played hockey and didn't care. Or that you just...didn't care what I do."

"I didn't care about what you do...until I found out you worked for my father," I say, sputtering.

"Shit, shit. This is terrible." He shakes his head, not even bothering with the spilled artichokes and glass on the floor. "I can't believe I did this. I can't believe I slept with the coach's daughter."

He sounds sick to his stomach. I feel sick to mine too. "I can't believe I slept with one of his players," I mutter, pacing around his living room, trying to untangle this mess and make sense of it.

My dad's been the coach of this team for the last five years. Players respect him. The league respects him. He's had a phenomenal career. And I can't get involved with a member of his team.

"I didn't know it was you," I add quickly when I stop pacing and head into the kitchen because it feels important to make that clear. I don't want him to think I've tricked him. "I really believed Birdie, and I'm guessing she told me you were a chef to protect you. She probably thought if she told me you played hockey that I might only be interested in you for that reason, since she obviously knew we were into each other."

He laughs humorlessly. "Trust me, she knew I had it bad for you the first day we met."

My stupid heart flips, but I don't let myself linger on the feeling—it's fleeting.

Besides, I want to impress this point on him. "I've been out of town. I went to college in Los Angeles. I even spent a year studying abroad in London. And since then I have been busy working on my career. I know hockey, but I don't know every single player. I'm not one of those superfans who can rattle off each team member and recognize every photo of them."

Miles just stares at me, stunned. "Did Birdie know who you are though?"

"I don't think my last name came up. I'm not close with her. We just talked about photos, and that was all."

He shakes his head, dismissing the thought of Birdie knowing his coach is my father, because why would she do that to her beloved grandson? "She wouldn't have done this on purpose...She knows how much I admire your father." Miles lets out a pained sigh and drops his head into his hands. "Holy shit, your father saved my career. He fought for me to be on this team when I was struggling in Vancouver. He helped me get over a problem on the ice. He hooked me up with a sports psychologist. Your father is the reason I still have a career."

"My father is the reason I have one good parent who cares about me..." I trail off, the weight of this whole mess pressing down on me.

We stand there in his kitchen, surrounded by a broken jar of artichokes, an open bottle of wine, and the ingredients he'd planned to make into our late-night dinner. A dinner that isn't happening now. A second date being cut short. A third that won't ever come to pass. Because it's not a matter of who says it first; when we look at each other, I know beyond a shadow of a doubt we're both thinking the same thing.

"This can't happen again," I whisper.

Miles nods, understanding immediately. "I know. Let me take you home."

I shake my head. "I'll catch a Lyft."

"Let me drive you."

"It's not necessary," I say.

"You're right. It's not. But I still want to do this for you. It's all I can do right now," he implores me, sounding more vulnerable than I expected.

It'd be silly to think either one of us fell hard in one day and night. And I'm realistic, above all. I believe in facts and hard work. I don't believe in taking risks with my future. But even so, everything about today and tonight felt real and possible, and it's hard to give that up. So, yes, I suppose his vulnerability makes sense after all. And I wouldn't mind a few last stolen moments with this man. "Okay."

He leaves the spilled artichokes on the tiled floor. "I'll clean those up later," he says.

"Shame. They're my favorite," I say as we return to his car.

He pulls out of his garage and into the night. I give him my address, and he plugs it into the GPS then navigates along the streets of San Francisco, now shrouded in a rare night-time fog. But that feels fitting.

He's quiet for a long beat. Once we cruise along Van Ness Avenue, he says, "This is a massive line I can't cross."

"It's a line for me too. I would never want to hurt my father or change how he might think about the team he loves coaching. The only thing he loves more than his team...is his daughters."

Miles manages a tight smile. "I wish he'd called you and your sister by your names the few times he mentioned you. And she's the only one he even mentioned coming to a game since I've been with the team."

"She's in high school so she still lives at home. And as for my dad...he's a private man. He's always been that way." His reputation is pristine. The respect he's earned from his players is well-deserved. I'm not going to ruin that.

A few minutes later, I'm at the front door of my building in the Mission District, a far cry from the Marina.

Miles sighs heavily, letting his head fall back against the seat. "I didn't mean that last thing—about wishing I'd known who you were beforehand," he says softly, then turns and looks at me with such longing in his eyes. "I'm glad I didn't know who you were, and I don't regret anything about tonight."

"Me neither."

With that, I leave the best date I've ever had in the past.

* * *

"Potatoes. Scrambled eggs. No butter, please—just oil. Well-cooked. Toast dry."

Before our dad can finish his order, Riley and I chime in unison from across the booth, "And a cup of fruit on the side."

The server at our regular café near Riley's school laughs. "Someone knows your order, sir," he says to my dad.

My father gives us a stern look, like he's challenging my sister and me to just try it again. "And coffee—"

"Black. No sugar, no cream," Riley and I say together, since we can't resist needling him.

The server chuckles, jotting it all down. "Noted."

"And for you?" he asks, turning to me.

I order pancakes. After last night went sideways, it just feels like a pancake kind of morning. "With extra syrup," I add.

My dad tilts his head in curiosity, studying me. "You always order eggs with artichokes and mushrooms."

A pang hits me in the chest, sharper than I'd like. Artichokes feel off-limits today, tangled up with the memory of Miles mentioning he'd make them for me last night. Then the jar breaking at his feet. The thought feels too fresh, too close.

Riley jumps in. "She usually does, but she mixes it up way more than you. You're a creature of habit, Dad."

"Nothing wrong with habits. Especially good ones," he says.

"True. But I need pancakes today, Dad. Maybe even whipped cream," I say, pushing the memory of last night away. I've been doing that all morning long. I feel like I'll be doing it longer than I'd like.

The server nods my way, like we're kindred spirits. "I hear you, girl. Some days, you just need all the extra sugar."

Yeah, like after you sleep with one of your dad's players.

But I try to shove that thought of Miles out of my mind. His hands, his ink, his eyes, the way he talked, the way he listened...I sit up straighter, focusing on keeping my hands still. I won't be seeing him again. My dad will, though—in two hours when he gets on the team bus, then boards the team jet as they head to their first pre-season game.

After Riley places her order and the server takes off, my dad turns his attention back to us. He's dressed for travel today, so he's wearing a charcoal suit with a light green tie that Riley and I gave him for Christmas last year. All his ties come from his daughters. "So now that you've mocked me for ordering the same thing—"

"Which you do every time," Riley interjects.

"It's breakfast. Breakfast is supposed to be the same. Mornings are for routine. You get up, exercise, eat a healthy breakfast," he says, like it's a mantra.

"And you already ran three miles, right?" Riley asks.

He rolls his dark blue eyes at her—we get our eyes from him. Our mom has brown eyes. I can't say it bothers me that Riley and I look more like him than the woman who barely wants to know us.

"Yes, Riley. You saw me come back from the run. You still live with me, you sass monster," he teases.

That's mostly true—that she lives with him. She also stays with his parents, who live next door to them. When our mom left nearly a decade ago to ostensibly focus on her handbag line, but actually to shack up with Dad's agent, he became our primary parent. He built a house for his parents on his property in Mill Valley so they could help raise us. I was fourteen then, Riley was six, and Mom had moved to Miami.

She did launch the handbag line with the money she protected in the prenup, and she's still running the wildly successful Simply Grace. But Michael, the guy she cheated on Dad with? Pretty sure he's been out of the picture for a long time. Well, she always loved accessories more than anything so I suppose her exit strategy worked out for her. It also taught me a valuable lesson—it's best if I depend on myself.

I focus on the most important people in my life—my father and little sister. Dad, however, is already focused on me. "So, what's on tap for today, Leighton?"

"I'm assisting a fashion photographer," I say, then tell him about some of the work I'm doing with a local designer. "And later this week I'm taking some dog pictures for a Bark in the Park event."

"Nice," he says, his tone proud. "And you had a shoot yesterday. How'd it go?"

I mentioned it when I last saw him, so it's only natural he'd ask. Only now, I feel like a complete traitor lying to him, maybe for the first time. "It...sort of fell apart."

"What happened?" he asks, and I'm sure he'll be ready

to dole out advice, too, on work and how to handle setbacks. Normally, I like his advice. He knows what it takes to collaborate, manage big personalities, and work with a huge team. Obviously.

Think fast.

"The model canceled, and then the client canceled," I say. Since he'll never know Miles stepped in, I add, "So it was a bust."

He sighs. "What did you do instead?"

Got absolutely wrecked on a chaise longue by one of your fifty-goal scorers. The guy you saved after an injury. Filthy mouth. Big heart. Smart too. Basically, a perfect date. "I just shot some self-portraits," I say, knowing nothing will shut Dad up faster than the thought of me in lingerie. He knows I've been playing around with that type of shot, but not that I want to build a business shooting boudoir.

Riley sits up straighter, then nudges me, her gaze drifting pointedly down to her hands. They're below the table. She signs, *What did you wear? Can you take me shopping for something pretty?*

I laugh, then say out loud to her, "Anytime."

Dad clears his throat. "I do know ASL too."

We all know American Sign Language, even though I don't *need* it now—I can hear them all well enough and everyone else—clients, friends, neighbors, strangers. I don't know if I'll ever truly have to use it. But my high school offered it, so I took it just in case. Riley and my dad decided to learn it too. Someday I might need or want to use ASL to communicate with them, even though I know I could also use conversational captioning tools on my phone. Either way, the future can barrel down on you. So I choose to be practical.

I turn to Riley, smiling as I say to my father, "You know it, but only if you can *see* it."

He rolls his eyes. "That's just mean."

I shrug. "You're a girl dad. We're going to have secrets from you."

"Get used to it," Riley adds.

"Daughters," he says with an over-the-top sigh then he moves on, turning to Riley. "And you have a chemistry test today."

"Which she'll ace," I add because she's a genius STEM girl.

"I don't know about that," Riley says.

"You kind of ace everything," I say, grinning.

"You do," Dad agrees, and when the server returns with his coffee, he thanks him. We chat more, carefully sidestepping any mention of hockey until Dad studies me for a long beat, then says with a chin nod, "Where'd you get that locket? Is it new?"

Oh. Right. I'm still wearing it. I stupidly couldn't bring myself to take it off. My cheeks flush as the lie slips out. "Oh, this? Just grabbed it at a thrift shop."

"It's pretty," he says.

"Yeah, I might have to steal it sometime," Riley teases.

I smile, but beneath it, guilt knots in my stomach.

The food arrives a minute later, and I'm grateful for the distraction. Before everyone digs in, I take a picture of Riley and my dad—a candid here at the table. They're so used to me snagging pics like this that they just keep talking as I frame the shot and snap it. Then, it's selfie time for all of us. They lean in close and I take the pic. I want to capture all life's moments, big and small. I want to experience everything, and sometimes that means being able to look back and remember a moment that's passed you by.

"The camera eats first," my dad says, faux grumbling.

"And the camera is very hungry," Riley adds with a huff.

"Please. You both love my pics," I say. "I've seen your smart hubs."

Riley rolls her eyes but bumps my shoulder—her subtle acknowledgement. As for Dad, I get his acknowledgement nearly every day. I gave them both digital photo frames for Christmas last year and they eagerly display the pics on them that I upload to our family album. And nearly every day my dad takes pics on his phone of the pics the frame scrolls through and texts us notes like "Remember that day?" or "That was fun!"

It's so meta, I love it. But I love, too, that the pics make him happy.

When breakfast ends, I have some time before I meet the other photographer, so I make a quick decision—I can't hold on to this necklace. It feels like it belongs to someone else. I take a bus to the Presidio and hike along Tennessee Hollow Trail until I find the lockbox I visited yesterday with Miles.

I try to remember the code, but he found it through an app. Dammit. I don't even know what app he used. Crouching by the stream, I go to the app store and search for geocaching apps. There are five.

I sigh, downloading them one by one, and after ten minutes of setup with the first one, I plug in the location and find the cache. Well, lucky me on that count.

I click on the info and there it is—the code. I punch it into the lockbox as a curl of hope rises up in me. Maybe he left something for me this morning. A note? A trinket? A small token that would show yesterday mattered to him.

Stop it, Leighton. This is so ridiculous. I'm not that girl —the one who hopes for gifts from guys.

"Just move on," I mutter.

I yank the box open...and it's empty. The bracelet is gone. My heart sinks heavily, but really this is fine. This is so fine. The bracelet didn't matter that much to me anyway.

But the necklace? It feels like it could have meant a lot. Like yesterday did. It's a day I don't want to forget. I have pictures of Miles and me in the studio, but none geocaching of course. That would have been too much to capture. I don't want to forget it though—how I felt when we were together. Effervescent, hopeful, heady. Like everything was possible. I run a finger over the heart locket, tracing the grooves and ridges of the metal before I take my phone out and snap a picture.

Something to remember yesterday.

Then, I let it go so someone else can have it.

I take off the heart locket and set it inside the box, its weight lifting from my skin. I close the box, leaving the necklace—and Miles—behind.

10

THE ABRIDGED TALE

Miles

It's not Birdie's fault. Not even a little. But still, as my grandmother slides an espresso in front of me—an espresso that is not at all vile—I figure she needs to hear the story. Well, the abridged version—no way am I spilling every detail of yesterday to her or anyone.

"Best date of my life, and guess what?" I say, leaning in. I glance over my shoulder, scanning High Kick's crowded tables. For what though? Coach McBride himself? The thought alone makes me shudder. But really, it's for anyone who might know me through hockey. Wrong ears and all that.

I nod toward the back room, and Birdie doesn't hesitate to follow. Once we're away from the espresso machine buzz and the morning crowd's chatter, I drop the bomb that still feels like it's dropping on me. "She's the coach's daughter."

Birdie freezes mid-step. "Shut your mouth."

"I only wish I were lying." I lift my arms in mock surrender, but my smile doesn't reach my eyes.

"No, no, no," she says, her brow furrowing as if she's rewinding through every moment since she met Leighton, searching for hints she might've missed. "That can't be right."

"It is," I confirm. "Some luck, huh? By the way, why the hell did you tell her I'm a chef?"

"Because I have to screen women for you, Miles! Make sure they're interested in the real you." She lifts her chin, looking a bit vindicated. But that's my grandmother for you—she's a lioness. Maybe because she's the *only* grandmother who's ever truly been in my life. My dad's mother vanished right around the time he did. But Birdie's always been there, from the days when I grew up in Seattle till our whole family moved down here. I get where she's coming from with the dating—looking out for me and all, especially given how things ended with Joanne and the things my ex said to me when we were unraveling. Then again, I wasn't exactly the best boyfriend at the end. I wasn't "emotionally available," as my ex liked to say. Well, she wasn't wrong. My emotion during that time was singular—my priorities during that time were me. Selfish, sure. But I was a fucking mess about my knee, and I have the scar and eventual therapy bill to show for it. As well as a grandmother who likes to vet all romantic prospects to make sure they're...compassionate.

Now, as if scolding herself, Birdie mutters, "But I guess I should've screened better this time. I'll need to up my game if I'm going to gain admission into The Underground Grandma Matchmaking Society you spoke of. Just never thought I'd need to check for family ties to your boss." She pauses, clearly still digesting this plot twist. "Really, the coach's daughter? That's bad."

I nod, but my thoughts drift back to yesterday. Sure Leighton's beautiful, but she was even easier to talk to the more I got to know her. Clever too. And, best of all, it seemed like she'd already decided to trust me—with her vulnerabilities and her desires. That trust part felt real. I felt different with her than I did with my ex, even in one mere day. Our connection seemed more meaningful. It made me want to keep seeing her. Made me imagine someday sharing my vulnerabilities with her.

That someday won't happen now though.

"Trust me, I know," I say to my grandmother, rubbing the back of my neck. "The last thing I need is to get on Coach's bad side—or worse, disappoint him." The thought's enough to make my stomach twist.

Birdie squeezes my arm. "Hey, at least there are other mermaids in the sea. I'll find a wonderful new one for you. Minus the tail. Really, mermaids are overrated— think about all the water pollution these days. The rising oceans. Oil spills."

I shake my head though I can barely keep up. "Please don't."

She sighs, her eyes softening with sincerity. "Let me do something, Miles. I feel like I need to make it up to you somehow. Think of this as a matchmaking debt. I need to repay it," she says, probably knowing I don't ask for help often, so she needs to push for me to accept it.

"To earn admission to the underground society?"

"Yes. Of course. But because I love you."

The last thing I want is a date with someone who's not Leighton. But now that Birdie's mentioned this alleged debt, there is something she could do. Something karmically helpful, considering the stunt I pulled this morning. Woke up early to make it happen, but I did it. There's only one detail I left out though, and I don't have enough time to handle this last piece on my own.

I check my watch briefly wishing I'd left this gold band back at Leighton's studio. A small excuse to see her again. But I shake the thought off. I can't keep coming up with reasons to see her.

Still, I need to take care of a proper goodbye before I leave town. "Here's what I need," I say to my co-conspirator.

After I explain, she nods dutifully. "I'll go, even though you know I don't hike."

"I do know that."

"But I love you more than I hate the outdoors. And I despise the outdoors. If you ever find me camping, just know the aliens have taken over my body. Speaking of aliens, I heard this great podcast on life forms from other galaxies the other day—might help take your mind off all this terrible news."

Maybe it would. I take the recommendation, and once I leave, play the podcast in the car as I make a quick pit stop. Then, I head out to the players' lot, mentally steeling myself to focus on hockey, and only hockey, from here on out.

Move forward.

Ever since my dad took off when I was twelve, leaving all of us behind with barely a word, I've lived by one mantra: move forward. Never back. And right now, that's exactly what I need to do.

* * *

An hour later, I board the team jet, keeping my head down. Maybe I can avoid Coach.

Yes, genius, you can avoid him the whole season.

I definitely can't avoid him today. He's in the fourth row, reading something on his tablet. Perhaps he won't see me. As I walk toward him, he looks up, nodding my way. "Falcon," he says, voice cool, composed.

"Hey, Coach," I say.

Then he returns to his tablet. That's it. Just *Falcon.*

Just my last name, like he greets all of us.

He says "Lambert" next for our goalie, Max, then "Bryant" for our right winger, Wesley, then "Callahan" for our left winger, Asher.

The parade of last names, each said in his confident, commanding voice is a reminder that I only want him to see me as a part of the team. Like every other guy. I don't want to stand out in any way other than being excellent on the ice. And that's what I'm here to deliver on this road trip.

We play New York the next night, where I'm fast and calculating from the second the puck drops. I hunt for openings, flipping the puck to Bryant for an early goal. In the second period, Callahan's barreling down the ice, but when the defensemen swarm him, he spins around and passes me the puck right as their D-man barrels toward me.

Only move forward.

So I do. I move the puck forward, sending it past the goalie's skate, and it lodges in the net.

Callahan high-fives me, and Bryant swings around for a pat on the back. Over on the bench, Coach gives an approving nod. He's rarely one for cheering.

When I hop over the boards for a line shift, Coach pats

my shoulder. "Good job out there, Falcon. You keep that up. Set the pace," he says.

A wave of discomfort tightens in my chest. I fucking hope it won't be like this all season. This kernel of guilt, this secret—it's only natural I'd still feel the press of it now. A few more weeks and it'll fade. I'm the kind of guy who learns from his mistakes, so I'm going to learn to be smarter, ask more questions, and never lose sight of my goals again.

"Yes, sir."

The next night, we play hard against Montreal, and when the game ends with a W, Coach hands me the puck in the locker room. "You capitalized on the power play. Do that this season. That's what we need."

Later, he pulls me aside in the corridor as we're leaving. "I mean that. You know you can do that, right?"

That's what he helped me most with when I joined this team after Vancouver put me on waivers—basically hockey's way of saying *anyone can have this guy we don't want*. I get it though—after my ACL tear and recovery, I'd lost my edge on the power play and Vancouver didn't believe I'd improve. But Coach McBride saw my potential, helped me see it was fear of injury slowing me down rather than anything physical. I worked with him and the team psychologist so I could get over that mental block after not being fast enough post-injury.

I don't struggle like that anymore. I'm even faster now, post-rehab.

But what would he think if he knew about the other night? Well, he'll never know. "I can, and I will, sir," I say as my teammates stream down the hall toward the exit.

"Good. That's what we want."

That's the *only* thing he'll want—for me to play at peak performance. That's what I want too.

When the road trip is over, we head home with three wins and one loss, and one short text message from Leighton thanking me for the gift I dropped off.

I don't answer it. Because I'm moving on.

INTERLUDE: WHEN WE PINE

In The Fall

11

JUST IN CASE

Leighton

"The Sports Network offered me a regular freelance spot. I'll be covering the Renegades," I say the second I step into my dad's office, a bit breathless from rushing over. It's early November, and I've been hustling nonstop for the last couple months.

I hand him the coffee I just picked up for him. His face lights up as he rises from behind his desk, his eyes twinkling in that way that tells me he's genuinely thrilled. I'd texted him that I had news, and, since I was in the area, he'd convinced me to bring him coffee, declaring that the coffee in the arena "tastes like it's been dragged through the locker room." So here I am, playing delivery girl. Not that I mind.

"That's fantastic! I'm not at all surprised. They loved you when you interned for them a few summers back," he says, pulling me into a hug.

He's not wrong. The producers there gave me glowing

recs. "And look who's making it on her own," I reply, a smile tugging at my lips. My dad's offered to help me out with rent more times than I can count, but, as tempting as it sometimes is, I've turned him down. Maybe I'm stubborn, maybe just proud, but I don't like depending on him. And since I don't have to, I choose not to. I've landed work on my own, and I'm making inroads by pushing hard.

He starts asking about my work, and we chat until he nods toward the open door, indicating someone's here. For one electric second, I wonder if it's Miles. My skin prickles at the thought, my pulse quickening as I remember our night together. But when I turn, it's not him. It's Everly Rosewood, the team's publicist.

"Hey!" she says brightly, stepping in for a quick hug. I tell her my new job news.

"So, does this mean I can officially add you to my photographer roster now?" she asks.

Dad's eyes spark in that knowing way, clearly pleased with the prospect.

"Of course," I say to her, since I'd be a fool to turn down her suggestion. But I'm also not convinced anything will come of it.

After Everly leaves, Dad leans back in his chair, studying me. "Would you want to do that? Take on some work here?"

I hesitate. It's a tempting offer, but there's that nagging thought—if I work here, I'd probably see Miles around, maybe more than I'm ready for. Still, I'm practical, and I know how valuable connections can be. Denying Everly's offer, especially when I can back it up with my talent, would be...well, foolish. The world runs on connections, and I'm hungry to prove myself. After all, I wouldn't be where I am without my father instilling confidence in me from day one.

"I think I'd be up for it," I say with a dry smile.

"Thanks for making me wait for that answer though."

"Someone has to keep you on your toes," I shoot back, smirking.

"You say that like my players don't." He fixes me with a mock stern look.

Since the next question is safer signed, I switch to sign language, asking, *Is someone giving you trouble?*

He signs back, *I work with a pack of grown men with elite skills. They always give me trouble.*

Briefly, I wonder if he's talking about Miles. But then, from what I've read, Miles is having a good season.

We exchange a few more signed words before his phone rings.

"It's the GM—Clementine. I should take this," he says with a wink.

"Even the boss has a boss." I grin, turning to leave his office.

But as I step into the hallway, I walk straight into the man who left me these earrings in a pretty box in my building's foyer. My stomach tightens as I meet Miles's gaze. His stare is locked on me, like he can't look away. He's wearing workout shorts and a Sea Dogs T-shirt. He must be on his way to the weight room.

For a moment, it's like that night all over again—the world narrowing down to the weight of his stare, the way he swallows roughly, clearly taken off guard to see me in my dad's office.

Maybe I should move first, make this less intense, less charged. The hallway feels small and close, and his gaze is heavy, like he's struggling just as much as I am to look away.

I glance at the stairwell and then nod toward it, wordlessly asking him to follow me. As we walk, I catalog the sounds—the hum of the heating system, the faint sound of voices from nearby offices. But when I open the door and it shuts, we're shrouded in silence. I don't mind it. Silence is comfortable for me.

"Hey," he says, taking a big breath, then tilting his head. "You wear them." He sounds mesmerized. Surprised too.

"Yeah, I do," I say, my voice feathery and I lift a hand, the silver bracelet sliding down my wrist as I touch the tiny earring on my right ear. It sits above the long, dangling star earring that I'm wearing today. It's a delicate, intricate flower given to me one morning by this man, along with the bracelet I left in a lockbox. "Every day," I say.

And then I instantly regret it because it feels like I'm confessing far too much. Who admits something like this? That they wear something every day from a one-time-only lover? Apparently, this girl does.

But his lips lift, like I've said the exact right thing. "You do?"

"Well, yeah, they're really, really pretty," I say, as if that excuses the significance of wearing them daily. But then again, he's the man who retrieved my bracelet from the lockbox the morning after. That's why it was empty. He had both delivered to me along with a note—*I wanted you to have your bracelet, so I got it for you. And then I couldn't resist giving you these too. -M.*

"I had a feeling they'd look good on you. They reminded me of you and your tattoos when I saw them that morning." His gaze stays locked on my face. "They're so pretty."

My stomach flips, but my throat aches annoyingly. I say nothing.

He's quiet for a spell too, rubbing the back of his neck, glancing at the stairwell door as if he's aware time is slipping away.

Aware, too, that even talking here, like this, is a risk.

I shouldn't linger in this stolen moment for too long. But something has always nagged at me since that morning—how quickly he must've pulled it off—retrieving the bracelet *and* getting me a gift. And, of course, I didn't say anything because we haven't been talking. "Did you just go out to the trail that morning?"

He smiles, like *you caught me.* "I did. I wanted you to have your bracelet back."

"Even though I said it was no big deal?"

"It was yours. It belonged on you," he says, like there was no other option but to retrieve it for me.

I love that he was so determined. And that's why I admit the next thing. "I went there too," I say softly.

"You did?" He sounds borderline thrilled, and I'm not sure why given that I returned the locket to the lockbox. "Why?"

"It didn't feel right keeping the necklace," I say honestly.

"Because it was someone else's?"

"No. Because it reminded me too much..."

He pauses, absorbing that, then says, almost like he's caught me on a technicality, "But you wear the earrings."

I shrug. "With a note like that, it was kind of hard to resist."

A smile shifts his lips, and he says, "I understand that completely."

And I suppose I do understand why he sounded borderline thrilled moments ago. Maybe because he suspected the real reason I went down that trail nearly two months ago. I don't like letting down my guard. I don't like showing myself to most people. But since Miles put himself out here this morning, I do something risky too. "But if I'm being honest, I suppose I went there because I was kind of stupidly hoping there'd be something left there. *For me.*"

His smile widens but is tinged with regret. "A note? A trinket? A treasure?"

"Any of the above," I whisper.

He takes a step closer. Close enough that I catch the scent of him. Soapy and clean, like he showered at home before he came here to work out with the guys. "I was in such a rush to get it done that I forgot to take something to replace the bracelet. I had to convince Birdie to take another bracelet later that day."

I crack up. "The thought of your grandmother in a pink boa and heels trudging through a hiking trail in the Presidio doesn't compute."

"Trust me, it didn't compute for her either. But she did it. She felt pretty bad about...everything."

"It wasn't her fault," I say softly.

He scratches his jaw, glances at the door again. "She tells me you're doing some work for her? Besides the photos you took?"

I smile. "I am. She hired me to take pics of her shop and the different drinks and food offerings every week— then she posts them on socials for the week."

"That's awesome," he says. "Maybe I'll see you around."

"Maybe," I say.

He's quiet for a beat, then perhaps resigned to this new normal, he says, "I should go. I really shouldn't be here like this."

I nod, understanding completely. "I know."

Before he leaves, he tilts his head and says, "Do you know sign language?"

"I do. Did you see me talking to my dad in his office?"

"Yeah. But I didn't know what you said," he admits.

"That's the point," I tease. But I can tell he's asking seriously, in the way that means he wants to understand me.

"Have you always?"

"I learned it in school." I don't usually share the next part either. I hesitate, unsure if I want to put myself out there like this, unsure if I want to admit this to anyone besides my family. Still, maybe there's some safety in telling him. He's not my boyfriend. He's not a guy I'm dating. He can't really hurt me. He can't run away since we've already parted. "Just in case."

His eyes flicker with something somber. "In case?" he prompts gently.

"Well," I say, then I pause. "I don't know what the future holds. I always want to be able to communicate with my family."

He winces, his throat tightening. "I understand. I do."

I'm not sure if he really does, but I appreciate how open he is about it, how comfortable and non-judgmental he seems. How caring he is when he talks to me. And how hard he tries.

"I should go," I say, feeling the moment close in.

He leans in, like he's going to kiss me, and honestly, I wouldn't stop him.

I'm both sad and relieved when he doesn't.

12

DOG YEARS

Miles

Don't look at her.

Do not look at her.

Do not *fucking* look at her.

That's what I tell myself all morning as I pull weeds and plant pea shoots for The Garden Society at an abandoned lot turned community garden on the edge of the Mission District.

I'm here with a bunch of guys from the team and a few from the Renegades football team too. Everly set this up, and I know it's part of her efforts to give our goalie, Max, a makeover. He's grumpy as hell and needs an image boost, so she's been tasked with that, and it looks like she hired Leighton to snap promo pics for this community outreach event.

I really should just focus on these clowns I play hockey with and not on the beautiful brunette. "Hey, Callahan, you thinking of planting some lucky coins here?" I tease, giving Asher a hard time. The winger is the walking definition of superstition.

"Maybe you should. Might help your prospects," Max tosses back.

Ouch. He can't know it hits below the belt. "Nothing wrong with luck," I say. The older I get, the more I learn to happily take the days when fortune is on my side.

As Wesley digs a small hole for a plant, he tosses a wry look my way. "True, true. And since you're older, Falcon, we should listen when you speak from the fountain of old-dude wisdom."

I thump him on the side of the head. "Did that hurt?"

"That *hurt*," he whines.

"Good, it was supposed to."

"Old dudes know how to hit," Max deadpans.

I narrow my eyes at our goalie. "I'm only a few years older than you, asshole."

Max shrugs. "But you know how it is for hockey players. Years are like dog years. So you're..." He pauses, thinking.

"Twenty-one years older than you," Asher supplies to Max, who's thirty.

I point at Asher, who's supposed to be the nice guy. "And you're thirty-two, asshole. You're closer in age to me."

"Still seven years younger in dog years," he says.

"That's it. We'll have a bench-press contest tomorrow," I say, egging them on.

"So you can get enough sleep first, right?" Wesley asks, smirking.

I have no choice. I punch his arm, but then I hear the click of a camera. It's Leighton, and she's smiling serenely.

"Are you publishing that?" I ask, but my voice doesn't sound like it's coming from me. It sounds like I'm trying too hard to talk normally. Or maybe more like I'm trying too hard to keep it even, to talk to her like anyone else would. But how the fuck would my teammates talk to her? How the hell do they talk to the coach's daughter? I've got to get out of my head around her. Especially since she's here in a work capacity, and if she's here now, she might be around again.

She tilts her head, an amused look turning her lips. "Don't worry, I don't publish everything I shoot. But it's cute to get pictures of you guys clowning around. How would you feel about this?" She bends to show us a picture of us goofing off. "I'll need Everly's approval, of course, but I think it's fun."

She's not looking at me as she says this, and I stay quiet too, because I don't want to let on what I'm thinking about. My mind has wandered to the pictures she took of us. The ones she was supposed to send me. I can't think of anything but the one time I stood right next to her, looking at pictures on the back of her camera.

Those images are lodged in my head the rest of the morning as we plant peas and other veggies. They won't leave, and the more I think about them, the more I have to know. What did she do with those pictures?

Later, when the event wraps up, she's packing up her gear. I walk past, then stop, unable to resist. "Do you need a ride?" I ask, my voice low but my eyes locked on hers so she can read my face if she needs to.

She looks around. Everly's deep in conversation with a reporter, and Max is with her. "I can take the bus or ask Everly to drive me home," she says, glancing back at them.

"But I'm offering." I try to keep my tone casual. "It's no big deal to give you a ride."

She nods. "You're right."

A minute later, she's sliding into my car, and we're leaving the parking lot like we're escaping. Something in me relaxes as soon as we're out of there, on the streets of San Francisco with my team far behind, and I can't hold back. "What happened to the pictures?"

She glances at me, as if she's feigning confusion. "Which ones?"

"You know which ones," I say, feeling an uncharacteristic edge in my tone. There's a part of me that thinks she might have deleted them, erased that day like it didn't happen. The possibility's been gnawing at me all morning. Even though we can't be together, it's like I need to know that we might have tried. That even in spite of both our relationship baggage—because I know I have plenty of checked luggage, and based on what she said the day we were together, I've got a hunch she has a carry-on too —we'd still have tried. The thought that I could be wrong about that is a bruise I can't stop touching.

"Don't make me spell it out."

"You're going to have to be more specific," she says, arching a brow. "I take a lot of photos."

At the red light, I turn to her, my irritation slipping through in my tone. "The ones from that day."

She looks at me, her gaze calm, steady. "And I'm asking you—*which ones?*"

Like she's forcing me to admit I can't stop thinking about *all of them*. Well, easy enough. "Every shot. What happened to them?"

A small, devilish smile plays on her lips, and it's clear she has the upper hand and knows it, maybe even likes it. "I kept them."

She *has* them, and I don't. That's not fair. She gets to revisit that day whenever she wants, and I'm left with nothing. I'm irrationally annoyed. "Why didn't you send them to me?"

"You said we weren't going to talk."

Technically, we said *date*, but pointing that out would be a dick move. Especially since I never responded to her thank you text. And yet, I'm kind of a dick, when I add, "You said that too."

"Yes, *we* both said that," she corrects me softly.

And she honored that, and I have mad respect for her self-control. But still, I'm so tightly wound right now. Since the second I saw her peering at the back of her camera, it's all I've been able to think about—the pictures. Except, no. It's not even the pictures that are driving me wild. It's what she might have done with them. That's what I need to know. If she's as affected by that day as I am.

The light flips to green, and I press down on the gas a little harder than before. "Do you look at them?" I ask, barely above a whisper but loud enough, I hope, for her to hear.

"What do you think?" Her voice is light but tinged with something more.

"Why aren't you answering me?"

"Why are *you* dying to know?"

The answer bursts out of me. "Because I'd look at them if I had them. I wouldn't stop looking at them," I say, not bothering to play it cool.

Her gaze softens, but there's something bittersweet in her tone as she says, "That's why I held on to them. To look at them."

The light ahead changes to red, and I slow down, the weight of her words sinking in. "I want them."

She raises a brow. "Are you sure?"

"Yeah, I'm sure. Why? Are they bad photos?"

Her lips twitch into a smile. "No, they're good."

"So I'll like them," I say, feeling...relief, but a wild excitement too.

"Maybe too much," she adds.

I'll consider myself warned.

* * *

That night, I'm dog-sitting for my mom and Harvey, so I'm walking their four rescue Chihuahuas—Bippity, Boppity, Boo, and Cindy—along Marina Green when my phone pings. It's a message from Leighton. I know I should focus on these tiny terrors, let them get their walk, but every fiber in me wants to check. With each ounce of self-control, I ignore it while they finish up.

The second I get home, I unclip their leashes, send them off to their heated dog beds—because of course they have heated dog beds—and finally open the message.

I was *not* prepared.

Holy shit, I was not prepared for this. And I need to enjoy the fuck out of it. I head over to a dark oak cabinet next to the TV I rarely watch, grab a bottle of scotch from my collection of the finest vintages, and pour two fingers. With the amber liquid in the tumbler, I return to the couch and take a long pull that I savor, feeling the good burn. Then, I open the pictures again, ready to savor them. As I look, my breath catches, a fire starting, then blazing in my chest as I scroll through the shots, each one more intense than the last.

One by one, I study every frame: the way I looked at her, the way I wanted her, the way I moved behind her, my hands brushing her arms. Then, there it is—the moment I kissed her, my hand on her throat, the trust in her gaze, and her whispered desires captured in every pixel.

I can't take it much longer. I'm rock hard and far too aroused while my mom's dogs watch me staring greedily at the photos. Setting down the glass on the coffee table, I replay my memories of the day, then...fuck it.

It won't be the first time I've done this to thoughts of Leighton. Probably won't be the last. I unzip my jeans, take out my aching shaft, and tug.

It's a relief, but only for a few seconds. I breathe out hard, giving in to the lust that grips me, the want I feel for her...my coach's daughter.

For a few seconds, I freeze over those words—*coach's daughter*.

Don't go there again. Get it together. Stop fucking thinking of her.

But the dick is sometimes stronger than the will.

I ignore that voice because it doesn't matter what I do when I'm home alone. It's what I do when I'm with her that counts. I haven't crossed the line again. And baggage or no baggage, we're not going to be a thing. But her admission that she looks at the pictures too? It's what I wanted. It's what I needed. It's also all I can have of her.

So what's the harm in giving in tonight? Faster, my fist shuttling harder, I jerk to the pictures of Leighton melting in my arms. To her asking for what she needed. To me giving it to her.

To us knowing what was happening between us that one perfect day.

But really, I just need to finally, *fucking finally*, get that day out of my system.

* * *

That's easy enough for the next couple months since I don't see her. I don't run into her at any more promo events. I don't bump into her at High Kick, though I definitely try. But I'm never there when she's taking her pictures for the week. I don't spot her at any games. She doesn't text me again.

I don't text her.

Impressive, I know.

I keep busy with hockey of course, and geocaching with a local club of fellow cachers, and taking some classes at a local university when I have free time. I've always liked school, and I try to take a new class every few years, usually in psychology or something related. My teammates don't call me The Professor for nothing. In January, I enter the Annual Win a Date With a Player auction, along with Asher, who's determined to go for the highest bid to keep his streak alive. I've done this event since I joined the team. The proceeds go to local nonprofits—animal rescues, food drives, and our team's support for libraries.

As I'm striding across the stage at a fancy hotel in the city, the color commentator for our broadcast partner touts my stats, then talks up my love of hiking, playing pool, and my affection for my hometown of Seattle. But when I spot Leighton, off to the side in the front row, snapping pictures, I falter, pausing for a step.

I do my best to tear my gaze away, and when the emcee mentions I like urban treasure hunts, my chest tightens. I know I won't be taking the winner geocaching on a date.

When a woman bids sixty-five thousand dollars on me and wins, I figure that's good money for a good cause. But something about it feels wrong, especially when Leighton turns her gaze away instantly.

At the end of the auction, after I've given Everly my info for the winner, she says, "We need a pic with you and the winner."

Natasha, the woman who won, tells me how much she loves the Sea Dogs, how excited she is, how she's followed my career from the start, and how glad she is that this team picked me up. She's nice—really, she is. And she's not the coach's daughter.

But I still feel like a piece of crap when Leighton takes our photo backstage. She's all business, entirely unreadable as she takes the pictures for socials.

"Thank you, Miles. Thank you, Natasha," Leighton says, then spins on her heel and heads off. But she's wearing those earrings—and that bracelet.

I can't read her, but it feels vitally important that she knows my mind. I'm not even sure why, but maybe it's this pressure in my chest. Maybe I can let go of it if I just...*say something.*

I loosen my tie but don't head for the parking garage. I march down the hallway, searching for her, and catch her as she's leaving the hotel. In the quiet hallway, I say her name but she must not hear me so I reach out and grab her arm. She startles.

"Sorry," I say, looking around. Coast is clear. "I wasn't loud enough." I feel bad now.

"It's okay," she says, then shrugs like she's saying *it happens.*

But I don't want it to happen with me. I'll have to do better with communication with her—make sure I'm speaking at a reasonable volume for her. But I also want to communicate well in *this* way. "I don't want to go on a date with her," I say because it feels important that Leighton knows where I stand.

She gives a resigned smile. "You should, though, Miles."

My jaw clenches. I want her to be as annoyed as I am. I want to know she can't stop thinking about me either. I want to know our one date fucked her up too. And I also want her to be happy. I drag a hand through my hair. "I'm not going to," I repeat.

"She won a date. You should." She sounds like she legit means it.

"I won't like it," I say.

"Maybe you should try."

"What about you? Are you trying?" The words spill out before I can stop them.

"Are you asking if I'm seeing someone?"

The thought that she might be makes me want to throttle...well, the world. "Are you?" It's like eating nails.

Gently, she shakes her head. "I'm not."

"Me neither." I don't even know why this matters—we can't be together. But maybe I can get the closure I need if I admit it to her. "I'm still hung up on someone else."

I feel lighter. And then entirely thrilled when she says, "Same here."

A couple weeks later, in February, I go on the date with Natasha, and we talk about hockey the whole time. It's completely platonic—so platonic that I break my no-texting rule.

Miles: It wasn't like going out with you.

Leighton: Good.

. . .

I try, I swear I try, to forget her. It would be easier if I didn't see her at a game next month, hanging out with Asher's temporary wife, Maeve. She's become friends with Maeve, as well as Everly, who's now with Max officially. So Leighton's around more. I see her more.

During warm-ups, I catch myself staring at her, wondering what it'd be like if she were here to see me play. Asher catches me and gives me a look that says "Are you going to keep doing that?"

It's a valid question and the answer really should be no.

And it *mostly* is no, until the end of the summer when I get a text from Asher inviting me to his wedding party. He and Maeve accidentally got married after the player auction and stayed married, falling in love for real over the last several months.

Now Maeve's aunt is hosting an official party for friends and family.

Including Leighton. And the whole team. Which means Coach will be there.

I almost don't go. But after one year in human years and seven in hockey-player-dog years, this will be my proof that I can handle it. I'll go to this party and finally put her behind me for good.

NOW: WHEN WE RESIST

The End of This Summer

13

LITTLE DICKS

Leighton

When I walk into Moon Over Milkshakes, an oldie-but-goodie is blasting louder than usual at the retro-themed diner, and I wince. The song isn't bad; it's just that loud music and I don't play well together.

I scan the room for my friends, since we're meeting for a pre-wedding party lunch. But as usual, I'm the first one here since I arrived early. I like to pick the table if I can, especially with this song about beaches and California sunshine blaring. A booth in the back opens up as a group stands to leave, and when the hostess swings by, she asks, "How many?"

"There'll be five of us," I say, pointing. "Any chance we can snag that booth in the back?"

"Of course, doll. I'll have it ready in a jiffy. What's your name?"

"Leighton. Thanks," I say as she enters my name into a tablet.

Turning to my phone, I adjust my hearing aids to restaurant mode, which is supposed to amplify speech and filter out background noise. Sometimes, though, the setting just amplifies everything—like, well, the music. Ugh. The song's even louder in my ears now, so I tweak the settings again, trying to enhance soft sounds. I save the adjusted program, hoping this time it'll work.

When I look up, the hostess is standing a couple of feet away from me, head tilted my way and eyebrows raised expectantly. I recognize her expression. She's waiting for me to say something because she just said something—something I missed. A kernel of embarrassment twists through me, but I do my best to ignore it. Besides, it's not hard to figure out what she said, so I ask to confirm, "The table's ready now?"

"Yes, it is! Right this way," she says with a smile, leading me over and asking a question without looking over her shoulder. I catch most of her, "How's your day going so far, hon?"

Even though I'm a bit frustrated I can't make out every word, it's not her fault. "Great, thanks," I say, but my mind is still whirring as I slide into the mint-green booth while she heads back to the front.

I'm tempted to ask someone to turn down the music. But that wouldn't be fair to the fifty or so other people here enjoying it. Besides, my friends are easy to talk to; I'll manage. And really, this is a reminder that I always have to be vigilant when I'm out and about. I don't have the luxury of fiddling with my phone if it means I might miss something I need to hear.

I'm adaptable and I've had to be since I was diagnosed at sixteen with mild to moderate sensorineural hearing loss. I didn't go to many concerts as a kid (none, actually). I didn't blast my eardrums out. I didn't have ear infections when I was younger. It was simply random.

That means I'll deal with the acoustics and the volume since I've had to for years, and I've learned where to sit or stand at restaurants and movies, in living rooms and at parties. I've figured out how to focus on different people who speak at different levels, and, most of all, I've learned how to pay attention. That's my best asset—my own internal focus. With it, I've figured out how to handle all sorts of situations.

How I'll handle seeing Miles later? That remains to be seen. Just being near him, even at the rink, still sends a spark down my spine. A spark I hope will burn out.

It would just be easier if it did.

Before long, my friends filter in, and I pop up to say hi to Everly, Josie, Fable, and Maeve. I met them all through Everly after we reconnected last fall. After I took photos at the community garden, she introduced me to her girl squad, and we clicked. I even did boudoir shoots for each of them. Hard to believe that just ten months later, they're my ride-or-dies. Maeve even sub-leased her apartment to me for a while, though the lease recently ran out, so I'll be moving in a few weeks, but back into the same apartment with my old roomies again. It's like a merry-go-round with my old roomies—one I'd rather not get back on. That'll be a pain. But some things are easy—like the fast friendship I've formed with these women.

Josie, who's a librarian, is always full of quick wit, and clever solutions. She recently got engaged to Wesley on the team. Everly's a warm and supportive badass babe. She's engaged to Max, the team's goalie. Fable's delightfully sarcastic and direct, and is dating her boss, the owner of the Renegades. And Maeve's our artist friend, full of beautiful chaos and love. She just had her second wedding with her best friend, Asher, who's also a hockey player. Yes, their *second* wedding. They got accidentally—well, maybe not so accidentally—married in Vegas and then decided to stay married for appearances. Last week, they renewed their vows, and that's why we're here today. Tonight's the wedding party. But we also need to review the party favors—definitely a priority alongside lunch.

"So, are you ready for the most *you* wedding party ever tonight?" I ask Maeve as the music shifts to something catchy from another era. I concentrate hard on hearing over the music, especially with the clatter of dishes. But it helps, too, that my friends know I prefer eye contact when we're all talking.

Her grin spreads wider than a city block. "I can't wait," she says.

"The venue couldn't be more Maeve unless it were a funhouse," Josie adds, setting her library book down, her huge diamond engagement ring glinting in the light.

Maeve's hazel eyes widen. "Why didn't I think of a funhouse?"

"Maybe save that for wedding number three," Fable says to her, tucking a strand of red hair behind her ear.

"Hey, don't tempt me," Maeve says, smoothing a hand over her T-shirt that reads *I Speak Dog*. "I just might renew my vows every year."

"Well, I agree," Everly chimes in. "A coffee shop with room to dance is very you. And now that they carry your art? Iconic."

Maeve gives a playful shrug. "That's me." She's lighthearted about it, but the shop carrying her paintings is a big deal. Maeve's made serious inroads as an artist in the last several months, and that includes landing placement on coffee shop walls. They're the *new* art galleries.

"And the party favors?" I ask, turning to Fable, focusing fully despite the loud music. I'm in vigilant mode. "Are they as amazing as we hoped?"

Fable and I planned the favors, but she picked them up.

"Even better," she says, pausing as the server arrives. We order quickly, knowing our go-to dishes. Then Fable returns to the topic of the favors, meeting Maeve's gaze. "You wanted classy chocolates, and we delivered." She dips a hand into her bag, fishing around before pulling out a robin's egg blue box and setting it on the table. She slides it to Maeve with a perfectly straight face. I keep my expression even too. "Here's a sampler. Open it."

"We wanted you to try them out before tonight. Just in case," I add, since that's what Fable and I planned when we plotted out these favors.

Maeve laughs. "I never say no to opening a present before Christmas—or dessert before a meal." She opens the box, her expression blank for a beat. Then her eyes pop, and a wicked smile forms on her lips. She raises her head. "You didn't?"

"Oh, we did." I smile too. We planned the favor together at the shop the other day, and seeing her reaction makes it worth it. "Do you like it?"

"I'm sure I'll love it." Maeve opens the box to reveal a set of chocolates from Elodie's Chocolates, each one cheekily phallic. "Aww. You know me so well."

"We do," I say, and oddly, I feel that way despite only having met her a relatively short time ago. It's a good feeling. The best feeling. I feel like they'll be around for a long time, and I like that reassurance.

Maeve pops a little chocolate dick into her mouth, chews, and sighs like a food show host.

"So...are we handing these out tonight?" Josie asks innocently.

We all burst out laughing. "As much as I love dicks, the answer is no," Maeve says. "There will be adults there."

"Surely you don't mean the hockey team by adults?" Everly teases.

"You don't want the whole team getting tiny dicks as a gift?" Josie deadpans.

"The Sea Dogs can eat dicks all night long, but it's more like my aunt and her friends that I probably shouldn't give mini cocks to," Maeve clarifies, since her aunt's hosting the party. "Let's keep these just for us," she says, giving Fable a pointed look. "These are a joke, right?"

"Do they taste like a joke?" Fable counters, then relents. "Of course. They're just for us."

Everly sobers, leaning in, her blonde ponytail swishing closer to me. "Your dad will be there too?"

"Yep," I reply, shrugging. "Everyone's going."

She gives me a knowing look. "So...that means Miles too? How's that going to be for you?"

Inwardly, I feel a twist of nerves but I keep my expression neutral. They know the basics—I've told them about the one perfect date we shared. A date that couldn't be repeated. But I haven't told them how hard it's been to keep my distance. What's the point? I need to keep moving forward.

In life, in work...in everything.

I shrug, forcing a smile. "It'll be fine. Good, even. Let's just say it'll be interesting."

The food arrives, and as I eat my veggie burger, my mind wanders once more to tonight. I've seen Miles a handful of times in the last year—in the stairwell, in his car after the community garden event, in the hallway post-auction.

Tonight will be different in one big way. There won't be a chance to be alone.

*   *   *

MainLine is buzzing, the spacious coffee shop packed with friends, family, and...the team. Lights glint off glasses and silverware, and the space feels sparkly with celebration. The music is softer here, with an old standards vibe, and I'm grateful. But I'm still on edge, knowing *he's* somewhere in the crowd.

It's summer and hot for September. I'm wearing jeans and a silky black sleeveless top—at least, that's what I tell myself. It's not that Miles likes the ink on my arms so much he once bought me earrings that reminded him of my tattoos—earrings I'm wearing tonight.

I don't have to look for him; he's already here, chatting at the counter with the guys. I should've been ready for it —that jolt I felt when I saw him earlier tonight—the first time I've seen him since the season ended. But it surprised me again tonight, maybe because he looks so good. Like he's worked out even more in the off-season. His arms are stronger, chest broader, and his hair a little longer and messier.

I'm not complaining.

I'm acutely aware of him across the coffee shop, which is closed for the private party but serving champagne and, naturally, coffee spiked with liquor. But I stick with a group of friends, where Maeve is thanking us for the real party favors—chocolates shaped like paintbrushes, hockey sticks, and a ring for their marriage.

"You're the best, and I love you," Maeve says, pulling us into a group hug. When we let go, I grab my camera from my bag and snap a few pictures. "I can't resist," I say, since I want her to have pictures of tonight.

"You're the best," she says again, then nods to my camera. "And you better send me those."

"Obviously," I say. "Also, just try to stop me from taking more all night long."

"I'm afraid I can't do that," she says.

"Good."

"But I don't want you to feel like you have to," she adds, and it's thoughtful the way she looks out for me professionally. There's no need though.

"Trust me, I want to," I add.

"Thanks." Then she leans closer, her gaze straying across the room briefly before she turns back to me, saying in a lower voice, "And someone can't take his eyes off you."

My body reacts instantly—a tingle slides down my spine, chased by excitement. I shouldn't want this. I really shouldn't. And yet I want to eat up her comment with a spoon.

Stupid. So stupid.

"Well, he should probably stop, since my dad is here," I say. That's why I can't talk to Miles tonight—I don't want to give a thing away. This is just a party, and I'm just another face in the crowd tonight.

"And your dad's walking toward him right now," Maeve adds.

Tension flares in me. Worry, too, for no reason. It's not like my dad is talking to him about me.

Still, I whip my gaze to them, curiosity gripping me.

Yep, there's the coach talking to one of his star players, and since I have a solid view of my dad's face, I'm pretty sure I can make out most of the words my father's saying to the team's center. *Especially if you become co-captain.*

I blink, then mutter, "Holy shit."

"What?" Maeve asks.

Of course she doesn't read lips. I do. I turn to her. "I think Miles is up for the captaincy."

14

SHUTTERBUG

Miles

I'm still reeling—in a good way—from the twin bombshells Coach just dropped here at Asher's wedding celebration. First, he told me the Sea Dogs traded for my brother, Tyler, from the Los Angeles Supernovas. Then, he hinted I'd be playing alongside him as *co-captain*.

Usually hockey teams have only one captain and a handful of alternates. But Coach said last season that he'd like to do things differently here with the pecking order. Change it up and have a true co-captain to lead alongside our current captain. I scan the crowded coffee shop across from that guy—Christian Winters. Christian's been a Sea Dog for years, and everyone on the team looks up to him. With two young kids at home, though, I know he'd be glad to share some of the responsibilities that come with wearing the "C."

And I'd really like to be that guy he shares them with.

It feels surreal. A few years ago, I was in Vancouver, watching the game from my couch, my knee still screaming post-surgery, my mind dark. Joanne was pulling away from me, and I from her, and my whole body aching and broken. Back then, I would never have believed I'd hear words like these.

All I wanted was to play again—just one more time. But to squeeze out a whole career after an ACL tear? One that's—knock on all the wood in the world—going pretty damn well? I'd never have let myself believe it. That felt like too much to hope for. Too good. And now? Damn.

Really, I should say something to the man standing in front of me.

"That's...great," is all I can manage, though, as I stand at the coffee counter with my closest teammates and good friends—Asher, Max, and Wesley.

Coach McBride gives a professional smile, then claps me on the shoulder. "We'll talk more at training camp, Falcon," he says, his shrewd eyes glancing around at the party, teammates and friends toasting Asher and Maeve's happily ever after. Then he turns to Asher with a nod. "No one wants the boss around too long. Congratulations, Callahan."

"Thanks for coming, Coach," Asher adds, and the other guys say their goodbyes. With that, Coach McBride heads out into the night, leaving me to process his news. I need to call my brother soon, but selfishly I'm a little fixated on what Coach just said about me. Max and Wesley are too, since they give me their congrats before peeling away.

Asher turns to me, his eyebrows raised. "Dude."

I manage to nod. "Yeah." Like that means anything. Then I add, "I've got...nothing."

Asher laughs. "And they call you the articulate one."

He's not wrong. I'm the guy they come to for advice. The veteran. The player who's supposedly seen it all. The game's highs and lows, the different teams, the changing styles. And...the potential scandals. My gaze drifts to Leighton on the other side of the room. She's snapping a pic of some of the guests, then she lowers her camera. My pulse surges with one look at her. Her chestnut hair spills down her back in waves. Her black top shows off her arms and creamy skin I want to kiss, touch, explore. Her eyes spark with mischief and intelligence, and this feeling tugs in my chest—a desire that won't go away and hasn't since I met her. A desire to get to know her better. It's annoyingly insistent, more so when she turns my way briefly. Her lips are glossy pink and tipped up in the hint of a smile. A knowing one—and I wonder what's behind it. But I shouldn't. Really, I shouldn't wonder. Not my place to think about her, especially with this potential captaincy on the line.

I tear my focus from her, squinting at Asher through my glasses, trying to get my bearings. "What did you say?"

Asher cracks up, shaking his head. "You are so screwed, man," he says.

"No kidding." I scrub a hand across my jaw, trying to play it cool. But clearly failing. Asher doesn't know everything about what happened with Leighton. In fact, he hardly knows anything. But I did tell him one night that I had it bad for her. So he knows enough.

Asher leans in, lowering his voice. "Here's a tip for you—"

But Maeve shoots him a just-for-her-husband look that must be far more interesting than this conversation.

"Go see your wife," I say, exonerating him from this convo.

"Catch you later," Asher says, then joins Maeve, and follows her out onto the dance floor, leaving me to wonder what his tip about Leighton might be. And leaving me with my so-very-screwed feelings.

Watching Asher dance with Maeve, I grab another drink from the bartender, switching to water. I look back at the crowd, at my friends dancing or laughing with their partners, and I think about what it means to be captain, the work ahead, the season I want to have. And what it'll be like to play with my brother. I tap out a text to him. *Anything exciting going on?*

He'll appreciate the irony whenever he reads it, which might be tomorrow since he's the world's worst texter. But he might be busy with the kids, so I'll wait to hear from him before I call.

As the night winds down, my friends start drifting away one by one, couples and groups slipping out. And still, I find myself...not leaving.

I stick around, offering to help with the favors, making sure guests have their chocolate boxes, as well as their bags and purses. I'm just doing it to help a friend. This is a big night for Asher. As I hand out boxes, Leighton snaps a few pics.

Soon, most of the guests are gone. When the happy couple takes off for the night, Leighton's at the door, capturing the moment. Then, she waves goodbye and turns around.

Hardly anyone else is here—her, me, the catering staff, a few others.

She glances around at the mostly empty space, littered with champagne glasses, cake plates, and the remains of mini mango tacos. An Ella Fitzgerald tune plays softly overhead. I don't know the song, but I recognize the vibe —it's something about longing. Leighton lowers her camera, smiles, and gives a small wave.

Seems foolish not to talk to her. Tonight is proof I'll see her around. Might as well get used to it. Really, it was one day we shared a year ago, so what's the big deal? I shouldn't carry it with me all the time. Resolved to put the past in the past and forge a new—friendship, perhaps— with the coach's daughter, I head her way.

"Are you playing the role of shutterbug tonight?" I ask.

Her smile disappears. Her eyes glimmer with dirty memories. And, fuck, it's like a jolt of electricity shooting down my spine as I remember calling her that when we were together. *Shutterbug.*

The shift in her expression tells me she remembers it too. How I said it. When I said it. Images of her threading her hands around my neck as she sank onto my dick have the audacity to flash in technicolor before my eyes. Heat charges through my body.

"Maeve didn't ask me to, but I wanted to get some pics for her." She brandishes her camera almost apologetically. "I also kind of can't resist taking pictures. Actually, that's not true. I'm downright addicted."

She's moved away from the implications of that nickname, so I do the same. "Sounds like you chose the right profession."

"Definitely," she says. "It's a job and a hobby."

"Are you always the one taking pictures of friends?"

"Always," she says emphatically. "When we're out and about. When we're at home. When we're anywhere. I do the same with my sister too. Making sure I have pictures of us doing even everyday things, whether thrifting, or wandering around Japantown eating crepes. Because crepes are really good and sometimes you just need to capture the good stuff."

I laugh. "Two for one—pictures and crepes."

"Exactly."

"So photography is also a passion," I add.

"It is. Sounds like your job too." She shoots me a playful look. Or maybe it's playfully chiding since she says, "Though who knows—you never really talked much about it."

Her tone is teasing, letting me know she's not annoyed I never mentioned it that day. I'm so damn glad I didn't. In that case, ignorance was definitely bliss.

"Still don't regret that. Also, it's definitely a passion."

She takes a beat, then tilts her head. "So, you might be captain?"

My brow knits. "How did you know?" The question bursts out, but then, of course, the answer arrives obviously. "Your dad told you?"

I hadn't thought about that before—that she might know things about the team before others do. But it makes sense.

She laughs lightly, shaking her head. "No. He doesn't really give me tips like that. Nor do I seek them out."

It's a little bit like a rebuke, but that's fair, I suppose. "Sorry, I didn't mean to make it sound like..."

But I'm not sure what I didn't mean to make it sound like—that she's got the coach's ear? Of course she's got the coach's ear. That's different though than hunting for info, which still leaves me wondering. "How did you know then?"

She rocks back and forth on her black boots, a slight smile gracing those lush lips again. It's that look I saw the day I met her—confidence. "Want me to let you in on a little secret?"

That word—secret—sounds too sexy on her lips, and I am helpless to resist it. Or, really, her. "Yeah, I do."

She looks around, then says in a soft voice, "I read his lips when he was talking to you earlier tonight."

My jaw drops. That is hot and impressive. "You did?"

But of course, she did. The look in her eyes is devilish pride, and deservedly so as she says, "Yes."

"I am impressed."

She gives a no-big-deal shrug of her shoulder. "Girl's got skills."

"You do," I say. I knew generally speaking that she could read lips, but didn't realize she was so damn good at it. As someone who loves learning, I'm fascinated with how people pick up different skills. "Did you set out to learn how or have you always been able to? I honestly don't know how that works."

"I don't want to say it just happened. It was more like one day I realized that's what I had been doing all along by watching people form words—you wind up learning the way lips move when they make certain sounds. It's most helpful, though, to know the context of a conversation. But you're not likely to pick up one hundred percent of a conversation just from lip reading—the movies kind of exaggerate that. When you read lips, you have to combine it with what you expect someone to say, their facial expressions, and so on. In the case of you and my dad, it was easy enough—putting two and two together for what he might be saying to you, and I could make an educated guess."

I let out a low whistle. "You could be a secret weapon though."

"Accurate."

"Like reading things other teams say, plays they call."

"I'm pretty sure sports teams have tried that before, which is why other teams cover their mouths when they talk."

"True, true," I say, taking a beat to just...look at Leighton. Her blue eyes are something else—deep pools that have me transfixed. It's hard to look away from them but I do, only so I can take the rest of her in. While her hair mostly falls over her ears, I do catch a hint of silver above her long earring. I'm tempted to point out that she's wearing the flower ones I gave her. But that feels dangerously close to flirting. Everything with her does. Mostly because of how annoyingly fast my pulse surges when I'm near her. Funny, how you can be burned from a past romance, but then once you meet the right person you're ready to charge headfirst into a new one. What's not so funny is that I met the right person, but I can't have her.

Best to focus on the present then, and this moment since that's all I can have. "Anyway, we'll see what comes of the whole co-captain thing."

"I'm rooting for you," she says.

"Thanks. Here's hoping for a good training camp and a good year. It's an honor that I'm being considered."

"I'm not surprised you're being considered," she says, in a cheery tone, a supportive tone, and I wish I could read her more easily. I wish I could read her like I could the day I spent with her.

Since then, she's gotten better at holding back. I try once again to focus on this whole friendship thing. "Turns out, my brother was traded here too. Haven't played with him in a long time. Feels a little surreal. But it'll be interesting."

"To play with him instead of against him?" she asks, getting it completely.

"Exactly. He's been the enemy for ages."

"You know what they say in hockey—keep your team-mates close, and your family on the bench beside you where you can keep an eye on their every move."

I laugh. "Exactly. Gives new meaning to my brother's keeper." I pause, scratch my jaw then add, "You think you got some good pictures tonight?" I just don't want to stop talking to her. She's not making a move toward the door, so I hope she's feeling the same damn way.

"I do. I think I might make Asher and Maeve a surprise photo album or something. Or frame some of them."

"Can I see them?"

She looks around at the servers cleaning up at the nearly empty coffee shop, sensing they probably do want to close this place down. "I can show you outside," she offers.

I should probably keep my distance, but when the woman you can't have—the woman who's lodged front and center in your brain—offers to spend more time with you, you don't say no.

"Let's go," I say.

"Let me grab my things." She snags a box of chocolate from the counter, then a second box, dropping them into her bag, then we leave.

But it's crowded outside in Hayes Valley, with people pushing past us along the sidewalk.

It's a warm summer night, the kind that feels like it shouldn't end too soon. I don't feel like looking at her camera out on the street, so I nod to a bar at the corner. "You want to just duck in there?"

I have no earthly reason to want to look at photos of Asher's and Maeve's wedding party. But when Leighton says yes, I feel like I've won a game I barely realized I was playing.

And I do like winning.

I walk, fast and determined, toward the bar with her.

15

THINGS HAPPEN

Miles

A shot of the newlyweds dancing, Maeve's head tipped back as she laughs. A photo of Max whispering something in Everly's ear, her expression...serene. An image of Wesley standing behind Josie, his arms wrapped around her, amusement in her eyes. Pictures of Asher's dads sharing a slice of cake. Maeve's brother lifting a glass to toast.

"These are great," I say, admiring the way Leighton captures a moment in time, each one rich with emotion and connection.

And then there's a shot of me, elbows resting against the counter, looking pensive as I survey the scene. Alone, but watching. I try to place when it was taken, but I'm not sure.

"I don't know what I was looking at," I say, trying but failing to remember that moment. Mostly it feels like...the whole night. There's a glass in my hand in the photo, and I'm just...watching.

"As a photographer, I'm more interested in what you were thinking," she says, studying the viewfinder on her camera with the shot of me on it.

"What's your take then? What was I thinking?" I ask, turning the question back on her, here in this corner of the bar.

We're at The Spotted Zebra, tucked into a small booth in the back. The lights are low here, the vibe very much after dark, the music a little sultry. It might not have been the wisest choice for resisting, but the more I fall into Leighton's orbit, the less I'm thinking rationally.

She has that effect on my brain—she makes everything warm and hazy.

She studies the picture a little more, then looks at me next to her. Her gaze on me right here, right now, tightens the pressure in my chest. She looks back at the photo. I'm wearing my glasses, like I am now, with a faraway look in my eyes. "I think you're wondering," she begins, her tone thoughtful, "what's next for you. Where do you go from here? Will you live up to the captain job? And what will it cost?"

Talk about a mind reader.

"You got all that from a photo?" I ask, but she's shockingly right. Those thoughts all ran through my mind.

"Yes, but in all fairness, I was looking for it too. I wanted to remember that moment in time. So I was trying to find your thoughts on your face and capture them in the picture. When I was taking it, I knew what to look for —the idea that you had a lot on your mind."

I let out a low whistle, impressed with her artistry, her approach. "You're good. I knew that, but I keep learning it.

You seem to know how to...read a room, but really—to read people."

"Thanks," she says. "I hope so. But I also love it. Trying to find a story in what's going on with the people I'm photographing. Sometimes it's easy to just assign all these stories to people. But I think you have to know what you're looking for, or at least be open to finding the stories they're telling themselves."

I think on that for a moment, linking it with what she said a few minutes ago about always taking pictures—like she did of us, of our first kiss. Like how she held on to those photos. "Do you look back at the pictures you take? I've read stats on the number of images humans now take every day and most seem so mundane. A receipt, where we parked our car, a schedule for a workout class."

"A lot of photos are just notes. But the thing is, you *could* look back on those later, and read the story of your day, what was going on, what mattered to you in that moment."

That's one way of looking at disposable photos, but I don't think that's what she does behind the lens. "You're not taking photos for notes though, are you?"

A soft smile shifts her lips as she shakes her head, looking like she appreciates being understood. "Not really. I want to capture experiences if I can." Excitement builds in her tone as she says, "Think about how fast the world moves now. Our days fly by so quickly, filled with simple, incredible moments we don't realize are special until later, when it's too late. So I try to capture what's happening now—what's exciting us, worrying us, making us think. Then, someday, I can look at a picture and that memory won't be lost. When I take pictures, I try to find the story of that moment, that *unlost* moment, so that I can feel it again later."

I peer at the photo she took of me with new perspective. I'm pretty sure, against my plans, against my judgment, I was looking for time with her at the party.

No matter what I told myself.

It's true I stayed to help a friend. But it was also a lie I told myself to be close to this woman. That was the story of my day. That's the *unlost* moment.

With her so close, her hair cascading down her shoulder, that vanilla-brown sugar scent teasing me, it's hard to remember that tonight I'd intended to put this thing between us squarely in the past, where it belongs.

That plan seems like a blur now. In a round booth at the back of the bar, with the lights low and us talking about the things that make us tick.

I swallow roughly. "I was looking at you."

Her breath hitches. "You were?"

"Yeah," I admit. "You're not wrong. All those things went through my head, but mostly I was trying to look at you...while not looking at you."

She licks her lips, glancing toward the bar's front door, then back to me. "Were you successful?"

"Not in the least." A *fuck it* mentality takes over as I slide a hand along her thigh under the table. It's such a relief to touch her again. Such a privilege. It blots out everything around us.

She shudders, and the way it runs like a wave through her body spurs me on. I shouldn't be touching her like this in public, but I do it anyway. No one can see my hand under the table.

But *she* can feel it.

So I run my hand down to her knee, cup it, then move my palm back up, covering her thigh.

A gust of breath escapes her pretty lips.

Her eyes float closed for a few dangerous seconds, and I'm tempted, so damn tempted to succumb to this...spell.

That's how I feel with her.

Like there's nothing else beyond The Spotted Zebra's doors.

Like we're immune to the world.

And I could lean in. Kiss that gorgeous mouth. Feel her melt under my touch. And forget the promises I made myself mere hours ago so I can take her home and fuck her again the way we both want.

Goddamn, I need to stop this train of thought.

Instead, I inch closer to Leighton, squeeze harder, touch more.

She shudders again and lets out the most intoxicating sound. My brain short-circuits. I'm not thinking. I'm just *doing*.

"I'm about as successful in not touching you as I was at not looking at you," I murmur.

She turns her gaze slightly, her hair falling as she looks at me. "I've noticed."

My touch turns softer now, more teasing as I drag my fingers slowly down her leg once more. "You're a little irresistible, Leighton."

Just like when I said I was a little into her.

"And you really should resist me," she says, moving closer to me. We've created this vortex where we can give in—a no-man's land, free of rules and consequences.

A space in the hazy glow of night where drinks flow, soft music pulses, and Leighton's heady scent drifts around me.

"Yes, I should," I say, breathless. Then she drops her hand under the table too, finding mine and then covering it.

Fuck me.

This wicked seduction should not feel so good. Her hand on mine sends electric pulses through my body. I swallow roughly, breathing out hard as she slides her fingers between mine, watching me the whole time.

My god, she's so fucking sexy. Does she even realize what this simple touch does to me?

My money's on yes. Her eyes are full of instinct, awareness, and passion as she glides her hand under mine so that our palms touch, our fingers clasp.

Heat roars in me.

I'm ridiculously turned on by this woman holding my hand under the table. This is how you touch someone's hand before you fuck. This is foreplay. We steal touches and pile kindling on a fire while the flames crackle.

"I really should stop," I rasp. Instead, I let go of her hand and trail my fingers along her forearm, tracing her ink there, and she trembles.

Her gaze drifts down, and she watches me touch her while seconds stretch into a fever dream. "I should go," she says. "Maybe that's easier."

Her resolve spotlights that she's better at this than I am. She's got a stronger handle on this...thing between us.

I slump back, drag a hand through my hair, and swallow the longing I feel. My gaze falls absently on the two glasses on the table. Bubbly water for her. Iced tea for me. Was that intentional? Maybe I knew that if I got buzzed, I'd give in.

"I'll drive you home," I say.

She arches a brow, but she smirks too, wordlessly asking, *Are we really going there?*

But I toss some bills on the table to cover the tab and leave the bar before either of us can say *should* or *shouldn't*.

Once we're in my car, I ask, "You still live at the same place?"

She shakes her head. "Actually, I moved into Maeve's little apartment for a while. My former roomies were having really loud sex, like, all the time."

I laugh as I turn into traffic. "That must have been annoying."

She gives me the address and watches me plug it into the car's navigation, then adds, "But Maeve's windowsill is inhabited by some seriously randy pigeons. So I can't seem to escape loud banging. You'd think for a girl with hearing loss, this wouldn't be an issue. But you'd be wrong."

I love that she can poke fun at herself. "I guess you're not a voyeur, then?"

"You are correct," she says, then adds, "but I'm moving back in with the loud sexers in a few weeks."

"Need any help? With the move?" I ask without thinking. I know we shouldn't be alone again, but here I am, offering to help her.

You're alone in the car with her right now, you dickhead.

"I think I can manage," she says. Her independent streak excites me, even though I kind of wish she'd say yes.

Her place isn't too far away. I park on a side street and turn off the car. "Thanks for showing me the pictures," I say, "and getting that drink." Am I stalling? Maybe.

"Glad you liked them." Her tone is teasing, playful. "Are you going to demand them from me again?"

"Did I demand the last ones?"

She rolls her eyes. "You were kind of demanding, Miles."

I think about the night she sent me the pics and the many nights I've spent with them since. "Worth it." I hold her gaze and lick my lips. "So worth it."

She doesn't look away. I can't say who breaks the stare first. But the next thing I know, my lips are crashing down on hers. She meets me, pressing closer, and I curl my hand around the back of her head.

I expect something like our first kiss in the studio—a sultry tango of a kiss, like a slow sip of brandy.

But this kiss is a shot of tequila. It streaks straight to my head, and I see stars. It's white-hot, full of teeth and moans.

Leighton maneuvers a hand between us, grabbing my shirt collar and jerking me close. My glasses are in the way, so I wrench apart from her to rip them off, setting them—maybe—on the console. "Fucking glasses," I mutter.

"They're still hot," she murmurs.

This woman.

She gets me going more than anyone ever has. "C'mere," I say. "Need to kiss you again."

"So do it," she taunts.

I grip the back of her head again, and she gasps. Then I seal my lips to hers once more. I growl into her mouth, and the sound seems to excite her. She pulls me closer. I grip the back of her head tighter. We kiss deeper, our tongues skating together. Mouths exploring. Breath coming fast.

I slide my fingers into her hair and tighten my fist at her nape, tipping her chin to the perfect angle. I coast my lips down her throat, kissing the soft, delicate skin there, my free hand tugging at the top of her shirt.

I should stop. Really, I should.

But she lets go of my collar, wraps her hands around my head, and jerks me closer to her chest.

Fuck yes.

I groan against her skin and kiss her more—the hollow of her throat, the dip of her collarbone, the side of her neck. Her jaw next, grazing my teeth along it, before I meet her lips again.

One more shot, I tell myself.

One for the road.

I raise my face and then drop my lips more gently onto hers. This is me hitting the brakes. I slow down as our mouths meet again and run my fingers along her arms, savoring one last kiss.

Then I let go.

We're both panting.

Eyes are glazed.

Windows are fogged.

I've already gone further than I should.

I shoot her a rueful half-smile, then do what I should have earlier instead of giving in to this wild need that inhabits me when I'm near her. "We probably shouldn't be alone together again." I somehow manage to choke out the words, hating each one.

"No," Leighton says. "We definitely shouldn't."

She sounds resolute. Thank god, because I'm sure as hell not.

"Yeah," I say dryly. "I guess you're more than a little irresistible." I lift my thumb and forefinger to show a sliver of space.

The callback to earlier makes her chuckle. "You too."

The words warm my chest. Leighton lifts a hand and slides a thumb along my jaw, brushing over my stubble before letting go and picking up my glasses. "Here you go."

I slide them back on and blow out a breath. "Bye, Leighton," I say, then shake my head, frustrated with myself. "And I'm sorry."

"For what?"

"For breaking our...deal not to do this again."

Her sigh is heavy and a little wistful. "I broke it too. Things happen."

She's letting me off easy, but I'll take it. "I guess they do."

"We'll make a new promise," she says.

"That we won't be alone together." I offer my hand to seal the agreement—and to test whether I can touch her without pulling her into my arms.

She shakes my hand, proving it's possible. "Good night, Falcon."

"Good night, Shutterbug."

She collects her bags and climbs out of the car, heading to her building. At the door, she gives a brief wave goodbye before going inside.

I don't leave right away. I sit behind the wheel. Drag a hand through my hair. Stare out the window while I replay the night.

Finally, I go too.

When I get home, I call my brother and refocus on my responsibilities—to the team, to my family, to myself. And...to the coach. I won't let them down. It's time to move forward. That's the only way I know.

16

NOT SO FAST

Leighton

The thing about pigeons pornicating is this—their cooing sound is right in my wheelhouse.

It's low and a little rumbly, like thunder, and it wakes me up like high-pitched banging never would.

Fortunately, I'm a morning person, so I pop out of bed and turn off the alarm that is about to go off anyway.

In the living room, I pause at the window to check out the feathered friends with benefits. I suppose I should give them their privacy. But look—if Ms. Peck and Big Bird want discretion, they could pick a different place to get it on. I press my hand to the cool glass as I peer at the scene on the windowsill. "Get it, girl," I say when Big Bird hops up on her back to seal the deal.

I'll miss these little exhibitionists when I leave. Shame that this place is going co-op. I don't mind Maeve's quirky apartment—ducking in the low-hanging shower, and the sideways toilet. For these last several months, it's been my own space.

I head out. I have a shoot later today, but I need to make a quick stop at the arena before I go to the studio. Dad texted me after he left the wedding party last night, telling me he'd forgotten to take home a box of chocolates and adding a sad face emoji so I'd grab an extra box for him.

The sweet-tooth treasure in hand, I hop on a bus. I gaze out the window at the city passing by, but in my mind, I'm watching yesterday's highlights—the moment in the diner with the hostess, then stolen moments with Miles at the party, in The Spotted Zebra, in his car...

My stomach flips, but I shake off that weakness. I'm in full game mode by the time the bus pulls over at the Sea Dogs home, and I bound down the steps and toward the arena's main entrance. Ruben, one of the security guards, greets me and quickly scans my bag before waving me through.

"Thanks, Ruben." I hand him one of the boxes of chocolate I snagged from last night's party. "And this is for you."

"Whoa!" Ruben's grin is a rare break from the serious expression I normally see on him. "What did I do to deserve this mid-morning snack?"

"You're you," I say, smiling as I head inside and take the escalator down to the quiet concession area. Training camp hasn't started yet, and it's almost eerie here without the usual buzz.

I pass the huge posters of the players on the walls, deliberately avoiding eye contact with Miles's larger-than-life image. I don't need more thoughts of him crowding my brain, especially with my dad walking toward me. On game days, he wears a suit, but today, he's in a button-down and slacks. I know Riley picked out those trendy sneakers—he wouldn't know that style or brand on his own, much less choose it.

"My chocolate supplier," he says with a grin.

"Junkie," I tease, handing him the box.

He hugs it to his chest. "You're my favorite daughter today."

I roll my eyes. "Such high praise."

He tips his head toward the corridor to his office. "I got coffee for me. Tea for you."

Dad clearly wants me to stay for a bit. "Very strategic," I observe.

Reaching the management level, he scans his employee card, then holds the door open for me. "That's because I am pretty strategic, Leighton."

Yes, that's his job.

As we head down the hallway, I spot Mako, the team's photographer. We've worked together on a few projects when Everly hired me for freelance shoots. He wears a Sea Dogs T-shirt and a hat with the Japanese flag, and when he sees me, he smiles like he has something up his sleeve.

"Just the person I wanted to see," he says.

It can only be a professional thing, and my father excuses himself from the shop-talk and tells me he'll be in his office.

"What's going on?" I ask Mako. "How is Sarah's pregnancy going?" Last time I worked for the team, he and his partner were expecting their first child.

"Knock on wood—" He raps the concrete wall. "She's

supposed to deliver in a couple weeks, and I just got approved for paternity leave. Three whole months."

"Nice," I say.

"I'm pretty excited about it." His dark eyes twinkle as he rubs his palms together. "That's why I wanted to talk to you. I requested that you fill in for me. I just gave the director of marketing a heads-up, so—"

I freeze. "You did what?"

He grins. "I gave Chanda your name. You know I love your work. And I trust you to maintain the high quality I expect."

I need to hear that again. My head is spinning, and my heart skips in disbelief. "You recommended me for your job?"

He narrows his eyes and wags a finger. "Not my *job* job. Just a temporary fill-in."

"Right. That's what I meant." I mentally flip through my portfolio of sports photography. While I've shot plenty of action pictures over the years, I'm not at the level required for pro sports. "I don't have your experience with action shots though."

"No problem. Rae will do the on-ice photos and videos during the games themselves."

Rae is the other photographer. She and Mako usually rotate between promo work and on-ice shots, trading off as it suits them.

Slowly, I process this unexpected news. What does Rae think about doing all the games? And there's my dad —will he mind if I do more work for the team? From his reaction when Everly first hired me for a freelance assignment, I'm pretty sure he'll be elated.

But I don't want to assume anything, so I ask Mako for more specifics. "What do you have in mind exactly?"

"With the season starting up soon, our promo needs are heavy—headshots, photo opps, all sorts of training camp and pre-season events to hype up the fans. There's so much to do that we figured my stand-in should focus on the promo shots while Rae concentrates on the games." He pauses to give me an excited, expectant look. "Want to do it?"

My mind races through my calendar for the next few months. I have some studio work booked with brands and for my boudoir work. But I'm not busy all day, every day. "I have some shoots on my schedule. But if the hours here are flexible enough, I think I can fit it all in."

Holy shit. Did I just say yes to a new temporary job?

"Chanda is pretty cool about working out the hours and all that. Especially since it's not a typical nine-to-five." He rocks back on his heels. "It's not a done deal yet, but can I tell Chanda you're interested? Because you're the only one I recommended."

Wow.

The only one.

I'm floored. Especially since the Sea Dogs pay well. *Really* well. Eleanor Greer owns the team with her husband, but she bankrolled it and makes the final decisions—and she's committed to hiring women and paying above marketplace rates. I know this firsthand from freelance projects.

I flash back to yesterday at the diner and the frustrating moment when I didn't hear the hostess. It's a too-familiar flicker of fear—what if moments like that become more frequent over time? Maybe not this month. But next year, and the one after? What if I miss more and more over the years?

I need to snag as much work now as I can and save for my uncertain future.

"If she wants me, I'm in," I say decisively.

Mako offers me a hand to high-five. "I'll tell Chanda. Hopefully she'll reach out soon."

"Thanks, Mako."

We exchange goodbyes, and I walk a little faster toward my dad's office, excited to tell him.

Once I'm there, he slides a cup of tea across his desk. "What was that about with Mako?"

I take the cup and a seat, then tilt my head. I'm fairly sure he doesn't know, but just in case..."You don't already know?"

He scoffs and laughs. "No. I stay out of anything that doesn't involve winning games."

"Fair enough," I say, then tell him the whole story.

The more I share, the more his eyes twinkle. "And I said yes," I finish. But then hold up a hand. "This is all presuming Chanda wants to move forward with hiring me."

My dad punches the air and doesn't sweat the details. "That's great!"

I laugh. "Dad, why are you such a goofball?"

"Can I help it if I like having you around?"

"You don't think it'll be weird if I work here? If it happens, I mean. It's just three months to cover his paternity leave."

"If 'weird' means 'good,' then yes. I do think so."

I roll my eyes, but it does feel warm and fuzzy that he likes having me here. "Are you sure? I don't want to step on your toes. This is your space, after all."

He sticks out a sneakered foot. "Step on them, please."

I am so grateful for his support. He's always been that way. Where other parents would be protective or hesitant, he's always had my back.

"Fine, I guess I will." I was already leaning toward yes. I'd only needed to know he was on board. "*If* she offers officially," I add.

"How could she not?" he asks. "I've seen your pics."

True, but I have a hunch he skims over the boudoir ones on my website, focusing mostly on my other work. At first, while I was dabbling in boudoir photography I didn't mention it to him. I wasn't sure what he'd think of me building a business around sexy photos. I've since told him, and he wasn't weirded out at all, so maybe the worry had all been in my head. A fear that the one parent who adores me might not want to think of his little girl taking, and posing, for sexy shots. But now that I think back on it, maybe the real worry was that he'd be disappointed.

Like Mom was. When she invited me out to New York for the launch of her newest handbag line a year ago, she took me to lunch at a see-and-be-seen eatery on the Upper East Side and asked what I was up to career-wise. When I told her, she tutted, shaking her head over her arugula salad and Perrier, then said, "Darling, I just don't understand why you spend so much energy on...*that.* Imagine what we could create if you channeled your talent into something lasting—like handbags. Real art. Something people actually value. You have so much potential, and it's such a shame to see it wasted on photos that end up hidden away in bedside drawers. Now, let's put your abilities to real use."

So, yeah. I guess that's why I didn't tell my dad at first. Once burned, twice shy and all. Turns out I didn't have anything to worry about. His response? "That's terrific. You're so talented and it sounds like you find it empowering."

I should have known he'd be behind me—he's always supported my dreams.

Like now, and it's great he's so thrilled about this opportunity. It makes it easier to imagine working here—though I'll need to be extra cautious with Miles, for both my sake *and* my dad's. I can't risk causing any complications for him. This is his turf; I won't mess that up.

"Thank you. I actually really want it to work out," I say, but I don't tell him how badly I want to make my mark *now*. The future is too uncertain.

He takes another sip of his coffee. "Now, maybe we can get Riley a job here too? She could be an usher. Scan tickets, maybe?" I can see the wheels turning in his eyes.

"Yes, let's definitely encourage her to drop her science and chem homework for that," I say dryly.

He snaps his fingers, pointing my way. "You're right. We'll let her finish school. Get a couple degrees. Then get her in here when you're full-time, and she can be too—she can be chief statistician for the team."

I just laugh and drink my tea. "Keep dreaming," I tease.

"Speaking of dreams, how's the search going for your own place? I can help with rent if you want." Steam wafts from his coffee mug as he speaks.

"Dad," I warn, though I wonder if I'm being stubborn by refusing his help.

"Leighton," he says, giving it right back to me in a firm voice too. I bet it's the voice he uses with his players.

"Noah," I say, sterner this time, matching him.

He parks his elbows on his desk, fixing me with a serious look. "What's the point of me working this hard and making good money if I can't spend it on my daughters?"

I don't really have anything to say to that—except, well, *this*: "I need to learn how to make it on my own."

He growls but relents. "Fine. Then I'll just save more for you."

Like I figured he was doing anyway. "Sure, threaten me with your money market accounts, Dad."

"I will," he says, lifting his coffee for a long sip. It's probably scalding, but he doesn't seem to notice. That's so him. He's impervious to heat, to cold, to spice. He's both iron and ice.

The other thing that's so him? He's ridiculously happy we're working together, and, honestly, so am I—or I will be if it all works out. "Thanks again for being cool about the job. I won't come in every day asking questions, and I definitely won't step on your toes."

He laughs. "I wasn't worried."

"I know, but I want you to know I respect your role," I say, then briefly wonder if I'm overselling my *above-the-boardness*.

My father tilts his head, studying me, like he's trying to figure out why my words don't quite add up. Shit. I am overselling myself.

I gulp as he says, "I'm not worried about *you*, Leighton." His tone transforms from lighthearted to serious. "Just watch out for the guys."

Tension slams into my body. I shift in the chair. "The guys are fine," I say as casually as I can while I pick at unseen lint on my shirt. "I'm used to them."

"I know you are, but they're elite, ultra-competitive athletes with a lot of...let's call it...*energy*."

Testosterone, he means. But I don't want to say that either, because I understand him completely. "I get it."

"And you'll be working closely with them. They can be," he says, sighing thoughtfully, "charming."

It was inevitable, I suppose, with this job possibility. The *don't date a hockey player* warning. He's given it to Riley and me before, packaged as part of his occasional dad dating advice. *Athletes tend to be obsessed with the sport. They're married to the game. Most aren't ready to settle down. I know these guys. I was one of these guys.*

We don't talk about the last part much, but there's no real need to. His age tells the story. I was born when he was only twenty and in college. My mom was young too, and she stayed home with me while my father chased his ice dreams with her support. He'd already been drafted, but he stayed in school and finished classes. He played in the Frozen Four and went to the minors all as a young dad while Mom did most of the parenting, setting aside her handbag dreams. But I wonder if that led to her resenting Riley, him and me. To her cheating on him with an athlete-turned-agent. To her leaving us for that guy and the handbag dream she'd wanted to fulfill.

Since she's not with Michael anymore, I don't think Riley and I got in the way of romance for her. But maybe we did get in the way of her dreams?

I'm already twenty-four and out of school, so our situations are different. Still, I understand where my dad is coming from.

"I understand," I say, finally responding even though the last thing he said is *they can be charming.*

Yes, they absolutely can. One in particular.

"I'm glad. Like I said, most of them aren't ready to settle down," he says, giving me a resigned smile. "I don't want to see you hurt. Ever."

My throat tightens from the protectiveness in his voice, the care in his eyes. The heartfelt emotion behind his words.

"Same for you, Dad," I say softly.

But his warning is heard and noted.

A week later, I'm tidying the studio at Hush Hush, returning silk robes to the wardrobe rack after a boudoir shoot, when Chanda calls and makes an official offer for me to take over for Mako for the next three months, covering training camp through Christmas.

"When he said you'd be the perfect choice, all I could think was *yes, she's the one.*"

I beam at the praise. "And I would love the project."

We work out the timing and hours as I organize the black pumps on the shoe rack. "Everly is coordinating with the social media and marketing team," Chanda says. "She'll send you details soon about the photos they want."

"That all sounds great," I say. Those were details I wanted to see before I started on Wednesday.

After I hang up, I stare at the phone, still amazed this is happening—a plum temporary job taking pictures. This is my dream. On top of that, the pay is good—better than expected. I'll have time to keep up with my freelance work, and my boudoir shoots if I'm clever with scheduling, but it shouldn't be too hard. Most of my boudoir clients prefer evening or weekend sessions to fit around their work schedules. Plus, moving back in with my old roommates means my rent will be even more manageable.

This is a smart move. A responsible move. And, most of all, it's a chance for me to make my mark.

It's also a responsible move to tell Miles.

A couple nights later, I finish the official Sea Dogs paperwork, pack up another box in my apartment, and text him.

> Leighton: We might need to revise our deal about not being alone together.

> Miles: Details???

I start to tap out a reply, but this really deserves an in-person conversation, despite our promise. Where though? If I have him pick me up, we'll end up parking on the side of the road and making out until we miss all our appointments. Meeting at the arena would be a disaster—my dad, Chanda, or a teammate could walk by at any moment. And where would we even talk? The equipment room? That's asking for trouble. I'm pretty sure equipment rooms are meant for stealing kisses with sexy hockey players you're supposed to stay away from.

I pace my living room until the answer slams into me. I smile a little wickedly. Yes, that perfect place. We won't be alone together there, not at all.

> Leighton: Meet me at High Kick tomorrow morning at 10.

Miles: I'm there.

I still take pictures for the shop, so it'll be the perfect cover. Plus, there will be zero temptation with his grandmother and all her customers in attendance. It will be like a business meeting. That's all.

17

STALK ME ALL NIGHT LONG

Miles

Funny how I haven't run into Leighton at High Kick in the last year, despite my best efforts.

Now, we're meeting deliberately, and I don't know how to feel about it. I know what I *do* feel, and it's not what I *should* feel.

Catching my reflection in the shop window, I pause and run a hand through my hair, giving it a quick, unnecessary tousle. I tug at the hem of my Henley next. Everything looks fine, but here I am, adjusting anyway.

This is a fact-finding mission and nothing more.

Still, I'm eager to hear Leighton's reason for revisiting our "no being alone together" promise.

I've been up for a while—I met with my local geocache club to search for a new stash over by the Ferry Building. Found it in thirty minutes, so I'm early. Anticipation feels like I've downed a couple of espressos, but it's all about seeing Leighton.

Inside the café, I head to the counter, where my grandmother sets a plated toffee brownie in front of a customer, paired with what smells like a caramel latte.

"That'll be nine dollars," Birdie says. The woman has double French braids in her hair and a dusting of freckles across her cheeks. She hands over a ten, and while my grandmother makes change, the customer glances at me, then glances again, her eyes lit up with recognition.

"Oh my gosh! Miles Falcon, right?"

"That's me," I say evenly.

"I'm a huge fan! I'm so excited that hockey's back tomorrow."

"Me too," I reply, keeping things polite and low-key.

"My friends will be thrilled when they hear I met you! My sister Cassidy likes Tyler, but you're my favorite."

"Ouch." I pretend to be mortally wounded. "And he hasn't even played his first game as a Sea Dog."

"I know." The woman shakes her head, so very disappointed in Cassidy. "I've told her I have better taste."

She bounces on her heels, looking at Birdie, who takes her cue. "Want a picture?" my grandma asks, always my number one hype girl.

"I'd love one." The woman thrusts her phone at Birdie like the offer might disappear. "I'm Kendra, by the way."

Kendra steps in beside me, wedging herself close. I give the camera a practiced smile.

Birdie takes the photo and hands back the phone, adding, "Be sure to tag the shop if you post it. 'Sea Dog Spotted in the wild at High Kick Coffee, home of the best toffee brownies and caramel lattes.'"

"I will! Thank you so much!" Kendra says, then heads off to a corner table with her drink and brownie.

I turn to Birdie, shaking my head. "So much for lying low. You totally blew my cover."

She rolls her eyes. "Honey, sometimes people recognize you. You'll just have to cope with some crushes on the Falcon brothers. I can't help it if you inherited my fabulous facial structure." She sets a hand on her chin and turns her head to show off those cheekbones. "So, to what do I owe the pleasure of this visit?"

"I'm meeting Leighton in a few minutes," I say, trying not to give away my amped-up feeling.

Birdie's eyebrows shoot sky-high. "Are you seeing her again?" she whispers, eyes gleaming.

"Relax, no."

She pouts. "Then why are you meeting her?"

I shrug, keeping it casual. "She wants to discuss something. I don't know what," I add before she can ask.

Birdie gives me a long, scrutinizing look. "But you think it's a date."

"No, I don't," I scoff. "Why would you say that?"

She grins smugly. "You're dressed for a date, you keep checking the door, and you've got that 'I'm trying hard to look good for the woman I can't get over' vibe."

I scowl, annoyed she's hit the nail on the head. "Don't pretend you can see into my soul."

"It's not hard. You're transparent," she says, seeming completely unfazed.

"And you're trouble," I mutter. "Besides, nothing's happening. Same deal as before. I'm focused on earning the chance to be co-captain."

She pats my hand. "And you will." Then she gives a subtle nod toward Kendra, smirking. "Want me to set you up with her then?"

I roll my eyes. "Is that your way of getting back into The Underground Grandma Matchmaking Society?"

She laughs. "Please. I was reinstated the moment I matched a couple of my regulars. This shop is basically my own dating app."

I shake my head at her antics. "Just don't meddle with this, okay?"

With a knowing smile, she nods toward the door. "Darling, here comes your favorite match."

I turn to see Leighton walk in, looking effortlessly put together, and my heart jumps. That's seriously inconvenient. I remind myself she's not mine. She can't be mine.

She makes her way over, flashing a small grin at me before turning a brighter smile on Birdie. "Hey, Birdie! How did the Earl Grey lattes work out on social? I hope everyone flocked here after those pics."

"With the showgirl latte art in them, no one could resist." Birdie waggles her plucked eyebrows. "Want one?"

Leighton chuckles. "You know I'm a green tea girlie."

"Live a little. I promise—if you love tea, you'll love my Earl Grey lattes."

Leighton's eyes catch mine with a hint of amusement. "Does she always get her way?"

"Every single time," I say.

Birdie grins. "Perfect. One espresso and one Earl Grey latte."

As she sets to work making our drinks, I turn to Leighton. "Let's snag a table. I'll grab the drinks when they're ready." I pause for effect. "Even the vile one."

She laughs lightly. "Thank you for keeping its vileness from me."

"Of course, Leighton. I'll always protect you from coffee drinks."

"Like I once said, you're gallant."

Her references to the day we met go right to my head. They're not romantic inside jokes, I remind myself and gesture to the back of the café. "After you."

Leighton walks ahead, and yeah, I'm not going to lie—the view's nice. But Leighton's like a Christmas tree in the middle of a department store—she looks good from any angle.

She picks a table tucked into the back corner, away from the chatter closer to the sparkly counter. Retro photos of showgirls decorate the exposed brick walls, adding to the vibe. The scent of coffee mingles with vanilla and cinnamon. Whenever I come here, I hardly ever want to leave.

Leighton sits, and I join her and notice her fingers tapping lightly on the edge of the table. She's focused but seems a little distracted.

"How's your day going so far?" I ask. Manners come before curiosity, after all.

"Not too bad. Yours?"

"Can't complain. Training camp starts tomorrow."

Her posture straightens, and she flashes a cheery smile, but there's something professional about it that pings my radar.

"That's what I want to talk to you about," she says.

Scratch that. The radar is screaming. Before I can ask, Birdie calls out, "Hot chef!"

Leighton laughs, her eyes brightening with a warmth that makes my chest ache. "She's so very Birdie."

Dragging a hand down my face, I mutter, "She is."

I head up to the counter, grab our drinks, and shoot my grandmother a look. "Did you really need to use that nickname?"

"It amuses me." With a sly smile, she sets a plate with a caramel toffee bar onto the tray. "And here's a little something special on the house. For the two of you."

"Birdie," I chide, low, a warning.

"What?" she asks, feigning innocence.

"You're playing matchmaker again."

She waves a hand dismissively. "Oh look, I see other customers. Bye, bye." And with that, she hustles over to the register.

I shake my head, bringing the drinks and pastry back to the table and setting the tray down. "A little surprise from Birdie."

"For the hot chef," Leighton teases with a hint of softness.

"For us," I correct her, sliding the plate to the center of the table.

We share a look that lingers longer than it should, and I feel that familiar pull between us, something warm and charged we're both trying to deny. Leighton picks up her Earl Grey latte, admiring the swirl of foam shaped into a woman high-kicking. "Almost a sin to drink it."

"But everything's ephemeral."

She arches a brow. "Aren't you philosophical today?"

"It was my major. Well, it was one of them."

She tilts her head, her eyes registering surprise. "One of them?" she repeats.

"I double majored. Philosophy and psychology."

"Who even are you?"

I laugh. "I was kind of into school."

She lets out a low whistle. "I'll say. Two? Wow. That's amazing."

Fine, it's just a degree or two. But I like that she's a

little impressed. "Honestly, I was going to get a master's or go to law school, but hockey called."

"I don't meet a lot of athletes who decided between graduate school and the pros."

I square my shoulders and take the compliment because, yeah, it's a fucking compliment and it feels good. "I like to aim high," I say, leaning back in my chair.

"You really do," she says, then sighs, a little thoughtfully. "You're a planner?"

"I suppose I am."

"Me too," she says, her tone warm. "I like to have options too. Opportunities."

"Exactly," I say. "You never know, right?" Then impulsively, I let down my guard and add, "I considered going back to school after my injury. I thought my career was over."

She gives me a sympathetic smile. "I get that, but I'm glad it's not. You have a lot of hockey left in you."

"I hope so," I say, then return to her comment. "You're the same? Planner?"

"Definitely. I don't like uncertainty, I guess, so I try to plan for it. I want to be ready for anything. Be able to make it on my own." Her tone is unusually vulnerable. It's clear her independence matters deeply to her.

Her manner shifts though. "Which leads me to why I asked to meet. I took a job with the Sea Dogs. A temporary one," she adds quickly, then takes a drink.

I blink, processing the news. "You did?"

She nods, her eyes searching mine carefully. "I'm filling in for Mako while he's on paternity leave." She pauses to gauge my reaction, her mouth pulled into a tight line. "I'm telling you in person because I didn't want you to think I took the job just to be near you."

The thought hadn't even crossed my mind, but now it's hard to ignore. "Why would I think that?"

"You're used to people...hanging on to you, right?" She waits for me to answer, and I give a reluctant nod. "I saw that woman taking a picture with you before I came in."

"It happens, true. But I'm not used to *you* hanging on to me."

Her smile echoes my regret, even though she says, "I'm just trying to be cautious. Since people do that with you, but also in general. They try to get close to people for all kinds of reasons."

I raise an eyebrow, half-smiling, then say dryly, "This meeting is doing wonders for my ego."

She rolls her eyes. "I don't mean it like that. I just didn't want you to think I was...stalking you."

A laugh escapes me, and I lean in, meeting her gaze. "It's funny that you think I'd be bothered by that."

She dips her face briefly, and when she raises it, she says, "Good to know that stalking is approved by you."

I wave vaguely in the direction of the Marina. "Feel free to wander past my home at night. You remember where I live, right?"

She laughs. "Sort of."

My jaw drops. "You didn't write down my address?"

"No," she says, laughing harder.

"That's going to make stalking me tougher, Leighton." I know better than to flirt with her like this. But I know better than to fight on the ice, and sometimes I do that anyway too.

She studies me, a playful glint in those gorgeous blue eyes. "You're making this hard. We're supposed to have a deal."

A gulp of espresso emboldens me. Or maybe that's

her. "I'm not breaking it, am I?" I challenge her, teasing her. If this is all I get, I want to make it good.

"Technically, I suppose not," she admits.

"So, you're free to stalk me as long as there are people around? I'll send you my address just to be safe."

Another laugh tips her head back, exposing her throat. That throat. Her neck. The softness of her skin. Memory crashes into me, and I wish I could kiss her again.

"I appreciate the invitation. But I probably shouldn't," she says, a little wistfully before she shifts to a more serious tone. "Anyway, I didn't want you to be surprised when you run into me tomorrow at the rink. And I took the assignment because it's a great opportunity professionally."

"Absolutely. I should have said congratulations. It does sound good for you. I'm proud of you."

"Thank you." She sips her drink while I finish mine. Her gaze is still thoughtful, and it's clear she's not done yet. "What I really wanted to say, though, is we won't be able to completely avoid each other." She glances around, checking for prying ears and eyes, then lowers her voice. "My dad gave me *the warning*."

My chest tightens. I can guess what that is. "The 'don't get involved with a hockey player' one?"

She winces but nods. "Yes. It was a little...weird."

"Does he know? Or suspect?" I ask carefully, my jaw ticking.

"No. God, no." She takes a beat. "He's just doing his due diligence, I think. It was more like *I know how hockey players are—charming and most don't want to settle down yet, so be on your guard.* That kind of thing."

If she only knew I'd settle down with her in a heartbeat. My failed relationship with Joanne wouldn't even stop me. I know how to work hard and learn from the past. So if I could, I'd explore the fuck out of this ludicrous chemistry that crackles and sparks every time we're near each other. I'd see her every night and prove the lie in her father's statement.

But I also get that proving him wrong has to be earned.

Over time, with evidence, and probably not while I'm trying to become co-captain. It's too complicated. That's the big issue—I've got responsibilities, plans, and most of all, a second chance.

I don't want to fuck with something that required so much work and so much rehab to get.

"Your dad's right about one thing," I say, keeping things light.

"What's that?"

"I'm charming as fuck."

"So cocky." She shakes her head, amused.

"You're not denying it."

She leans forward, locks eyes with me. "I think we've already established I'm charmed by you."

"It's the same for me."

I say it quietly, but she hears me. Her smile is soft, borderline sexy. We're silent for so long that it threatens to tip over into something else, something warm, something dangerous.

But then, Leighton sits taller and clears her throat. "Anyway, the promise we made to never be alone together might need revising due to work circumstances."

The idea of working closely with her sparks excitement that has no business zipping down my spine. I should focus on the team, the potential captaincy, my family, the increased media scrutiny from Tyler on the team, two Falcons playing together. Already, the press requests are coming in fast.

"We'll need to interact one-on-one sometimes," I say thoughtfully. "Maybe the best way forward is to focus on building a genuine friendship."

Her smile spreads, nice and easy. "I'd like that, Miles."

I arch a playful brow. "So no stalking?"

"I don't think friends stalk each other."

"But they can have coffee and pastries," I say, offering her a fork.

She takes it with a reluctant laugh, but a flicker of something warmer in her eyes. "Let's be friends. It'll be easier that way."

If friendship is all I can have with Leighton, I will take it. Oh hell, will I take it. "Everyone can use a friend."

"They can," she says, then hands me the other fork.

We dig into the caramel toffee bar at the same time, the tines of our forks clinking. That feels a little like a metaphor.

And since friendship starts with talking, I point my fork at the bar, saying, "Caramel *and* toffee? Do you think Birdie's saying you don't always have to pick sides."

Leighton thoughtfully polishes off a bite. "So you're saying this pastry is kind of subliminal messaging?"

"That feels like Birdie's style."

She laughs, warm and bright, and peers down at the treat. "I don't think she's wrong. Too much of a good thing doesn't necessarily make a bad thing. Maybe it just makes a very good thing." She wiggles her brows. "How's that for philosophy?"

"Very philosophical, Shutterbug," I say.

She digs in her fork again, nodding to the front of the shop. "Have you two always been close?"

"Definitely. She helped raise us—my brother, sister, and me—after my dad left."

Leighton sits up straighter, her expression shifting to something tender. "Wow, that's...big. So she wasn't just a grandmother who took the kids to the park and gave good birthday presents."

"Exactly," I say, my voice softening. "She helped Mom a ton. Picked us up from school, took Tyler and me to hockey, did animal rescue events with Charlie—my sister has always been into animals. Birdie did all that before Mom remarried. And after too, honestly."

"That's great. Not that your dad left," she says, her tone caring. "But that Birdie was a big part of the family."

"Now and then. And she still is. When everyone moved down here from Seattle, she moved too." I pause, flashing back on the life and times of my grandmother. "I think she misses the rain though."

"Does it really rain there a lot? In Seattle?"

"All the time. Constantly. It never stops," I say, then lower my voice, as if sharing a conspiracy. But I keep my gaze locked on her. "It's our best-kept secret to keep people out."

She laughs. "Smart. I won't say a word."

"Appreciate that," I say dryly, then add, "what about you? Are your grandparents around?"

She takes another bite before answering. "Same as you. When my mom left, the grandparents jumped in to help out. They still give Dad a hand with Riley when he's..." She stops and winces as a storm cloud seems to pass over her. "On the road with the team. It really means a lot to us both. They made sure I didn't have to be the grown-up, you know?"

My throat tightens. I know what it's like to carry that kind of weight, whether someone hands it to you or you take it on yourself. "I'm glad," I say, leaving the dad comment untouched.

"It really is." She pauses, her brow scrunching like she's debating something. "Your dad...is he—"

I shake my head, fighting the latent anger, resentment, and, yep, grief that still swims up when I think of him. "He took off with barely a word when I was twelve. Didn't hear from him at all during high school," I say, then swallow past the ancient hurt. "He died when I was seventeen."

"Oh, Miles," she says, her voice hitching. "I'm so sorry."

"Yeah, it sucked. And...thanks." What sucks the most —which I don't say—is that I never got to ask him why he left, why he told me to be the man of the house, why we weren't enough for him to stay.

But the world only spins forward, so I keep moving on.

I switch gears. "Your mom's still around? Do you see her?"

Her smile seems forced as she says, "Usually only if she wants me to take photos of her or whatever her new handbag line is."

"Ouch."

"Yup," she says. "And if I don't want to take pics, she's excellent at passive-aggressively pointing out how I'll make time for other things. Like myself, and my dad, and my sister. Ironic."

"That sucks," I say with a sympathetic sigh.

"It does. But I try not to let it bug me," she says.

"I hear you. I do the same. To try to let go of the things I can't control."

"You get it," she says. Understanding passes between us as we hold each other's gazes. I can see some of what drives her independence. And I suppose she now knows more about me than she did before.

Leighton points to the half-eaten pastry and the crumbs of our enjoyment scattered all over the plate. "I like not choosing between caramel and toffee."

"She's got a lemon raspberry cake too." I want to ask her to come back and try it with me. As friends. But I'd only be using friendship to cover up the date I wish we were having.

After we leave, I send her my address, as I'd said I would. But deep down, I'm hoping someday she'll wander past my home.

* * *

The weights clank as I set down my dumbbells during that afternoon's workout. On the bench, Tyler pushes through another set and then sits up, a resolute grin on his bearded face. The dude loves working out and always has.

"So, how's the adjustment going?" I ask. He's only been here a week, and he's had the kids most of the time, so he's had a lot to juggle. "Settling in okay?"

Tyler nods, grabbing a towel and wiping the back of his neck. "For the most part. Agatha just arrived, so that's good." Agatha is the kids' nanny—an older woman who's worked for him since his ex went back to college. "And Elle—she's doing well in med school. I think she likes the change—new city, fresh start."

I get that. I desperately needed that feeling when I moved here. "Seems like things are coming together."

He runs a hand through his hair, which is longer than mine now. "Just gotta, you know, play good hockey for a new team. No big deal."

"Right, no pressure," I deadpan, grabbing a heavier set of weights. "I mean, you only have to live up to my impressive stats. And that's not easy."

Tyler smirks, tossing his towel at me. "You'll be thanking me when I'm carrying you through the season."

I snag the towel and fling it back. "Oh, you think you're carrying the team? I was here first. Makes me the better Falcon."

Tyler raises an eyebrow. "Better? You mean...older?"

"Oh, please." I flex in mock confidence before I lift the weights. "I'm in my prime."

He shakes his head, grinning. "Sure, keep telling yourself that."

"I fucking will. Especially tomorrow when we start," I say, already feeling the thrill of stepping back on the ice.

I'm ready to make this year my best yet. Especially with Leighton there to capture it all.

Maybe, possibly, that's why I switch to even heavier weights. Well, there's a good chance she'll see me shirtless.

18

THE MILES FACTOR

Leighton

Even though I'm not Riley's third parent, I like to steal as much time with her as I can. Since her school starts late on Wednesdays, we grab a lychee bubble tea for her and tea for me before the first bell at school, and before I'm due at the Sea Dogs arena.

As we walk toward Harris Academy on the outskirts of Japantown, the streets dotted with cherry blossom motifs on banners, I ask about her classes. "How's chemistry treating you?"

"Nope," she denies me, grinning. "We're chatting about you. It's my turn. I have advice for you."

My eyebrows shoot up. "Oh, you do, missy?"

"Definitely." She gives a little skip. "I know most of the hockey guys."

I blink, surprised. "You do?"

"Hello! While you were away at college, I had to hang out at the arena. Go to games and all."

Right. Fair point—she's probably been to more games than I have."Okay, Miss Mini Coach, tell me everything," I say as we pass a small bakery, and I catch the faint aroma of matcha. Riley lifts her nose. She's a matcha girl too. "The guys on the team are kind of like uncles to me."

"Then wouldn't that make me their niece too? Because I'm not loving that," I say, shuddering at the thought. I definitely don't want to be seen as a niece, especially with one player in particular.

"Fine, you're like an aunt, then."

"Riley, I know you're good with genetics, but I don't think I can be an aunt or a niece."

My sister makes a swirling gesture with her hands, her fingers covered in rings. "My point is, remember: Hugo is the team teddy bear. His wife makes amazing cookies— we ordered them for the science competition last year."

"Right," I say. "Those cookies were delicious."

"Then there's Christian. Everyone looks up to him. Very serious."

"Got it." I nod, knowing this to be true about the current team captain.

"And Max, of course. The city loves him because everyone loves a goalie—even a grumpy one."

"Is he still grumpy? Didn't falling madly in love with Everly mellow him out? I watched him in that *Ice Men* documentary, and he definitely gives less battery acid vibes than before."

"True. But he's still the king of glowers," she says with a laugh.

"Fair enough," I say, then tap my temple like I'm noting these details.

"But Rowan Bishop definitely attended the Max Lambert School of Grouchy-ness so he's been picking up the slack in that department," she says, mentioning one of the veteran defensemen on the team.

"Noted. This is seriously helpful."

"Apparently the only time he even smiles is when his little girl comes to games."

That makes me smile. "That's adorable."

Riley taps her chin, as if she's deep in thought, her ponytail swishing as we walk. "Then there's Tyler. I don't know much about Tyler, but I did some research, and apparently some Supernova fans call him 'Daddy.' Like, actually call him that. They sometimes play that 'Daddy's Home' song on socials when he jumps onto the ice." She hums the tune.

I cringe. "Okay, I actually never want to hear you sing that again."

"I'm just giving you all the intel," she says, counting off on her fingers, delighting far too much in her knowledge of the team as we pass a small group of tourists snapping photos in front of the Peace Pagoda. A few families are gathered there, some kids playing tag as Riley continues with her team trivia.

She tells me about Ford, a veteran on the second line who I don't know terribly well, but who's had a rock-solid career. "He's recently divorced, so he gets marriage proposals from fans every few games," she says.

I laugh. "That's one way to find a husband."

Then she gives me all the details on Wesley and Asher, even though I know them well enough since they're involved with my friends.

I brace myself, knowing exactly who she's going to bring up next. "And then there's Miles," she says casually. "Basically the hot nerd of the team."

"'Hot nerd,' you say?" I tease, tugging on her ponytail. "You're judging him for the glasses?"

"I don't make the rules, okay? I'm just saying. He was photographed once in, like, slacks and a gray cardigan with those glasses, and he gave off total professor vibes. My friends all talked about it."

I shoot her a disapproving look. "You're sixteen. You can't think someone on Dad's hockey team is hot."

Honestly, I can't either.

"Don't worry," she says dryly. "Hockey players are not my type."

Ah, this is a better topic—her. "So, what's your type?"

"I'm totally into nerd kings. Give me a nerd, and I'm happy," she says proudly. "But seriously, stop distracting me. What about you?"

"You're asking what I'm into?"

"Yes. You haven't dated really since you've been back in town. Is it because dating is miserable, and the apps are full of liars?"

I pull her into a quick hug. "I've raised you well. But there are good ones out there. Just...not the guys I dated in college." Like Nick, the guy who, on our third date, told me my hearing aids were an embarrassment. He's definitely one of the reasons I'm not interested in dating anyone here. But so is Jameson, the guy I went out with after him. Jameson was an engineering major, had a dry sense of humor, and loved to play board games. But one night, when we were watching a TV show, I asked him to turn on the captions. He looked at me like I was asking him to fly to the moon. A few days later, he broke up with me, saying romance was *too complicated*. Was it the captions or was it just a line because he wanted out? I don't know. Either way, I didn't want to jump back into dating after him.

But I don't tell Riley any of that—she doesn't need another reason to feel disillusioned.

She's relentless though, she snaps her gaze to me, a twinkle in those blue eyes. "But have you noticed that, among your friends, you're the only one not dating a hockey player?"

Of course I've noticed. Of course I'm acutely aware of it. "Well, Fable's with Wilder. So not all of them," I say, pointing out the fallacy in her argument.

"Still. Odds are you're next in line," she says with a mischievous grin.

I shake my head. "Not a chance. Have you met our father? Have you heard his warnings?"

"He did tell me never to date a hockey player."

"What a surprise. He said the same to me the other day. *Hockey players can be charming*," I say, imitating him and his euphemisms.

"That's so him."

"And it's sound advice," I say, hoping that'll end the topic.

But Riley doesn't give up so easily. "Like I said, Miles is the hot one, so...I could kind of see you with him."

Her comment catches me off guard. Even my sister thinks we'd be a good match. And maybe, if things were different—if I had a different last name—I'd be able to think so too. Which means I'm going to have to double down on the friendship plans with Miles in, oh, say, thirty minutes when I arrive at work.

"You've always had a good imagination," I say, giving her a quick squeeze as we reach her school. "Now go, before you're late."

Once she's past the doors, I check my phone. There's a text from my father with a photo he's snapped on his digital photo frame, likely this morning. It's a picture of me heading into work at the boba shop I worked at during high school. *Look what my frame showed me this morning! A first day of work pic! Good luck today!*

I smile from the note. I think it's the only time Coach McBride uses exclamation points—with his daughters.

* * *

With my camera bag slung over my shoulder and my brand-new temporary employee badge in my hand, I stop at the doors into the corridor of the arena that leads to the locker room, the weight room, the rink. I've been here a hundred times, but this is the first time my stomach has flipped like a pancake so many times. I'm not usually a nervous person, but I'm made of nothing but jitters right now.

It's not simply the Miles factor. It's that I want to prove I belong here—that I'm not a daddy's girl or a nepo baby. It's not like anyone's said it outright, but I know what people might think. And that sliver of doubt, that little *what if*, keeps gnawing at me. And there's this bit of a worry too—what if I don't hear something someone says?

I swallow before I open the door, slide a hand into my jeans pocket, and check my phone. My hearing aids are fully charged, and the program is set for speech. It'll be fine. I don't usually have a problem. And besides, pro athletes aren't usually soft-spoken.

And really, it's not like asking *what did you say* is the worst thing.

I tuck my hair over my ear, then stop, breathe, and untuck it. Better to let it fall long and loose.

I'm ready, and the second I push open the door, I spot Everly on the other side. She's laughing with Jenna Nguyen, the promotions manager, who wears glasses and has her sleek black hair cinched back in a clip, and Chanda Kumar, the director of marketing. Chanda's wearing a bright red blazer over her blouse, and has a tablet in hand, her usual energy practically buzzing in the air around her as she scrolls through notes, presumably. I head over to them. I know them all already, but I still feel all the first-day-of-school vibes.

When I arrive, Everly turns her gaze to me. She's friendly but professional as she says, "Hey, Leighton. Welcome to the team. We have a busy day for you."

"I'm ready," I say, and I slough off all my nerves since I *am* ready. Ready to focus on work and to safeguard my future. Starting with photos for a series of social media posts around the "we're back" theme.

I've got the talent, the vision. I've been doing this long before I ever thought about working here. This is just another gig. Another opportunity.

Twenty minutes later, I'm walking into the weight room to take pictures of the guys working out. The smell of rubber mats and a hint of fresh laundry fills the air. Machines line the walls, clanging as weights are adjusted, while a couple of players—Hugo, one of the defensemen, and Alexei, usually a center on the second line—laugh in the corner, catching their breath between sets. Rowan, as promised by Riley, is stoic as he finishes up some preacher curls next to them.

And then I see Miles pushing off a weight bench, standing, taking off his shirt.

My pulse jackhammers.

Must. Not. Stare.

This is a test. The universe is simply testing me. And really, I've been around hockey players my whole life.

I ignore the curl of lust twisting through my veins. Stepping farther into the room, I take a quick, steadying breath, and say, "Hi, guys. I'm Leighton."

Kill me now.

My voice comes out all annoyingly breathy. My cheeks flush as I square my shoulders, soldiering on and willing the splash of heat to get the fuck off my face.

"I'm a photographer," I add, waggling my Nikon bag like it's show-and-tell in kindergarten, but I still sound high-pitched, like talking to a group of high-octane, testosterone-fueled elite athletes is all new to me. "I'll be here taking all sorts of promo photos throughout training camp, pre-season, and the start of the season. And then for a few months."

And...I sound like a kid listing the timeline of my job, like anyone cares.

I feel even more like one when Chanda steps in beside me, saving everyone from my over-eager prattling. "Leighton's filling in for Mako. So, just do your thing, guys. I'll send out a daily schedule of photo opps, but expect that she'll be taking pics of drills, practices, ice time, and lots of fun behind-the-scenes stuff," she says, and I focus on the whole weight room, and all the guys in here, rather than the one with his shirt off, his hand resting on the silver bar

—the one who's looking at me. "Anything you don't want posted, just let us know," Chanda adds. "But we'll start with the workout since, well, fans love a workout shot. Good?"

Why didn't I just say that? She sent me those details too.

"You're not wrong. My girlfriend loves shirtless shots of me. I like to make sure she has plenty *every day*," Alexei says, and the Saint Petersburg-born player is definitely not lacking in the confidence department.

Chanda laughs, amused by him. "Great. Leighton will make sure Freya has even more for her collection, and the rest of our fans too."

Alexei turns to me, pressing his hands together in a mock prayer and giving me an imploring grin. "Also, I went on a special training regimen this summer. Can you let Coach know? Really, I'm in peak form."

Hugo rolls his eyes at him. "Dude, Mini Mac is not here to curry favor with the coach on your behalf." Then, the big-hearted, burly defenseman shoots me a grin. Hugo plays for Sweden in international competitions, and has lived in the U.S. since grade school. "But if you were passing on nice words to your pops, just know I lifted every damn day and did sprints. I could throw in a box of my wife's cookies to sweeten the deal. Big Mac loves those."

Rowan rolls his eyes their way as he moves onto biceps curls. "Or you could try playing better, assholes."

"Language, Bishop," Christian calls out from his spot by the leg-press machine, shaking his blond head like he's had enough of these guys, and like he thinks I haven't heard worse. But he's the captain, so it's his job, I suppose, to keep these guys in line. He's also Josie's big brother.

"Ignore these idiots, Leighton. Just like I do. Let me know if you need anything."

"I will," I say as he strides over and sticks out a hand. I shake it. "And it's good to meet you, Christian."

"You too, Leighton," he replies.

"Welcome aboard, Mini Mac One," Alexei adds, all serious now.

"Nice to meet you, Mini Mac One," Hugo calls out, waving.

"Hey," Rowan grunts.

Now I see why Miles didn't know my name. My sister must be Mini Mac Two. And it's clear "Leighton" probably isn't going to stick with any of these guys. I'm not even sure if Miles is going to acknowledge me. What do our brand-new friendship rules call for? No clue.

But then the man I deliberately looked away from clears his throat and takes a step closer to me. "Welcome to the jungle, Leighton," he says, meeting my gaze with a steady, no-nonsense look of his own. He turns to the guys. "Let's let her do her thing."

And yes, it is a jungle in here. All the man-imals know I'm essentially the boss's daughter, even if Miles is calling me by my name.

Looks like I'll have to earn their respect the old-fashioned way—with talent, grit, and by pretending a certain player's shirtless workouts don't make me blush.

Oh, and one more thing—throwing a little gasoline on their competitive fire.

"Let's get some pictures. We can let the fans decide who worked out hardest in the off-season," I say, and there's a flurry of activity as the guys instantly snap into focus to prove who's the strongest, toughest, best among them.

* * *

Not only do I survive the first shoot, but I capture one hell of a story—competition. The guys push harder, lift more, and do extra reps. Intensity etches across their faces, muscles strained, beads of sweat trailing down their skin.

Fine, it's sexy in an eye-candy kind of way. But through my camera lens, it's more than that. It's a scene of a team reuniting, training together from day one with a single purpose—to be the last team standing by season's end.

When the workout winds down, the guys file out one by one, with Miles the last to leave. He's wearing a shirt now, but it clings to his sweaty chest. He glances over at me. "What's the story here?"

"Determination," I say simply.

He nods, approval in his eyes. "Determination," he repeats, his lips twitching with the hint of a smile. "Fitting."

It feels that way as he turns and walks down the corridor to the locker room without looking back.

That feels like an act of determination too.

For him.

And for me, as I draw a steadying breath and head in the other direction.

19

ICE VISIONS

Miles

One day down...however many more to go.

To celebrate keeping my promise to resist Leighton yesterday, I rewarded myself with a new book. After the evening class I've been taking at the local university ended, I stopped by An Open Book and picked up *Villain Era*, a sci-fi spoof with a dastardly looking tabby cat on the cover. It's an allegory about resistance in the face of a tyrannical leader—not the cat; the cat leads the rebellion —and the irreverence of the storyline sealed the deal. Last night at home, it was just me, that book, and my mom's dogs crawling onto my lap and sleeping on my head.

In the morning, I return the little stinkers on my way to the arena, bounding up the steps to her home near Dolores Park with a quartet of little yappers on a long braided leash for four. Whoever said Chihuahuas aren't spicy never met a Chihuahua.

Mom swings open the door, greeting her dog children with open arms.

"How was *The Last Single Guy in New York*?" I ask over the chaos. Tawny Bippity yips at Mom, Boppity, the long-haired cinnamon mix wags her tail, and the blond hellion, Boo, howls his greeting. The black-and-white harlequin, Cindy, licks Mom's ankles like she's been starved for affection, even though I gave her heaps of love. Drama queen.

"It was amazing," Mom says, drawing out the last word. "The songs were so good. Thank you again for watching my unholy terrors." Then she tilts her head, eyeing me slyly. "Did you take them to the bookstore to meet women? You know you can use them for that. Think of them as an opening act."

I roll my eyes. "You too, Mom? As if I don't get enough from Birdie."

"They're both relentless," Harvey calls out from the kitchen, where I can see he's brewing coffee. "Best to give in."

"Thanks, love," she says to him with affection in her tone.

"I'm always on your side, dear."

"Smart man," I yell down the hall, laughing.

"So," Mom says, like a dog with a bone, "it's been a while since Joanne. Surely, you're ready to date again."

That's not even the issue. But now's not the time to get into it. "I'm fine with dating," I say, hoping to leave the convo at that.

"It's the apps, right? They're getting you down. That makes sense," she says, not even waiting for me to answer her apps question. She scoops up Boo and Cindy, alternating in petting the demanding pups. "And you know... I've been listening to some podcasts and hearing more and more about this hotshot new matchmaker that some singles are using. Her name is Isla Marlowe and she's supposedly got the Midas touch."

Are we really having this conversation right now? "Mom," I begin, a touch of warning in my tone.

Harvey snickers from the kitchen. "Good luck, Miles," he mutters.

Mom barrels on. "It's apparently a wise approach to dating apps fatigue. That's a real thing these days. I heard all about it on another podcast," she says, since my mother is the queen of show tunes and podcasts. "And with all the dating apps fatigue, there's sort of a revival in traditional ways of meeting. And non-traditional. One man even put up a billboard touting himself."

I roll my eyes. "Mom, I'm not putting up a billboard."

"Of course you aren't. I'm just saying—it'd be nice to see you out there again. You weren't in a great place at the end with Joanne. And that was understandable. But you moved on and learned, and now look at you," she says.

And she's not wrong, but I can't get into it with her now. Or really at any time. The words *"There's only one woman I'm interested in and she's the coach's daughter"* would open up a can of worms that's best kept closed.

I check the time on my watch. "I need to go hit the ice."

"But you'll think about it?"

Ah hell. I hate to be a dick to Mom. Years ago, I swore I'd look out for her and my siblings. I held to that promise and in a lot of ways I still do. Now that I'm older I like to think that promise also means I won't lead her on. *But* I can have a little fun. "Mom, maybe save the matchmaker for Tyler when he's ready to date again," I say, fighting off a smile as I throw my brother under the bus.

"Oh, good idea! And don't forget to pick him up on your way to the arena," she says, reminding me in that same mom tone she used when I was a kid and she'd ask me to walk Tyler to school while she went to her real estate job, pounding the pavement, trying to sell as many homes as she could and pay for our lives since Dad was having none of that. Or us.

"Don't worry, Mom. I won't forget Little Ty-Ty," I tease, using a name my big, burly defenseman of a brother would hate. I bend down to scoop up Cindy, who licks my face right on cue and whimpers like she'll miss me. Yup. Drama queen. "See you soon," I tell her, and I'm off.

After hopping back in my electric car, I swing by Tyler's rental home in Pacific Heights, and he's already on the front porch, giving his daughter, Luna, a goodbye hug at the sky-blue door, then his son, Parker. Their nanny, Agatha, waves to me from the foyer, her eyes crinkling in a smile. Tyler jogs down the steps and slides into the passenger seat.

"You ready for me to school you in skills today?" he taunts, smirking.

"Why am I driving you?"

"Because you never stopped being our extra parent after Dad took off," he replies, his tone half-teasing but pointed.

"Ouch. Way to psychoanalyze me."

He shrugs. "You were always the helper. Into cooking, making sure our homework got done, dragging us to sports..."

No kidding. "Excuse me for being supportive," I mutter as we merge into traffic.

"Not a criticism," he says lightly. "I appreciated the

fuck out of it. And you know you liked it," he adds. "Being the man of the house. That's your thing."

I tense. *Man of the house.* Those were Dad's words to me, right before he left. But I've never told that to Tyler. No need to dig that up now.

I change the subject. "Anyway, nice to see you too. How do you like being a Sea Dog?"

"It's definitely nicer than playing on a team with Fletcher Bane. That guy's a dick," he says of his former teammate, one of the league's supreme fuckfaces.

I still remember the fight Bane started with our goalie Max the season I joined the team. I'd wanted to punch him myself, and I had. The whole team piled onto the ice to defend Max. Along the way today, Tyler and I shoot the breeze about past fights as I pull into the players' lot. "Sure is. So, who's the big dick here?" I ask, curious to know what he thinks of the guys I've gotten to know over my three years with the Sea Dogs.

"No dicks yet, but the day's young," he says as I park. Then he shoots me a smirk. "Maybe it's you."

"And I don't feel guilty at all for telling Mom to intervene in your dating life."

His smirk vanishes. "Dude."

I just shrug. "I'm not always the responsible one."

"Sometimes you're the troublemaker," he mutters, as we head toward the players' entrance, where I catch a glimpse of a city bus pulling up a few blocks away. Leighton's a bus person. I bet she's on it.

Impulsively, I clap my brother on the shoulder. "I'll meet you inside," I say, already turning toward the bus stop.

Tyler raises a brow, looking curious, but I shrug it off. A man's gotta do what a man's gotta do.

I jog across the parking lot and up to the arena entrance, timing it perfectly as she steps onto the sidewalk. No sign of her dad, which is good, though I feel a flicker of guilt. *We're friends, or trying to be, anyway. This is part of building our new relationship,* I tell myself. *I'm not pursuing a romance with her. This is fine.*

Her gaze lands on me as she heads toward the entrance, slowing down, and I fall into step beside her. She doesn't reach for her phone or fiddle with her headphones, like most people do, making me wonder if she's the rare person who doesn't listen to anything on her commute. Someday, I'll ask since someday I'll know everything about her.

No, you won't. You're just going to be friends with her.

"Morning," I say, keeping it casual. "How was yesterday? First day in the big leagues?"

She gives me a small smile that doesn't quite reach her eyes. "Not too bad," she says, then sighs. "But you know... first-day nerves. I probably looked like a total rookie."

I shake my head. "Didn't notice," I tell her honestly.

She laughs, raising a brow skeptically. "Really? I felt like I was trying way too hard."

"Nah, it's normal. There's a lot of pressure to get it right."

She nods, then lets out a breath. "And everyone sees me one way—as 'Mini Mac,' the coach's daughter."

I can't argue with her there. "Yeah...I guess that started because your dad would mention his daughters sometimes. He never used your names though. Always called you Mini Mac One and Two."

She cringes but smiles. "That's disgustingly adorable and completely mortifying."

"And my mom practically gave me a lunch pail and

told me to get along nicely with my brother today," I say. "Parents can be a little embarrassing."

She grins. "Truer words."

I shift back to her as we walk across the concourse toward the main entrance. "But honestly, you did great yesterday. You'll post the shots this morning?"

"Definitely. After I get some on-ice shots of the team doing drills and stuff," she says as we near a statue of a fierce dog—our mascot. "Fans don't just want workout shots. They want the real thing—players on the ice. Ice is what makes hockey...hockey. It's hard and unforgiving. Cold. Cruel."

I give her a sidelong look. "Sounds like you're talking about a bad relationship."

She laughs. "Maybe. And honestly, I could be."

I growl. "Who is he and when do I kill him?"

She laughs again. "There's no need to commit light murder, Miles."

"I didn't say it'd be light," I say, clenching my fists.

She shoots me an approving glance. "The good news is exes are exes for a reason, you know? Anyone who was awful is in the past."

"Good," I say, then circle back to her earlier comment. "All right, so we're talking about ice, not romance."

"Exactly. Because ice is what separates hockey from most other sports. Just lacing up is symbolic. My dad took me skating for the first time when I was little," she says. "Helped me lace up for the first time. He told me how his heart was racing before his first NHL game, like it was going to explode. I thought he was so tough, you know?"

"And?"

A fondness passes over her expression. "And he is. But he choked up. He told me, 'Real men tear up. Real men get emotional. Real men don't hide behind macho personas.'"

That's another reason I need to focus just on this budding friendship. Because I want Coach to be proud of me too. "That's...that's pretty incredible."

"At the time, I didn't totally understand, but I liked it when he tied my skates, patted my head, and said, 'Let's go for a spin.'"

"How'd you do?" I ask, picturing her on the ice—fierce, and determined.

"I stood up, wobbling like a foal, but after an hour, I was gliding around, my cheeks cold, my heart racing."

We're quiet for a beat, her words hanging between us, then she adds, "I understand why it means so much to the fans too. Seeing their favorite players lace up again gives them this sense of resilience. Every season, it's hope. Hope forged from ice. And hope isn't some soft thing—it's a blade. It's a stick. It's hard won, and worked for. I want to do it justice."

I swallow past a surge of emotion. "You're a poet."

She laughs, shaking her head. "No. I just think about ice a lot."

"Me too."

Before we go inside, I glance around. Hardly anyone's here yet. I tell myself this is just a friendly gift, and maybe, *maybe*, I believe that as I reach into my pocket and pull out a small brown paper bag and offer it to her. "Actually, I got you something," I say. Her brows lift in surprise, and she takes it, opening the bag carefully. It's a gift I picked up at the jewelry shop near An Open Book. The same one where I bought her earrings a year ago—flower earrings she's wearing today, like she was yesterday, like she did the day before.

Inside the bag is a delicate ankle bracelet with a tiny camera charm. Her expression softens as she stares at it. "It's beautiful," Leighton murmurs, her fingers brushing over the charm. "I...I didn't expect this."

"I didn't either. It's...a friendship bracelet," I say, making that up on the fly, keeping my voice low, as anticipation bounces around in my chest. *It's just a friendly gift, it's just a friendly gift.*

"Oh, it is?" She gives me a look like she'll play along.

"Of course."

"I love it," she says, a little spark in her eyes as she closes the bag. "Thank you. I'll put it on later."

"I could put it on you," I offer, impulsively. The image of hooking this onto her slender ankle is lodged in my brain and won't go away. The idea of finding an excuse to touch her is too hard to resist.

Her smile fades, and she's serious now. "Miles, is that such a good idea?"

"No," I say, and I'm not the impulsive guy. I'm the guy who thinks through things. Who weighs pros and cons. Who makes measured decisions for my life. Except, when I'm on the ice—then I think fast, react, and simply *do*. I feel like I'm skating down the rink right now, hell-bent. "But so what?"

She laughs softly, a little unsure. "Maybe later?"

I'll take that *maybe* and hold it tight in my hand. I'm glad, too, I'm not one of those exes who is awful. I'm glad, too, I have this new chance with her.

"I'll be looking forward to that later."

She seems to fight off a smile that tells me she is as well, and we go inside.

20

PRANK ME ONCE

Miles

A little later, I'm lacing up next to Rowan, debating what to list first on the DickNose board—the whiteboard hanging in the corner of the locker room. Technically, it's for last-minute strategy sessions before games, but usually, it's just a canvas for our finest immature artwork, and we are absolutely skilled at drawing faces with dicks for noses.

I take a quick glance around, gauging the room; everyone's in a good mood, so this is the perfect time.

"For the rookies, I'm thinking...new drills for the season?" I suggest, keeping it casual, though I'm itching to see what we can get away with this year when it comes to pranking the rookies—who are working with the assistant coaches right now so they aren't in here. I remember the pranks my first team played on me—cutting my laces at the bottom, filling my skates with ice overnight. Did I like being the butt of a joke? Hell yes. I felt like I'd arrived, but those pranks are child's play compared to what we've devised here at the Sea Dogs the last few years. It's a tradition, and we've got to keep it up—we invent the most ludicrous drills for the noobs.

And...this falls under leadership skills. At least, in my book it does—keeping up morale among the guys. The team that pranks together wins together.

Rowan's dark eyes glint with interest. "One-legged figure eights again? That was some of our best work, Prof," he says, using the nickname the guys gave me a while ago —The Professor. I don't mind that they think I give off a teacherly vibe.

I laugh as I tighten my laces. "Watching them try to skate full speed on one leg was gold. I swear, even you cracked a smile."

Rowan growls, not breaking his usual stoic expression. "Don't get used to it."

Across the room, Max, tugging on his chest protector, chimes in, "Once a season. That's all you get from Rowan for a smile."

With a knowing laugh, Asher pulls on his practice jersey at his stall. "Truer words. Rowan's got grumpy *and* mean covered."

Rowan snarls, making Asher's point.

I clap Rowan on the shoulder. "And you wear the title well," I say, then lower my voice. "Though I know you've got a heart of gold."

He growls. "Do not."

"Liar," I say.

"Fine. I do with Mia," he says, seeming to fight a stupid grin as he turns to the pic of his kid leaping in front of some graffiti art that he keeps in his stall. He taps the photo, his good luck charm.

"As it should be," I say.

Ford's here too, taping up his stick. He's a forward on the second line and as sarcastic as they come. "Stick-tape sabotage was my favorite back in the day."

"I don't know if anyone goes back that far," Rowan chirps.

"Slippery tape on their sticks. I love it," I say, then nod to Ford. "I trust you're doing that right now?"

An evil smile comes from the vet. "I guess the rookies will find out."

My brother is next to me, keeping quiet for now as he laces up. I get it. It can be hard to be the new guy. I was in his position not too long ago. I turn to him, hunting for an easy way to bring him into the convo. I could do it with the kid angle, since he and Rowan are both dads. But I've got a better idea—one that's broader, more team-centric. "Speaking of pranks, if memory serves, we pulled some fast ones back in junior hockey. Remember those?"

Tyler smirks. "We could do one-skate sprints."

Rowan stretches out an arm toward my brother, offering a fist for knocking. "Sweet," Rowan says as Tyler knocks back. "Let's do that. Make them take one skate off and sprint across the ice."

"Good plan," I say, feeling very captain-like indeed. Team bonding, here we come.

"We're definitely going to need pics," Max insists while pulling on his leg pads. "Or it didn't happen."

"We could ask Mini Mac One to get some shots," Rowan says, helpfully suggesting what I'm already thinking. "Or one of the media team."

Before anyone else even gets the chance, I raise my

hand quickly, claiming the responsibility. "I'll take care of that assignment."

"Captain Suck-Up," Asher mutters from his stall, smirking. He knows a little about my one-time fling with Leighton—mostly that I've got monster feelings for her—but he's not letting on in front of anyone, of course.

I roll my eyes. "All right, let's get these drills listed on the DickNose board so the rooks think they're legit," I say, looking around for the whiteboard marker. Max spots it on the floor and lobs it my way. I catch it and crouch in front of the board, scribbling the drills. As I'm finishing, Coach strides in, freezing mid-step as he spots the board and me.

He's seen it before, of course. It's not a secret. But we usually erase it fast when we're just messing around.

The man in charge cocks his head and clears his throat. "The whiteboard has a name?"

The DickNose board is practically fight club—known but never mentioned in front of management. But if I'm going to make co-captain, I figure I'd better own it.

"Yes, sir," I say, standing up straight. "And we take very good care of it."

Coach raises an eyebrow. "Is that right? And what exactly are you using it for?"

"Notes, sir. On ways to improve our game," I say, squaring my shoulders, and taking one for the team.

"Notes, huh?" he says, walking deeper into the locker room and eyeing the list. "What's up there right now, for instance?"

I exchange a quick, desperate look with Rowan. "One-legged drills, sir."

Coach's lips twitch, as if he's barely holding back a

smirk. "That sounds like a fantastic warmup. Why don't you all give it a try?"

The groans from the veterans echo around the room, long and loud.

And just like that, my first shot at "leadership" has all of us—everyone but the rookies—doing one-legged drills on the ice.

21

WELCOME BACK

Leighton

With an ankle bracelet burning a hole in my pocket, I walk down the corridor alongside a lineup of powerhouse women. Eleanor Greer, the owner, leads the way, her stride confident and steady. Next to her is Clementine Carmichael, our sharp, no-nonsense British GM, and Zaire Mandavi, the VP of Communications. Chanda's here too, organizing every detail, and Everly walks beside me, nodding along as we listen to Eleanor's goals for the season. Today's a big PR day, and Eleanor's energy is contagious, so I try not to give another thought to Miles's unexpected gift.

"I didn't trade for Tyler Falcon this summer to lose," Eleanor says, stopping at the edge of the tunnel. Her eyes are fierce as she surveys the arena, but her tone is full of her trademark boundless zeal. "I traded to win." She gestures to Zaire and Chanda. "And I want our marketing to reflect that—bold energy, passion, the excitement of a new season. Not just the Tyler trade, but the whole atti-tude of this team. Fierce, and electric. Are we up to it?"

"Absolutely," Zaire says, nodding with confidence. "We're ready to showcase that energy from day one."

"And the photos will bring that to life too," Chanda adds.

Eleanor's face softens just a bit. "Excellent. Let's see what we can capture today." She turns to lead the others down to the ice.

Chanda tells me to stay back as she follows them down too, but I'm already setting up in the tunnel. Today, my job is to capture the guys as they head out for their first practice—those exciting shots that tell fans, *We're stoked to be back.*

"Go get 'em," Everly mouths before she joins the others. I nod, giving her a thumbs-up. I so have this. I start framing shots in my head the way I would for a boudoir session—anticipating the poses, the mood, the angle that will capture just the right moment.

Then, the faint scent of soap mixed with a hint of sandalwood reaches me, sending my senses into over-drive. I glance up, and my breath catches when I see Miles striding toward me in full gear, towering in his skates, his broad shoulders filling out his Sea Dogs jersey. I've seen him in uniform before, but up close, it's something else. That royal blue looks too good on him, making my chest flutter and my stomach flip. Or maybe it's just him. Absently, I run a hand down the front pocket of my jeans, feeling the faint outline of the bag with the bracelet.

Miles stops barely a foot away, face serious, as if he's got important business to discuss. "We're pranking the rookies today, and I volunteered to give you the inside scoop," he says in that deep, businesslike tone.

I match his professionalism with a smirk. "Sounds fun. So, you want pics, I presume?"

"Yes, but..." He pauses, a wry smile breaking through. "Your dad got to us first."

I snort-laugh before I can help it. Miles shrugs with a *that's life* expression, nodding toward the ice. "You'll see."

As he heads out, I lift my camera, capturing the perfect shot of him walking through the tunnel, a man on a mission. One by one, the rest of the guys follow, game faces on, but I catch the faint grumbles and eye rolls, a mix of annoyance and resignation.

After snapping a few more shots, I hustle up into the stands, adjusting my camera settings as I slide into the second row, staying on my feet. Anticipation buzzes through me as the guys fly around the rink, taking a few practice laps, getting their ice legs back. Just as I get set up, my dad joins them on the ice in skates and a warm-up suit. That's unusual—most of the time he sends an assistant coach out to run the practices. This time he's joined by a row of rookies, who look both nervous and eager as they wait by the boards.

He blows his whistle, sharp and clear, then shouts, "Drills, vets. Show the rookies how it's done."

Even from a distance, Asher's clearly sighing heavily. Max is rolling his eyes. I imagine they're all groaning out loud, the kind of reluctant groan that comes from getting played by someone sharper, wiser, older. Without another word, they each stick one leg out behind them, balancing awkwardly before racing down the ice on one leg. The sound of their blades slicing into the ice cuts through the crisp air, even reaching *my* ears.

The camera nearly shakes in my hands as I stifle laughter. The guys wobble and flail, including Miles, but manage somehow to keep it together while the rookies stare, wide-eyed.

Then my dad blows the whistle again. "One-skate sprint, now."

I nearly break, laughing behind my camera as each of the guys unstraps a skate, clutching it in one hand as they try to balance and shuffle across the ice on one leg as fast as they can. It's a hilarious, clumsy disaster, and I make sure to capture every glorious second.

When the one-skate drills wrap up, my dad's whistle pierces the air again. "Rookies! Sprints, now!" The new guys scramble into line in no time.

For the rest of the practice, everything is business as usual, with all the players sprinting, then practicing shooting drills. I snap shots of every moment, documenting the energy and excitement, per Eleanor's marching orders.

Later that evening, Chanda posts a "We're Back" carousel, officially welcoming the rookies to the Sea Dogs with a lineup of shots that shows exactly what kind of team they're joining.

And I sink down onto the couch at the apartment I'm leaving soon, taking the bag out of my pocket at last. Holding the slim silver chain up to the light. Running a finger over the camera charm.

Closing my eyes and picturing Miles putting it on me. I clutch it tight for a beat, my imagination running away.

When I open my eyes, I sit up, bend over and hook it on, the cool metal sliding against my skin, drawing my eyes to my legs.

Probably his, too, if he were here.

* * *

Over the next several days, I capture shots of the team running through drills, reviewing plays in the video room, talking to the media—day after day until I finally make it to the end of the week. I've somehow managed to juggle this job with my other work, too, including a boudoir session for Katrina. She finally made it, a year after booking, and left the studio absolutely thrilled. The thing I didn't do this week? I didn't spend time alone with Miles. I didn't give in to kissing him. I didn't flirt with him.

Now, I'm almost packed and ready to move this weekend. Just one last task today: a shoot of the players doing volunteer work outside the arena. After that, I'm done for the week.

The shoot goes smoothly, and as I'm heading to the bus, Miles pulls up in his car, rolls down the window, and grins. "Need a ride home?"

He's a friend. We've proved this week we can do this friendship thing. "Sure."

Once I'm in the car, he glances down at my ankle, mostly hidden beneath my jeans. "Is it on? The friendship bracelet."

I raise an eyebrow, the teasing glint in his eyes daring me to answer. "Do you really want to know?"

"I do," he says, his gaze steady.

I tug up my jeans just enough to reveal the delicate anklet with the tiny camera charm. He lets out a low, sexy rumble.

"I really wish you'd have let me put it on you," he says, his voice thick with suggestion.

A suggestion that's hardly friendly at all. I flash back to the day he gave it to me, to the words I said to him. "Maybe later," I say, but that later feels like now.

22

A KISS, TECHNICALLY

Miles

When we're a couple of blocks from her building, the clock feels like it's plummeting. Each tick brings me closer to dropping her off, ending this stolen moment. I cast about for a reason to stretch it out as we pass a pool hall.

"Do you play pool?" I toss out casually.

"Not well."

"Want to play?"

I'm angling for more time with her, and judging from the arch of her brow as she turns toward me, she damn well knows it.

"You want to play pool with me?"

"Or we could geocache," I suggest, leaning into the familiar.

Leighton peers out the window. "It's not dark yet. Sure. Since you're clearly afraid to take me on in pool."

My jaw drops. "You just said you didn't play well."

"Take the win, Miles. Take the win."

And I do. I snag a parking spot by her apartment.

"Good. Let me drop off my camera bag," she says, already out of the car and bounding up the stairs. I watch her the whole way, feeling both victorious and like I'm getting away with something.

As I exit the car, there's a tiny dark cloud over my head, and a voice whispering: *What if someone sees you? How are you going to explain this?*

I talk back to that voice. *This is friendship. We're behaving like friends.*

I believe it. Mostly. But when Leighton comes back downstairs in a hoodie and white sneakers, looking effortlessly cute, I'm not thinking friendly thoughts.

This is just a casual outing, I remind myself. Nothing more. But with her looking at me like she's glad I asked her to hang out, smiling that way like this is what she wanted tonight too...friendship feels like a line I'm barely toeing.

At least I'm not acting on my non-friendly thoughts though. There's that, and I'll hold onto that little detail so damn hard.

She gestures to the sidewalk. "All right, what have you got?"

"One of the guys from my geocache club mentioned there's a cool cache at the nearby park."

She holds up a hand, blinking. "Wait. Did you just say geocache club?"

"Yes," I say tentatively.

She snickers. "That's adorable."

I scoff. "It's not adorable."

She scoffs back at me. "No, Miles. That's literally the definition of adorable. The big, bad hockey player hanging out with a geocache club."

"One, we don't *hang out*. We cache," I point out, but that only makes her snort-laugh harder. "And two, thank you—I'll take big and bad in that compliment sandwich."

"It wasn't a sandwich. There's nothing wrong with adorable," she says.

I set a hand on her back. "Enough with the adorable. I'm not adorable."

"You hunt for urban treasure with a group of other hobbyists. Just accept your adorableness."

I heave an over-the-top sigh. "Let's go, Shutterbug," I say, checking my geocaching app. "If you say adorable again, I might have to spank you."

She wiggles her brows and for a second, or several, I'm a little lost in the intoxicating image I walked right into. Judging from her eager expression she is too. But then she seems to shake it off.

"Okay. Let's check out that park. It's pretty cool. The clubhouse has a living roof," she says as we walk along her quiet block—a little alley tucked away from Hayes Valley's main drag. Trees line the street, shading colorful building after colorful building—some pastel yellow, some baby pink, some mint green. "Solar heating, too, and parts of the playground are made from recycled pieces of an old playground."

I shoot her a curious look. "How do you know all that?"

"I took photos when they revamped it last year," she says.

"The park hired you?"

She smirks. "Don't act so surprised."

"I'm not. I'm kind of amazed, actually. You're only twenty-four, and you've photographed so much already."

She stops, turning those sharp blue eyes on me. "Are you good with having a friend ten years younger?"

I laugh. "Yeah, I think I'm good with it. That is, if you can keep up with me on this cache."

Her mouth drops open. "It's on."

We reach the park as the sun dips lower, painting the sky in soft pinks and oranges. Together, we check the clue—something about *making it rain.*

"It's a water-related hint," I say as we walk past the playground, searching for something that might be a cache but finding nothing. Then we venture near the clubhouse and around a sculpture made from an old slide, but we come up empty. "Maybe a hose? A sprinkler system?" I ask.

Leighton squints at a water fountain attached to the clubhouse, then dashes over to it, but shakes her head after a quick inspection. "Nothing here."

We venture toward the gardens and stop in front of a small one full of native plants. Leighton huffs, stomping her foot. "Where is it? We've been looking for twenty minutes, and this isn't even a big park."

Then I spot a silver watering can nestled near the plants. Something clicks in my head. "This is a low-water garden, right?" I ask.

"Yeah. Part of the sustainability mission," she says.

"You don't need much to make it rain here. Maybe you don't need much water at all." I nod toward the can.

Her eyes sparkle. "Let's see," she says, grabbing my wrist and tugging me toward it. And yeah, that's really nice—her hand on my arm. Like an unexpected bonus of this so-called friendship thing.

We crouch down, and I reach inside. It's dry, and

tucked inside it is a small plastic tube and a pen. I pull out both and show her.

She squints at it. "A test tube is the treasure? Or a pen?"

I don't think so. "Open it," I say, handing her the tiny tube.

Taking it, she uncaps it and pulls out a tiny rolled-up notebook. Her brow lifts, a spark of curiosity in her eyes. "That's it? Just a notebook?"

"That's all it is," I tell her. "This one is a log-only cache. Just a record that you were here. Cool, right?"

Her brow lifts. "Tell me why that's fun to you."

"Because not everything is about the thing. Sometimes it's about the journey. About the satisfaction of reaching the goal," I say.

"And the goal was...?"

"To spend time with...my friend." I open the notebook, take the pen, and think carefully about what to write. Then it hits me. I jot it down and show her: *I am a thief, and today I stole a moment.*

She takes the pen and scribbles her own words beneath mine: *The moment was the treasure.*

I flash back to our treasure hunt a year ago when we found the locket—a treasure for a treasure. She's harkening back to that, and, well, I always am.

We're crouched close, our heads nearly touching, sharing the same air, the same quiet thrill of discovery. It's just us and the evening light, and the memories of our one day together between us.

A memory that's getting a reboot. It's no longer just our past. It's our new present. I could lean in, hold her face, catch her lips in a kiss. The pull is so intense, it's hard to resist. Sometimes, I wonder why I'm so drawn to her. Other times, I know. Deeply.

Because she's fearless. Because she's here with me, treasure hunting, saying yes. She's stealing moments too —moments off the clock, moments that aren't planned or predictable. Moments that are just...exploring the city I've come to love.

As we crouch there, the evening light softening around us, I reach out toward her ankle, brushing my finger against the silver bracelet. I trace the cool metal and her soft skin, her eyes flickering with sparks of desire— sparks that mirror my own. "Maybe now?"

"It's already on me," she teases.

"A technicality."

She nibbles on the corner of her lips, her gaze drifting to a nearby bench. She rises and makes her way over to it. "Then take off the technicality."

I'm there so fast. Bending, reaching, then fiddling. I have steady hands. I could take this off quickly.

But I don't.

She lifts her leg slightly, resting her ankle on my knee.

I linger, taking my sweet time unhooking the bracelet with the camera charm, letting my fingertips trail over her skin. I glance down, and goosebumps rise along her ankle. My throat goes dry. I'm dying to lift her foot to me, to kiss her bare ankle, to brush my lips on her skin.

Instead, I let the anklet fall into my hand. "A technicality," I murmur, my voice thick with tension.

"Such a lovely technicality."

Then I bring the charm to my lips, press a kiss to the tiny metal camera while holding her hot gaze, and return my hands to her ankle.

Her breath comes fast as I put it on her again, my fingers grazing her skin as I hook the clasp.

She didn't need it redone. It's another reboot, another stolen moment.

But really, it's another loophole.

When it's on, she stretches her leg out, twisting her foot to admire the charm. "It's like a kiss."

I let out a long breath. "I wish it were."

Her voice is soft as she says, "Me too."

As the sun fades, we leave, and I walk her home. "When are you moving back into your old place?" I ask so I don't ask other things, like *can I come up*, and *do you think about me all the time too*?

"This weekend. I only have a few things. I've managed to fit almost everything into two suitcases."

"Impressive," I say. "Do you have to use those packing cubes?"

"Of course. How else would one pack?"

"I can't even imagine," I say, making small talk, but also wondering something. "How are you getting it there? You don't have a car." Then it hits me. Her dad does. He's probably helping her.

My stomach churns as I wait for her to say his name. The man I respect. The man I work for. I can't cross a line again. I really can't.

"I'll just Lyft. It's no big deal."

I probably shouldn't go there and acknowledge the issue, but there's also no point *not* acknowledging it. "You won't ask your dad?"

"Nah. If he sees the apartment and how small it is, it'll just set off a new round of *I really wish you'd let me cover your rent, find you a place, help pay for things*," she says, and holy shit, it's uncanny—her imitation of him.

I part my lips but I'm too shocked to speak for a few seconds. Finally, words form. "You sound just like him."

She laughs. "Well, I don't think that's too surprising."

It's not, but still, it's another reminder. "True," I say, then shift gears. "Do you need a ride?"

For a brief moment she pauses, clearly thinking. "I'll be okay."

Not going to lie—I wanted her to say yes. But I don't want to let on I'm disappointed, so I ask, "Will it be weird moving back in with them? And the loud banging?"

"Ask me tomorrow night," she says.

That feels like an opening. One I know I'll take even if she doesn't need a ride.

We reach her place a minute later, and the evening slouches toward its inevitable end.

I wish I had another reason to make it last. But I don't. So I say goodbye. And think about her for the rest of the night.

23

MY LYFT IN SHINING ARMOR

Leighton

The Rubenesque woman lounges on the soft white cover on the bed, propped on her side in a zebra-print teddy, her red lips curving into a come-hither smile, her gaze dark with desire. A story of seduction unfolds before my lens, and I capture it frame by frame.

"Beautiful," I say to Cora, lowering the camera briefly. Then, I turn to her partner, Aliza, a lithe woman in a leopard bodysuit, who's standing just out of frame. "Why don't you move over to the bed and watch her as she poses?"

Aliza grins. "Sounds perfect."

She perches on the edge of the mattress, her expression softening into something tender with a touch of fire, too, as she gazes at her girlfriend. I lift the camera again, snapping away. These voyeuristic shots—the ones that tell the tale of desire from another's perspective—have become some of my favorites. I've been adding them to my repertoire more often lately, ever since that shoot with Miles. There's something intimate and raw about them, something that resonates deeply with clients.

It's not just about looking sexy; it's about being wanted. About knowing someone is captivated by the sight of you, unable to look away.

And isn't that what we all crave? To feel adored, like we're someone's entire world?

I take a few more frames, capturing them together but apart. When I'm finished, I say, "Do you want to come back this afternoon? I can do a soft edit and show them to you."

It's morning, and I have one more shoot, but I can squeeze in some work on their pics after that.

They say yes in tandem, then take off. A few hours later, they return to the studio with eager, hopeful eyes. We sit down at the table where I edit on my laptop and I hold my breath as I show them their pics. This is one of my favorite moments—the payoff.

It's a moment—most of the time—when clients see themselves in a whole new way. Cora gasps. Aliza covers her mouth with her hand, her eyes glassy. They turn to each other, and I watch them. "You look incredible," Aliza says to her love.

"So do you," Cora says.

"You both do," I add.

With obvious emotion, they say together, "We do."

This reaction makes it all worthwhile. I give them a quick rundown of when their final photos will be ready, as Cora heads to the door, then asks, "Want to join us for a glass of wine? Our treat."

I shake my head with a rueful smile. "I'd love to, but I have to move tonight."

Aliza gasps, her jaw dropping in mock horror. "You worked and you're moving in one day?"

I wave off her concern with a laugh. "It's easy. Everything fits in two suitcases."

"I still think you need wine," Cora says.

"You're probably not wrong," I say.

They leave, and once I've straightened up too, I exit Hush Hush, locking up, then blinking when I spot a bottle of chardonnay by the door. I reach for it, grabbing the tiny pink card next to it. I flip it open, smiling as I read: *I always get my way. Love, Cora*

I tuck the bottle into my canvas bag. It'll go to good use; I'll pour a glass as I unpack. Hopefully, my once-and-again roomies won't be there.

Maybe Indigo and Ezra will be busy at the bike shop they manage together—the one near the apartment where they make bespoke bamboo bikes. A woman can hope.

As I walk home, the city hums around me and I listen to it, soaking in all the sounds—the honks of horns, the buzz of traffic, and the chatter of pedestrians. I replay the session in my mind, the way Cora's face lit up when she saw herself through Aliza's eyes. The way that reminded me of the impromptu session with Miles once upon a time. I sigh, letting my mind wander back to that day, when I felt the same sort of adoration. What would it be like to feel that again? To feel it freely, and regularly? But then, I let the idea go. Now isn't the time to get caught up in romantic fantasies. I have work to do, money to save. A future to prepare for.

I'm better off behind the camera anyway. I prefer being the storyteller. It gives me more control, and that's what I need most in this wild, unpredictable, noisy world

—a world that someday might become a whole lot quieter for me.

* * *

And I lied.

So much for "two suitcases." Not only have I stuffed two massive pieces of luggage to their breaking points, but I've also filled a collection of reusable grocery bags with kitchen supplies. Who knew tea paraphernalia could take up so much space? Actually, someone probably knew. I just ignored it.

Don't even get me started on toiletries. That stuff multiplies. And the nightstand drawer? Let's just say I had no idea how many "friends" were crammed in there. I definitely need another suitcase.

I could call Maeve, Everly, Fable, or Josie to borrow one. But no. I've got this. More grocery bags will work fine.

I stand in the middle of the apartment, which now looks less like a home and more like a battlefield of boxed-up chaos. The couch with the broken spring is scheduled for donation—it'll probably end up in a college rental, right next to a Ping-Pong-slash-beer-pong table. The bed will be history tomorrow, too, since Maeve didn't need any furniture after moving in with Asher.

This apartment was only ever supposed to be temporary. A stepping stone. Still, as I stand here, taking it all in, a strange ache pierces my chest. This was my space. The place where I rebuilt myself after life fell apart.

I glance at my camera bag and decide to memorialize it. One last picture.

I snap photos of the couch Josie called "The Kid" after the villain from *The Giving Tree,* the window where Big

Bird and Ms. Peck curl up together (post-coitally, I'm sure), and even the bathroom with its annoyingly short shower and its toilet that faces the wall. This apartment isn't much, but it's mine. It gave me space to grow, to hustle, to prove to myself that I could make it on my own without my father's support.

My phone buzzes in my hand just as I lower the camera. When I glance at the screen, my stomach does a weird little flip.

> Miles: How's the move going?

It's thoughtful of him to check in, so I write back.

> Leighton: It's going great. Or it will be once I call a Lyft in a few minutes.

> Miles: Glad to hear that. Do you need anything? A pizza at your new place? Artichoke pasta? Housewarming gifts come in many forms, you know.

I smile, a warm flush spreading through me. Both sound amazing, and I'm about to say so—and politely decline—when my phone trills in my hand.

He's calling.

I stare at the screen, his name glowing there. My thumb hovers over the answer button for a second too long. Something tells me that picking up this call will change the rhythm of my carefully choreographed evening.

And maybe—just maybe—I'm not as annoyed by that idea as I should be.

I swipe to answer.

"Hey. Ready for your Lyft?"

I furrow my brow. "I haven't requested it yet. I'm about to."

"No, you're not."

"What?"

"I'm your Lyft. I'm outside."

I'm speechless for a long beat. My first instinct is to say thanks but no thanks. But I tamp that down.

Because he showed up for me.

Instead, I say, "I'll be right there."

* * *

"You're joking," Miles says as he cruises across the city toward the Mission District, still stuck on the names of my roomies.

"Not even a little bit," I say.

He takes a beat, shaking his head. "They can't actually be named Indigo and Ezra."

"Believe it," I say, smiling at his disbelief.

"How is that even possible? Those names scream, *I spend all day tending sourdough starters.* No, wait—with names like that, I bet they run a sourdough-starter daycare."

"Where they babysit sourdough starters when their owners go out of town?" I ask, getting into it.

"You know that's their side hustle, Leighton."

I laugh as the city lights streak by. "Honestly, I could see that. Maybe I should suggest it to them? But that would mean they're around more often, and my hope is that they stay busy at the bike shop."

"How about this? Suggest they run the sourdough daycare *from* the bike shop. These two-in-one shops are all the rage. I went to one in New York that was both a flower shop and a bike shop. They called it *Bikes and Blooms*."

"Nice," I say, momentarily picturing Miles on a bike. The image is unexpectedly hot—maybe because of his glasses. He's such a hot nerd with them on, like right now. But a hot athletic nerd? That's ten million times hotter. Which is Miles, with his two degrees, and his *I was kind of into school* understatement in a nutshell.

"So Indigo and Ezra make bamboo bikes," Miles says, "and they're also loud as hell in bed?"

"So loud," I say, groaning. "And so...specific."

He makes a rolling gesture for me to continue. "Do tell."

I flash back to the last time I lived with them and shudder. "They had this thing about using all the proper terms for body parts. No slang. She'd give him instructions like, *Squeeze my nipple really hard, then bite it, then lick the areola.* And he'd say, *Communication is so hot. Tell me exactly how to administer oral sex.* Then she'd lay it out in excruciating detail, step by step, from the vulva to the clitoris."

Miles shoots me a quick side-eye before returning his attention to the road. "I mean, communication is nice and all, but..."

"I prefer cock and clit," I say, laughing so hard my stomach hurts.

"I prefer my—" He stops himself, but I think we both know where he was going.

I relax into the seat, surprised at how easy this is after all—accepting his help. I'd planned to do it all myself, mostly to prove that I could. But maybe I don't always have to. Sometimes it's nice to let someone else step in. Then again, the answer might be a whole lot simpler: I like being with Miles.

It's not just the sandalwood scent of his cologne, or the way his wild hair flops over his eyes, or even the way his eyes are so expressive and thoughtful. It's all of it—*him.*

"Thanks again," I say, glancing at him once more, my chest a little fizzy with gratitude, "for showing up as my Lyft in shining armor."

"Happy to do it," he says with a casual shrug.

"I didn't expect it."

"I know," he says, seeming a little amused.

"I wasn't sure what to say at first when you arrived," I admit.

"The correct response is—*Miles, you're fucking amazing and I've found a portal to a parallel universe where I can ride your cock tonight.*"

A laugh bursts from me. "Yes, take me to that portal right now."

He taps the GPS on the car's console, then says in an authoritative tone: "GPS—take me to the secret sex portal where there are no consequences."

The GPS doesn't answer, of course, but I do, speaking in a cool, robotic tone, "Take the first left at the light."

With the panache of a man who wants a woman, he flicks on the turn signal for a hot second, before turning it off with a resigned sigh.

Not bothering to hide my appreciation for his effort, I

add, "You were kind of determined to give me a ride, it turns out."

"I was," he says, owning it.

"I thought I could do it all myself," I say, an admission.

"Yeah, but you didn't have to."

"Thanks."

"Anytime," he says, and I believe him—that his *anytime* means he'll show up. I like that feeling—the belief that he'll do what he says. On the one hand, I'm used to it from my dad and my sister; on the other hand, I certainly never felt it with my mom, or any of the guys I've dated.

The GPS guides him onto my block, past a Mexican restaurant and a mural painted on the side of a building. It's of a high heel kicking the word *Patriarchy*. I point to it. "That's one of Maeve's murals and one of my favorite things about this neighborhood. That, and the nachos."

"You had me at nachos," Miles says, his tone teasing, before he adds, "but that's a cool mural too, and so's the sentiment. Maeve's got skills."

"She truly does."

He shoots me a more serious look as he pulls over outside my building. Spanish music filters out from a nearby corner store. "And yeah, I was determined," he says. "Because when I asked if you needed a ride, you said you'd be okay."

I flash back to last night and the words I'd brushed off. "That's true."

"But you didn't say that you didn't need one," he says with a knowing grin.

"Another technicality," I tease.

"I'm excellent at loopholes." His voice is low and raspy, and the sound weaves through me. But it's those dark brown eyes that catch my attention most—they're deep and soulful, and he looks at me like this—*here*—is the only place he wants to be.

Well, besides that portal.

And maybe I like his persistence because it's familiar. I understand it. It's what drives me too. Showing up the way he did seems to say that he understands me—that I won't always ask for help, but I might actually—*gasp*—enjoy it. And perhaps need it too.

"Plus, it's what a friend would do," he adds.

"And we're friends."

"We are," he says.

I toss him back a smile. "Then, let's put those muscles to use carrying my suitcases."

"With so much pleasure," he says with a wink that makes my damn stomach flutter.

Again.

24

SUSTAINABLE PLEASURE

Leighton

Great. Just great. My once-again roomies have commandeered the living room for a public therapy session.

Indigo stands with her hands clasped to her chest, her long braid trailing down her back. "I am feeling frustrated," she says in a calm, measured tone, "because I reminded you this morning to move the bamboo out of Leighton's room. It upsets me that you didn't do it."

Ezra hangs his head low, his man bun drooping in solidarity. Even his beard looks defeated.

"It's okay. We can move the bamboo," I offer, trying to sidestep the roomie drama on night one. I really just want the bamboo out of my room. Miles is in there, setting down grocery bags.

Indigo lifts a hand in a regal *stop* gesture. "Thank you, Leighton. But Ezra needs to honor my feelings about this."

My head spins. Too much honoring happening.

Ezra pushes his horn-rimmed glasses up his nose—they're for show; I know he doesn't need them. He looks up at Indigo, and I expect him to cave. Instead, he says, "I should have moved them, Indigo. But I was frustrated about the kombucha top left on the counter. I felt defiant and acted out."

Oh, for fuck's sake. I do not need this confessional nonsense.

Apparently, neither does Miles. He strides out of my room, hauling the bamboo like a lumberjack with a stack of wood, his jaw set in that calm, no-nonsense way. "Where do you want this—couch, floor, or table?"

Indigo startles. "Um…"

"The table, man," Ezra says, brightening. "Sweet! That would have taken me half an hour."

"Because you get distracted by your folk music station every time you do chores," Indigo snaps.

"Oh, now you're mocking my music? Pretty sure you were the one who asked me to blast it the other night in bed."

And the gloves are off.

She gasps. "Ezra! Use your 'I feel' words."

What a great idea. "*I feel* like it's time to set up my room," I interject, darting past them.

Miles grabs two more of my grocery bags from the foyer, then follows, shutting the door behind him with a necessary finality. He sets the bags down by the door and leans his shoulder against the wall, arms crossed, watching me. "Good call on escaping the folk music and kombucha detente."

The chaos of the living room is replaced with the quiet clutter of my room, my life scattered in suitcases and bags.

I breathe easier, but the space feels smaller with Miles here.

And it's not a bad sort of small. But it is a tempting sort of small. I need to be careful with him so close. I need to remember the friendship plan. "It's always a good idea to escape them," I say quietly.

"Yeah, they're fun," he says, taking in my room with its futon, scratched-up bureau and not just secondhand, but fourth-hand chair that was passed on from a friend of a friend of a friend.

"Evidently they've moved from fucking it out to therapying it out," I mutter, glancing at the door. "Let's put on music so they can't hear us talk about them."

"Good idea," he says, pulling out his phone. "What do you like?"

I shrug, my chest tightening. "Honestly, anything. Well, not folk music."

"Heard. But seriously—any artists you're into?"

I wince. "I'm not a big music person."

He tilts his head, his expression softening. "Do you dislike it, or...does it distract you from hearing?"

I relax, but only somewhat. It's a relief that he's naturally curious and doesn't cringe, but it's still uncomfortable to talk about this with anyone outside family or close friends. Honestly, I don't even love talking about it with my girlfriends. It makes me feel even more vulnerable than I already am with the hearing loss.

But Miles is so earnest and patient, so I give him the truth. "Yeah, it's that. I don't listen to music much while I'm out and about because I'm afraid I'll miss something important. Same at home, I guess. It's silly."

He nods, thoughtful. "It's not silly. Not one bit. I get it." He touches the arms of his glasses. "Sometimes when I go to bed at night, my mind wanders to what if I need to see —really see well—in the middle of the night. That's why I never wore glasses when I was a teenager and lived at home. Just contacts all the time."

The tension in my chest unknots somewhat, replaced by something like empathy. "Because...you wanted to be able to look out for your brother and sister if you had to?"

"And my mom," he adds.

My heart softens and pulls toward him.

"I'm not saying it's the same," he quickly clarifies. "I know they're different senses. I just...I want you to know that I want to understand...you. That I like understanding you." He pauses, then like he has to say it, adds, "As a friend."

My heart thumps hard, my throat thick with emotion. "I don't listen to anything when I walk around the city," I say, and it is an admission.

His lips curve into a soft grin. "I was wondering the other day if you did."

"Yeah?" I ask, wanting to kiss that grin. To touch the corner of his mouth. To run a hand over his stubble.

"It had occurred to me."

"Now you know," I say, and it feels safe to tell him. Like my vulnerability doesn't make me weaker.

"I'm glad you told me," he says, then cocks his head, studying me. "What if we don't listen to music? What if we listen to ocean sounds or birds or something? Would that help?"

No one in the entire world has ever suggested anything like that. Maybe because I haven't given anyone the chance. But he took the opportunity. "How about rainfall?"

His smile grows wider. "You speak to my Seattle soul."

"You really do like the rain?"

"Fucking love it. Rain is a beautiful thing."

I picture him in Seattle—no umbrella, a cup of coffee in hand, Nirvana playing in his headphones, impervious to the drops of water the Washington sky flings on him. It fits him so perfectly it makes me smile. "Do you like Nirvana?"

He scoffs. "Do you like shiny things?"

I gasp, mock affronted. "Miles Falcon! How dare you!"

"How dare I figure you out already?" He smirks, moving closer. Lifting a hand, he lightly brushes my flower earrings, then my bracelets, and finally glances down at the anklet he gave me. I shiver from the dusting of his fingertips.

I feel almost...marked by his touch. It's a heady sensation.

"Yes," I say, primly.

"Get used to it, *friend*. I'm very observant," he says, queuing up rainfall sounds on his phone. The gentle patter fills the room, soft and private.

"Is this bickering new for them?" he asks, nodding toward the door.

"They've always been...talky. But yeah, this public therapy phase is new."

He raises an eyebrow. "And it's still going on."

Oh. "I hadn't realized," I say, swallowing, my cheeks warming with some embarrassment. "Sorry you have to hear it."

His smile is soft, full of understanding. "It's all good. The rain covers it up. Another reason I like rain."

And I appreciate so much that he didn't try to make

me feel better about missing what they're saying. I appreciate that he's not making a thing out of it. "Agreed." I grab a fitted sheet to toss onto the futon, then wrinkle my nose. "Does my room smell like beard oil? Like tobacco and pepper?"

Miles sniffs the air. "A little, now that you say that. Also, that's specific."

"I have a good nose," I say, offhand.

"I'm impressed."

"Eagle eyes and a bloodhound nose to make up for what I lack," I say.

He gives me a soft smile. "I'll have to make sure I smell extra good around you."

I lift a playful brow. "News flash: you do." But so I don't get caught up in flirting, I quickly add, "Anyway, when I was at Maeve's place, they sublet to a guy who made small-batch beard oil."

"Of course they did."

"Same circles," I say.

He smirks. "Figured as much."

Miles shifts to help me pull the sheet tighter on one corner of the futon. As we make the bed, it strikes me—he's already done so much for me today. I don't want him to feel obligated to hang around.

"You don't have to stay," I say, catching his gaze across the bed.

He shoots me a look, his hands still resting on the edge of the futon. "Have you met me?"

I laugh. "Yes, Mister Determination. Do you always get what you want?"

"When it's important," he says, straightening up, his voice soft but firm. "Besides, if memory serves, we're having pizza. Artichoke hearts, right?"

I laugh harder. "I thought your Lyft services were your housewarming gift."

"Turns out I'm giving you two housewarming gifts."

"Fine. But I'm paying."

"Not a chance. It's a housewarming gift, Leighton."

"Then I'm providing the wine," I say.

"*I feel* good about that."

The sound of rain muffles our laughter, and I'm suddenly keenly aware of the ease between us. It's dangerous. Too tempting. As if we could fall onto my bed, like a couple, enraptured by laughter, then turn to each other and kiss like it's all we've wanted to do all day. Will it always feel like this? With him both so safe and so dangerous at the same time?

I clench my fists once, twice, to try to ignore the desire swirling in me.

As we finish with the futon, Miles grabs his phone and asks me a few more pizza questions. When he finishes ordering the food, his attention seems to snag on something beneath the chair. He crosses the room, rummages around, and pulls it out, holding it up to the light.

Something long. Pink. Silicone.

I slap a hand to my face. "Oh no."

He dangles the dildo between two fingers, looking amused. "Yours?"

"God, no," I groan, grabbing an old T-shirt of mine to wrap it up. Marching to the living room, I interrupt Indigo mid-sentence as she says to Ezra, "Is it hard to listen to my feelings?"

Girl, it's hard for me. "Here. This is either beard oil guy's or..."

Indigo snatches it from me, her eyes flaring. Like she's going to lash into Ezra. But then her expression softens.

Instead, her gray eyes twinkle, and she whispers reverently, "This one is my favorite."

"Mine too," Ezra says.

"I thought it was missing," she whispers.

"It's a sign. It's come home to us," Ezra agrees.

"This whole night is a sign," Indigo says, turning to me with an air of absolute sincerity. "You're a good-luck charm."

Then they run off to their room, leaving me stunned. I retreat back to mine, shutting the door with more force than necessary. Miles looks up from his phone, grinning. "Rain sounds louder?"

"Yes. Please."

I pause, glancing at the gorgeous, thoughtful hockey player as the sound of rainfall fills the room. I definitely feel like I don't want this night to end.

* * *

Fine, *fine*. There's more to unpack than I'd thought. But Miles is helpful with my digital photo frame, my laptop and monitor, and the few books I have, though I'm more of an e-reader gal. As he plugs in the digital frame, he tips his head toward the bedroom door. "So, those two seem... *really* into communication. But almost too much?"

I laugh while hanging up clothes. "Right? Sometimes I think they're onto something, but most of the time they just remind me that relationships are really complicated."

"Tell me about it," he says, as he connects the frame to the router.

Well, I can't resist that. I probably shouldn't poke around in his relationship history, but I'm admittedly curious. He's never shared much online and I maybe, possibly, checked out his socials. "Okay, tell me about it," I say, nerves jumping through me. But I'm too curious. I want to know who captivated him at some point.

He stops his work on the frame, gives me a thoughtful look. "You want to know?"

"I do."

He takes off his glasses, pinches the bridge of his nose, then says, "I was involved with someone for a long time in Vancouver."

My stomach dips unpleasantly, but I say nothing. I simply wait.

"We were pretty serious. Lived together and all. But after my ACL tear, I was in a bad place. I wasn't able to focus on anything but myself. First, I kind of wallowed and that took up all my headspace, then I tried to heal. I wasn't...nice to be around. And so...she left."

I stop hanging, swallowing roughly. "Just left? It was too much for her?"

"Yeah," he says, heavily. Then, he slides his glasses back on. "I guess I understand in retrospect. I was...deeply unhappy."

My heart squeezes with pain for him. I step away from the closet and move to the edge of the bed, closer to him. "I'm sorry. That sounds awful all around."

"It was," he says, then shrugs. "But breakups are, right?"

There's resignation in his voice, like he's accepted the way things ended, and the way he felt. But there's real hurt there too. That has to be a factor as well in why it's best if we stay the friendship course. "They are," I say with a heavy sigh too, then add, "are you happier now?"

He nods instantly. "I am. Saw a team psychologist. Turned my career around. Got my head on straight. I'm good. I've always prided myself on moving forward. On picking up the pieces, you know?"

"I do."

"So that's what I did." He tips his chin my way. "Your turn. You tell me about it."

I wince, not sure I want to get into the romance details. I wave a dismissive hand. "Oh, I just had a couple college boyfriends. One wasn't even a boyfriend."

"The one I'm lightly murdering?"

I laugh at the memory. "Yes, that one."

He makes a "spill it" motion with his hand, his fingers curling toward himself. "Tell me about his crime."

I roll my eyes to make light of it, but that's just self-protection. I swallow my pride and bite off the truth. "This one guy said my hearing loss was an embarrassment."

Miles's face turns white. Wait. No, it's more like white-hot anger I see etched into the set of his jaw. "I will find him and kill him."

"He's not worth it," I say.

"No, but you are," he says easily, locking eyes with me like he would march into battle and slay the dragons of exes if that's what I asked.

My stomach swoops. "Thank you."

He rises, comes around the bed, and sits next to me. "He didn't deserve you or appreciate you. You know that, right?"

The thing is—I do. That's why it was easy to tell Nick thanks for the wine and to walk out in the middle of our third date. "Yes. Want to know what I said to him when he told me that?"

"I do," Miles says, eagerly.

"I said, *then it won't embarrass you when I walk out and leave you with the bill.*"

Miles's smile spreads nice and easy, his dark eyes full of pride and appreciation for my payback. "You're a fucking goddess," he says.

I preen a little. "I am."

* * *

The bottle of wine is nearly empty, and the pizza box is heading that way too with Miles reaching for the last slice from his chair a little later.

"Best pizza ever," he declares.

"Because of the artichoke hearts or the company?" I ask.

He pauses, tilting his head like he's genuinely considering it. "Hmm. Tough call."

I grab a small pink pillow from the futon, holding it up like I'm about to throw it.

"Try me," he says, leaning back, all confidence. "I have excellent reflexes."

"So cocky," I tease, then take him up on his offer, lobbing the pillow.

He catches it easily with his free hand, then eyes it. "Pink, huh? You don't strike me as a pink person."

I glance down at my black jeans and gray cropped tank, smirking. "I like pink too. I'm full of surprises."

His eyes darken, his gaze raking over me like he's remembering the surprises from that day—the way I like him to touch me: rough, hungry, possessive. "Good surprises," he says, his voice low and rough, leaving the words hanging in the air between us.

He's definitely thinking about that surprise too. I could

linger on those memories all night long. But they're too risky to our budding friendship, so fragile right now, but so important.

I can't afford to go there. Nor can he. Especially after what we both shared earlier. But especially him—I don't want to cause a single complication in his career, especially since he nearly lost it a few years ago.

I clear my throat, desperate to keep our vibe in neutral territory, returning to the safer topic of pillow catching. "And I suppose it's no surprise your reflexes are good. I'll allow that cockiness."

His grin returns to playful. "Thanks. I worked hard on them. I busted my ass to get back up to speed after my injury."

Opening a bag of books I'll set on the nightstand, I glance at him as he takes a bite. "Thanks for sharing those details. I'd read about your ACL tear, but of course didn't know the toll it took on you."

After he finishes a bite of his slice, his smirk spreads again, too pleased. "You looked me up."

Far too pleased.

"I did," I admit, trying not to give him the satisfaction of a blush—because we're being friends here, nothing more.

"And what did you learn?"

"That you had an ACL tear," I deadpan, rolling my eyes. "What did you think I'd find? That you like piña coladas and beach vacations?"

He laughs, shaking his head. "Fair point. But for the record, I do like piña coladas."

"You don't strike me as a beach guy. You're more... mountains."

"I'll take that as a compliment," he says, grinning.

"Because you're cocky," I tease.

"And you like that."

"In a friend," I add, since I need to remind him. But also me. "So...the tear itself was pretty bad?"

The pizza freezes halfway to his mouth, and his expression shifts. That easy confidence dims, replaced by something heavier. "Yeah. It was."

I try to imagine losing photography for six or nine months—how dark I'd feel, how lost. "That can change your perspective on a lot of things," I say.

A shadow crosses his face, and for a moment, it's like he's somewhere else. "I thought my career was over. It happened at the end of the season, so I was out for half the next one. And when I came back...I struggled to play well." His jaw tightens. "Which is why I ended up on waivers."

I swallow, feeling the weight of his words. And my dad —his coach—picked him up after that. I tread carefully, unsure if this is a door we should open now. "I'm glad my dad wanted to work with you," I say.

I've always admired how my father could see potential where others couldn't. And knowing that Miles respects him as much as I do adds another layer to the knot of feelings tightening in my chest.

Miles's features soften, but the storm cloud lingers. "He saved my career," Miles says simply, letting out a deep sigh.

The silence stretches for a beat—one where we're both clearly thinking of what's at stake if we give in to good surprises again. My relationship with my father is everything. And Miles admires him too, and needs him as well.

"And it's a hell of a career," I say.

"Thanks," he says, his tone full of gratitude.

Miles finishes the slice, wipes his hands, and points at the last unopened bag. "One more. Let's do it, Shutterbug."

I step toward it quickly, raising a hand. "I'll get that one."

Too quickly.

His brow arches as he reaches for it before I can stop him.

Oh no.

The moment he unfolds it, his eyebrows shoot up. "Oh."

Followed by, "Ohhh."

And then, with a grin so wicked I feel heat creeping up my neck, "Wow."

I close my eyes and exhale sharply. "There are...a lot in there, I know."

"A lot just became my new favorite saying." He's practically giddy, holding the bag out of my reach like a trophy. "Holy shit, Leighton. This is like Christmas morning and the Stanley Cup in one."

I laugh despite myself, lunging for it.

He spins away, holding it behind his back.

"Miles," I warn, though it's useless.

"I'll give it back...if you tell me what each thing is."

"Oh god, I thought you were going to say 'show and tell.'"

His grin turns devious. "Is that an option?"

"When you find that sex portal," I shoot back, grabbing the bag. I pull out the first item, holding it up. It's a standard vibe, but there's nothing standard about the Os it delivers. "This is the Dynamo. Made from recycled ocean plastic."

His brow furrows in surprise. "Sustainable pleasure— You're killing me, Leighton. I need to find that portal right now."

Want spreads in my chest, and even though we're flirting with trouble, I can't resist. I pull out another one with a curved end. "This is The Wand."

His smile falters. His gaze flicks between the toy and me, his eyes darkening. He's picturing me using it. "I bet it's magic."

I smile, but it burns off quickly as the air shifts. His steps are purposeful, closing the space between us until he's barely a foot away. Heat radiates from him, and I'm keenly aware of how small the room suddenly feels, how easily I could grab the neckline of his shirt and tug him against me. My pulse rockets.

"And that one?" His voice is low, gravelly, as he nods toward the rose-pink toy.

I hesitate, heat flooding my cheeks. "It operates with suction." I nibble on my lower lip. "It's *really* good."

His breath hitches, his chest rising as he drags a hand through his hair. He steps closer again, pressing his palm to the wall like he needs the support. When his eyes meet mine, they're molten.

"If I stay much longer..." His voice is rough, scraping the air between us. "I'm breaking the friendship rule."

My pulse thrums everywhere, my whole body on fire. "You should go."

But he doesn't leave.

He cups my cheek, his hand warm and steady, his thumb brushing against my skin as his gaze roams my face. "Send me a picture when you're done."

The words hit me like a hot kiss, leaving me breathless.

Before I can respond, he's gone, the door clicking shut behind him.

I stand there, my pulse pounding and my skin tingling. The need rises higher in me, so high it's impossible to ignore.

* * *

Later, I'm quiet as I imagine him pinning me down, fucking me hard, taking me apart.

My toes curl. My legs shake. A moan rises from the depths of my dirty soul. I swallow the sound as I come hard.

Then, with my cheeks still flush, my lips parted, my hair fanned out, I take a photo of my face and send it to him.

Ten minutes later, a reply lands.

> Miles: Fuck me.

I roll my lips together, savoring his reaction. Then another drops.

> Miles: You're so fucking sexy.

My smile grows stupidly bigger. A few minutes later, my phone pings once again.

. . .

Miles: It's not the first time, and it won't be the last that a picture of you has come in quite handy.

25

THE GREAT SOCK DEBATE

Miles

I could really use a Border Collie.

The second I step into the locker room for our season opener on a Wednesday in early October, it's buzzing with noise—gear clattering, banter flying. Herding these guys for the opening night team pic feels like wrangling twenty-plus rowdy sheep. A canine companion would make this so much easier.

But Coach asked me to round everyone up, so here I am.

"Boys," I call out, stepping into the chaos, but my voice barely registers over Hugo's loud declaration.

"For once and for all: you can wear sandals with a suit," Hugo argues from his locker, peeling off a sock with cartoon cupcakes on it, "but you can't wear socks and sandals with a suit."

"Why are you discriminating against socks?" Wesley shoots back, yanking off his Corgi-butt socks like they're badges of honor. "Socks are elite. Do you hate the coolness of socks?"

"Socks aren't cool," Tyler says from across the room, earning him a withering glare from Wesley.

"Maybe you didn't get the memo, Little Falcon," Wesley fires back as he tosses his suit jacket into his stall. I stifle a laugh at the nickname he just gave my brother.

Judging from the eye roll, Tyler's not too fond of it, but Wesley doesn't back down. Nope. He holds up his Corgi-butt socks once more like evidence in court. "I have monkey socks, giraffe socks, dumpster fire socks, librarians-like-it-hard socks, I-read-banned-books socks, Christmas socks, Halloween socks, and zombie socks. Socks are motherfucking elite."

"Thank you, Wesley, for that rundown of your sock drawer. Exactly what we all needed today. Now, as I was saying, we need to get our asses in gear for the team pic," I say, gesturing pointedly toward the exit.

Max stops loosening his tie. "Yes, but did you know I have I-hate-everyone-but-you socks?" he says, smirking as he holds up his foot to show off said socks. "Everly gave them to me." It's hard for him to hide the obvious adoration he has for his fiancée.

"Yeah?" Asher snorts. "Well, I've got giraffe briefs, monkey boxer briefs—but not Corgi butts. Hmm. I need those too. I might pitch that idea to CheekyBeast." He whips out his phone, muttering a note to himself to send to, I think, his underwear sponsor, before turning back to Tyler. "So yeah, man, socks with animals are definitely cool."

"You literally just bragged about your underwear, dude, not socks," Tyler shoots back, scratching his head.

"And you should wear fun underwear too, man. Tip of the day from yours truly," Asher says.

"I have black socks. And black briefs," Rowan contributes dryly.

"Black—like your soul," Asher says with an eye roll.

I plant myself in the center of the room, stick two fingers in my mouth and let out a sharp, piercing whistle that cuts through the chaos.

"Boys," I say firmly, drawing all eyes to me. "Let's settle this, yeah?"

Christian sheds his suit jacket in his stall near the back, raising a brow. But he stays quiet as the scene unfolds. It's subtle, but his presence is felt—the watchful eyes of the current solo captain. This is a test, I realize. He's waiting to see how I handle this circus—this show of leadership. Usually, he's the one rounding up the unruly children, but if I'm going to be co-captain, this is absolutely part of the job. And since our first game of the season is tonight, I want to set the tone.

I turn to Hugo first. "You're right—don't wear socks with sandals and a suit. That's just painful to my eyes and, frankly, all eyes."

Then to Tyler: "Socks are cool. Deal with it."

Tyler blanches, then swallows roughly, nodding. "Fine," he grumbles.

Wesley sits up straighter, grinning Tyler's way. "See? I told you, Little Falcon. And Big Falcon agrees. Socks are the G.O.A.T."

"And Asher," I add, pointing a finger. "Corgi butt idea? Golden. Get that happening ASAP."

Asher salutes me with his phone. "On it."

I turn to Rowan. "Your black soul is exactly what we need on the ice."

The defenseman gives a workman-like nod. "And it's what you'll get every single game."

Finally, I return my focus to my brother since it's time for some tough love. "Listen, man. The issue isn't your socks. It's your sandals," I say, gesturing to the offending footwear he kicked off that I kind of can't believe he wore with a suit on the first day. "They're giving major number-one dad vibes. And I think that's the real problem."

The room erupts in laughter as Wesley slides across the bench to sit next to Tyler. "He's right. Your sandals are the weak link, bro. Don't worry; I can help. I don't want you left behind in the sock-or-sandal revolution."

"But no socks with sandals and suits," Hugo cuts in. "Big Falcon said so." He points to the DickNose board, then turns to me, his eyes like a puppy dog's. "Can we make that a rule?"

Seizing the opportunity to wrap this debate up and move on, I grab the marker from the board. "Dress code rules. No socks with sandals while wearing a suit," I write at the top, underlining it. "And...dress like a cool dad."

"Ouch," Tyler groans, clutching his chest as if he's been stabbed. "Way to twist the knife."

"We're just looking out for you," Hugo says, smirking. "One dad to another. Also, for the record, my wife dresses me, and I'm not ashamed to admit it."

"Cookie Melissa?" Wesley asks, his curiosity piqued. Pretty sure he has developed a cookie addiction courtesy of Hugo's baker wife.

"Damn right. She's got great taste in cookies *and* clothes," Hugo replies, and an idea forms in my head.

I snap my fingers. "We should send Leighton over to shoot a video of that," I suggest. "Cookie Melissa picking out the defenseman's clothes. That's gold for social."

"Fashion tips from the players' wives," Wesley muses. "Hell yeah."

"Right. I'll pass it on to Everly first and see if she approves," I say, pointing my thumb toward the locker room exit, and moving on from this talk of Leighton, since I can't let on that I've thought about her nearly nonstop since the night at her place more than a week ago. "But right now, we need to get to the ice for a promo pic. Get your jerseys on and let's go."

They groan, but one by one, they pull on their jerseys and uniform shorts, lace up their skates and shuffle out of the room. I stay behind, making sure every last one of them gets their ass in gear, including Christian, who claps me on the shoulder as he passes.

"It's no joke being co-captain potentially, huh?" he says, his voice low enough for only me to hear. "I won't miss this stuff. I'll delegate rounding up the boys to you."

I glance at him, smirking. "So you're putting me in charge of the sheep herding if I get the gig, Winters?"

"Fuck yes, Falcon. I'm keeping the good stuff for myself," he says, then strides out, leaving me alone with the faint echoes of chaos still ringing in my ears.

I guess I'm the Border Collie. And...I don't really mind.

* * *

But honestly, the real Border Collie is Scuppers. He's the team's mascot—part Border Collie, part Husky, and all rescue. When I step onto the ice a minute later, the black-and-white dog is already rolling on his back, legs flailing, begging for belly rubs.

"Aww, Scups," Asher says, crouching to pat the four-legged critter. Scuppers paws at him, demanding more attention, while Leighton snaps picture after picture a few feet away. I keep my cool, careful not to look at her gorgeous face. We've been doing a solid job sticking to our friendship rules. Besides, a little dirty sexting doesn't count. It was only once, anyway.

Shame, that.

"Did you put dog food on your face?" Wesley asks Asher.

"Nope. I'm naturally dognip," Asher says, grinning as Scuppers flips over and pops up to lick his face.

"And I figured my natural animal magnetism would be enough," Rowan says, with a deep sigh.

I clap him on the back. "Tough break, Bishop. Stings not being the chosen one, huh? Maybe do some journaling later. Get to the bottom of it."

He scowls, then calls to get Scuppers's attention again. But the dog whips around, surveys the scene, and bounds over to me instead, skidding along the ice, all paws and excitement, then plopping into a perfect sit at my feet, tail wagging furiously even in the cold.

"See? He knows what side his bread's buttered on," I say, scratching under Scuppers's chin as Leighton's camera clicks away.

She's good at this—moving seamlessly among the guys, blending in to capture candid moments. Still, the closer she gets to me, the more my bones hum, the more my insides churn, the harder my pulse thuds. Her dad stands just a few feet away, arms crossed as he watches her work. It's a reminder to keep my cool.

Everly clears her throat from the players' bench, breaking the moment. "All right, guys, let's get some team pics before the first game of the new season!"

She outlines the poses, but half the guys are already

distracted. When she's done, I turn around, and face the clowns. "Listen up, boys. You do a good job and focus right now, and drinks are on me tonight when we win."

That gets their attention. Everyone snaps to, striking their best game faces for the team photo.

"Excellent," Leighton says, her voice calm and encouraging as she snaps away. "That's right. Just like that."

She lowers the camera, turning to the bench. "How about one with you, Coach McBride?"

The guys react instantly. Hugo snickers. Alexei cracks up. Rowan snorts.

I shoot them both a glare. "Focus, boys."

Coach gives a crisp nod, skates onto the ice, and lines up with us. Like magic, every single guy straightens up, standing at attention.

Leighton doesn't miss a beat, snapping a couple of quick shots. "Good job," she says, lowering the camera with a satisfied smile.

Because we all want to impress Coach. He's that kind of guy.

A few minutes later, as I'm leaving the ice, Coach catches up to me. He nods, his expression unreadable. "Good job rounding them up for the shot," he says. "That's what I wanted to see."

The subtext isn't exactly subtle. This is what he wants in a co-captain.

"Glad to hear that, sir," I say evenly.

"And remember, I'll need you to take point on the press too," he adds. "That's part of the responsibility— being willing to talk to the media, even when we lose. Even if you've had a bad game. It's about being the face of the team."

"Understood," I say, stoic and sturdy. Exactly what he needs me to be.

"And accessible as well," he says, his lips quirking in the faintest smile.

My gut twists. Would he still smile at me like that if he knew the things I've said to his daughter? The things I want when I look at her? The things I've done with... photos?

Hot shame slices through me, and I force all those traitorous thoughts aside.

* * *

When it's game time, Leighton's standing in the tunnel again, camera at the ready, snapping pics as we head to the ice, stopping at Scuppers along the way. The mascot hangs out at the end of the tunnel next to his handler, offering a paw for high-fives. Every player stops to high-five—high-paw—the dog for good luck. When I stop to offer a hand, I fight like hell not to turn my head back and look at Leighton one more time. I'm ready to high-five myself for my resistance when I reach the gate, but then something—a force more powerful than me—draws my attention back to the beautiful brunette with the Nikon around her neck.

Some days I wish I didn't want her so much.

But it's so much more than want—this feeling that won't go away. I linger on her for another second, then I hit the ice.

* * *

"C'mon, c'mon, c'mon," I urge as a Phoenix defender swarms Callahan before he can take a shot, but he flips the puck to Bryant, who ferries it around the back of the net, hunting for an opening.

Like, say, me.

I sneak past the defender chasing Callahan, getting open for Bryant. He flicks the puck my way, and I lunge for it, then line up my shot, but it bounces off the post.

"Fuck," I grumble as Phoenix recovers it and streaks down the ice. My skates dig hard into the surface as I race to cut off their momentum, the burn in my legs a distant hum beneath the adrenaline. The crowd roars, but I tune it out. There's no time to think about anything but this play.

Lambert looms in front of the net, his stick flashing out to bat the puck away before the Phoenix forward can even think about shooting. It rockets toward the boards, ricocheting off with a sharp crack that echoes through the arena.

Right to Tyler.

Sweet.

My brother's stick inhales the puck, and he's off like a shot, tearing down the ice with me flanking him. I'm open, so I call for it, a quick snap of my voice over the chaos. He doesn't hesitate. My stick catches it cleanly. My eyes snap to the goalie.

There. Right there.

The gap between one of the goalie's legs and the post is just wide enough.

I pull back and fire. The puck cuts through the air and slams into the net. The lamp lights, and the crowd cheers.

"Yes!" I shout, pumping a fist in the air. My pulse races

—not just from the play, but from the relief I feel every single time.

Ever since my injury, I play on a different level of awareness. I don't take my health for granted like I honestly did before the ACL tear. Now, there's a low-level buzz in my brain, a memory of what could go wrong. So when things go right, I want to kiss the sky.

Relief and gratitude flood me. This team took a chance on me, and I'm determined to prove they made the right call. I'm determined to prove it every season, every game, every play.

Bryant skates over, knocking fists with me, and Callahan follows. But it's Tyler's assist that steals the moment. I grab him, pulling my brother into a hug that turns into a group pile-on. When we break apart and skate to the boards, I knock fists with him again.

"Nice job. It's going to be a good season," I say.

"I hope so," he says as we hop over the boards.

The game isn't over yet—we've got a few minutes left to play—but he gives another nod, maybe believing it at last, possibly feeling like he's fitting in.

I tap my stick to the floor. "It's not easy joining a new team," I say, just for him.

"Especially when your brother plays on it," he says.

"But you're finding your way," I say.

"Thanks. I hope so. I really want this to stick," he says, genuine hope in his voice. Tyler had a good career in Los Angeles, but he carries a lot on his shoulders with two young kids. This career isn't just about him—it's about the life he's building for his family.

I glance toward the stands, following his gaze to where Mom and Harvey sit with Birdie and Charlie, and Tyler's kids, Luna and Parker. Tyler yanks off his gloves, waving to all of them, but his eyes linger on his son and daughter. He makes a heart gesture with his hands, and they wave frantically back at him, practically bouncing in their seats.

Somewhere in the arena, ovaries explode.

"Proud of you," I say, admiring how he balances all the things. "You're a good dad."

"They're good kids," he says, and that's just like him too. Deflecting.

I turn my focus back to the ice.

The game isn't over yet, but something in the way we're playing tonight tells me it's going to be a good season. I just have to keep showing that the ACL injury didn't break me. I feel that way every season here though. It hangs over me. A question the press might ask. A worry teammates might have. A concern for the coaching staff.

I don't want anyone to worry about me—ever. I want to leave that guy recuperating far in the rearview mirror.

As the next line gets ready for the faceoff, with Winters poised and ready, I glance at the stands and spot Leighton. Nikon in hand, she lowers the camera, and her gaze lands on mine. Excitement flashes in her eyes. Maybe pride too. But that smile...hell, it digs right into my soul. It's beautiful, and I wish I could flash her the public grin I want. Blow the kiss I want. Haul her in for a hug after the game, like I want.

This is getting ridiculous. I've had one date with the coach's daughter, and she's etched into my mind and heart.

It's hardly one date. You've been sneaking hits of her all along, hanging out with her, talking to her, getting to know her.

And now is not the time for voices in my head.

I've got to get over all these feelings for her.

I jerk my gaze back to the ice.

Focus.

The game's not done, and there's still more to prove.

I turn back around to watch our team destroy Phoenix until "Tick Tick Boom" plays, signaling our win.

We cheer and knock fists and smack gloves as all the guys look to me, including Winters.

"Drinks are on you," is the repeated refrain.

The captain grins, clearly amused as we head off the bench and into the tunnel. "You keep promising drinks, you're gonna have empty pockets by the end of the season."

"Sounds like a perfect tradeoff," I say, then head through the tunnel, where my heart hammers—and it's not from the win. It's from the photographer at the other end, taking pictures.

This is going to be a long season.

Torturous even being so close to her.

And the thing is—I am here for it.

26
___

THE ONLY ONE

Miles

Talking to the press is easy enough—I'm used to it by now. It's more fun when we win, though, and even better when I can credit an assist from my brother. After answering a round of questions from local reporters in the media room, I glance at Gus, one of the more seasoned guys on the beat.

"And I think our mom is here, so we should go say hi to her," I say, flashing him a grin.

That earns a rare smile from Gus, who's been covering the team since before I could skate.

"Can't leave Mom waiting," he mutters, pecking away at his ancient PC.

"You understand," I reply, then head out. On my way, I spot Everly down the hall, catching her just before she leaves.

"Hey, I had an idea for Hugo and his wife. At least we could start with them and see how it goes," I say, then tell her about the fashion concept that Leighton could shoot. "Might be something they'd enjoy."

Everly's eyes light up. "Oh, that's fun! Appreciate that. I'm sure Leighton will love it too."

Her smile broadens at the mention of Leighton's name, but then it fades quickly, like she's trying to reel it back in. It pricks at something in my brain. I frown slightly, filing the moment away, then continue into the hall, where my family waits.

Mom, Charlie, Harvey—and Birdie, of course—are all there. Birdie's decked out in a silver sequined Sea Dogs jacket. It's over the top in the best way and so very her.

"And to think, I always wondered who would buy the sequined jacket," I say, heading over to give her a hug.

"What a silly thing to wonder. It had my name written all over it," she replies, flicking the sequins for emphasis.

"It sure does," I say with a laugh, then turn to Mom. "How are the kids tonight? Did you get a dog-sitter?"

Charlie steps in before Mom can respond. "Sometimes she can leave them alone for a few hours, you know."

I blink, pretending to be shocked. "Our mom? Leaving her 'children' unattended?"

"Oh, hush," Mom says, waving me off. "It's been known to happen."

"You mean her favorite children," Charlie corrects pointedly before flicking her pink-tipped blonde streaks off her shoulder.

Glancing at the group, I switch gears, nodding in the general direction of my teammates. "I'm taking the clowns out for drinks. But if you all want to grab some food first, I can meet up with them later."

Charlie yawns. "I have to be up early. Expansion plans are calling my name."

"How's everything going with that? You're opening, what, twenty new locations?"

She rolls her eyes. "Two, but you know...it feels like twenty."

I turn to Mom, and she shoots me a no-go smile.

"And it's a miracle I'm even awake at ten," Mom adds, making a show of checking the time on her watch.

"I think what she's trying to say is that she misses the dogs," Harvey chimes in, cupping her shoulder affectionately.

I laugh but I'm a little serious as I ask, "How are you going to survive two weeks away from them?"

Mom frowns, then turns to Harvey. "Miles has a good point. Let's cancel the cruise and stay with the dogs. Or, better yet—can you book us a private yacht so we can take them?"

Harvey rolls his eyes with fond affection. "Of course, Lauren. No problem."

"Seriously, Mom. Does your dog-sitter know to send you photos every hour on the hour?"

"Dania has been well-trained in the care and feeding of a neurotic dog parent," Harvey says, answering for her, since, well, he's well-trained, too, in looking out for Mom.

"And we'll help out Dania when she needs to see her clients," Charlie puts in. Dania is a professional pet-sitter who specializes in cats, but Mom convinced her to take on four demanding small dogs and stay at their home when they travel. Charlie and I have always tried to pitch in and take the critters when Dania needs to make the rounds of the cats across the city.

"You two are the best," Mom says, then eyes the exit longingly. "Since my husband isn't getting me that private yacht, I should go spend as much time with the kids as I can."

"You really don't even pretend we're your favorites," I say.

Her expression goes surprisingly serious. "Why would I?" Then her lips curve into a grin as she steps closer. "You played great tonight. I'm proud of you for coming back. Sticking with this. You've always been so resilient. I never doubted you'd recover."

That's me. Take it on the chin and keep going. It's a good thing, I'm sure, my ability to just keep moving. That'll help me stop obsessing over Leighton. *Maybe.*

"Thanks, Mom," I say. "Appreciate your faith in me."

"You've always worked so hard. You've always been so focused on..." She stops, pauses, maybe collects her emotions. "Everyone else."

I swallow roughly, getting her meaning but not wanting to look like a martyr. "Good thing I like hockey though."

"You play like you love it," she says.

"I do love it. I'm glad I can play again, thanks to Coach," I say, since the reminder is good for me.

But I'm not the only one I care about. It's a good reminder because...how would Coach feel about his daughter if she were involved with a player? Would he be pissed at her? Would it put a strain on their relationship? Leighton adores him, rightly so. And I know he dotes on her. That's another reason I need to stay in this friend zone—I don't want to harm the relationship she cares most about.

Mom knits her brow. "It's all you, but I get what you're saying."

My mom, Charlie, and Harvey say goodbye, then take off, joining Tyler and his kids at the end of the hall.

Birdie clears her throat, stepping forward with her usual flair. "I'm a night owl. And I can drink any hockey player under the table."

"Truer words," I say, gesturing for her to lead the way. "Go on, Birdie. Set the pace."

Her serene smile turns mischievous as she declares, "Where is my favorite shutterbug? I should invite her and her friends. Yes, I think I'll do that."

"Birdie," I say, but she's already gone, her sequins shimmering as she marches off to hunt down Leighton.

I should stop her—but I don't.

A little later, most of the team has claimed the pool tables at Sticks and Stones, the local bar we all hit up after games. I've covered a round of drinks—and maybe a few more—and most of the guys are gathered around the tables with their wives, girlfriends, or partners, laughing and talking trash.

Asher's here with Maeve, and they're a fearsome duo, taking on team after team and wiping the floor with them at pool. They look like they're having the time of their lives.

As for me, Birdie's corralled me into a corner booth, and before I know it, she's calling over Leighton.

Birdie flashes a mischievous smile as Leighton slides into the booth across from me. "So," Birdie says, clasping her hands dramatically and turning to Leighton, "tell me everything. How's it going with the team? Do you love it as much as you'd expected?"

"I do," Leighton says, her voice warm. "The only thing that would make it better is if they served your green tea at the end of every shoot."

"Oh, you flatter me," Birdie says, waving a hand and glancing at her phone. "Would you look at the time? I need my beauty sleep. Coffee shops wait for no one."

Before either of us can respond, she's already scooting out of the booth, her sequins catching the light as she goes. She disappears in the blink of an eye, leaving a trail of meddling-grandma energy behind her.

I turn to Leighton, raising a brow. "She's so subtle."

"The subtlest," she deadpans, her lips curving into a smile.

Now it's just the two of us, tucked away in this booth a little removed from everyone else. Like Birdie planned the whole thing.

"So," I say, leaning back against the seat, "it's going well?"

"It is." Leighton nods. "The GM has told me a few times how much she likes the pictures. So has Chanda. It's all good." She pauses, tilting her head. "You did well tonight. How was it playing with Tyler?"

"Honestly?" I let out a breath, feeling it hit me all over again, fresh and sharp. "It was kind of a dream come true. I don't think I realized how much I wanted it until it happened. But it was great—to play together in a regular season game. We did so much as kids, and then we went our separate ways in college, and of course the pros. And really, there aren't that many brother combos playing at the same time."

"It's rare," she agrees softly. "That's why I wanted that picture with you two high-fiving at the bench. Did you see it?"

"It's on socials?"

"Chanda and Everly posted it right away. Let me show you," she says, grabbing her phone.

Her polished silver nails fly across the screen, catching my attention as I linger on her hands and murmur softly, "Silver."

She stops, her face tilting toward me. "What did you say?"

I do better at meeting her gaze. "Your nails are silver. They're usually black."

"They are. You noticed."

I can barely think about the reasons this is a bad idea. "I notice everything." I tip my forehead toward her earrings. "Your earrings." My gaze drifts to her ink. "The flowers on your arms."

She rubs her right hand along her left forearm, licking her lips as though waiting for me to say more.

"The way your hair falls," I continue, the words spilling out before I can stop them.

And I can't stop. "The way you smile. Your different smiles. You have so many."

"And what are they?"

Images snap before my eyes. "There was one earlier tonight. When I scored—I think it was pride."

She rolls her eyes, but she's smiling again. "So cocky," she whispers.

I tip my chin toward her. "There's that one. The smile you give me when you say I'm cocky."

"I do have a smile like that," she says.

I cycle through her smiles in my head, then let out a satisfied sigh. "The one you have when you flirt."

She gasps dramatically. "I flirt?"

I slide maybe an inch closer. There are teammates

here, co-workers. But the pull toward her is magnetic, and my resistance is tenuous at best. "You know you do, Shutterbug."

"So do you," she counters.

"I am guilty as charged," I admit. But the words hit differently as I say them, guilt cutting into me. Not just guilt for wanting her—for being drawn to her—but for the fear that I couldn't stop even if I tried. And what that might mean—for us, for the team, for everything I've worked for my whole life. I take a steadying breath, square my shoulders, and pivot the conversation. "Everly kind of gave me this look earlier when your name came up."

Leighton startles, but she goes with it. "And?"

And I'm not sure what I'm looking for. But now that I've said it, I know I'm searching for breadcrumbs. "Fuck it," I mutter, since there's no point pretending with Leighton. "It made me wonder if she knows..." I trail off, hoping she'll pick up the thread.

"She does. I told her," Leighton admits softly. "A while ago."

"What did you tell her?"

"That...I'd have seen you again. If I could."

"Every fucking day," I say, shaking my head and scrubbing a hand over the back of my neck. Then I look at her again, laying all my vulnerability on the table. "I should stop thinking about what that'd be like. Really stop. But it's hard. I want to know I'm not the only one who feels this way. That I'm not the only one who hasn't gone on another date. There was the auction date, but it was platonic. It was a PR charity thing. I want to know I'm not the only one who feels like nothing else could compare..."

She runs her hand along her arm, her fingers tracing

the flowers as if she's grounding herself. Then her eyes meet mine. "Do you know why I have these?"

I'm dying to know every detail about her, especially with how deliberately she shifted gears. "I don't."

"One day, my sister and I went to a flower farm. We had the best time, checking out all the flowers. I took pictures of us. It made me so happy. But it also stayed with me because I understood then why I love flowers so much."

"Why do you love them so much?"

"Because I can smell them—all of them. I can tell the difference between each one. The delicate scent of jasmine. The peppery scent of calendulas. The creamy, crisp scent of lilacs. I could tell them all apart. I could smell everything."

Her voice carries a longing. But there's gratitude too, for the way she can detect every scent.

"That's why you have flowers on you," I say softly.

"Yes. Because...I can enjoy them completely. Experience them completely," she says, closing her eyes. When she opens them, they're full of emotion. "I haven't seen anyone either...since you."

"Leighton, let me drive you home." I sound like I'm begging and I don't even care.

She shakes her head, a small, bittersweet smile on her lips. "I don't think that's a good idea." She takes a beat. "And you don't either."

I drop my head, knowing she's right. Appreciating she's looking out for both of us.

But I walk her to the curb anyway and wait until her Lyft arrives. I hold the door open, watching her climb inside, the ache settling deeper in my chest. Letting her go is the right thing. It's what we both need.

When I go back inside to join the guys, Asher pulls me aside to a corner of the bar. "Be careful."

I arch a brow, feigning confusion. "What do you mean?"

"You know what I mean," he says, his tone low but firm. "You're not exactly subtle, Miles. The way you look at her—it's only a matter of time before someone says something."

I sigh, dropping the facade. "Thanks, man."

He's right. That's something I'll have to work on this season, even if it feels impossible right now. Especially when an image lands on my phone a little later—the shot of my brother and me. I like the pic, but I love that she sent it.

27

THE FUCK IT STAGE

Leighton

Two weeks, four wins, two losses, and thousands of photographs of hockey players later, my savings account is finally growing.

It's working, this plan to squirrel away money.

It's working because *I'm* working nonstop most days—bouncing from photo shoots with the Sea Dogs, to freelance shoots for The Sports Network covering the Renegades, to Birdie's shop for coffee art, to boudoir shoots at Hush Hush. Word of mouth is my favorite thing, and since Cora and Aliza passed my name along, along with Katrina, who told her single mom support group, I'm booking boudoir sessions into December.

On Wednesday afternoon, I'm at Melissa Bergstrand's house, AKA Cookie Melissa. Since video is nearly as easy to shoot on my phone as photos, I'm recording her as she takes me through her husband's walk-in closet. Her nail art is pink and mint, inspired by unicorn cookies she made earlier today—she told me she always matches her nails to her cookies.

"Ooh, this will be perfect for the next home game," she says, plucking the shirt from its hanger. "It's a little team spirit without screaming, *'Put me on the Jumbotron.'*"

I nod, smiling, and ask—off-camera, of course—"And what will you pair it with? Inquiring fans want to know."

She taps a nail against her lower lip thoughtfully. "We can't go too literal—team colors can't carry the whole look," she says, pivoting to a rack of suit jackets. "This charcoal gray suit is the perfect finishing touch. It's dark, so we can lean into his defender role on the ice."

"And now the big question. Tie or no tie?"

"I'm a no-tie woman personally. He's playing hockey, not presenting a PowerPoint."

I stifle a laugh, and since she's such a good sport, I toss out one more question. "And what about when he's not playing hockey? Do you pick his clothes then too?"

With a confident smile, she says, "Of course. For the weekend when we take the kids to the farmers market for face painting, I'll put him in a peach polo. It's my favorite color, and he likes wearing my favorite colors. There you go."

I stop shooting and meet her gaze. Her face is freckled and heart-shaped, a perfect match for her warm, open nature. "That's so sweet that he likes wearing your favorites."

"He's such a great dad and husband," she says, and these two are seriously couple goals with their affection for each other and their support. "I love to be able to help him shine since that's what he does for me." She pauses, her brow furrowing, and for a second, it looks like she's about to ask me something. But instead, she smiles brightly. "This is so much fun. What a great idea."

"It was Miles's idea," I say, giving credit where credit's due.

"But you're the one who's putting it together. Never underestimate that what goes into the cookie is just as important for its success as the idea for the cookie."

That's good advice there. "Thanks, I appreciate that."

I shoot some B-roll of her in the closet, selecting clothes for the upcoming road trip, and on the way out, she stops me at the door, a curious glint in her warm brown eyes. "I've seen your photos..." she begins, her tone unusually tentative.

I wait for her to say more. I figure she means the pics on the team feed.

"And they're so gorgeous. The lighting, and the sensuality, and the poses," she blurts out, like it's a relief to have said it.

"I'm so glad you like them," I say, pleased she means the boudoir work.

Melissa exhales a little laugh, glancing at her nails. "I've thought about doing one of those shoots. You know, for him. But I don't think I'd have the guts."

That surprises me. She's always so poised and self-assured. "You'd be amazing at it," I say sincerely. "And if you ever decide to try, I'd make sure you feel completely comfortable."

She brightens slightly, though there's still a flicker of uncertainty in her eyes. "Maybe someday. For now, it's probably more my speed to offer cookies in the shape of bras or panties."

"Sexy and sweet," I say with a smile.

"Yes!" Then she gives me a goodbye hug since she's a hugger, and I head on my way.

I edit the video that afternoon, tweaking every detail until it's just right. Chanda posts it that night, and within hours, it's racking up views.

My phone blows up with messages from Chanda, Everly, and even Zaire, all gushing about how great the video turned out. It hardly feels like my doing. Melissa is just...likable. Still, I reply with thanks and exclamation points to everyone.

The next evening as the team flies back from a quick trip to Chicago, I head to pole class with my friends. Along the way, a text from Miles lands.

> Miles: Nice job, Shutterbug. We just boarded the flight, and Hugo is losing his mind over the video. He's sent it to his family, his neighbors, his elementary school teachers—basically anyone he's ever met. Also, Cookie Melissa is thrilled.

> Leighton: I'm glad he loves it! She was easy to shoot, and you had a good idea.

> Miles: You're the one who made it happen.

That's similar to what Melissa said, so I accept the compliment for what it is.

> Leighton: Thank you. It felt good to contribute.

. . .

And truly, it did. I like being useful. I love being good at my job. And I absolutely adore having happy clients.

I turn off the phone when I arrive at Upside Down, grateful for the chance to spend time with my girl gang, working on new pole tricks at the studio Everly owns and dances at. I haven't seen much of them since I've been working so hard, and I need the girl time.

I'm not a regular at pole like Everly or even Josie, but I like to go once a week. I'm not wild about the floor work—choreography isn't my thing—but I love doing the tricks on the pole. They take strength, and that's my jam.

As a new instructor named Jewel demonstrates a spin while blasting a sultry tune, I have to watch her moves more closely than usual. It's hard to hear her instructions over the music. No, make that impossible.

I could ask her to turn it down, but this is a me problem. I don't want to draw attention to it. Besides, this is an opportunity to figure it out using my other senses.

My eyes.

I study her every move carefully and then imitate her. On the first try, I nail the move. Yes! It feels incredible to be strong enough to pull this off, to hang upside down with my hair spilling toward the floor.

Briefly, I wonder what Miles would think if he could see me like this. A sly smile creeps across my lips, knowing he'd probably lose his mind.

He'd stare hotly, like he did at our boudoir session, his eyes locked on me, waiting patiently for the moment I'd finish—just so he could close the distance between us, claim my lips, and murmur that I'm incredible.

I feel kind of incredible—both from the thrill of this fantasy and the satisfaction of nailing this move.

Maybe it doesn't matter that I can't always make out the instructor's words. I have a rich interior life, and really, that has to be enough.

When class ends, I leave with my friends, Everly praising us for the progress we've all made over the past year.

"Are you all still enjoying class?" she asks, clearly hoping we'll say yes.

Nerves race through me. I could mention the music volume to her. This is my chance, but something stops me. I don't want to make my issue someone else's issue. I have a workaround, and that's good enough.

"I'm loving the tricks," I say.

"You're so good at them. The dance stuff not so much?"

"Not really, but I do understand it's the foundation."

"I like the floor stuff since I'm least likely to break all my bones on the floor," Josie chimes in brightly.

Everly laughs, and Fable nods toward our favorite diner at the end of the block. "Does anyone want to take this into Moon Over Milkshakes?"

"Anything to keep me out of my own apartment," I say, jumping at the chance—even if the music is blasting there too.

Josie pats me on the back as we walk. "We love being your escape pod from your roomies."

"What's the latest with them?" Everly asks with some concern.

I sigh. "They either fuck or fight. The other night, I came home to Indigo giving a detailed, painful monologue about how running out of mustard reminds her of childhood loss."

Maeve rolls her eyes. "I get that we all have emotional wounds, but you can't use them as crutches for everything in your life. Sometimes you just have to deal when there's no fucking mustard," she says, yanking open the door to the retro-themed diner.

Exactly.

Which is why I don't ask the pole instructor—or the diner—to lower the music. Sometimes you just have to deal.

After we slide into a booth, a server pops over.

"I'll take a chocolate milkshake as big as my head and the large fries," I say.

When everyone else orders, Josie shoots me a sympathetic look. "As big as your head? You really need to numb the pain of your roomies, don't you, friend?"

"I do," I say, but the time with them does the trick— eating, gabbing, playing with Maeve's tarot cards, and catching up. When it's my turn to share, I tell them about my growing business.

"Get it, girl," Everly says with a shimmy.

"So proud of you," Fable adds as I spoon the last dregs of my milkshake.

But Maeve holds my gaze. "And how's it working with the Fucking Falcon?"

I nearly spit out my drink. She's called him that before —after learning about our day together. But it's been a while.

"Yes," Josie says, her eyes gleaming with curiosity. "Are you stealing moments in the stairwell? Nipping off to the equipment room? Making doe eyes across the ice?"

"No," I say pointedly. But there have been close calls.

Maeve snaps her fingers. "Dammit. I wanted some good tea."

"I wanted tea and solidarity," Everly adds with a pout. "Max and I did all those things before we were officially together."

"We know," Fable teases her, then turns to me. "I'm impressed with your restraint."

I wish restraint wasn't my strong suit. Sometimes, I wish it were easier to throw caution to the wind. But Miles has worked too hard to take this kind of chance. I've worked too hard as well. My dad's not an unreasonable man, but at the same time, this *thing* with Miles is too uncertain. It's not something I want to bring up to my father, so really, this *thing* is best left in the friend zone. "We've mostly behaved. Though, not to sound full of myself, I think if it were up to him, we'd have broken all the rules."

Maeve's eyes widen. "So he has it bad for you?"

I shrug. "I think so. He's pretty upfront about it." My chest flutters from memories of his intensity—saying he can't stop thinking about me, that I'm the only one. It's heady to be the object of his longing, but risky too.

"Sometimes, I feel like I have to be the one who remembers what's at stake. Like he'd be willing to throw caution to the wind, even though he has a lot on the line too."

Everly sighs knowingly. "He's in the fuck-it stage, isn't he? I've seen how he looks at you during photo shoots."

I can't resist asking, "How does he look at me?"

"Like he can't help himself," she says, smiling.

I fight a grin, fizzy inside. I like that his feelings are obvious to her, even if they can't go anywhere. "Nothing can happen, though," I say heavily. A wicked smile creeps in. "But is it terrible that I love that it's obvious?"

They laugh, shaking their heads.

"I just hope it's not obvious to my father," I say, wincing.

Everly shakes her head. "Men don't usually pick up on that stuff."

We lift our glasses in a toast to that truth.

As the clock ticks to ten, I wish I could slow time. I don't want to go home to my roomies, especially since this night has been exactly what I needed.

All good things must end though.

After we say goodnight, I head home, terribly hopeful that my roomies will be asleep when I crack open the door.

A girl can dream after all.

But the universe gives, and the universe taketh away. When I unlock the apartment with a quiet snick, I step right into the alligator pit. The two of them are perched on the living room couch, facing each other, with Indigo's hands folded into a prayer.

"I do understand that because you have a penis, you pee standing up and you lift the lid. But when you don't put the lid down, I inherently feel like I'm being punished for having a vagina."

I would like her to be punished for having vocal cords.

Keeping my head down, I smile blandly, and point to my ears, signaling that I'm listening to something. But Indigo pops up, grabbing my arm before I can reach my room.

"What's going on?" I ask innocently.

Indigo turns to her guy. "Please ask Leighton if your behavior is okay."

Kill me now.

Ezra shoots me a helpless look as he mumbles, "If you walked into the bathroom and you saw that the toilet seat was up, what would you do?"

I'm so annoyed that they're actually asking me to intervene that words fly out of my irritated mouth before I can hold back. "I'd kick it down."

But that's the exact wrong answer because Indigo gasps. "Where is the female solidarity?"

Not the point, but for the sake of keeping the peace, I backpedal. "What I meant is I would solve the immediate problem and then I would ask the offender to please put it down next time."

Indigo frowns, her expression saying I've failed the test. "And you don't think him leaving it up is a sign of the patriarchy?"

For fuck's sake there are bigger battles to fight than toilet lids. "It isn't my place to intervene," I say, trying once more to head straight for my room and learn to love rock music to drown out the sounds of them for all eternity.

"Please, Leighton. Please help us," she says, her lower lip quivering.

I groan privately, then give in since it'll just be easier. "Maybe give him a consequence if he leaves it up and a reward if he puts it down. K, thanks, bye."

I hustle into my bedroom and slam the door, breathing a huge sigh of relief.

But five minutes later, the sound of the flushing toilet, a theatrically loud snap of the closed lid, and a squeal from Indigo filters under my door.

Seconds later, she's saying—no, shouting, "That makes me so hot."

He brays right back. "I knew it would, babe. Let's both enjoy the reward...of passionate sexual intercourse."

That's it.

I groan, exasperated, but as I slip into bed and tuck my hearing aids into their charger, I revel in the blissful quiet.

Sometimes, it's a blessing to have this kind of control over the noise. The hum of the refrigerator dims, the noise of the street fades, and the distant sound of voices drifts away.

Except...

"Oh god, yes! Play with my balls, baby."

I wither inside. They must be having a really good time if he's not saying "touch my testicles."

"Fuck me harder, honey," she shouts.

Somehow, some way, they're louder than my loss.

* * *

In the morning, when I trudge, bleary-eyed and yawning, toward the shower, they're already in the kitchen, arms crossed, arguing by the coffee maker.

"I feel that when you make coffee, you should make enough for me." Ezra adjusts his man bun like it's a crown before crossing his arms.

Indigo flicks her sleep-mussed braid off her shoulder. "I feel you should ask me to."

"I feel you should know."

"I feel we should ask Leighton," she says.

They both brighten, snapping attention to me like I'm the solution to all their woes.

I hold up my hands, and shake my head as I sidestep them on my way into the bathroom since I feel I should get new roommates.

* * *

I slump down on the players' bench at the Sea Dogs arena as my father flops down next to me, skates still on. He reaches for the coffee I brought him.

He works out there in the mornings, still snagging ice time for himself.

Perks of being a pro coach, I suppose.

I down another thirsty gulp of my tea, then sigh. "I think the tea is working—finally," I say, but my voice sounds dead tired to me.

That's no good.

"Rough night?" Dad asks.

"I barely slept, but the guys and I have a shoot today with senior dogs from Little Friends. It's for the rescue's campaign to highlight overlooked older pups. Worth it, but whew, I need more caffeine."

"Is it the futon? Those things are the devil's work," he says.

I crack my neck, shifting it side to side. "I wish it were the futon."

He shoots me a sympathetic look. "What is it then?"

After a semi-truck-size yawn seizes me, I blurt out all my frustration. "I've become their mediator," I say, then tell him all about my roommates' constant bickering.

I leave out the dirty details.

When I'm done, there's a serious look in his dark blue eyes. He's quiet for a beat, and I can tell he's devising a plan. His coach mindset runs deep in him. His strategic mind never rests. He takes a fortifying drink of the coffee, then sets it down on the bench. "I know you want to make it on your own, and I respect that, but this situation sounds miserable. What if I helped with rent? You could find a place you actually like."

My heart tugs. His offer is so ridiculously tempting. "Thanks, Dad. Let me think about it, but at first blush, I still think I need to do this whole life thing on my own."

I switch to sign language because this feels intensely personal. *Know what I mean?*

His smile is kind, a touch sad. *I do know.*

He taught me how to navigate the world. He gave me the skills and the faith. Now it's up to me to show that I can do that—carve out a life for myself. I don't know what the future holds; no one does of course. But I know I need to be independent. And I know, too, that he respects that.

He wraps an arm around my shoulders and squeezes. I set my head on his shoulder, feeling safe for the moment, like I did growing up.

But even though I know deeply that I can always count on him, I need to be certain, too, that I can always count on myself.

28

HE'S GOT THIS

Miles

As I pop in my contact lens in the morning, I'm mentally running through my schedule for the next couple weeks. Mom's dog-sitter, Dania, sprained her ankle freeing a stuck cat from a curtain, so Charlie and I offered to handle the dogs during the cruise. We'll trade off taking the hellions based on my travel schedule—the dogs arrive this afternoon, I take off in two days for a road trip, then I'll have them again for a few more days when I return. It's a lot but it's doable with the two of us.

There's just that day after I return from the road trip when I'll need to hustle up to Charlie's home, which is an hour away. I'll have to get the critters so she can deal with her stuff, but I'll be cutting it close since I have a luncheon with a sponsor. Tyler offered to help out if I need it. But I can probably get on one of those dog-sitter apps and find someone to transport them.

Yep. That's what I'll do. I'll download an app when my

eyes are in. I uncap the left lens as my phone trills. It's Charlie. She never calls—always texts. This can't be good. I swipe to answer, blinking away the sting that comes with the first lens of the day.

"What jail are you in, and how quickly do you need me to find a lawyer?" I ask, half joking, but already on edge.

"I'm in expansion jail. And if you can find my business lawyer, that'd be great."

There's definitely something wrong. I straighten, turning away from the contact lens case. I'll put the other one in after this call. "What's going on?"

"So, you know how we were going to share dog-sitting duties for the four horsemen of the apocalypse?"

"Yes," I reply, already wary. I know where this is headed.

"I have to go to Los Angeles to oversee the expansion there. Some issues with permits and stuff. I'm so sorry."

I drag a hand down my face. "Shit."

"I know. I feel terrible. But I'll help you find a dog-sitter. I promise. I know we can't board them."

"Understatement of the century," I mutter, since the pack can't handle boarding. Boo was banned from the dog hotel because he tried to hump all the other guests. He's neutered, of course, but no dog likes a rando canine's come-ons. Add Boppity's anxiety and Bippity's sneaky Houdini ways and the pack spells trouble at the dog inn.

"Maybe Birdie can help out?" Charlie suggests.

"That's an option." Birdie's pretty busy with High Kick, but she could help me out a night here and there. I'll keep that in my back pocket.

"Let me make some calls. But if you know anyone, let me know."

"I can ask around," I say before hanging up.

I wash my hands, clean the lens, and pop it in.

Time to solve this problem. Just like I taught myself to cook when Dad left—I get things done. And now it's on me to make this happen.

* * *

First stop, my brother's place. I swing by, pick him up, and the second he slides into the car, he harrumphs.

"What's going on?" I ask. I want to ask him to help out more with the four tiny terrors, but he's got his hands full with his own kids, as well as making his mark with a new team.

"You have no idea how hard it was to get the kids to school this morning. They heard we were visiting dogs, and now Luna's begging me to bring one home."

"Well, maybe you'll find one for her."

He shoots me a withering look. "I'm barely keeping it together. I can't add another mammal."

And clearly, I can't ask him to help chauffeur them. "You're doing a good job managing," I say, since he needs the encouragement, and really, it's not fair to ask him to help with the dogs after we return with everything he has on his plate. I've got to handle this for Mom, like I promised I would. She deserves to go on that cruise. And she's leaving in two days so I need to solve it fast. I can't drop the ball. Not when it matters to her, and not when Charlie's in a real bind. It's a lot, but I've done it before. And I'll do it again.

When we arrive at Little Friends, I shove that worry aside for the moment. Time to focus on the team and the work we're trying to do in the community. But once we're inside the shelter, my focus snaps instantly and irrevo-cably to the brunette with the camera waiting in the dog playroom. One glance at Leighton, playing with a frosty-faced old dog who happily seems to melt into her affec-tion, and my heart does funny things.

An insistent longing tugs at my chest, but I do my best to push it down, dismissing all these feelings as she shoots pics. I keep it together as Tyler, Asher, Max, Wesley, and Rowan pose for pictures—with a Frenchie with its tongue hanging out, an Aussie Shepherd who has arthritis, and, as the shelter manager tells us, a Lab-Border Collie mix recovering from an ACL tear.

That comment catches my attention just as I lock eyes with Leighton. Recognition, sympathy, understanding—they all pass between us in that fleeting moment. "He'll find a good home," Leighton says softly, just for me.

And that doesn't help my efforts to keep it together.

I scratch the dog's soft chin. "I hope he finds a second chance," I say.

Just like I did. And since I can't take them all home, or any dog for that matter, I write a big check before we leave.

* * *

Later, after practice, I'm still making calls, trying to find a reliable dog-sitter in the area at the last minute. Surely my mom's mutts aren't the only ones who need specialized care.

But I'm not making much progress. The call I'm on with a dog hotel asking for recommendations seems to be going nowhere as I pace down the corridor outside the weight room. "Thanks anyway for checking. I'll look at the pet-sitting apps," I say, even though I've been on them all morning to no avail. I hang up, frustrated and annoyingly helpless.

I heave a sigh as Coach turns around the corner, then stops when he sees me. "How's it going? Everything okay?" he asks with real concern.

So it's that obvious? I'd better get it together since I don't need him to see me struggling. But then again, he can already see that I'm frustrated. Maybe part of being a leader is admitting when you need help. It's not easy, but here goes.

I scratch my jaw. "I'm in a bind with my mom's feisty little dogs. I need a dog-sitter I trust who can stay at my place when I'm on the road during their cruise," I say, then add the dates.

I don't usually share stuff like this with him. Is he going to brush it off with a half-hearted "good luck," or is he actually going to give me some solid advice?

Because I could seriously use it right now.

Coach's lips twitch. A glint flickers in his eyes. "I've got someone for you."

29

A THANK YOU GIFT

Leighton

I should turn down this opportunity to stay at Miles's house when he's on the road, but I can't find a single compelling reason to. Especially since we won't be there at the same time—no temptations, no complications. We'll be ships passing in the night. Exactly what I need and what he needs too.

"You get a break from your roommates and make some extra money watching the dogs," my father says, resting a hand on my shoulder here in the corridor by the locker room. "And Miles gets the help he needs, plus someone to take excellent pictures for his mom. In fact, he's willing to pay a bonus for photos."

Funny thing—the bonus happens to cover exactly half the rent my dad's been trying to get me to agree to if we split a place for a month. He's too clever for his own good.

I can't poke holes in his logic, no matter how hard I try. But does Miles really want this? I'm weighing how to pull him aside and ask if he's truly okay with me staying there when Dad cuts through my overthinking with a simple, "You'd be helping so much."

It's said earnestly, with a hint of pleading in his voice I've never heard before. So I say yes.

* * *

Two days later, I'm bouncing in my seat as the bus trundles along Marina Green, the bay sparkling under the bright October sun. My pink duffel bag rests beside me along with my trusty camera bag. A buzz zips through me. The idea of wrangling four small, wild dogs has me grinning—far more fun than managing the relationship antics of Indigo and Ezra.

When the bus groans to a stop three blocks from Miles's place in the Marina, I leap up, grabbing my bags like I'm stepping off a bus in some old Hollywood movie, ready to take on the world. I hit the sidewalk and collide —literally—with a wall of man.

A familiar wall of man.

Broad chest, unruly dark hair, and a tattooed forearm topped off with that vegan leather bracelet I didn't let him trade in more than a year ago at the lockbox. The best part, though? Miles is standing in front of me wearing a black T-shirt and jeans. Not only do I get to stare at his ropey arms, but I also get to admire the denim. No one in the world looks as good in jeans as Miles Falcon. They hug his thighs, snuggle against his firm ass, and love his legs like they were tailor-made for him. Which, knowing how hockey does unholy things to men's asses, they probably were.

Before I can say anything, he grabs my bags. "Let me

get those," he says, already slinging the duffel over his shoulder.

I don't even bother protesting. "I told you I'd be here at eleven," I say, tilting my head at him. "How'd you know exactly when the bus would arrive?"

He shoots me a crooked grin. "I checked the schedule and waited. I wanted to carry your things for you."

My chest flutters. It's such a small gesture, but it feels so...him. Thoughtful. Quietly intentional. Like showing up when I needed to move a few weeks ago, or finding me after work to offer a ride home.

I try not to overthink it, but there's a dangerous warmth spreading through me. "Well, I get it. As a dog-sitter for four wild Chihuahuas, I'm a rare breed."

"You must be protected at all costs," he says, flashing me a playful smile as we start walking toward his house.

The warm fall air carries the faint scent of saltwater as I glance toward the sparkling bay, glimmering by the Golden Gate Bridge. "God, I'm not going to mind this view for the next week or so," I say, taking in the shimmering water.

"The balcony on the second floor is perfect for a cup of tea in the morning," he says. "You'll love it."

"Oh! Great idea. I need to pick up some green tea—I didn't bring any."

"You don't need to," he says, his grin widening. "I already stocked up on your favorite."

I blink at him, caught off guard. "How did you know my favorite tea?"

"I asked Birdie what you always get."

The pride in his voice is obvious, and honestly, he deserves it. My heart does a little flip as I look at him. "That's...really thoughtful. Thank you."

"Of course," he says, like it's no big deal. But it feels like a big deal. A small part of me wonders if this is just a *thank you* for taking care of his mom's dogs. Another part knows better when he says, "I want you to have everything you want."

My heart stutters. It feels like this isn't just for me as the dog-sitter. It feels like it's for me as *me*. I clear my throat. "Thank you, Miles."

His eyes swing toward me as we walk, a spark flickering in them. "And since you're such a rare breed...there's pasta in the fridge—sun-dried tomatoes, artichokes, all the good stuff. I made it for you this morning. So it should be pretty fresh. Just heat it up when you're hungry."

"You made pasta?" I stop in my tracks, turning to face him, because it's more than just pasta—it's the meal that never happened.

"You never got to try it over a year ago," he says, holding my gaze for a long beat. Heat thrums through me. "Trust me, I'm a phenomenal chef."

The warmth in my chest turns into a full-on blaze. "I can't wait."

A minute later, we're walking through his front door, and my mind is spinning. The tea, the pasta, the way he showed up at the bus stop—it's like he's orchestrated this little world where everything is easy for me while I stay at his home to help him.

As much as I want to say I can do it all myself—I can buy my own tea, make my own dinner, carry my own bags —I don't. Because for once, I don't feel the intense, driving need to prove my independence. Before he opens the door, I impulsively reach for his forearm.

His jaw tightens when I touch him, like he's at war inside.

"Miles," I say, and his name comes out warm, breathy even.

"Yes?" His voice is strung tight with desire, but I don't let go of his arm.

"Thank you. For everything."

"No, thank you. You're helping me."

I curl my hand tighter, my thumb sliding softly across the hair on his forearm, tracing the arrow tattoo on his fair skin. "We both know you're the one helping me."

He dips his head, swallows roughly, then raises his face, blowing out a soldiering breath. "Come inside."

When he opens the door, it feels like I'm stepping into something entirely new between us. But the moment evaporates as four small, barking hurricanes barrel toward us, and they have a lot of opinions.

* * *

An hour later, Miles is upstairs changing into his travel suit, getting ready to head to the team jet. He's already given me the lay of the land and a litany of instructions for my charges—all of which I plan to follow religiously. He showed me their heated dog beds—he calls them their hot tubs—then sent me all the details on their food, on Boppity's meds, and the code for the front door, as well as the location of the security camera. It's in the living room, and he turns it on when he leaves in case he ever needs to check the interior of the home while he's away. "I'll make sure I don't walk naked past it," I said when he showed it to me.

"Or make sure you do," he replied.

But that'd be trouble, so I won't. Besides, I don't generally parade around anywhere naked, so it'll be easy to keep my clothes on.

He showed me his scotch collection, telling me to feel free to have some. I stared at him like he'd lost his mind. "Things that will never happen," I said. "I'm convinced scotch is espresso's cousin. Meaning it is *also* vile."

He rolled his eyes. "I'm going to pretend you never said that."

"It won't work. The truth of scotch and espresso will forever haunt you."

"You might try to ruin my two favorite drinks, but I'm made of tougher stuff than that."

"Is that a challenge?"

He laughed. "No, because you'd smile at me and win."

"Good. Because I have excellent taste in beverages. I'm a white wine girlie till the day I die."

"I'll remember that."

No doubt he will. He remembers everything.

He even installed the app on my phone for the dogs' GPS trackers, assuring me they'd never escaped but his mom likes to have them wear them just in case. Makes sense—it's always good to be cautious. My sister has an AirTag on her water bottle, so I sure as hell understand putting a GPS tracker on a precious pet.

With all this intel filed away in my brain and my phone, I focus on making Miles's mom happy. I snap pics of the pack as they burrow into the blanket forts I built for them on the couch. I'm going to be the best dog-sitter ever. I'm going to take the best pictures ever. I'm going to ace this job.

"Smile for the camera," I say to the dogs, making a clicking sound to get their attention.

Four little heads tilt toward me in perfect unison.

Yes! The money shot.

I snap the picture with my phone, already imagining how much Miles's mom is going to love this one.

"Oh, I can see you're already settling in." Miles's voice drifts behind me as he enters the room.

I lower my phone and turn around...

And my jaw falls open.

It's not the first time I've seen Miles in a suit—I've photographed him and the other guys on game days enough to know he cleans up well. Those shots always blow up online, and for good reason.

But this is different.

He's standing in front of me in a tan suit that looks like it was made to worship his body. The crisp fabric stretches just right over his broad shoulders, and his tie hangs undone at the collar, leaving him looking effortlessly sexy. His travel bag is slung over one shoulder, and the jacket rests casually on his elbow.

My throat goes dry, and my skin hums, every nerve ending sparking like a live wire.

"Hi," I manage to say, though it comes out soft and breathy—so not me.

His lips quirk, and he gives me a look that's warm and just a little too knowing. "Hey." His tone is lower than usual, like he's reading the shift in the air between us and leaning into it. Or maybe causing it. Intentionally. The man does everything with so much intention.

I stand, brushing invisible wrinkles from my jeans, as if that'll make me less underdressed next to him. My black zip-up hoodie is covered in dog hair, and he looks like he's arrived for a photo shoot for a luxury watch ad. As I tuck my phone into my back pocket, my gaze sails to the gold watch on his wrist. I don't even know why wristwatches are so sexy, but there's something about them. So strong and masculine. But it's also...personal. I haven't seen him wear it yet this season.

"You have on your watch," I say, pointing to it, like it holds the key to this charge between us.

"You noticed," he says, amused, maybe touched, definitely calling back my comment from the night at Sticks and Stones.

The tip of my tongue darts out, wetting my lips as I weigh my response. "It's a nice watch. Once upon a time you left it behind at the studio," I say softly.

A faint noise seems to rumble from his chest. "You remember."

"I do," I say, a smile teasing at my lips as we dance around our memories of the day we spent together.

He looks down at the gold band, runs his thumb across it. "It's a reminder...of that day."

A whimper threatens to escape my lips. But I swallow it down, instead gesturing toward him—the whole ensemble. "You look..." I start, but the words are lodged in my mind and don't make it past my lips.

His dark gaze travels up and down me. "You always look..."

He can't seem to finish either.

We're both at a loss for words as my pulse thunders in my ears. The charged silence stretches, and I fight the urge to look away.

He shifts the bag higher on his shoulder, the casual movement breaking the spell just enough to let me breathe again. "I should get going, but I need to tell you —" he says.

"What about your tie?"

He looks down like he's just noticed it's undone. "I guess I should do something about that."

"Let me," I say. The command—or is it a plea?—comes out unbidden and full of unchecked desire. A desire that's stronger than my restraint and all my reasons to resist him.

"Do it," he says, his voice both raspy and urgent.

I close the distance between us, checking behind me to make sure the dogs don't need anything, but they seem transfixed too, staring at us like they've stumbled onto a show they can't stop watching. I can't stop either.

Miles sets down his bag.

I reach for his tie—it's blue, a deep, dark shade like the color of a lake under a clear morning sky. The silky fabric is soft against my fingers as I run them up to his collar. "Nice tie. I like the color," I say. "It looks good on you."

He swallows, his Adam's apple bobbing. He parts his lips but doesn't say anything at first. His arms hang at his sides, but his fists are clenched. I fiddle with the fabric, but the scent of him—soap mixed with sandalwood—hits me with such force, I can't, for the life of me, remember how to tie a Windsor knot.

I look up, and at last, he says, "Your eyes."

I'm...lost. "What?" I've heard him, but I'm not sure what he's saying.

"It's the color of your eyes. The tie," he says, reaching for one end of the fabric, showing it to me.

My chest rises and falls as the full meaning registers. "You got it because it—"

"Reminds me of you."

I'd like to say I'm strong enough to resist him. To walk away. To remember how utterly risky this is—for him, for others, and for me.

I'm only strong for a moment—a moment in which neither of us moves. My hand is on one end of the tie, his on the other. Then, in no time, our hands collide.

We clasp, and it's like a match to kindling. We ignite in a fiery kiss. Holding on to his tie, I jerk him closer.

He ropes an arm around my waist, his other hand grabbing my jaw.

Our mouths explore, tongues skating, bodies pressing together. Need rockets through me. Then it shoots to the sky when his hand slides down my jaw, over my neck, and around my throat.

He doesn't squeeze. It's a gentle caress. I arch against his palm, a subtle way of asking for more.

His fingers curl a little tighter, but he still doesn't squeeze. He just...holds me in place as he owns my mouth.

My hand climbs into his hair, sliding through that wild mess of locks, curling around his head. He groans, the sound raw and desperate, like he's utterly lost to the sensation. Lost to the connection between us, crackling and snapping like twigs underfoot in a forest.

The sound drives me on. I tug on his hair harder, rougher.

"Fuuuuck," he groans against my lips. But then he pulls back, letting go of my throat and my mouth too. He's staring down at me, his eyes carnal, his mouth a hunter's. "Leighton," he says, his voice a warning.

I frown, my breath coming fast. "I know. You need to go."

He shakes his head slowly, deliberately. "No. I need to touch you." He lets go of my waist, tucking a finger under my chin and tilting my face toward his. His dark eyes hold mine, and his voice drops to a pleading rasp. "Let me. Before I go. Just fucking let me, baby. Please."

It's the *please* for me.

No, it's the *just let me.*

Actually, it's everything.

It's the complete and utter despair in his voice over the thought of not having me. Pretty sure I didn't have much resistance left in me, but any shred I might have had has vanished in his need. I need him too. More than I want to walk away.

I grab his wrist, checking the time on the watch. "You have eight minutes," I say.

His lips curve into a wicked grin. "It. Is. On."

Before I know it, he's scooped me up and carried me to the side of the room where he sets me down, pressing my back to the wall.

In no time, he's unzipping my jeans, pushing them down my hips and sliding a hand over my panties. He growls when he feels how ready I am. "You're so fucking wet, Shutterbug," he says, using that nickname so deliberately, as if saying he's been thinking dirty thoughts every other time he's said it.

Knowing that, deep in my dirty soul, makes me even wetter.

"That turned you on more, didn't it? When I said *Shutterbug*," he rasps out, cupping me, flicking a finger against the damp—now damper—panel of my panties.

"You weren't kidding when you said you noticed everything," I say, by way of answering him.

"With you, I really fucking do." He drags his fingers to the top of my panties.

I steal a glance at his watch. "You'd better get moving, Mister Cocky. You're down to seven."

"You doubt me?" He sounds wickedly delighted.

"Let's just say I'm the kind of girl who likes proof," I tease, since this man seems to thrive on challenges.

His hand slips inside my panties, traveling down, then gliding over my wet pussy.

My breath hitches.

"Talk about proof, sweetheart. You're so soft. You're so fucking wet. Fuck, I'm dying to taste you," he says, as he strokes and I shudder again.

Pleasure twists inside me, climbing higher in seconds, like a switch has been flipped. I wriggle against his fingers, then grab his face and haul his mouth close to mine. "Kiss me while you make me come," I say, giving him an order.

With a hot groan, Miles seals his lips to mine and strokes faster. As his mouth claims me, his fingers draw dizzying circles around my clit that have me groaning and rocking against him.

Then, he slides two fingers along my clit and pinches me.

Breaking the kiss, I gasp, the sound quickly turning into a long, needy moan that thrums through my body.

His eyes darken with heat. "You like that?" he asks, wholly rhetorical. It's clear I do.

"So much," I say, bracing myself against the wall as he finger-fucks me.

He pulls his hand back, away from my pussy briefly. There's not much room so it's only about an inch, but then he gives a quick smack against my clit.

I jump in a good way as the sharp sting radiates blissfully through my cells. "I've never...no one has ever..." I can't quite form sentences, but I don't need to.

His lips twitch in satisfaction. "Good. Want another?"

I want it all. He sounds like he wants to give it all to

me. "Yes," I say, swallowing roughly past all this heat and longing, laying my desires bare.

His hand is still inside my panties, but he pulls his fingers back, pausing, making me wait for it before he slaps my clit again.

I cry out. My toes curl. My knees weaken. I reach for his collar, holding on. "Again," I beg.

"Anything for you," he rasps out, and it sounds like he means it in every single way.

Right now, though, I can only focus on *this* way. The physical. My gaze slides down our bodies, to his hand fucking me inside my panties, then to the way his arm looks in that crisp dress shirt.

Strong and so fucking sexy.

An idea takes hold of me, and as he strokes my wetness, I quickly undo the button on his right sleeve, fold the cuffs back and push up the sleeve, giving me a view of his arrow tattoo. "I like your arms," I say quickly, like my action requires an explanation when it's obvious I like them.

But his smile is pleased. "Then enjoy them, Leighton. Enjoy everything. I want to make you feel so damn good," he says, his deep, sexy voice tinged with the desperation I feel too.

I arch into his touch, urging him to go faster. He reads my cues, picking up the pace as he kisses my jawline, saying, rather than whispering, "I can't believe it's been a year since I got to touch you like this."

My heart flips a little harder from how he speaks so clearly as he finger-fucks me. "More than a year," I say, just to tease him.

He pulls back, meets my eyes, and shoots me the most serious look. "It's been a year, one month, and five days."

My knees go weak, and I ache from the bare admission. From the awareness that he's been counting down the days. I grab his stubbly jaw and kiss him messily as he strokes and smacks, strokes and pinches, then slides two thick fingers inside me, filling me up and making me want his cock again.

"Fuck my hand. Do it now. Clock's ticking," he demands.

I grip his strong forearm and ride his hand, using him till I'm shaking, shuddering, and falling apart. An orgasm seizes my body, rocketing through me in hot neon waves, stars bursting behind my eyes, Miles's sexy scent filling my head.

And his lips brush mine with tender, possessive kisses as he coaxes the last of my climax from me.

When I come down and we inch apart, he slowly eases out his fingers, then brings them to his mouth and reverently, carnally, licks each one. "Even better than I imagined when I fucked my fist to you," he says.

That image sears into my brain, and even though I know we shouldn't do this again I grip the hard outline of his cock through his dress pants and say, "I want to taste you coming."

He groans, grabbing my palm, pressing it tighter against him. Letting me feel what I've done to him through his clothes. "You make me so fucking hard," he says.

I squeeze his pulsing cock again as I glance at his watch. That took a little more than seven minutes. I sigh, frustrated we don't have enough time. But I can't risk him missing his flight, and knowing this man, he'd take the chance for me.

So I squeeze his cock one more time, then say, "You should go."

He sighs heavily but nods. "I know."

As he heads to the kitchen to wash his hands, I straighten up, zipping my jeans. On his return, he checks out the pack of pups, still silently staring at us.

"Weirdos," he says, but it's spoken with such affection as he strides over to them, petting each one on their little heads. The image is social gold.

Impulsively, I grab my phone. "Can I take a picture? For the team feed if they want it?"

He turns his gaze to me. "Sure."

I tell him to sit on the couch, and he obeys. The dogs pile onto his lap, and the shot of him in his suit, covered in pups makes me swoon.

And I know I won't be the only one. He rises and says, "I definitely should go now."

"You should," I say.

But once more he gives the middle finger to the ticking clock, coming right up to me in the living room, stroking my cheek and saying, "I know that broke the rules. I know we shouldn't do that again, but right now I have something to tell you."

"Okay," I say, urging him to keep going. This must be what he wanted to tell me earlier.

"I want you to sleep in my bed when I'm gone," he says, and he already told me that when he showed me around.

He clearly *really* wants me to.

"I will," I say.

"I want you to send me a picture of you in my bed. Can you do that?"

"Yes."

"And I want you to fuck yourself on my bed while I'm not there."

I tremble from his filthy request. "I will."

"Did you bring your toys?"

"No. That seemed presumptuous."

His lips twitch in the hint of a grin. "Call me presumptuous then. Because I left one in the nightstand drawer for you. As a thank you gift."

This man. This fucking man.

Then he hauls me in for a hot, passionate kiss that ends far too soon. When he breaks it, he says, "We shouldn't do that again."

But he doesn't sound convinced one bit.

I'm not sure I am either.

30

A ROOM OF HER OWN

Leighton

I could get used to this life.

The next morning, I'm standing on the second-floor balcony, sipping a steaming cup of Jasmine Downy Pearls —AKA the world's greatest tea. The sun's rising above the bay, and I tell myself yesterday was a mistake I won't make again.

A delicious, toe-curling mistake. But even so, it can't be repeated. Especially since he's now my employer. It's temporary, but who knows? It's best if I don't get more tangled up with a man who's already so deeply entwined with my family and my job. Now, my *jobs.* But I also don't want to take a chance with my future or with his.

He's worked too hard to risk the uncertainty that comes with a fling with the coach's daughter. I care too much about Miles and my dad to put either one of them in that position.

Today I'll return to the friendship we'd been building. I have to. It's the only way.

The morning light casts a golden glow over the water —a good signal for this shift back. Wanting to capture this moment before it passes me by, I lift my phone and snap a photo.

I send it to Miles with a friendly message since we've talked about inspiration before.

> Leighton: This view speaks to my photographer's soul.

> Miles: Yeah? What's the story you're telling with this picture?

> Leighton: It's the story of a girl who had a good night's sleep in a soft bed with four perfect roommates. They burritoed themselves under the blankets and didn't say a single word all night long.

> Miles: They are the perfect roomies. I'm glad you got some peace and quiet. I sent the pics you sent me to my mom—she says you're a better dog-sitter than I am.

> Leighton: What every dog mom really wants—pics.

> Miles: OK if I set up a group chat with her?

I type back a quick, **Of course.**

I reread the exchange. It's friendly, casual. Safe. A new day where we move past yesterday's not-so-friendly encounter when he put me up against the wall and finger-fucked me so well I saw distant galaxies.

Maybe we slipped yesterday, and fine, maybe I stoked the flames last night when I sent him a photo of me in my cami, sliding under those soft, fluffy covers.

But today, Montreal is a country apart from me. An international border separates us, and three time zones too.

We'll be back to the way we were—just like that.

* * *

After leashing the pack by the front door, I count them. "One, two, three, four," I say. Miles insisted counting them regularly keeps you sane and he's not wrong. It helps.

We head out to Crissy Field, the dogs trotting beside me, their snouts sweeping the ground for scents, their gazes surveying the landscape for enemy dogs.

AKA—any dog that isn't them.

Boppity, the long-haired pretty girl, spots one a hundred feet ahead—a Doberman Pinscher jogging past with a woman. Boppity growls, low and menacing, all seven pounds of her (and that is mostly hair), before launching into an ear-splitting, *how dare you walk past me* bark. Boo joins in, backing her up.

"Boppity, you think you're a German Shepherd, don't you?" I ask.

She prances ahead, tail wagging sassily—a German Shepherd trapped in a Chihuahua body. I take a pic and send it to the dog chat captioned: ***Chihuahua Confidence Level—100.***

So friendly.

I'm acing this return to friendship land.

Thirty minutes later, we're back at Miles's home, which is so delightfully quiet and free of roomie shenanigans that I could weep with happiness. I double-check the head-count as I lock the door behind us. "Everyone's here." I unclip their harnesses and set the gear on the dog shelf by the door.

A buzz from my phone distracts me—a photo from Miles's mom of her hand holding a piña colada, the wide-open sea in the background, with a heartfelt thank you for the dog pics.

I smile. She's loving her trip.

Miles sends a message just to me.

> Miles: Thank you. Seriously, just thank you.

Sometimes text has no tone, but not this one. I can hear his gratitude, and it makes me feel shimmery.

* * *

After showering and applying a little makeup, I let the dogs out in the backyard one last time before gathering my camera bag so I can head out to a boudoir shoot. It's Monday and I don't usually do boudoir then, but with the team out of town, it was easy to schedule one for this morning.

But when I return to the living room, I only count three.

"Where's Bippity?" I scan the room. No tawny, yippy pup cuddled with the others.

"Bippity?" My voice is light, but my chest tightens. I check the kitchen first—she's not by the water bowl. I move to the little library. No tiny pup curled in the corner.

My pulse climbs as I race upstairs. "Bippity!" I call louder. Did I leave the balcony door open? The thought makes my stomach drop.

I fling open the bedroom door, relieved to see the sliding glass door shut tight. But still, no dog. Yanking the phone from my pocket, I toggle over to the dog GPS app Miles installed. As it loads, my heart pounds and I search the en suite bathroom. Then Miles's walk-in closet filled with suits and dress shirts I should absolutely not touch later, then under the bed.

Nothing.

What if she Houdini-ed her way outside? What if she's stuck somewhere?

In the app, I click on Bippity's photo and then ask for her location. While it answers, I rush back down the hall, yanking open the guest room door. It protests with a groan, but I push it harder and hunt under the bed, then the closet, calling her name.

No luck.

The app brags unhelpfully: **We found Bippity! She's at home!**

With an exclamation point, no less.

That's good. Of course that's good, but my pulse barely settles. I still need to find her and the app doesn't pinpoint location to a room. After I dash downstairs, I check the backyard, pushing the door open in a nanosecond. No Bippity.

"Where are you, Houdini?"

But the dog still doesn't answer, and my throat tightens with fear. I don't want to do this, but I need help. I call Miles.

"Hey," he answers immediately, the sound of traffic and voices in the background. French, I think, since he's in Montreal. "I was about to call you."

What? Why? "You were?" I ask, barely masking my panic.

"Yeah, sorry to be a spy, but I'm guessing you can't find Bippity. I got a camera alert from the dog-cam in the living room, and you looked a little frantic."

Relief washes over me, mingling with irritation. "Where is she?"

"Check the guest room."

"I *did!* And the app says she's in the house, but I can't find her."

He chuckles softly. "That's her spot. The guest room. She likes to hide there sometimes. I should've told you— I'm sorry."

My heart races as I tear down the hall and reach the closed door. Weird. I definitely left it open moments ago. "How can she close the door on herself?"

"It's the angle. It always falls shut, so I keep it closed, but if she slips in while it's open, she gets a room of her own."

I twist the knob and shove the door open. "She's not here!"

"Look between the pillows," he says, unbothered.

"That doesn't make any sense!" I grumble, but I yank the pillows off the bed—and there she is. A little tawny peanut-butter-and-jelly sandwich between two big pillows.

"Little stinker," I mutter, scooping her up and

clutching her close. She licks my face, entirely unapologetic.

Miles laughs in my ear.

"You're laughing at a time like this?" I snap. "You should've told me about the Houdini pup!"

"I was going to. I even *started* to yesterday, but then, well, my brain kind of drained out of my head when you grabbed my tie."

"That's not an excuse," I say, but I'm already smiling as I carry her down the stairs.

"I know. I'm sorry," he says, a smile in his voice. "But *je ne regrette rien.*"

He's speaking French. I don't know the language, but I can figure it out. "You regret nothing?"

"Yep."

He sounds delightfully smug. And the memory of yesterday flickers before my eyes, hot and bright. Pleasure curls in my belly, a reminder of what he did to me.

I'm supposed to be moving on. Resetting. Yet I have no regrets either. "Same here," I admit as I set Bippity on the couch with the others.

"Yeah?" he asks, sounding...happy.

"Even though you're the worst."

"I'll make it up to you," he says smoothly.

I'm too intrigued by his promise to let it go, though I should. I'm sure I should. Instead, I ask, "How?"

Even with the noise of the Canadian city, I can hear a low rumble in his voice—god bless deep sounds. Then he says, "You could let me taste you properly."

I gasp, faux annoyed, but really, I'm turned on. "We're not supposed to do that," I say, but it sounds like the lady doth protest too much.

"You don't sound mad," he observes.

"I *was* mad. I thought I was a terrible dog-sitter," I say, trying to steer the conversation back to safer territory.

"You're doing great," he reassures me, dropping the flirting. "That was my fault."

"Next time, leave instructions for the escape artist," I say, not truly annoyed anymore.

"I will," he promises. "I was distracted yesterday. But that's on me. I should have given you a heads-up about her tricks. I'm glad you called, though, even though I was about to call you."

"Spy," I mutter, though a part of me likes how much he was paying attention.

"I only used my dog-cam for good," he says, then pauses. "Anyway...I'm glad you called because it's good to hear your voice."

I told myself I was resetting, moving on. But now, all I want is to talk to him. "How's Montreal?"

"*J'aime cette ville,*" he says.

"I love it here?" I ask.

"I love this city, so close enough."

"And do you speak French?"

"Only enough to be dangerous."

"How did you learn it?" I ask. "Or if I go into your library, will I find books written in French?"

He laughs. "I'm not that good. I read in English, but I know enough to get by since I went to McGill."

Oh, right. "I remember that."

"You remember it?"

"I looked up your bio. After I met you," I admit.

He laughs softly. "That's the nicest thing you've ever said to me."

I roll my eyes. "Stop. I've said plenty of nice things."

"True. You have. But that's up there."

"Wow. I need to raise the bar for myself then," I say, petting Bippity to calm her—and, if I'm honest, myself.

"No, don't change a thing," he says. "I'm also good with languages. It comes easily."

"I'm not jealous at all," I say.

"You know another language," he points out.

I smile. "True. I do." Then I glance at the time, sighing. "I should go. I have a boudoir shoot."

"Too bad," he says, sighing with some reluctance. "I was going to the Museum of Illusions with the guys, and I stepped down an alley behind an old church to talk to you instead."

"Me over illusions with the guys. Quite the compliment," I say, but inside I'm giddy.

"I'd always choose you," he says, and the air escapes my lungs. I'm quiet for a beat, the stillness humming in the air.

It's like his words have settled into the distance between us, bridging the miles. "I don't know what to say," I whisper.

Because what I really want to say would make this even more complicated.

I want to say—*choose me.*

"It's okay. I just wanted to say it," he replies, then adds, in a tone full of longing, "thanks for calling. You can call anytime."

I know he means it. I hang up, and before I go, I snap a photo of Bippity, lounging with smug indifference in her heated dog bed now, alongside the others in a row of little dog hot tubs, and send it to him with a caption: **Your fur sister has zero remorse.**

Miles: What can I say? She's got my stubborn streak. But I promise I'll make it up to you.

I think back to the deal we made, to the reset I promised myself. But here I am, breaking my own rules. And the truth is, I regret nothing too.

Leighton: Counting down the days.

Even though I shouldn't.

* * *

"You looked beautiful," I tell Sophie once more as she lingers in the doorway of the studio. She booked the session as an engagement gift for her fiancé. *He got me a ring; I'm giving him silk and skin,* she'd said earlier, spinning around in red and black lingerie—his favorites.

"Is it weird that I felt beautiful?" she asks, her hand resting lightly on the red door.

I shake my head, smiling. "Not weird at all. That's fantastic. I'll be in touch soon to show you the whole set."

"Can't wait," she says, and with a bounce in her step that wasn't there when she arrived, she disappears down the staircase.

That fills my cup. I started doing boudoir photography in the first place to empower women—capturing the moment when a client starts to see herself differently, beautifully. I don't want that moment to slip through my fingers. To fade into a blur. I want women to be able to hold on to it always. To remember it. And, when I look back at photos I've taken, I can feel their joy. Right now, I carry her joy with me as I straighten up the studio.

The door snicks open, and the click of heels interrupts the quiet as I'm re-hanging a robe. I glance up to see Mai Akamai, a statuesque Japanese woman, striding in with a whirl of jet-black hair and an oversized recycled-plastic purse that she tosses onto the ruby chair.

"Did you hear?" she asks, skipping pleasantries entirely.

I brace myself. Good news rarely starts that way. "Hear what?"

She gestures broadly at the lush studio we've curated so carefully, with its sapphire chaise longue and ruby-red chair. "The landlord is raising the rent."

The silk robe freezes midair in my hand. "Seriously?"

"Twenty percent," she says, her voice dripping with disdain. She flops into the chair, throws her head back dramatically, and lets out a groan. "I didn't know landlords were taking villain lessons these days."

My stomach sinks. "Twenty percent? That's highway robbery."

"And his reasoning? Get this." She smirks. "Costs have gone up. Like, what? Air costs more now?"

I hang the robe with deliberate care, gripping the hanger tightly. "It's space. He already owns it."

My mind spins. Twenty percent more rent isn't just an inconvenience—it's a threat to everything I've built here over the last year or so. Everything I need to make it on my own. My chest tightens with worry.

But there's no point in stressing. Time to solve this problem. "We could look for another space. Maybe band together with the other photographers here and find something better?"

Mai's eyes light up. "Yes! Girl, yes."

The truth is finding another space could be just as expensive—or worse. My to-do list feels endless already: dog-sitting for Miles, this studio, shoots for the hockey and football teams, my editing backlog. Can I handle adding a studio hunt on top of everything else?

No idea, but I'll have to find a way.

By the time I arrive at the Sea Dogs arena, after stopping at Miles's place to let the four-pack out, I'm no closer to an answer. But I do my best to set the studio issue aside when I run into Melissa at her cookie concession cart. It's closed now, since there's no home game of course. But she's hanging up some new signage with Christian's wife, Liv, who's got two little twin toddlers sitting nearby on the floor, listening to a story that Melissa's school-age daughter—I'm guessing that's who the blonde with pigtails is—reads to them from a kid's book.

"Hey, Leighton!" Melissa calls out, urging me over.

I stop, checking out the pink and purple typography on a pretty white sign advertising cookies. "Hey. How's it going? The new sign looks good."

"Thanks. I bribed Liv to help me out," Melissa says, nodding to her friend. "With my new sexy and sweet cookies."

"You did it? You made them?"

"I did. You're the inspiration," Melissa says.

"And they worked. I'd pretty much do anything for them," Liv says.

And the proof of that is right in front of me with Liv

helping out. "I'm so glad. I'm guessing you're not selling them here though?" I ask Melissa, since I doubt lingerie-shaped cookies will fly at a family-friendly sporting event.

They both laugh. "Nope. I'm selling them online," Melissa says, then bends down behind the counter of her cart and pops up quickly with a bag. "But here's some for you if you want. As a thank you for the idea."

I peer inside at a handful of pink, red, and white bra-shaped cookies. They're adorable. "I will enjoy these tonight."

I say goodbye, then tuck the treats into my bag and head to my temp desk to edit some evergreen content—more high-pawing shots of Scuppers and the team, as well as adorable snaps of players tossing crocheted rescue dogs into the stands at the last home game. The team partnered with a local charity to make and sell the dogs in the likeness of Scuppers, and the pictures are perfect for Chanda to post on off-days.

I narrow my focus to the task, only the task. But the number keeps circling in my mind—twenty percent, twenty percent. No matter how I slice it, it's too much.

I pause on a shot of Miles, flinging a crocheted dog to fans eagerly stretching their arms to catch it. He's having a blast. Something he didn't have in Vancouver with his injury. Something he's having now, playing for this team that my dad manages.

My heart squeezes.

He's not doing it on purpose and yet my feelings for Miles always find a way to complicate things—on the ice, off the ice, and somewhere in between. Then again, I complicate his life too.

All those complications *should* be reason enough to resist him. Really, they *should*.

By the time the marketing meeting starts, I've managed to finish the batch of photos. Everly, Zaire, Chanda, and Jenna gather around the conference table, and Chanda briskly runs through the week's schedule. It's all business until she glances at me with a grin.

"And," she says, excitement spilling into her tone, "the pics of the Sea Dogs with rescue pups were so popular we've decided to do a team calendar this year with Little Friends. And thanks to the fan vote on last night's picture..." She raises her eyebrows my way. "Miles, in his suit covered in puppies, was voted the cover model. Can you take on the project of shooting the calendar?"

Another project on top of everything else? But I'm not saying no to something that I made happen. I took that picture because I had a feeling it'd be social gold. And, I was right. That's enormously gratifying. And this project feels meaningful, no matter how busy it makes me. It's a chance to grow my brand, to prove I can handle work like this at a high level. And maybe, just maybe, it'll help me keep the studio afloat. Isn't that what a businesswoman does anyway? Adapt, expand, innovate. *Grow.* Like Melissa with her bustier cookies.

"Absolutely," I say as a part of me wonders if this is the start of more work with the team. And what if this turns into regular freelance assignments? If I leaned more into team photography, would that make our forbidden romance even more complicated? And more dangerous?

You're not having a forbidden romance, girl. You had one sexy day. That's all.

That's what I tell myself. Except, the math isn't mathing. I had two sexy days. But that doesn't turn this thing into a relationship.

And besides, the calendar can help with my bigger

goal: to make it on my own.

31

THE THING ABOUT ME

Miles

The thing about the Montreal team is they swear—and chirp—mostly in French.

The thing about me? I understand most of it.

Montreal's Armand Delacroix is one of the most aggressive forwards in the league—with his game play and his mouth. When Bishop strips the puck from him and races down the ice with it, Delacroix mutters something wildly insulting under his breath, but I ignore it. For now.

By the third period, though, Delacroix's chirps have gone from mildly annoying to flat-out nasty. The French equivalent of *"Your mom sucks my dick"* reaches my ears just as Bishop spins around, his voice sharp and cutting.

"Maybe learn to play better, fuckwad," Bishop fires back, his tone dripping with venom though he doesn't know exactly what Delacroix's said.

Our opponent's face darkens, and for a second, I think

he's going to peel off his gloves and throw down. It's hockey—fighting's part of the game, and sometimes the guys just need to settle it.

But Bishop doesn't give him the chance. Skates scraping against the ice, he snags the puck from Delacroix again—a clean, beautiful steal—and flips it to Bryant. Bryant tears down the ice and slams the puck into the net.

I pump a fist in celebration, and Bishop does the same, smacking gloves with Bryant.

As we hop over the boards for a line change, Delacroix skates by our bench and mutters, just loud enough for a few of us to catch, *"I'm seeing her tonight."*

I snap my head toward him, my voice clipped. "Enough with the moms."

Delacroix raises an eyebrow, a flicker of surprise crossing his face, like he didn't expect me to understand him.

Coach peers down the bench at the commotion while Bishop glances my way, a confused frown creasing his forehead. "He's saying mom shit?"

"Of course he is," I say, waving it off as I clap Bishop on the padded shoulder. "Ignore it."

But Bishop doesn't look like he's planning to ignore anything. His jaw is tight, and he's gripping his stick like he's imagining snapping it in half—or over Delacroix's head.

"Fuck him," Bishop growls, low and dangerous.

I lean in closer, keeping my voice calm. "Seriously. Ignore him. You start something, you're getting a penalty. Coach hates that shit. Don't give Delacroix the satisfaction."

Bishop lets out a noise somewhere between a growl and a huff, like a bull at the gates, ready to charge.

But when he's back on the ice for the next line shift, he stays cool. Delacroix keeps chirping, upping the ante with smirks and jabs, but Bishop doesn't take the bait. He skates hard, clean, and focused, ignoring the hell out of the French barbs.

And when Bishop strips Delacroix of the puck one more time and helps set me up for a goal, I can't help but grin.

The scoreboard's doing all the talking now.

* * *

"What was Delacroix saying to Bishop?"

The question comes from a podcaster. His phone's thrust forward and he's recording every word.

I'm seated at the table in slides, shorts, and my jersey, hair still damp with sweat. "They were debating recipes," I say, my voice dry.

The podcaster tilts his head. "Excuse me?"

"Poutine recipes," I clarify with a shrug. "It's an age-old debate."

It takes a second, but he cracks a grin. I haven't broken player code, and he knows I won't give him anything juicier.

Another reporter—gruff, no-nonsense—doesn't let up. "Bishop looked pissed out there."

I pause, raising an eyebrow. "Is that a question?"

The reporter doubles down. "Why was he so pissed?"

I lean back slightly, keeping my expression neutral. "His socks were cold, I'm guessing."

A ripple of chuckles moves through the room, but one or two reporters look annoyed. Doesn't matter. I'm done discussing it. I don't like playing diplomat, but it's part of the job—protecting the team on and off the ice. Sometimes that means playing verbal pinball with reporters too.

Another voice cuts in. "Did Delacroix's comments fuel your performance tonight?"

That's a fair question. A damn good one too. But I know better than to show my hand. So I keep my cards close to my chest. "Everything fuels me," I reply evenly. "That's the beauty of hockey—it's unpredictable, and you use it to your advantage."

The follow-up comes fast. "When you played for Vancouver, you tore your ACL. How's it holding up now?"

I clench my jaw briefly. I'll never escape that question. But showing frustration doesn't help anyone. I take a breath and let it go, reminding myself it's a valid thing for him to ask.

I rap my knuckles lightly on the table, grounding myself for a beat. "No complaints," I say, but I know that's not enough. Injuries *are* a big deal, especially major ones, and so is the work it takes to recover. They can haunt you, but they can also define you. If I downplay the injury, I disrespect all the effort I—and everyone who helped me —put in. "I work hard to stay healthy. Injuries like that— they take you out physically, sure, but mentally too. You don't forget what it's like to sit out for months. I'm grateful to be on the other side of it, but I take nothing for granted."

The room goes quiet for a moment, the weight of those words settling before Coach steps in to wrap up the presser.

As I head for the bus a little later, Coach catches me near the locker room. His voice is low, deliberate. "Good job out there."

The way he says it, I know he's not just talking about the game. He's talking about protecting Bishop—in the presser and on the ice. About being honest when it counted. Coming from him, those words mean everything.

"Thank you, sir," I say.

That's it. No more mention of the potential co-captain assignment. He'll decide when he's ready—and I'll just have to hope like hell I'm up to the task.

Later, on the plane, as the lights of Montreal flicker and shrink below us, my phone buzzes. A photo pops up from Leighton. I wait briefly for that flicker of guilt. For the unease that follows it—the sense that I need to keep all these feelings in check. That I *ought* to resist her. But those emotions don't come. I feel only the warm, hazy wish to connect with her.

I click on the photo, guilt-free. It's a shot of my bed, covered in four Chihuahuas sprawled like they own the place, with the caption: **They regret nothing.**

Fuck...I can't help it. I grin too big, angling the phone away even though no one's looking in the dim light of this short flight to Toronto.

It's not just the photo. It's that she knows me. She knows what I need after a game, and she gave it to me.

I probably should be thinking about her relationship with her dad, and my relationship with him too. I ought to be thinking about my career—the work, time, sweat, and tears I put into it—and how grateful I am to still have it, like I told the media tonight. I should definitely be wary of the past, and all the ways romance can go wrong.

And yet—it's like I'm a little bit high, a little bit hooked. I don't dwell on any of that. And I don't look her dad's way, not once, as I type back: *I'm calling you later when I land.*

* * *

The thing about travel is that sometimes time zones work in your favor. By the time I flop down onto the king-size bed in my Toronto hotel room, it's nearly one a.m. But on the West Coast, it's only ten p.m., still early enough to call Leighton.

I toe off my shoes and loosen my tie, the dim light in the room perfectly matching my mood.

I don't bother telling myself I'm only checking in with the dog-sitter. Settling back against the headboard, I hit Leighton's contact. She answers almost immediately.

"So, Delacroix was talking shit about Bishop's mom?"

I love that she cuts straight to the chase. "However did you know?"

"An educated guess. I know what asshole hockey players are like."

"You'd be right. Did you catch the whole post-game press conference?"

"I did."

Something about that warms my chest, like the sun breaking through on a cold morning. "Do you normally watch post-game press conferences?"

I didn't go to law school—though I took the LSAT— but I know the rule: *Never ask a question on cross-examination unless you already know the answer.* I'm ninety-five percent sure Leighton doesn't normally tune in to those things. Which means...she had a reason tonight, and I can't resist fishing for it.

"No, I don't," she admits.

My grin widens, and I keep teasing her. "So you just *happened* to tune in this evening?"

"Well, I guess you could say that," she says, her tone light and playful. "It was just playing in the background while I kept the dogs entertained."

"Oh, of course, right. That makes perfect sense," I say, going along with her. "You probably didn't even care about the game since you don't seem to know anything about hockey..."

"Nope, not at all," she says breezily. "Not even when that guy wouldn't stop chirping at Rowan in the third period."

I smirk. "Uh-huh. Guess you caught more of the game than you'd thought." She watched the whole game and the presser, and I am eating up her interest.

"I guess I did," she says dryly.

"And you know what? I really don't regret saying yes to talking to the press now."

She laughs, and the sound fills the quiet of my hotel room, doing something strange to my chest—making my heart flip in a way I like too much. This feeling—it's addictive. I spend so much of my day working hard. Hell, I've spent so much of the last few years working hard, focusing, moving forward and moving on. But when I talk to Leighton, I feel...peaceful and just happy in the moment. I feel like I'm finally enjoying the present for what it is.

"How was the rest of your day?" I ask, leaning into the conversation. "I hope I didn't stress you out with the dogs or anything earlier. And Bippity's...escape artist situation."

"No, you didn't," she assures me.

"Did she give you any more trouble?"

"She was perfect," Leighton says.

"Am I still in the doghouse for not telling you about her habits?"

"Hmm. If it means more of your hot chef skills, maybe."

"I take it you liked the pasta?"

"I had it for dinner two nights in a row. Loved it," she says.

That makes me unreasonably happy—being able to do something as simple as cooking for her. "Good. I'd be happy to make it up to you again. What did you do the rest of the day?" I'm craving all the details of her. I've spent so long resisting Leighton McBride that I can barely help myself now. I want to inhale all her stories.

"I had a photo shoot, then I had some things to deal with at the studio..."

I sit up a little straighter, the tightness in her voice catching my attention. "What do you mean?"

"Oh, nothing," she says quickly. "I'll sort it out."

"What is it?" I ask, pressing gently. I want to be the one she turns to when something's on her mind. I want to be the one who helps her when she needs it.

"Nothing to worry about right now," she says, and it's clear she doesn't want to get into it. I table my concern for the time being, but I'll find a way to bring it up again later.

"Besides," she adds, her tone lighter, "I got good news later in the day! I'm going to be photographing you again soon. For a team calendar. Apparently, you won the fan vote."

"Yeah, Everly mentioned that. I got an email about it. So, I guess we're going to spend more time together." I try to play it cool, but I know I'm failing. Hell, I've always failed at playing it cool with Leighton.

"You really don't mind?" she asks, her voice quieter

now. "That we're going to spend more time together at work?"

"I don't mind at all," I assure her, my chest warm, my heart bouncing around fearlessly in it. I swallow, weighing how much to say, how far to give in, then finally say, "If we're splitting hairs? I fucking love it."

I can feel her smile, even though I can't see it. It's in the pause, the soft sigh, the rustle of what I assume is the duvet. It's in the ache in my chest—the wish that I were there with her.

"I guess I don't mind either," she says.

I close my eyes for a beat, letting myself linger in the way everything feels so damn good right now. *This* is what I truly can't resist—this connection. "So how were the dogs the rest of the day?" I ask.

"Do you want me to show you?"

"Video call?" I ask, already reaching for the button. "Fuck yes."

A few seconds later, my phone lights up with her video. When I accept, it's the best night ever.

She's exactly where I want her.

In my bed.

Her chestnut hair is fanned out over my pillow, four little dogs wedged at her sides like they belong there. Like *she* belongs there.

In that moment, I know two things: I'm inextricably fucked, and I don't care about anything but stealing moment after moment with this woman.

We talk longer—about the calendar, the game, her dinner, the view, my mom's cruise, and a million other things. It feels like we've slipped into our own world, warm and hazy, where nothing else matters.

But then, she abruptly says, "I have to go."

It takes me a second to process, to connect this cozy moment with her sudden shift. Reality hits—sour, unwelcome. We don't have a relationship. She probably really does have to go.

"Okay. Good night," I say, keeping my tone all business.

"Good night," she replies softly, and then the line goes dead.

I stare at my phone, like I can find some kind of answer in it. Like it's a magical device that can replay her voice and translate her words into what I want them to mean. That she's found *that* portal, and it's not just a sex portal—it's a romance one too.

Like I want desperately.

But it's quiet. Silent. No insight into her, no window into her thoughts.

Sighing, I climb out of bed, head to the bathroom, and go through the motions of getting ready to sleep. My mind keeps circling back to her—the way she sounded, the way the call ended too soon.

Then, this longing in my chest. This gnawing desire to talk to her, to be a part of her world, to see her, hear her, touch her.

Get it together, man.

I resolve to go to sleep and reset my mind in the morning. But when I return to bed, a notification on my phone blinks up at me.

Dog-cam: Person detected.

My first instinct is to ignore it. But then—fuck it—I tap the notification without thinking twice.

And there she is.

Leighton's in the living room, standing purposefully in

front of the camera, like she's checking out her reflection. She's wearing my jersey.

My jersey—*my fucking jersey*—hangs off her shoulders, the hem brushing her bare thighs. She shifts, her fingers teasing at the fabric, lifting it just enough to make my heart pound.

She knows I'm watching.

The way she looks into the camera, her lips quirking in the faintest smile—it's not just casual. It's deliberate.

My chest burns hot, and I can't look away.

She's not stripping. Not yet.

But this?

This is for me.

32

DOG FACETIME

Miles

I stare so hard I'm pretty sure I've stopped breathing. I can't look away. I can't stop. The scene unfolding in front of me is every fantasy I've ever had about Leighton come to life. She closes her eyes and lets a hand drift down the fabric of my jersey, her fingers brushing over the number twenty-one, then teasing the top of her panties.

They're black. Lacy.

My body roars with need, heat surging through me at the thought of stripping them off her.

But she's setting the pace—slow, deliberate, deliciously torturous. It's a striptease that's like honey, a drizzle of sweetness that's driving me insane. She tugs at the hem of the jersey, inching it up, up, up, revealing a sliver of pale skin. Then more.

When she reaches the bottom of her breasts, my throat goes desert dry. The lower curves of those perfect globes peek out, and it's enough to wreck me completely. I make a sound—raw, feral, full of need.

She smiles. She knows what she's doing to me even if we aren't talking.

And then—just as she starts to pull the jersey over her head—the camera blinks off.

What the fuck?

An alert flashes on my home camera system. *Dog-cam: Offline.*

I'm not just turned on anymore; now I'm worried. My pulse is a mix of lust and panic as I call her immediately.

She doesn't answer.

The worry tightens in my chest for the longest thirty seconds of my life—until a new notification pops up.

Dog-cam: Online.

Merry fucking Christmas to me.

Leighton's in my bed, sitting on her knees, picking up right where she left off. The dogs are off the bed. Thank fuck.

With one swift, seductive motion, she pulls my jersey over her head and tosses it aside, leaving her bare from the waist up. Her gorgeous tits bounce and my mouth waters.

I'm done for.

Wait. Nope. Make that I'm absolutely ruined when she leans forward, her face closer to the camera and she slowly lifts a finger, making a shushing sound.

"Sweetheart, I'll be so goddamn quiet," I mutter to myself as she turns around and crawls across to the nightstand, giving me a perfect view of her ass, covered mostly in black lace. When she spins to face me, she's running her hand along a thick, peach vibrator made from sustainable plastic, and the look on her face is the sexiest thing I've ever seen.

The toy I gave her.

Lust cranks higher in me as she slides the head inside, then down her panties, gliding it across her pretty pussy. I can't see it touching her, but I can imagine. Oh hell, can I imagine.

She takes it out and brings it closer to the camera, showing me...

My pulse rockets to the moon—the toy glistens.

A rumble works its way up my chest. I can't stand the electric pressure in my cells. I can't take this rabid want pulsing in my veins. I palm my cock through my boxer briefs, then hit her name on the phone. She stretches across the bed to answer on speaker.

"Hi."

I waste no time. "Sit on it. Fuck that toy so I can see your perfect body and your gorgeous tits bouncing. So I can watch you ride that toy thinking it's me."

"Are you sure you want that?" she asks, her voice breathy, playful. She knows the power she has over me.

"Positive," I say through gritted teeth, tension mixing with lust inside me.

"If you say so," she says, then slides the toy back into her panties again.

I groan, long and loud.

She murmurs, and it's a sound of appreciation. "You like that."

"Fucking love it," I say and I'm careful to speak clearly, not to whisper. To make sure she can hear and enjoy every word. I don't want her to miss anything. Especially when I say, "Take them off, Leighton. Take them off, now."

With a heady murmur, she says yes. Then she slides

from the bed, still in view of the newly positioned cam, and slips off her panties.

My groan echoes from Toronto to San Francisco. "Yes, fucking yes, sweetheart. Now get on the bed and fuck that toy. *For me.*"

"It works so well, Miles," she says as she moves back onto the mattress.

"You used it last night," I say, a question, but a statement too.

"I did." Her tone is full of heat.

"All I could think when I was going to sleep was you fucking yourself on my bed."

She grabs the toy and slides it between her thighs. My dick throbs, jumping in my boxer briefs at the sight.

"Did you jerk off thinking of me?"

"Yes," I say, shameless.

"Don't touch yourself yet," she says, a quick, clear directive.

I understand completely. "I'll wait for you, sweetheart. But you'd better ride that toy good and hard right now."

She looks at the camera, licks the corner of her lips as she positions the dildo between her bare legs. Then she smiles wantonly as she sinks down onto it.

I fucking shout in pleasure. "Yes, baby. That's so fucking hot."

"Feels so good," she says, holding the base of the toy with one hand, her other hand sliding up her stomach to palm one breast.

A shiver visibly runs through her as she rises up, exposing more of the toy's shaft and giving me a view of how wet it is.

I can barely follow her instructions, I'm so aroused. I grip my cock, giving it a necessary squeeze to relieve some of the tension. Then, letting go, I focus on my woman. "Grind down on it, sweetheart," I say.

With a nod she sinks right down on it. I nearly lose my mind as she takes it all. It's the most erotic sight I've ever seen as Leighton rises up and down, the battery-operated cock in her hand while she squeezes her left breast. Her eyes flutter closed, and her sweet, beautiful pussy that I miss so much seeks more of the toy. She fucks it with abandon, grinding down faster, rising up, riding that toy like it's everything she needs.

"I'm close," she gasps out.

"That's right, sweetheart. It's my dick you're riding. It's my cock that's making you come. Take me deeper and fucking ride me until you scream."

She's a blur of flesh and desire, fucking and seeking, then calling out my name as she loses herself to the gift I gave her.

Watching her on camera like this, seeing her come as a voyeur who has been invited in, is a wicked thrill.

But what's even hotter? It's the way she moans, sighing in the aftermath of her orgasm. When her eyes open, she says in a sex-drunk voice, "My turn. I want to watch you."

I switch to video so she can see me as I push down my briefs and take out my aching cock. "Stay on video, baby. Lie back on my bed and watch me."

"Gladly," she murmurs and drags a hand down her chest as she takes the phone and stares at the video call while she settles down onto the pillows, enjoying the show.

And I give her one.

I grip my shaft nice and tight, stroking it then sliding a thumb over the head, gathering a drop of liquid arousal and spreading it over the crown.

Her eyes widen, flaring with a brand-new desire. "Do that again," she says, clearly mesmerized.

I comply, spreading the pre-come down my shaft. My balls are aching. My cock is throbbing. My brain is demanding. I can barely take this anymore and my fist flies faster, harder, sliding down my length until my hips are punching up.

Alone in a hotel room at two in the morning in Toronto, I fuck my hand until I spill all over my palm, picturing all of the things I want to do to the woman in my home who drives me wild.

The woman who seems just as surprised as I am since she says, "I didn't plan that. But I couldn't resist you."

"Welcome to the club," I say. "We have jackets."

33

FIRST-DEGREE SEX

Leighton

The hiss of the espresso machine mingles with a show-stopping number on the High Kick Coffee sound system, nearly drowning out the sounds of my thoughts on Tuesday morning.

They've been chasing me all morning—the *did you really do that?*—along with the realization that not only did I do that, but I *planned* that.

When I really should be planning how to both budget for the rent increase at Hush Hush and to grow my business. Blowing out a frustrated breath, I adjust my camera, then return to my job for today—capturing the warm morning light on a matcha latte and a plate of seven-layer bars for the shop's social media.

Taking photos grounds me when my thoughts are chaotic.

And today, that chaos is named Miles. Somehow, I thought that moment when he put me up against the wall before he caught his flight was a one-time thing. A *get it out of our system* moment of weakness. Toe-curling, knee-buckling weakness. But something that wouldn't happen again.

Last night though? There was no *fuck it* to last night. That was pure, premeditated, first-degree sex, when I should have been, I don't know, devising a plan for the studio. Or even sleeping.

But as I fiddle with the lens, I'm not thinking about numbers or budgets. I'm replaying the way I felt last night giving Miles what he wanted—*me*. I'm not even sure what I'm shooting anymore.

I lower the camera so *I* can refocus. And soon, the grandmother of the man I've been fantasizing about is staring at me inquisitively from across the counter.

"Where did you just drift off to?" Birdie asks as she measures oat milk for a latte, her purple feather boa flung jauntily around her neck.

I blink. "You could tell?"

She smirks. "Considering you've been standing there holding the camera without taking a single picture for the last minute? I had a hunch."

Busted.

Birdie sets the milk down, resting her hands on the counter as she studies me. "What's going on, Leighton?"

I can't exactly tell her the truth: *Oh, nothing much, just replaying the steamy details of what your grandson and I did last night.* Instead, Birdie takes the reins as she gestures to one of her employees and says, "I'm going to need you to handle the next few orders." She grabs a slice of coconut cake and two forks, along with a cup of tea, then slips around the counter and leads me to a free table. I suppose I do need a break.

"Romance is best discussed over cake and tea," she declares.

I laugh, following her lead. "So we're discussing romance now?"

"Please. You've been floaty all day. Clearly, love is on your mind." She slides the tea and cake in front of me.

Birdie's perceptiveness is both a blessing and a curse. I feel safe with her, but I'm not ready to spill every detail about what happened with Miles. She's not only his grandmother—she's also my client.

"Floaty, huh?" I say, deflecting.

"Don't even try it. Talk to me," she says, cutting into the cake and taking a bite.

I busy myself, fiddling with the napkin on the table, trying to decide how much to share. Briefly, I consider steering the conversation to business instead. Birdie is a businesswoman after all. I could ask her advice on the rent increase. But I don't want to look like I'm angling for more work from her. And, honestly, maybe I need to deal with what's front and center on my mind first. "There's... someone. But it's complicated."

Her eyes light up. "Oh, I *love* complicated. Who is he? Anyone I know?" she asks so innocently.

I give it back to her in the same way. "Maybe a little."

"And you like him?"

I hesitate for a moment, then nod. "I do."

A grin spreads across her wise, weathered face. "I bet he feels the same."

"He does," I admit, warmth spreading through me at the thought.

She takes another bite, then sets down her fork with a clink against the porcelain. "So what are you going to do about all of these complications? Because, honey, *compli-*

cations is just another word for stuff you're not ready to deal with."

"Why don't you tell me how you really feel?"

"I'm not in The Underground Grandma Matchmaking Society for nothing," she adds, winking.

I swallow hard. "Okay, so as a member, what would you tell me to do?" I know she's on my side. I know she'll say go for it. Maybe all I'm really looking for is permission.

Birdie leans back in her chair, her eyes softening. "Honey, you're young. Don't get caught up in the details. Someday, you'll be old, running a coffee shop, taking photos, and wondering about some guy who got away."

Her words hit like a hammer to my chest. I glance out the window at the morning crowds rushing by on Fillmore Street, people chasing their to-do-lists and their days, my throat tightening. It sounds so easy—like you can just throw caution to the wind. But it's not just *my* caution. There are others involved. My dad will always be here for me—to the end of the Earth and back. Which also means he would always take my side. But what if I try something with Miles and it falls apart? What would that mean for Miles on the team? Even if it works out, would it be awkward? Uncomfortable? Create a rift between them? Cause discomfort with the other players? Would they respect him less? Miles was affected by his injury. What if there was an emotional injury, too, from us? How would that impact him?

"I know what you mean," I say. "But it's not that simple."

"Of course it's not easy. If it were, you wouldn't be drifting off while taking pictures of lattes and treats." She smiles knowingly. "Speaking of, let's take a picture of that next drink I'm making. I think you'd benefit from focusing on something familiar."

Yes, she's right. Her insight grounds me, reminding me of who I am. I'm a photographer, a storyteller, a human who likes to remember all the special moments. Even the ones that might pass you by. Like this one, when a kind, sassy woman who believes in romance looks out for me.

She also gave me the answer to the question I didn't have to ask—what to do about the rent increase. The answer is the same as the romance one—*focus on something familiar.*

There is no magic solution to a cost jump. I need to keep taking photos. The more clients I gain, the better I can handle the ups and downs. Like Melissa is doing with the cookies. She jumped on the opportunity to add a new line of sweet things. She wasted no time.

Life keeps coming at you. And I'll keep dealing with whatever it throws my way. I glance down at the Nikon— with *this.*

This skill, this ability, this talent. It's mine, and I'll keep using it.

I pick up my camera again, letting the act of taking photos settle the storm in my chest, even if all sorts of complications remain.

* * *

Later, when I'm at his home, covered in four small dogs, editing the photos, my mind drifts again. To the way Miles makes me feel—desired, appreciated, and seen in a way I haven't experienced before. But maybe it's what I've been searching for with my camera all these years. I spend so much of my life being the lens, but what I've really been looking for is someone to see me.

And of course, seeing me really means...listening to me.

Miles listens. More than anyone ever has.

Over the next several days, Birdie's advice digs roots in me. Her encouragement—though of course she has her grandson's heart in mind—makes me think that maybe it's okay to give in to something that feels good, even if it's fleeting. Maybe it's okay to be with someone, however briefly, who listens.

I replay her advice as I work for The Sports Network, as I walk the dogs, as I make tea every morning and gaze at the sun rising while steam curls over the mug, imagining mornings like these with Miles.

Dangerous things, these daydreams. They nip at my feet as I go to the arena and plan the calendar with Everly. On Tuesday afternoon, as we're scoping out locations in the arena to shoot the images, we walk past the mural Maeve worked on last season. My attention snags on the Presidio looming at the edge of the mural—the site of our first date. The painted image pulls me back to that day. It reminds me of kneeling in front of the lockbox, clicking it open, discovering a vintage locket. I can see him lifting it, looping it around my neck, clasping it as his fingers brushed against my skin.

I still have the photo I took of it, so I dig around for it in my files, finding it without much effort. I stare at it, slipping back in time, falling into a memory of how I felt that day with him. It's comforting knowing that that perfect day isn't forgotten—it's captured perfectly in this image.

As I look at it, I shiver, just like I did then—before I

gave in to the way I felt with him. To the way he *listened* to me.

This mural feels like a quiet echo of that moment. Maybe it's a sign too. Have I been looking for one all along?

Everly glances at me, her expression curious but patient. She's always had a way of knowing when something's on my mind.

"How did you manage it?" I ask abruptly.

She furrows her brow. "Manage what?"

"The way you felt about Max...and your job."

Everly pauses, then smiles softly. "It wasn't easy."

I exhale, the weight of her honesty hitting me. "Yeah, that's the impression I'm getting."

She sips her London Fog latte. Then she says, "He sent me these every day. He brought them to work. Then to my home. It's a little thing, but it added up. I needed to know what I was fighting for, you know?"

Do I even know that yet? My throat tightens unexpectedly. "Some days, everything feels so tangled up," I admit quietly. "The way I worry about the future. The present. My family. My goals."

She nods, her voice steady. "It's always tangled. It's never easy. Everything is a choice. All you can do is make the best ones and know your friends will have your back."

I swallow hard, my heart tightening with unspoken fears. But I manage a small smile. "Cheese alert: I'm so glad we became friends."

"Me too." Everly throws her arms around me in a warm hug.

As we return to work on the calendar, she grins at me. "You know, complicated is my middle name."

I laugh, the tension in my chest easing for now. But

later when I'm on the bus heading toward the Marina, questions swim up—what happens when Miles returns late tonight? I'm supposed to go. We even planned for me to go when we set up this arrangement in the first place. We figured I'd leave a few hours before he returned. That will make it easier, we'd both said.

To avoid temptation and all.

But are we still avoiding it?

* * *

I don't have the answer to that question as the evening rolls on. As I straighten up, all I know is that I should leave in a little while since he's due home in a few more hours.

I'm making sure towels are hung properly in the bathroom when my phone pings with a notification from the front door cam. A delivery arrives—grocery bags. After the delivery guy leaves, I head to the door and grab the goods so I can put them away before Miles returns tonight.

A proper dog-sitter task will be good for me. It'll remind me why I'm here—putting things away, taking care of the home and the creatures in it. But there's a note attached to one of them with my name on it. They're not just for him? My heart skips a beat as I open the bag and find a note tucked inside:

For when I cook for you.

It's presumptuous. Cocky, even. But it's also so wonderful that my pulse soars. All the floaty feelings return, flooding every cell in my body. So much for a dog-sitter task. This feels like a task for a—

I stop myself before my mind dares to say other words. *One other word*, really. That starts with a G.

But I can't fight off the smile that pulls at my lips as I text him: *Can't wait to see what you whip up in the kitchen.*

Then I add one more sentence—*For us.*

The giddy haze stays with me a little while as I unpack the groceries—artichokes, hearts of palm, mushrooms, tofu, asparagus, pasta—all the things I love. He really did shop for me. There's even a bottle of wine—white, of course. A Riesling that's so light and pretty my mouth waters.

That lovely feeling turns into something else. Something warm, something safe as I settle onto the couch, pick up a photography book and slide under a fleece blanket that's like a magnet for the pack. Soon, the heat from four small animals burrowing under the cover with me warms me from the inside out.

The words and images blur on the page as my mind drifts to the locket, to that one perfect day, then to all the days I've spent with him since.

And the nights too.

Like this night when he sent me groceries, and I hardly feel like I should leave anymore. I close my eyes and drift into sleep until there's a click of the door at the edge of my dreams.

34

HOMECOMING

Miles

My muscles ache. My bones are tired. This is how I usually feel after a long road trip that starts in Montreal and ends in Denver in the afternoon.

The difference this time? My mind won't settle. Normally, when I come home, my thoughts calm, ready to crash right along with my body. But tonight, when I punch in the code and hear the soft click of the lock, something inside me both settles and speeds up.

It's a surprising feeling—contentment and excitement mixed into one intoxicating cocktail.

And anticipation. Will she be here? Did she leave already, like we'd planned? Even if she did, I know where I'd be. I'd get in my car and find her. I'd bang on her door until she let me up, curl up beside her, and beg her to tell me about the last several days.

That certainty powers me forward as I slowly, quietly push open the door to my house.

The room is cloaked in that in-between glow of
twilight, where the edges of objects blur into the quiet.
Only a few lights are on, their dim glow casting soft,
golden pools onto the hardwood. Shadows stretch lazily
across the walls, unthreatening, folding the room in calm.

I step inside, careful not to break the spell of the stillness or disturb whatever traces of her linger. The scent of
vanilla and brown sugar is a warm, sweet tether to her.
Her things are here: a couple of books on the table, her
phone too, but also her duffel bag—and that feels all
wrong.

I tense at the sight of it, but it also awakens something
in me. Something urgent.

I toe off my shoes. Cindy's the first to notice me. She
pops her head out from under a soft, gray fleece on the
couch and bounds toward me, her tiny body wiggling
with joy. I scoop her up, nuzzling her warm little face, but
when I glance back at the couch, I see why the others
haven't followed.

Leighton is there.

She's asleep, curled up in the corner of the couch, her
face serene in the dim light. A blanket tangles around her
legs, and a photography book rests on her chest, her
fingers still loosely curled around it. Bippity meets my
gaze but lies pressed against her side, tail thumping lazily
as she refuses to budge.

I know the feeling, girl.

For a moment, I just stand there, utterly charmed by
how seamlessly Leighton fits into my life. She looks like
she's been a part of this house—of my life—for years.

My steps are quiet but my heart thunders as I close the
distance. I kneel, brushing a stray hair from her cheek,
and Bippity's tail picks up its tempo. Still, Leighton doesn't

stir. Her steady breaths fill the room, a soft cadence against the hush of the home.

I start to step back, not wanting to wake her, but her eyes flutter open. They're unfocused at first, heavy with sleep, but then they meet mine.

"Hey," I say, my chest squeezing.

She sighs softly, her lips curling into a faint, dreamy smile. "Hi," she whispers, her voice rough and warm with sleep.

My chest tightens. It's the most perfect moment I've experienced in ages—more perfect than a goal, more than a hat trick—and I don't want it to end.

"Don't go," I say, my voice barely above a whisper.

Her smile deepens, and she nestles back into the blanket. "I won't," she murmurs, her words wrapping around me like the night itself.

And just like that, everything feels right.

Yes, there are reasons to hold back, beyond the obvious. She could leave me, like Joanne did. She could decide she'd rather not cause any complications with her father. She could also figure she'd rather not try something brand new with a hockey player whose body has already been broken—someone who's been injured and could be again. Someone who, by his own admission, was deeply unhappy when he wasn't playing.

She could choose all that and not choose me.

But none of that stops me from wanting her. From wanting to open up to her. From wanting to know her more, better, again and again.

"How did it go?" I ask softly, tipping my chin toward the pack.

She yawns, stretching lazily, and murmurs, "They're kind of into me."

Her gaze drops to the dogs snuggled against her, Bippity tucked into her side and Cindy now curled at her feet.

"I get it," I say, meeting her eyes so she knows just how much I mean it.

She smiles as she pets Boo, who pokes his head out from under the cover. "You do?" she asks, like she already knows the answer.

"So much." There's a pause, then I ask, "Nice to have a quiet house, huh?"

"It was bliss. Not once did they argue about their feelings—except over who gets fed first and which dogs they hate on walks."

I laugh, leaning closer and resting a hand on her hip. She responds immediately, a slight tremble under my fingers. It's gorgeous, like her body's telling the truth her words won't quite yet. I let my hand curl around her, squeezing gently.

"I'm glad. *I feel* like your roomies are awful."

"They are." She pauses, breathes in deeply like she's inhaling something sweet. "Your place is the opposite," she says, her voice soft. "I love the quiet."

There's something poetic about her loving the silence. It's tempting to comment on it—to point out why—but maybe it doesn't need to be said. Maybe she just likes the quiet.

"Do you want me to stop talking?" I tease.

She shakes her head, her smile easy, and says, "Tell me about your trip." She lifts her hand above the blanket, sliding it down to my palm on her hip.

Her fingers curl through mine, and all the air rushes from my lungs. Everything in me feels hot, needy. Our fingers link, and I don't censor myself—I give her the truth of the trip. I tell her everything she asked. I don't skip over the parts about her dad.

"Coach seemed pleased with how I handled the press conference in Montreal," I say, my voice steady, "and with how I've been talking to the other players."

"That's good. It's happening, isn't it?"

I take a deep breath, letting the weight of this opportunity sink in. I'm proving myself as a co-captain. "I think so. It's kind of wild. I'm glad...and ready to lead." Except...I hesitate, then admit something hard. "Most of the time. Other times, I'm not so sure."

Her expression softens. "Why would you think you're not ready?"

Her question is gentle, like she knows how hard it is for me to say this out loud. Normally, I project confidence. That's how I get through life. I'm the resilient one. The optimist. I work hard, focus, stay responsible, and move forward. But sometimes, I'm not that guy.

"I wonder if I'm taking on too much," I say. "And if the guys will listen to me." There's more to it though. Something I can't avoid. But tonight is for honesty. "And I wonder how the team would see me..." My gaze roams up and down her. "If they knew. About this."

She exhales heavily, her grip on my hand tightening— a reassurance, like she's saying we're in this together. Or maybe I just want to believe that.

"But I know you'd make a great leader," she says firmly. "You care enough to worry—that's the difference. You have this calm confidence, this sense of purpose. You always seem to know exactly what to say. You're going to be great, even when it's hard. I really believe that."

Her faith lifts me up. It's everything I needed. "Vulnerability isn't easy for me," I say.

"I think you are with me though. Vulnerable."

I take a deep breath. "I'm a lot of things with you that I'm not with other people."

"Like what?"

Like falling for her—that's what. I want to take care of her, watch her shine, cook for her, come home to her. But I can't put all of that on her—not yet.

"Vulnerable," I repeat. "Open. A little obsessed."

That's a lie. I'm a lot obsessed.

"Yeah?" she asks, sounding enchanted.

"Yes. I've been thinking about you. I think about you all the time, Leighton. I probably think about you too much."

She lets go of my hand, reaching for my face, her thumb gliding along my jawline, her touch featherlight and maddening. I stay still, frozen in her touch, but the tension vibrates through my entire body as she looks at me. When her lips part slightly, everything in me tightens and unravels at the same time.

And then, I break.

I bend, leaning in, and crush my mouth to hers.

35

DOWN, BOY

Miles

My brain short-circuits. A hum vibrates through my body as we kiss, hot and deep. Our lips seal together. The taste of her sweet mouth is almost too much. Her vanilla and brown sugar scent drives me wild. And soon my thoughts disintegrate as my right hand slides into her hair, careful to avoid her ear. My fingers tangle in those strands I've missed, tugging gently at the ends. She moans into my mouth—a frantic sound that obliterates the last shreds of my control. Not that I had much to begin with.

I kiss her even harder, the way I know she likes it. The way I know she *wants*. She moves with me, her tongue seeking, her lips just as hungry and greedy as mine. It's a kiss that's wild, reckless, and so much more than the sum of its parts because we're in perfect sync. We want the same things—in bed and, I'm starting to think, out of it too.

I break the kiss to trail my mouth along her jawline. I

should take my glasses off, but I can't be bothered to stop right now. My pulse hammers mercilessly as I find the hollow at the base of her throat and press my lips there. That spot reminds me of the locket we found the day we spent together.

"That locket looked so good on you," I murmur against her skin, remembering it, wishing I could see it on her again.

"You'd look good *in* me," she replies, her voice a blend of tease and heat.

A laugh bursts out of me, and I pull back just enough to look at her. She's so fucking perfect for me. She keeps me on my toes—snarky, smart, kind, brave, passionate—and it feels like ages since I kissed her, even though it's only been... "How the hell did I last a year without kissing you when it already feels like forever since I kissed you nine long days ago?"

Her hand slides against my chest, right over my heart. I don't know if it's intentional—where she lays her palm—but it doesn't matter. It makes that organ in my chest slam hard just the same, especially when she says, "Time doesn't work the same way when you can't stop thinking about someone."

And now my heart is beating outside my chest. It's beating so damn loud she's got to be able to hear it. I want her so much. I need her so completely it's terrifying and wonderful at the same time. A part of me wants to tell her, to blurt out *you're the one*, but no way am I scaring her off before we figure out what *this* is.

Before I know if we're both this caught up in each other.

I force myself to focus on the physical, and that's not hard at all. I glance down at her shirt, my restraint hanging by a thread. I want her stripped bare. I want to take her apart, fuck her, make love to her, have her in every way. But I need to know—even in spite of her *you'd look good in me* remark—that we're on the same page.

"Tell me I can take all your clothes off," I say, my voice rough, my hands playing with the button on her jeans. "Tell me I can eat you. Tell me I can fuck you till you're begging for more orgasms."

She blinks, then shudders. "I would think you already know my opinion on that."

"Tell me this one. Tell me now."

My hand is restless at her waist, barely holding back.

She slides her fingers into my hair, her touch grounding and electrifying all at once. "I want all of you. I can't keep fighting this, Miles," she says.

And dear god, those are the greatest words any woman has ever said to any man. "Don't fight it. Let's fuck instead."

She ropes her arms around my neck, and I scoop her up and carry her up the stairs to my bedroom.

But it smells like her, and it somehow, incomprehensibly, already feels like *ours*.

What a heady thought.

What a fantastic thought.

I set her down on the bed. Every instinct in me screams to tug off her black shirt, to peel away those jeans, but I force myself to slow down. I run the backs of my knuckles down her cheek. "Tell me what you need and don't need from me," I say.

But she's already lifting a hand toward her right ear. "I'm taking them out," she says wryly. "I don't want to lose one—or both—when you fuck me into next year."

My heart hammers so hard it hurts. I'm falling deep

for her. The fact that she can make that joke right now—that she can let me see this unguarded side of her and still laugh—does it for me.

She rises from the bed, moving toward the bathroom with that confident sway I can't look away from. At the doorway, she pauses, glancing back over her shoulder. "Maybe I was presumptuous," she says, holding up a small case. "I packed my bag, but I left this behind."

"You should be presumptuous with me," I reply.

Her lips curve into a small smile before she steps into the bathroom and clicks open the case.

When she returns, her hearing aids tucked safely into their charger, she places a hand over my chest. "I can hear you," she says, looking up at me, her gaze clear and steady. "You don't have to yell or over-enunciate. But just know, if you murmur, I'm probably not going to catch it."

I laugh softly, the sound catching in my throat as my laugh burns off, replaced by something raw, tinged with need. "I don't think I could be quiet with you even if I tried."

"Don't be then," she says.

"I won't," I say, as my fingers find the loose strands of hair curled behind her ear. I tuck it back gently, my finger-tips grazing the shell of her ear for the first time.

It's such a privilege to touch her like this.

Her breath halts and when she looks up at me, the softness in her eyes steals the air from my lungs. This moment isn't lost on me. She's letting me in. She's trusting me when she's at her most vulnerable. I swear to myself I won't let her regret it.

First, though, I let go of her, take off my glasses, and set them on the nightstand. Then I grab her and haul her close, running my hands through her hair at last. "Fuck, this feels so good," I rasp out, grateful to have free rein in these gorgeous locks.

She leans her head back, savoring my touch. "It does."

I kiss her throat again then up her neck, then I nip her earlobe.

She gasps, melting into me. I kiss along her ear, flicking my tongue across the flower studs she wears every day. *Every damn day.* I've known this, but I haven't entirely felt the magnitude of it till now. "I fucking love that you wear these all the time," I say, then pull back to look at her.

"You have good taste in jewelry," she says, teasing, a little dry. Like she knows how to wind me up.

"I think it's more than good taste," I say, my fingers teasing at the hem of her shirt. "You like wearing something I gave you."

She rolls her eyes playfully. "If you want to see it that way."

"I know it's that way," I say.

She laughs, shaking her head, but then gravitas sets over her eyes. "I don't like taking them off."

"Don't. Don't ever take them off," I say before I can think twice about the *ever*.

But I don't linger on it. I move on as I tug off her shirt, growling at the sight of her in lingerie again. "Fucking missed this," I say as my gaze travels over her chest, the swell of her breasts, the white lace snug against her skin. I'm used to seeing her in black lace—well, the three times I've gotten her clothes off or halfway off. But white fries my brain too.

Her nimble fingers make quick work of the buttons on my dress shirt, but by the time she's halfway down it, I have no more patience.

I jerk it over my head, then peel off her jeans as fast as I can. "Can't wait," I say, as I help her step out of them.

When they're on the floor next to the bed, I rise up... and swallow roughly as I stare at the gorgeous sight.

She's wearing matching white lacy panties, and that's it. She's here. With me. Wanting me. Ready to say *fuck it* to all the complications.

The ones involving her, me, and everyone else. The weight of this hits me all at once, but it doesn't scare me. It makes me want to do right by her however I can, whenever I can.

My brave, bold, beautiful woman. "You're stunning," I tell her, my eyes locked with hers, but those two words hardly capture the depth of what I'm feeling.

Everything.

"So are you..." she says, but the words trail off as I cup a hand on the damp panel of her panties, her wetness soaking through them.

She shudders.

"You finally gonna let me taste you properly?"

Her lips part. "Have I been holding out on you?"

"Yes," I say, half joking, but also feeling like the world has been holding out on this blazing lust. "And I can't wait."

In no time, I slide her panties off, then before I can even be bothered with spreading her out on the bed, I get down on my knees in my dress pants and press a hungry kiss to her greedy clit.

"Oh god," she murmurs as her hands clamp around my head. I fucking love the feel of her grip, nice and tight, like she needs to hold on to me.

I groan as I taste her sweetness. She's slick and hot and

delicious. I flick my tongue around her clit, then suck on her.

Another needy moan falls on my ears and drives me on. I kiss her pussy more deeply. As I lap up all her arousal, she pants and moans, her fingers curling tighter around my skull.

I want her to be rough with me. I want her to use me for her pleasure. I wrench away, run a hand up her stomach, and meet her gaze for a hot, heady beat. "Pull on my hair, fuck my face, do whatever you want."

She nibbles on the corner of her lips briefly, then turns her gaze longingly to the bed. Specifically, the pillows piled by the cushioned headboard.

I pop up in no time. "Let me revise that, sweetheart. Sit on my face right now and ride me."

Her smile is wicked and wanton.

Soon, I'm stretched out on the covers and she's straddling me, looking down right as I curl my hands around her hips.

"Use me like you did that toy on the video. Fuck my face even harder than the toy," I tell her, then I jerk her pussy right to my mouth and groan.

"Miles," she murmurs, half surprised, half protesting, but all blissed out.

Leighton doesn't need much encouragement. As I grip the flesh of her hips, she rocks against my face. My eyes roll back in my head as she goes to town on me.

Rocking, groaning, fucking.

Lust roars through me, the temperature in me shooting higher.

She presses one hand against the cushioned headboard. The other finds my shoulder, and in no time, my woman's seeking her rhythm on my face. She's fearless and unashamed as she rides my mouth. With every thrust, my cock jumps in my pants, aching with the need for her. But right now, this is all I want.

I'm coated in her wetness, my stubble soaked with her juices, my mouth devouring her sweet pussy. I let go of her hips to grab her ass.

She yelps out a long, feral "yes."

I squeeze her cheeks, and she gasps, and then, I swear, I can feel her gush. She's even more aroused from the rough way I knead her flesh. So as she fucks my face, I raise a hand, pause, then come down on her cheek with a hard swat.

"Oh god, yes," she gasps.

My dick throbs as I raise my hand again and swat her once more, harder, firmer, louder.

"Yes, yes, yes," she chants.

I suck on her clit, smack her ass, and urge her to fuck me the way she needs.

Her cries grow louder, needier, and then...shakier. And soon, she's shaking, trembling and shouting that she's close.

Then, she's there, coming on me as I'm smothered in her, and there's no place else I want to be.

Well, except inside her.

With my hands on her hips, I ease her off me. She's all soft and pliant, melting into the moment like she's boneless. It's fantastic. "You're like a noodle," I tease.

"And you should take that as a compliment," she fires back, rolling onto her side and settling into the bed, her voice warm and just a little breathless.

I smirk, climbing over her. "Oh, I do. Trust me, I do."

Her eyes drop to my abs and then lower, lingering on

my slacks. Her lips curve into a slow, teasing smile. "Why are you still dressed?"

I arch a brow. "Do something about it."

"Gladly," she says, sitting up with a mischievous glint in her eyes. Her hands are on me in an instant, working the zipper of my pants with determined precision. The angle's awkward—because, well, real life—so I slide off her, shedding the rest of my clothes in one fluid motion once I stand at the side of the bed.

She doesn't waste a second. She's up on her knees, reaching out to help push my black boxer briefs down. When they fall, her eyes widen as my cock springs free. That look on her face? It's everything. My ego soaks it up like sunlight.

And then—just as I'm about to make a clever comment—she licks her lips and stares up at me, her gaze filled with heat. "You really did miss me."

I brush my thumb along her cheekbone, holding her face in my hand. "I really fucking did."

Her shiver tells me she believes it.

Her hand circling my cock tells me to get a fucking move on.

Climbing back onto the bed, as the sound of dog nails scratching on floors catches my attention, I whisper, "There's just one thing I need to do first."

"What?" she asks.

Of course I wasn't going to nail the communication one hundred percent the first time. I repeat myself at a louder volume. "There's just one thing I need to do first."

Her eyes roam down my body. "Protection?"

"Well, there's that." I reach for the nightstand and grab a condom, but before I put it on, I reach for her bra, flick the clasp open with practiced ease, and let it slide away.

Heat roars in me as I take her in—tight curves, perky tits, perfect dusky-rose nipples that practically beg to be kissed, licked, and worshipped. I want to spend hours on every inch of her, but I know there'll be other opportunities for that. There has to be, because there's no way this is just a one-time thing.

"Time doesn't work the same way when you can't stop thinking about someone," I say, repeating her words from moments ago.

Words that burrowed into my heart.

Words that define me.

She lifts a hand, her fingers brushing across my jaw, her eyes soft and wide as they meet mine. "Show me."

It's a statement, bold and confident, but her voice carries a quiet vulnerability, a kind of trust so complete it knocks the air from my lungs.

And for the first time, I realize I've earned something I didn't know I needed: her faith in me.

I'm not sure what we'll do with it—what we'll become —but I know one thing for certain. I want to give her everything. Starting with wringing another orgasm from her.

I slide my hands over her knees then up her thighs. "Part those pretty legs for me, sweetheart."

Her cheeks flush as she complies, spreading wide, and sparks explode across my nerves. "Fucking gorgeous," I murmur, staring savagely at the most beautiful sight in the world.

This woman, ready for me.

I roll on the protection. Settling between her thighs, I rub the head of my cock against her wet pussy, teasing her before easing inside.

Her back arches, her tits rising as a stuttered breath

escapes her. "Oh god," she gasps, reaching for my arms, her fingers gripping my biceps.

I slide in deeper, heat crackling through me as I sink into her, filling her completely.

And for several delirious, mind-bending seconds, the world goes offline.

Sensations crash over me—electricity, sparks, power. When I finally open my eyes, I look down at the woman I shouldn't want but can't resist. I'm so far gone for her. I want to give her everything—everything she needs, the hard fucking she craves.

I ease out, then slide back in, taking my time, setting the pace, watching her every reaction. Her breath comes in soft pants, her cheeks flush pink, and her eyes shine with raw need.

Her nails dig into my back, scratching upward, and it's fucking fantastic.

"So good," I growl. "Leave marks on me. Everywhere."

"You sure?" she murmurs.

"Do it," I urge, my voice thick with want.

Her nails rake down my back as I fuck her, and all I can think is how much I want to feel those marks tomorrow. But I also want her to feel everything tonight.

I rise to my knees, looking down at her, then assessing the situation. The position. My goals. "Sit on my lap. Ride me. I'll make you come so hard that way."

"So cocky," she says, but she's scrambling.

I shift to the edge of the bed, sit there and tug her toward me. I pull her into position, then guide her down onto my dick again, thrusting up into her with a sharp, desperate rhythm.

"I need to see your face when I fuck you. And when I do this." I lift a hand and smack her ass.

She gasps, then moans. "*Miles*."

My name has never sounded better.

"You want more?" I ask, holding nothing back.

"I want marks."

It's official. I'm a furnace. "You'll get them, sweetheart." As I drive into her, I lift my other hand, pausing, *pausing*, then coming down hard on the soft flesh of her ass.

She yelps, then whimpers. And that's all I want. I fuck, I smack, and then I kiss. Hard, ruthless, using teeth and tongue. I'm sweating, she's moaning, and we're coming together. Everything—every single thing about this moment—is filthy perfection.

Then, somehow, it gets impossibly better when she grabs my hands from her ass and says urgently, "My hair. Pull it. Touch it. Play with it."

The invitation. The meaning behind it. The desire.

I rope my fingers through her hair, tugging as she rises and falls on my cock.

She tenses, then keens.

My hands curl through those locks, messing them up, touching her everywhere—it's a freedom she clearly craves, and one I need too. The more I touch her, the faster her moans come, the quicker she moves, and the hotter we both become.

Until one more jerk, one more thrust, and she's tipping over, crying out. And that's all it takes. The switch flips in me, and I come so hard as she falls apart on me.

As she murmurs softly, something soft moves against my ass. Something...odd.

When I focus again, I look down. It's Boo. He's squirmed past me, licking Leighton's leg. Nope. He's no longer licking—he's gearing up to mount Leighton's leg.

"Down, boy," I say firmly, scooping him off her. "She's mine."

Leighton meets my gaze, one brow arching.

"Well, you are," I say, owning it.

She smiles, then says, "Then you should ask me to stay the night."

I haul her close, my voice firm. "As if you'd stay anyplace else."

36

A HARD BARGAIN

Leighton

I have questions. Starting with: "Where did you learn to cook? Did you go to culinary school while getting your philosophy and psychology degrees?"

Miles smirks, his lips curving upward as he flips the omelet in the pan. "Not at the culinary school level," he replies, his tone teasing, but it's clear he enjoys the compliment.

It's the best morning ever. Miles wears glasses, low-slung black lounge pants, and a snug gray T-shirt that clings to his broad shoulders. His ink peeks out from beneath the short sleeves as he flips mushroom omelets at the stovetop. Cindy's curled into a dog ball on my lap, snoozing as I sip my green tea at the counter.

It's the kind of domestic moment I never knew I craved until now—comfortably sitting across from someone, a man who makes me feel like I belong, the smell of breakfast in the air.

"I am, however, a tea sommelier," I quip, taking another sip.

Miles glances over his shoulder as he slides an omelet onto a plate. "Good," he says, holding my gaze a beat too long. "You should enjoy everything here."

There it is again. *Here.* The word lands, weighted with something unspoken. I spent the night—of course I did. He asked me to, and honestly, I was planning on it anyway. But the question of what comes next looms.

Like, tonight.

I should ask him, but my stomach growls as he sets the plate in front of me, the aroma distracting me, and likely enticing Cindy too much. I scoop her up and set her down in her hot tub, next to her fur siblings.

"So, how did you learn to cook?" I ask again once I return and dig in. The omelet is perfect—savory, fluffy, and impossibly good.

"I taught myself," he says, coming around the counter with a plate of his own, along with a cup of coffee, and sitting next to me.

It's nice eating breakfast together. It feels...easy. Like this is something we've done a hundred times before instead of something that might not happen again.

"Like, with YouTube and everything?" I tease.

He laughs, shaking his head. "Sweetheart, I started cooking more than twenty years ago. YouTube wasn't a thing. I learned from the Food Network and books."

"Books?" I feign shock, clutching my chest dramatically. "You had to learn from books? How old are you?"

Miles shoots me a mock-stern look. "Keep it up, and I'll put you over my knee."

"That only makes me want to tease you more," I reply,

grinning as I take another bite. "This is incredible, by the way."

"I'm glad you like it." He takes a bite of his, and after he finishes, he says, "I had to learn."

"Why?"

"My dad was the cook."

"Oh," I say, understanding dawning. Miles had mentioned at Birdie's coffee shop that his dad had left without warning. "And so you took it on then?"

"Yup," he says, then takes another bite.

That fits him so perfectly. That's what he does. He takes things on without complaining—responsibilities, people, pets, chores.

"I didn't want to make things harder on Mom than they already were," he adds. "I focused on school and helping out with Tyler and Charlie since they were younger. Mom was working full-time and already had enough on her plate. So to speak."

My smile fades. "School, your siblings, the house, hockey. That's a lot for a teenager. Did she ask you to step up?"

"No," he says, his tone a little clipped. "My dad did. Right before he left. He told me I needed to be the man of the house."

"That's a lot to put on you."

He shrugs again, as if shrugging off the memory. "Someone had to do it."

My chest tightens, a mix of admiration and something deeper—my own hurt over what he went through. I know what it's like to be left by a parent. But my dad took everything on for Riley and me, his parents helping out. I didn't have to become an early parent. Miles doesn't just step up —he sacrifices without hesitation. It's such a part of what he does and who he is that he thinks it's not a big deal. So I push back a little. "Sure, someone *had* to do it. But *you* did it. And it's a lot. I admire that," I say, since I want him to know it *is* a big deal what he did, even if he doesn't see it that way.

A smile teases at his lips. "Yeah? You do?"

"Of course I do. It's very you," I say.

His eyes are soft, a little vulnerable, almost like he's glad someone noticed. "I guess so." He heaves a sigh, scratching his jaw. Something's on his mind. Maybe something he's not sure he wants to say. But then he soldiers on. "I wanted to ask why he said that to me—*to step up. Why* he left me with that...weight. That responsibility. At first, I just did it. I stepped up. Cooked, cleaned, studied, helped out. But later, when I graduated from high school, I was a little pissed at him. I really wanted to understand *why*."

I reach for his hand, urging him to keep going. "I'd have been more than a little pissed."

"I wanted closure," he says, his voice heavy as he opens up, but also calm, steady. "I wanted to tell him how I felt. But when I tracked him down, I found out he'd died of a heart attack."

My heart squeezes—not for his dad, but for this man with me right now. "I'm sorry, Miles."

He swallows, sighs, then says with some resignation, "Me too." He pauses, holds my gaze. "And thank you. For asking."

It's said like it's what he needed all along.

"Of course," I say, then even though it might make him uncomfortable, I ask the next thing. "What would you have told him? If you found him? What's the closure you wanted?"

If he needs closure, maybe he can get it...with me.

Now.

Here.

He blows out a long breath. "Good question." His brow furrows, but it doesn't take long for him to find the answer. "I think I'd have said I wished he had the guts to tell me the truth before he took off. That it was unfair to leave like that. That it pissed me off." He looks away, then back at me. "But also, I think what I really wanted to say is —he missed out. It was his loss. I wanted him to know he had an amazing, clever daughter in Charlie who turned out to be a passionate advocate for animal rights, a son in Tyler who's funny as hell and ferocious on the ice, and more disciplined than anyone I know. A wife who is the best mom in the world. And he missed out on all that," he says, emotion in his voice, but it's clear the emotion is reserved for his family, not for the family member who left.

"And a strong, thoughtful, caring, smart, incredibly resilient son who's pretty passionate too," I add.

Miles's lips tilt in another smile as he moves in for a kiss. A soft, tender one that ends with a "thank you" whispered against my lips. When he pulls back, he adds, "For the closure."

"You're welcome," I say, then glance down at the food. "Oh! I should have added—who's an excellent chef too."

"A hot chef," he says.

"A hot tattooed chef," I add, my gaze drifting over the ink on his forearm as we resume eating.

"You like my ink, Leighton?" he asks, like he's glad I do.

"It's hot. What's this one for?" I ask, tracing the arrow tattoo that runs along his arm.

"Focus," he says. "I got it when I went to college. It was my reminder to stay on track."

"Well, two degrees and hockey—I'd say it worked."

"A little," he deadpans.

My attention shifts to a colorful tattoo on his bicep, a tree with bright fall leaves. "And this?"

"Family tree," he says with a sweet smile. "For my mom, Birdie, Tyler, and Charlie."

Not his dad. He doesn't have to say it; I get it. My life's the same.

"I love it," I say, glancing back at the plate in front of me. "And I love your cooking."

"I told you I'd cook for you," he says with a small, self-satisfied smile.

I flash back to last night, to the groceries he sent here with that cocky note: *For when I cook for you.*

"You were so presumptuous," I say, raising an eyebrow. But inside, I keep wondering—how many more times would he like to cook for me?

"I thought you said I was cocky," he counters, grinning as he lifts his coffee mug.

"Same thing," I reply, but my mind circles back to that word again. *Here.*

"Miles," I say, swallowing down the nerves. This isn't easy, but it needs to be said. "What are we doing?"

He sets his mug down, his eyes locking on mine. "I don't know. But I don't want to stop." His voice is full of emotion, mostly hope and longing.

Relief washes over me, followed by something brighter, sharper. "I don't either," I say, and it's hard being vulnerable. Truly hard, but how could I be anything else with him when he lays himself bare?

He leans forward, resting his forehead against mine

briefly before he pulls back. "Then don't go home tonight."

I laugh softly. "You've still got the dogs. You need my help, of course."

"Exactly. I have them till Sunday night. Stay and help me with them," he says, his grin turning wicked. His eyes make it clear we both know that's not why he wants me to stay.

I hesitate for a moment, wondering what happens after *a few more days*. Questions about the future circle me, but they always do. The future is my albatross, so I bat them aside. I narrow in on the present, weighing the practical risks instead. But really, there aren't many. Who would know the difference? No one. No one has to know where I stay.

"Yes," I say, my voice firm. "On one condition."

He arches a brow. "I give you countless orgasms?"

"That's a given," I shoot back. "But I'm walking the dogs, and I'm cleaning. You're not getting in my way."

"Who's bossy now?" he teases, his eyes sparkling.

"Let me take care of something for once," I say, softer this time.

His grin fades into something gentler, and he dips his head to kiss me. "You're making this hard for me."

Well, that I can't resist. I slide a hand over his lounge pants. And hello! He's at half-mast. "I see I am."

A rumble-growl crosses his lips. "I'll walk the dogs with you."

I squeeze his growing erection, then stand my ground. "But I'm cleaning."

With a happy sigh, he relents. "Fine."

"Also, thanks for breakfast," I say as I slide to my

knees, tug on the waistband of his lounge pants, then lick my lips.

His mouth curves up, and he pushes off the stool in seconds flat. "I bet you'd like me to fuck your throat, Shutterbug."

He knows me too well. I want to be manhandled. I want to be pushed around. "Only if you pull on my hair while you do it," I say, giving it right back to him.

His eyes darken to flames. I swear I can see lust radiating off his whole body, like an electrical charge. "You and your dealmaking."

"You love my dealmaking."

He pauses for a weighty beat, holding my gaze, then says, "I really fucking do."

It feels like he's talking about more than a blow job, but for now I focus on the task at hand. Or mouth, really.

I peel down his boxer briefs, his hard cock showing off how ready he is. I kiss the tip, lightly, feather soft.

Then I open wide, grab his hip, and urge him to fuck my throat. Miles doesn't hesitate. He threads one hand through my hair near my temple, yanking and tugging while filling my mouth.

Exactly how I want him to.

He's in control, but really, when I play with his balls, drag my nails down his thighs, and squeeze his ass, I'm pretty sure I'm the one in charge.

And the sounds he makes when he comes, the grunts, the groans, the long, carnal growl of my name, tell me how good this deal is for both of us.

* * *

Not going to lie—the dog walk is kind of wonderful. It's almost like a date, but I know it's safe. I'm just his dog-sitter, after all. No reason we can't be seen walking them together, if anyone even notices. But I don't think anyone does.

Besides, it's impossible to hold hands when you're managing the leashes of four tiny terrors. By the time we get them home, I need to head to the beach for the Renegades' volunteer cleanup event. They hired me to take photos, so it's a work thing, but still—it feels good to be doing something meaningful.

At the door, there's this awkward moment. How exactly does this work? Do we make plans for later here at his house? Since, well, that's all we can do. He's heading out to a luncheon with a sponsor, and I have a shoot. But before I can overthink anything, he says, "Any chance you'd want to meet at High Kick when you're done with your thing and I'm done with mine?"

"Like...in public?"

His confident grin somehow makes the question feel ridiculous. "She's my grandmother. We've been there before. Besides..." His voice softens. "Aren't we friends?"

We both know that's a lie. Friends don't make my heart trip like this.

"Sure. I'll text you when I'm done...*friend*."

His hand slips to the back of my neck, pulling me in for a toe-curling kiss that says we're so much more than friends.

What, though, I don't entirely know.

I'm not sure what I want this to be either. Or, really, what it even can be. And I suspect that's the same for him, since wanting and having are two entirely different beasts.

* * *

High Kick Coffee is quiet in the late afternoon, the stream of customers fading as the sun dips lower and caffeine needs dwindle. Birdie's signature showgirl music plays softly as I enter, passing Dolly by the door.

I smile at the sequined mannequin, remembering how she caught my attention the day I met Miles—when he carried her in here.

The second the door closes behind me, I shed the stress of the day. The shoot went well, though my mom sent a half-dozen texts teasing "exciting news." She hasn't actually told me what it is yet, and I'm not sure I want to know. For now, I leave her drama behind.

I glance around, but Miles isn't here yet. Behind the counter, Birdie catches my eye and beckons me over, pressing one finger to her bright red lips.

"I saved you a special spot," she says, her voice full of mischief.

"Thanks," I say, feeling suspicious. "But I'm meeting Miles here."

"I know, sweetheart. It's my job to know these things." She winks and waves me toward the back.

I feel a little fizzy as I follow her, my suspicion growing. She's up to something. Or maybe...in on it.

When I round the corner, my suspicions are confirmed. The table she's picked is tucked into a cozy corner, complete with a small mason jar of wildflowers. It offers a discreet view of the shop—and of Miles, waiting for me.

"Just for you two," Birdie says, sounding far too pleased before she takes off for the front of the café again.

Miles stands, pulling out my chair. "Hey," he says, and

the way he says that one word reminds me of last night when he returned home. It's full of hidden meaning.

"Hi," I say, hoping that one syllable conveys how much I like this unexpected moment too.

His fingers brush mine as I sit, sending a zing of warmth down my chest. I gesture to the tiny vase of flowers, focusing on it instead of the intoxicating feelings bubbling inside me. "Think she does this for everyone?"

He leans closer. "No. I brought the flowers. For you."

"Oh." The word gusts past my lips, my surprise unmistakable. No one has brought me flowers in years. Or maybe ever. "I love them. Thank you," I say in a rush.

"They reminded me of your tattoos," he says, a hopeful note in his voice. "Want to smell them?"

He knows why I love flowers. The thoughtfulness of it is so specific and so touching that my throat tightens.

"Always." I lean in, inhaling the gentle fragrance of the blooms and the meaning behind them. They're fresh, sweet, with a sun-warmed scent that feels like spring.

After I rattle off every note I can detect, I add, a little embarrassed, "I love flowers so much."

"I know," he says, his voice full of quiet pride. His gaze drifts to my arm, then to the rest of the shop, as if he's checking to see if the coast is clear.

It's just us right now—us and the jazzy music, the warmth of his gift, and the secrecy of our date.

Like a thief, he stretches an arm across the table. His fingers trace the intricate lines of my wildflower tattoos. I shudder, hoping this secret date never ends.

And for a while, it doesn't. Birdie's voice calls out, "Order for Boppity."

I laugh as she turns the corner, bringing us a warm toffee brownie.

"For Boppity," she says with a wink. "Compliments of the boss."

We thank her and she smiles, the far too pleased kind, before she leaves us alone again.

"I think she's trying to get her membership for The Underground Grandma Matchmaking Society reinstated."

"Trying?" I counter. "I think she has it."

His smile seems unstoppable. "I hope so."

Yep. This is definitely the bubble, and I never want to leave it. We talk, we laugh, and everything feels possible here in the cozy corner of his grandmother's shop. But that's just the good vibes talking. This is a mirage—the setting, the privacy, all of it. I can't let it fool me into thinking anything can truly last. But I decide to lean into the heady part—how good I feel when I'm with him.

As we're finishing, my phone buzzes. I glance down at the screen.

> Mom: Can you shoot the new handbags soon? Pretty please? You're the only one I trust with them. You're so talented, my love. I could fly you out to New York.

I sigh, setting my phone down, my gut churning with dread and temptation. "My mom. Again."

His gaze turns serious. "What does she want?" He sounds like he'll protect me from her, and the passion in his tone does something to me.

"She's in full force," I reply, rolling my eyes lightly, trying to mask the way her offer twists me up. I do need more work, and my mom pays well. But I'd probably have to ask for some days off to fly out to New York, and I don't know if that's feasible. And I'd be working for someone who doesn't think much of some of my business choices. The whole situation makes me feel...icky. But that's a lot to go into on a secret date, and I don't want to kill the mood. "She wants me to do some work for her. If I don't respond to her offer to shoot her new line, she'll text me ten more times."

He pauses, taking a beat before thoughtfully asking, "Will you say yes?"

"I don't know. It always feels weird working with her, but it's work, and I still have that whole rent situation to figure out..." My thoughts tangle.

"What's the rent thing?"

But today isn't about her or my rent or anything else. Today, I feel too good to dwell on the practical. "Just the rent is going up at the boudoir studio, but I've got it figured out. I'll work harder. And really, I don't want to talk about work right now."

His brow furrows. "You sure? I'm happy to talk about it."

My heart squeezes at his clear and obvious willingness to chat. I don't have a ton of romantic experience, but I do have enough to know how rare and precious a man like him is—someone legitimately interested, truly kind, incredibly smart, and, most of all, a great listener.

That's the rarest part of all. The one I value most.

Right now, though, I'd rather talk about other things. "Thanks," I say. "I'll probably take you up on it. But not now."

He nods, listening once more as he says, "Fair enough."

We don't talk about work anymore. In fact, once we're home at his place, we don't talk much at all. We touch, and that's much better. Especially when he curls his hand around my throat the way he alone can do.

I don't know why, but that move does it for me. It sends me flying. Later in bed, starlight twinkling through the windows and four small bossy Chihuahuas curled up with us, I turn to him. "No one else has done that to me."

"Made you come ridiculously hard?"

I laugh but shake my head. I slide my hand over my own throat, demonstrating. "This."

"Yeah?" He sounds too thrilled. It's a good sound.

"Yep."

He covers my hand with his. "Good," he says, then tilts his head, clearly thinking. "Why me?"

I'm not usually this open. I'm rarely this vulnerable. But he's earned it. "I trust you."

A smile plays across his lips, but he must fight it off, since his expression remains serious. "You let me do it the first time we were together." It's a statement but really, it's a question.

"I guess I've always trusted you."

He hums, a low rumbly sound in just the right frequency that I can still hear it. "Sometimes you just know."

37

MY TREASURE HUNT

Leighton

At pole class the next evening, I'm feeling pretty damn good. Hand necklaces and red-hot spankings just have that effect on a girl. The good sex sends me spinning—literally—as I glide around the pole for another mermaid spin at Everly's studio.

But when I finish, I realize I'm the only one spinning.

Oh.

My cheeks flush hot and uncomfortable as I plant my feet on the floor. Everyone else has stopped and is looking at Jewel, who's demonstrating the next move.

Swallowing hard, I glance around at my friends. They're standing next to their poles, focused on the teacher. Maybe no one noticed my extra spin. Maybe no one cared.

But I care. Because I can't fucking hear her.

Why does Jewel play the music this loud? How can

anyone hear over this thumping bass? Her voice is muffled, indistinct as she slinks around in leg warmers and tiny shorts, demonstrating some new choreo. I can't quite read her lips, because she's in motion, her hair swishing past her face as she goes. I'm standing here just... wondering what the hell she's saying.

The thing no one tells you about hearing loss? It's not just the volume you lose. It's the ability to pick out speech in a sea of sound. With this sexy, throbbing music blasting, Jewel's words are a garbled mess.

Faking it isn't working.

I swallow tightly, trying to push down the stupid rush of emotions I don't want to feel.

Shake it off, Leighton. No one even saw you. This could happen to anyone.

Right. Of course. I don't want to ask for special help since I don't want to draw attention to myself. But really, I just got distracted. A little too much Miles on the brain. This is my reminder: focus more, daydream less.

With my throat tight, I zero in on Jewel for the rest of the class. I don't miss a beat—not because I hear her, but because I watch her and everyone else like a hawk.

When class ends, Everly slings her workout bag over her shoulder. "Who's up for Moon Over Milkshakes?"

My first thought is the sound, the noise. My second is whether there's another diner I could suggest. But everyone's already nodding and saying yes, so I go.

It's easier that way.

Besides, I've learned how to manage here. Once we're inside the bright, noisy diner and seated at a booth, I discreetly adjust the settings on my hearing aids. It's not that I don't want my friends to know—I just don't want them to think they have to accommodate me. I'm fine. Really, I'm fine.

We slide into a worn mint-green booth. The scent of French fries and pancakes fill the air, and I inhale them, taking comfort in the way I can tell them apart no problem.

"So," Maeve says, whipping her gaze to me the second the server walks away. "You've got that freshly fucked glow."

Well, then.

In one spot-on assessment, Maeve takes my mind off my funk. "Do I now?" I ask playfully.

"You do," Josie agrees, drumming her *Kim's Convenience*-themed nails on the chipped Formica table.

Fable nods, her hazel eyes twinkling with interest. "Spill, girl."

"You all have freshly fucked glows too," I point out, shooting them knowing looks. Most of their boyfriends are back in town after the same road trip Miles went on.

Everly wags a finger at me. "And yet we're talking about your freshly fucked glow. So I'm guessing resistance proved futile?"

The earlier tension from class fades completely as I let myself focus on Miles and the whirlwind of emotions he stirs up. "He's kind of..." My stomach flips, my chest tightening with a mix of nerves and something far more dangerous. "He's great. Like, really great. And it's weird that he's so great. I don't know what to do with him being this great."

Josie raises a hand, her blue eyes curious. "Did you just skip all the sex part and jump straight to feelings?"

"I guess I did," I say, a little sheepish. Then I smirk.

"Do you want me to back up and tell you how absolutely incredible it was? Because it was. Best I've ever had."

Maeve claps her hands several times. "Thank you, because that's super important."

Fable nods sagely. "Never underestimate the benefits of a good banging." She grins, turning to Maeve next to her. "Put that on one of your mirrors, Maeve."

Maeve, who's expanding her art business with a line of mirrors featuring cute love lessons, taps her chin thoughtfully. "That is solid advice. But maybe I'll add, 'Never underestimate the value of a man who truly gives a shit about you.'"

There's a collective sigh around the table, and my heart goes a little squishy.

But then Everly gives me a concerned look, her brow furrowed. "What are you going to do about it, though? You know...your dad and everything."

The warmth in my chest is doused with a bucket of ice. There are so many feelings swirling inside me right now that it's hard to find space for them all. "I honestly don't know," I admit, shrugging. "I'm trying not to think about it."

The conversation shifts when the food arrives, and I let myself breathe. It's easier to join in when I'm not in the spotlight.

We're finishing up when an athletic blonde with shiny hair and a shinier ring walks past. She does a double take and turns to Everly. "Everly, how are you? It's so good to see you!"

"Sabrina!" Everly lights up, standing to hug the woman in a cute pink sweater and distressed jeans. She's all smiles and exudes a poised, magnetic energy that immediately draws attention. Also, her rock is as bright as a disco ball. It's on her left hand, so she must be engaged.

Everly quickly introduces her to the table. "Everyone, this is Sabrina. She's with *Glace*," she says, mentioning the Cirque du Soleil-esque ice show that's set up camp in San Francisco for a long stay. "And amazing, by the way. You should see her triple loop. Well, you will—she'll be at the rink in a couple weeks doing a promo."

Sabrina waves, her bright eyes sparkling with warmth. "It's so nice to meet you all. And here's hoping I can keep the crowd entertained while they wait for the boys to get back out there."

"Our fans love the intermission entertainment," Everly assures her, then gestures to me. "Leighton will be there too—she's taking photos for the event."

"Perfect!" Sabrina's smile widens. "Can't wait to see you then."

We chat for a few more minutes before she heads out, her effortless confidence stirring something in me. She reminds me of how I felt more than a year ago in the studio with Miles. I wouldn't mind getting that feeling back.

When we're done, I'm glad to have spent this time with my friends, but I'm also ready to go.

On the bus back to Miles's house, I'm mentally making plans for later when I see him while trying to close the loop with my mother on the handbag shoot. Last night, I finally replied to her text asking for more details, but as she sends me the dates now, I'm secretly relieved. They line up perfectly with dates for the Sea Dogs calendar's shoots. The money would have been nice, but it's not even an option. As we trundle past the cafés and shops on Chestnut Street I write back.

. . .

> Leighton: Sorry! I can't be in two places at once. But I appreciate the offer.

Her reply is lightning fast.

> Mom: That's disappointing! Usually you're so good at making time for these.

Yup. Still passive aggressive. But I stand my ground as I tap out a note.

> Leighton: That's not the issue. The issue is I'm working with the Sea Dogs, and I literally have a shoot on those days.

Really, that ought to be enough to settle her down. But my phone buzzes again as the bus nears Miles's home.

> Mom: Perhaps I can convince the Sea Dogs to move the shoot? I can be very persuasive.

. . .

Why doesn't she just move *her* shoot? That would make the most sense. And yet, she wants everyone to bend to her. Still, I don't know what she might try to pull, so I try to nip that in the bud.

> Leighton: Please don't. I'll try to make the next one.

> Mom: Brilliant! Send me your schedule and I'll work around you.

I roll my eyes—she finally gets it. But also, I don't want to send her my schedule. That feels entirely too personal for some reason, and I don't entirely know why. It just does. My schedule is mine. I don't share it with others. Still, I want to treat her the way I want to be treated by her— with respect. So I reply with that in mind.

> Leighton: I'll send you some dates.

Then, I set the phone aside as I hop off the bus and head inside, eager to execute my plans for Miles.

* * *

But as I'm setting up, everything feels too...girlfriend-y. Maybe it's because I'm alone in his house, adjusting my tripod, leaving a trail of lingerie for him to discover with geocache clues.

A bustier hanging in the closet next to his ties.

A satin nightie tucked under a pillow in the guest bedroom.

A thong slipped into a bathroom drawer.

It all sounded playful and bold in my head, but now my stomach twists, and I feel...off. Like I'm overstepping. Like I'm trying on a role that doesn't quite fit. Miles isn't here—he's working out with some of the guys on their off day and grabbing a bite afterward. So it's just me, the dogs, and all my uncertainty.

I wince, glancing around the bedroom. Boppity and Cindy sit at my feet, their cute, inquisitive stares somehow making me feel even more exposed. The queasiness settles deeper, a pit in my stomach that won't go away. It's not just that I'm staying a few extra days—it's that it's starting to feel like something more. And I don't know what to do with that.

We've been sharing his space, making breakfast, getting ready together—like we've done this a thousand times before. We're playing house, and I don't know if that's comforting or terrifying. Maybe both.

I look at the white duvet cover, crisp and unassuming, and then at the carefully written clues in my notes app. The plan was to surprise him with a lingerie treasure hunt, then pose for him, taking pictures he could keep.

But now all I can think about is how much space I'm taking up in his home, how presumptuous this all feels—the lingerie, the clues, this version of playful intimacy I've dreamed up in my head. The confidence I saw in Sabrina has melted away, leaving me feeling like I'm...overstaying my welcome. Yes, I know Miles wants me. But I don't know if he wants all of me, or all of this. My cheeks burn, and I reach to put the camera and clues away before he gets home.

The dogs erupt into a tornado of barking. Cindy and Boppity spin around and skid out of the bedroom, racing like a herd of Chihuahua-phants down the stairs.

Which means...Miles is home.

Shit.

I don't have time to hide the evidence. Especially not when the sound of him padding up the stairs, with a canine entourage reaches me. He turns into the bedroom right as I freeze, caught red-handed taking the camera off the tripod.

He's wearing jeans, a navy blue Henley, and his glasses. A smile spreads across his lips as he takes in the scene. There's curiosity in his dark eyes, but it's good— like he's delighted.

"What's going on?" he asks, unable to mask the grin as his gaze lands on the camera I'm still fiddling with.

My throat works like I'm swallowing a stone. I feel completely caught, but there's nothing in his expression that says I'm taking up too much space. Instead, he follows it up with a playful, "Is this for me?"

He sounds so damn hopeful that it wrenches something free in my chest—a sob I didn't even know I'd been holding in. Or maybe I did. Maybe I shoved it down after class and now it's breaking loose.

"I was going to do this whole lingerie treasure hunt for you," I blurt, the words tumbling out in a hot mess. "I had clues and everything. But then, in class, I couldn't hear the teacher, and I felt so stupid."

I don't know if any of what I said makes sense, but in seconds he's crossing the room, closing the distance between us, cupping my cheeks, the dogs at his feet. "You're not stupid. Tell me what happened. I'm here for you."

And just like that, I bury my face in his shirt and do something I haven't done in years. I cry. Big, sniffling, ugly, snotty tears.

"She plays the music so loud, and I hate it," I hiccup. "I hate a lot of music. I hate it because I can't hear people. And I don't want to miss something someone says. But I don't know how to tell her it's too loud because I don't want any attention. I don't want any special treatment. I don't want to be difficult, and I definitely don't want people to think about me differently. I don't want them to treat me differently. My mother treats me differently, and I hate it. I just hate it." My voice breaks, and I bury my nose deeper into his shirt, like an animal burrowing into a den.

"How does she treat you differently?" His question is gentle, full of concern.

"She talks really loud. Like, in an exaggerated way. And she thinks she's being considerate. But she's not. It's just rude, but it's so hard to explain that to her, and when I try, she just says, 'I thought I was being helpful.' And what if I ask the teacher to turn down the music and she starts talking to me like that?" I flinch at the possibility, raw and visceral. "I don't want anyone to look at me differently," I whisper. My voice cracks as I push out the words I've been too afraid to say. "And what if...what if one day I can't hear the music well at all?" The thought feels like a chasm opening beneath me, one I'm not ready to face even though his expression is so open, and he's willing to hear me. Still, I walk it back as resolutely as I can manage with, "I should just enjoy it now."

Miles tugs me closer, rubs my back, sighs softly. "Sweetheart. Are you enjoying the loud music though?" His voice is gentle as he lets go of the embrace to guide me to the bed. He sits down next to me, taking my hand in his, meeting my gaze as the pups jump onto the duvet one by one, settling around us like little bed sentries. "Do you like going to pole class?"

I blink at him, startled. I hadn't expected that question. Taking a big, necessary breath, I let it fill my chest as I think about his words. "I like a lot of it," I admit. "I like being with my friends, learning new moves, feeling strong. But the dancing? I don't love it. And that's okay. I don't have to love every part of it." I exhale slowly. "I just wish I didn't have to do every part of it with my eyes." I pause, feeling horribly vulnerable. "Do you know what I mean?"

"I do." He runs his thumb along the top of my hand, back and forth, soothingly. "Do you want to keep going?"

"Yes," I say without hesitation. "I like enough of it to stay. I want to be with my friends, use my body, and feel healthy. I love being able to exercise and do all the things in this body that I can do well."

He nods, then rises, grabs a tissue, and hands it to me. "I hear what you're saying that you don't want to ask her to lower it, but for what it's worth I don't think that makes you difficult," he says, his voice soft, free of judgment. I understand why they call him The Professor—his tone isn't confrontational; it's thoughtful, steady. It calms my wild beast of a heart.

"I don't know..." I fumble for the right words. "Maybe it does."

He strokes my arm. "You know I went to PT for my ACL tear, right?"

"Yes."

"I went to this sports medicine clinic in Vancouver. For whatever reason, it was so cold in there I thought I'd freeze to death. But I didn't say anything. I just kept bundling up. I'm an athlete, right? A pro hockey player, no less. We're supposed to be immune to cold. Then one day, this older guy—the kind of guy who would tell stories about the fish he caught way back when—was doing some rehab for his hip surgery. He walked in one day and grumbled, 'It's colder than Santa's seat on the sleigh at cruising altitude.'"

I laugh, despite myself. "Why can I picture this crotchety old man so perfectly?"

Miles grins too, the warmth of it melting some of the hurt inside me. Then his smile fades, his expression turning serious. "It's not just you. I get that you feel like it's you right now. But it's okay that you can't hear them over the music, and it's okay to ask to turn the music down. You might not be the only one who thinks it's too loud. A lot of people don't like loud music. And even if everyone else can hear your instructor...so what?"

My brow knits. "So what...what?" I ask, pushing him to explain.

"They can still hear the music even if she turns it down. You're not hurting anyone by asking for her to lower it." He hesitates, his fingers flexing slightly against mine. "I know it's easier to tell yourself it doesn't matter though. I used to do that all the time after my injury— pretend I didn't need anything because I didn't want anyone to think I couldn't handle it. Joanne tried to help me, but I wouldn't let her. I thought if I admitted I needed help, it meant I was weak." He frowns, and there's hurt in his eyes, but maybe not regret as he brushes over the back of my hand with his thumb. "I don't miss her—we weren't right for each other. But I regret how I handled that. She wanted me to be vulnerable. She wanted to help me. Instead, I fed my own pain. I pushed her away because I was in such a spiral. But it didn't make me stronger; it made me lonelier. It's something I try not to do anymore."

I blow out a breath, noodling on that for several seconds, on whether the situations are the same. But before I can ask that—if I'm even going to ask it—he keeps going, perhaps sensing my question.

"I'm not saying it's the same. I just want you to know that in my experience it's not always better to think we can do it all ourselves. Hell, I've been to yoga classes where people ask to turn the lights up because it's too dark. Or they ask someone to move a mat because there isn't enough room. I've been at restaurants where they only have candlelight on the table, and my mom takes out her cell phone flashlight to read the menu." He squeezes my hand again, and it feels like he's imparting strength, or maybe just the wisdom of years—a wisdom of experience that I don't have yet. Maybe that's some of the difference in the ten years between us.

"It's not just you," he says gently. "I know it feels that way right now, but it's okay to ask for something you need. It doesn't make you weak; it makes you your own best advocate."

I try to picture asking Jewel to turn down the music. I close my eyes and see myself walking into the studio before class, before anyone else arrives, and asking for what I need. It makes me feel like one frayed nerve. But it doesn't feel as terrifying as it did before I told Miles.

"Maybe," I say, on a shuddery breath. "Maybe I'll do it."

He runs his knuckles along my cheek. "Maybe is a good start." His eyes hold mine, his gaze calm, thoughtful, passionate too. "And for the record? I'd do it for you. I'd walk right in there and ask them to turn it down. But I know that's not what you want."

I smile, a small, sad one as I shake my head. "It's not," I say softly, grateful that he knows I'm not looking for him to slay this dragon. I'm the only one who can slay it, and I'll have to do it in my own time if I do it at all. "It's not what I want. But thank you for knowing that."

He pulls me close and presses a kiss to my temple. "Thank you for telling me."

My throat tightens. There's more I want to tell him. That was only the beginning.

I want to tell him that I'm not only afraid of feeling stupid, but I'm deeply afraid that someday I won't even be able to hear that music I'd be asking her to turn down. I meant it when I let that fear slip. But I didn't share all my fears. Not only am I terrified that I won't be able to pick out a single note of music someday, but worse, the voices of the people.

The people I love.

No one knows what this loss will look like in the future. The doctors and the audiologists can only say what the typical path is for people like me. It worsens, yes, and hearing aids and advances in technology will *usually* do the trick—but no one knows for sure.

Diving into that though with Miles? Telling him that I'm afraid of a world that might one day be silent? It's too much. Too heavy. I can't put that on him.

Instead, I say something else that's true. "I was going

to...do this whole treasure hunt for you. With lingerie and pictures and hints. Maybe another time."

He squeezes my hand. "Let's watch a movie tonight."

We head downstairs and settle in on the couch with the dogs, and even though I know I can ask him to turn on the captions, and I'm about to, he's already fiddling with the remote and selecting them.

Without being asked.

My heart swells dangerously bigger.

38

LITTLE SNEAK

Leighton

The next morning, my chest tightens as I carry a travel mug of tea and my dad's favorite coffee. I'm here at his office because he loves coffee. Because he'll soon be busy with college visits for my sister. Because I love him.

I'm not here to preemptively spin fables about where I'm staying...and not staying.

That's what I tell myself as I step into his office doorway, the faint sounds of Michael Bublé playing from his computer—his Dad music. "Knock, knock," I say, holding up the two cups.

"Favorite daughter," he says, turning down the tune, then popping up with a grin. He takes the coffee, then gives me a quick hug.

Guilt pricks at me, and I fidget with my own cup. It's okay to have coffee with my dad, I remind myself.

He nods toward the seat across from his desk, and

before I can ask anything, he says, "How was dog-sitting? I trust it worked out?"

Trust.

That word digs at me. My stomach churns as I answer, "Yes, it was great. But now I want a dog."

He laughs. "I doubt your roommates would like that. All the more reason to think about getting your own place," he says, his tone light but nudging—a reminder he wants to help me make that happen.

But his words remind me, too, that he probably still thinks I'm living with Indigo and Ezra, the roommates from hell. I am, though—I haven't moved out. I'm just... not there right now.

"Maybe someday," I say, evasively. Then, after a pause, I force a shrug. "But I'm not done yet. I am still helping out since his mom's still away," I add, the lie scorching my tongue like acid.

It's not entirely a lie—I *am* helping out. But it's necessary to keep the details vague. Dad's never been a fan of me dating hockey players. *Most aren't ready to settle down,* he's said more than once. And it's too soon to know what'll happen next with Miles—the man who listens to me, who cares about me, who looks out for me without stepping in the way.

If Miles wasn't a hockey player, I'd probably tell my dad about him. But with that thought, another question follows: *Would you?*

I don't share details of my dates or my past romances with Dad. We don't have that type of relationship, and that's okay. So, it has to be okay that I'm not talking to him about Miles. It's not the time to tell my father anything. A bit of evasiveness keeps things simple, which is better for everyone.

"Good. That's what I figured," he says, in that confident way he has.

Right. Of course. He brokered this deal.

"Thanks again. It was blissfully...quiet," I say.

"Good. You deserve some peace at home," he says.

I wince at that last word. For a moment, he studies me, a flicker of curiosity in his eyes.

Quickly, I turn the conversation around to ask about the road trip, Riley, and this morning's photo shoot for the calendar.

But even as we talk, I can feel the weight of the lies sitting between us.

I don't think he can. And I don't know if that makes me feel better...or worse.

* * *

Good thing I have a meeting with Chanda next. It'll give me something else to focus on as I swing into a conference room in the marketing department to review the plan for the calendar. She already approved the first series of photos—on a Zamboni—and I'll be shooting those today.

As she's discussing the next round—a locker room melee scene with the pups, followed by a playful shot where the guys will sit in the stands with senior pups sharing seats next to them as if they're all watching a hockey game—some of my tension begins to dissipate.

"Your concepts are great," she says. "Really impressed with your creativity and your work. Glad Mako recommended you, and I've already been telling colleagues about you. You'll be a hot commodity when he returns."

"Wow. Thank you," I say, both thrilled and grateful. But guilt prickles at the edges of my excitement, a little like whiplash—the emotions pulling me in opposite directions.

It should feel good. Really, it should.

But as I leave the meeting, the uncomfortable feeling creeps back—the sense that I don't deserve that praise. A feeling, maybe, that I'm taking advantage of my situation. If everyone knew I was sleeping with Miles, would I still have this work? What do I do about this feeling though?

I glance at the time, mentally shifting gears to prep for the Zamboni shoot. Maybe I need to see Everly, talk to her about this, and figure out how to handle it. Just as I'm about to tap out a text to her, a familiar figure catches my eye at the end of the hallway.

Miles.

He turns the corner, and when his gaze finds mine, a wave of calm washes over me. A burst of happiness too. He's the one I want to share my days with. A quick nod to the stairwell door from him, and I follow without hesitation.

"How did it go with your dad?" he asks, leaning casually against the railing.

I make a see-saw motion with my hand. "Okay-ish?"

"Sorry," he says sympathetically.

"Not your fault."

"But it kind of is."

Is it though? Or is it mine? I can't spiral into those questions now, and I shake my head firmly. "It'll be fine," I say, trying to sound more confident than I feel. I don't want to bother him with these feelings when he has a lot to lose too. "Don't worry about me."

"But I do," he says.

"Let's do the shoot." If we stay here, I'll give into the urge to melt into him.

"You sure?"

"I am." As much as I want to talk to him, I want to look out for him too. It's the least I can do for him.

"You go first," he says with a hint of caution.

I push the door open and step out into the hallway, where my heart seizes. Rounding the corner ahead of me is the power trio: Clementine, Eleanor, and Zaire. AKA the GM, the owner, and the VP of marketing.

Panic flashes like lightning, but I lecture my primitive brain sternly. *You're fine. You're not doing anything wrong. Put one foot in front of the other.*

They're not even walking toward me, but headed in the opposite direction.

I straighten my posture, keeping my steps even and casual, while my pulse sprints ahead. What would they think if they knew the truth? Would they care? Would Chanda be less inclined to refer me to others?

This romance with Miles isn't against the rules of the team or the organization, but it feels like it is. Deep down, I know all this sneaking around is bound to catch up with us.

39

THE ZAMBONI OUTLAW

Miles

If I wasn't a hockey player, I'd be a Zamboni driver. Actually, scratch that. I want to be a Zamboni driver whose dog comes to work with him every day, sitting right next to me like this cool dude Frank here. He's a Pit Bull-Boxer-Cattle-Dog mix with a brindle coat that looks like it was ordered from the Cool Dog catalogue, and the senior mutt is sporting an excellent frosty face. Fitting for an old guy, since his chill factor is off the charts. He's just sitting here, hanging with me as I take the Zamboni for a spin around the rink before our game tonight, while the world's sexiest, most captivating woman takes pictures for the calendar.

My life right now is basically perfect.

"Why did I wait so long to drive a Zamboni again?" I call out to Tyler, who's lingering near the edge of the ice, holding onto a leash attached to a three-legged German

Shepherd. The dog has a wild energy, faster than most four-legged ones I've seen.

"Because you're an idiot," Tyler shouts back.

"Why have enemies when you can have brothers?" I yell as I steer around the oval, maybe showing off my mad Zamboni-driving skills for the photographer.

"Now hurry up and get off that thing before you get arrested again, like the time you tried to steal a Zamboni," Tyler says, making a "get on with it" gesture.

"I wasn't arrested," I say, scoffing as I make another loop.

Leighton lowers her camera a bit to smirk at me. "Of course you weren't, Miles. I'm sure you talked your way out of it." Her playful tone says she knows me so well, and the sound makes my chest tighten. She also seems more relaxed than when I ran into her an hour ago. I hate the thought of her unhappy or stressed.

"Maybe not arrested, but you were banned from the rink for a week." Tyler will just not let it go. "Basically the same thing for a hockey player."

"What'd you do, Prof?" Rowan calls from the tunnel. "Try to actually steal a Zamboni?" He's cradling a fluffball of a dog—some kind of Pomeranian-Chihuahua mix. "You need to get better at being an outlaw, Falcon. I've driven a Zamboni countless times and never got in trouble."

"He can't misbehave," Tyler shoots back. "He's gonna be co-captain."

"Not if Coach finds out about his checkered past," Rowan adds.

My grip tightens on the controls as my conscience threatens to ruin what should be a fun shoot, not a therapy session for me to exorcise my guilt about sleeping with, shacking up with, and oh, falling ass over elbow for the coach's daughter.

"You guys need to be better sports about waiting your turn." I manage to keep my tone even. "It's still my shoot."

Leighton clears her throat, stepping closer on the ice. "I hate to break it to you, Miles, but your ride's up. Everyone gets their moment with the Zamboni."

It pains me, but I stop driving. I have to follow *some* rules at least.

Rowan whistles. "Take that, co-captain. Get your ass off the Zamboni. It's my turn with Wanda the Wonder Dog."

I glance at the tiny fluffball in his arms. He already seems halfway attached to it, and I'd bet good money he'll take that dog home, maybe to his daughter, Mia, or maybe for himself. Either way, it's happening.

I hop off the Zamboni, giving Leighton a quick nod. "Admit it though. I'm an awesome Zamboni driver, right?"

"The jury's still out," she teases as she busies herself with the camera. I step closer, leaning in to peek at the shots on the screen. As I do, the faint scent of her lotion— that warm and sweet brown sugar and vanilla elixir—hits me, and my brain momentarily stalls. It takes everything in me not to press a kiss to the hollow of her throat. The locket she wore on our day together looked perfect against her skin there, a symbol of a future where I'd run into her in the hallway and we wouldn't have to dart into the stairwell. Where we could talk freely, touch lightly, interact without worry.

But could we ever have that future? What would that take?

A throat clears, sharp and intentional. It yanks me out of my spiraling thoughts. I glance up, half-expecting Tyler or Rowan, but the sound comes from the tunnel.

Coach is heading onto the ice, his eyes scanning the setup.

Oh, shit.

I straighten, ripping myself away from Leighton and trying to look casual. "What's up?" I ask, my voice steady even as my pulse races for entirely different reasons now.

Coach's face is implacable, unreadable, and it's terrifying. Did he notice me inhaling the scent of his daughter?

Leighton is much cooler than I am. "Hey, Coach," she says, easily. "You want to show them you're the best Zamboni driver ever?"

She masterfully keeps the convo about the Zamboni, and I could kiss her.

Only that thought's not helpful either.

"Maybe I will. It'd be good for them to see how it's done," he says, a dryly sarcastic reminder that he's in charge. When his gaze shifts to me, my stomach drops with the fear that he knows something—that he can see it in my eyes. "Leighton said the dog-sitting went well?"

It's not a tricky question, but my gut twists anyway. "Yes, it went great!" I blurt too loudly. "The dogs love your daughter."

Behind Coach, my brother's eyes widen, aiming question marks at me. *Did you really say that?*

"They think she's great. They're obsessed with her." I can't stop babbling. What the fuck is wrong with me? Am I talking about the dogs or me? "They can't wait to see her again," I add, trying to cover up the reality—that the dogs saw her a couple hours ago when we had breakfast together after I had her.

For fuck's sake, brain. Give a guy a break.

Coach tilts his head, no doubt piecing together the holes in my story, like *how would I know the dogs are obsessed with her since I'm supposedly not at home at the same time as the dogs and Leighton?*

My pulse hammers in my chest, and I force a grin that probably looks as shaky as I feel. Leighton, on the other hand, is steady as ever, her voice smooth as she jumps in. "That's what I told Miles, of course—that they love me. Not as much as they love their heated beds though."

"Tough competition," Coach tells her with a smile. His gaze is more serious when it turns toward me. "Now you've got a dog-sitter if you need help again."

He sounds eager to play matchmaker once more and that makes me feel decidedly worse.

"Absolutely," I say, forcing a grin.

When Coach walks away, Leighton lets out a breath, then meets my gaze for a split second in a silent acknowledgment that we dodged a bullet—thanks to her. I could barely handle the softball questions, which is not good for a guy trying to be co-captain.

I take off, my pulse still racing. I head to the weight room to burn off some adrenaline on the stationary bike. Fifteen minutes later, Tyler looms in the doorway, gesturing to my AirPods.

I pop them out and he strides in, shutting the door. It's just us.

He's quiet for a moment. Thoughtful, like he's just walked in on his kids finger painting the whole kitchen. "What's going on with you and Leighton?" His tone is curious rather than accusatory. An observation from someone who knows me so well.

"We're friends," I say impulsively as I pedal faster, focusing on the burn in my thighs rather than the lie on my lips.

Tyler nods a few times, like he's taking that in stride.

"You seem friendly," he says, and that cuts close. "But also, like you *really* like being friends with her."

The *really* is doing a lot of work in that sentence. "She's cool," I say, as flatly as I can.

He arches a brow, a sign he's not buying what I'm selling. "I hear you. I really do. But hear this—be careful."

I sigh, slow my pace, and nod. An admission of sorts. "I will," I say.

"There's a lot at stake," he adds, like I don't know that.

"I know," I say.

Because what else is there to say? So I shift gears, asking how things are going with his nanny situation. Then, we dive into the strategy for tonight's game.

But the whole interaction is unsettling.

And when I play that evening, I'm determined more than ever to hide all these fucking feelings for Leighton McBride.

Good thing it's a tough, tight game. There's no time to linger on things like feelings. Or to look for her in the stands. There's only time to focus on making plays.

And I do, nabbing a goal on Ford Devon's assist to help our team beat Vancouver in our barn tonight.

"That's what I like to see," Coach says when the game is over and he flips me the game puck in the locker room.

It's like he knew I needed it for beating my old team. I don't feel like I deserve it though.

40

A SIMPLER NEXT

Miles

That night, Leighton's waiting for me at my place, which feels all kinds of right. So I do my best to shake off the wrong feelings from earlier.

This woman curled up on my couch with my mom's dogs, sliding her thumb across her tablet, is, well, everything. I don't even know what she's doing on her tablet, but it looks like a calendar template, so that tells me it's the pictures. I like that she's doing it *here*.

That feels entirely right too—a clear and bright realization, one that's almost enough to erase the heaviness I feel.

"Hey," I say softly—soft in tone, not volume.

She's looking at me, so she can hear me. "Hi."

It's wild how one syllable from her makes my heart thump harder. Makes me want to get closer to her. I toe off my shoes and advance toward her, unknotting my tie as the dogs pop up to say hello.

Leighton raises an eyebrow. "Let me do that."

My heart fills up again, that guilt and unease slinking away. I sink down next to her, the crew hopping back up and surrounding us. I focus on her though, inching closer, and she reaches for the tie and undoes the green knot.

Her fingers on the silk, her skin near me, the scent of her hair—it's all so intoxicating. I want to just drown in the sounds and scents of her. Forget the shitty way I felt earlier. The guilt I'm carrying that's all of my own making.

"You won," she says, stating the obvious.

"You were there," I say, stating the same.

"I know," she says, then kisses my jaw so tenderly that I feel unsteady in an entirely good way.

I close my eyes. "I wanted to drive you home after the game," I say on a wistful sigh.

We discussed that—if she'd waited for me after the game and we'd left together, it might look...too obvious. She leaves when she's done taking post-game promo shots. She takes a Lyft—I installed my credit card on her app when I was gone in case she needed to take the dogs anywhere—and comes straight here.

Worst case, if anyone saw her? She could say she was letting the dogs out. Plausible enough.

But I hated driving home without her almost as much as I loved seeing her here. I can't stand the thought of Sunday, when Mom and Harvey return from their cruise and collect the dogs. When she might leave.

Opening my eyes, I glance at the clock on the wall. It doesn't tick out loud, but I swear I hear every second. Right now, though, I want to inhale as much of Leighton as I can get. So I bury my face in her neck and kiss her slow and tender, leaving imprints of my lips all over her.

New tattoos on her skin. Marks I want her to always have. More kisses, more moments, more...her.

She sighs softly against me, her fingers twisting gently through my hair, lighter than how she usually touches me. Leighton's fiery and tenacious, and she touches like that, too, most of the time—like a warrior goddess who knows how to fight. The same way she likes to fuck.

Right now, though, she's soft, a summer breeze, a wisp of a kiss.

And when she sets her hands on my chest and gently pushes me away, I understand why—there's something on her mind. Before I drown myself in her, she's got something to say.

"What's going on?" she asks, her eyes full of insight. "I don't think this is all about you wishing you could have driven me home after the game."

"What do you mean?" I ask, dodging it because I really just want to touch her, to forget how awful I felt earlier. To lose my feelings in her.

She smiles, the kind that says she'll allow my innocent question, but not for long. "I can sense your sadness. Your...guilt?"

I drag a hand down my face, then slump back into the couch. Of course she sees it. She's one of the most astute people I know. She can read the room. She can read situations.

She can read...me.

"Is it what happened earlier? With my dad?" she prompts. "It wasn't easy for me either, seeing him there, but I felt I needed to..." She doesn't finish. She doesn't have to.

"Yes, but it's also..." I begin, then push the back of my head against the couch, frustration digging into me. "It's

Tyler too. It's the fact that I'm so fucking obvious. You're so good at handling everything. Measured. You've got your shit together in front of everyone. Even me. And I'm supposed to be a team leader, yet every time I see you at work I act like the guy in high school trying to impress the girl."

Her smile is amused, and she's clearly delighted, but then it fades as she turns serious. "It's hard for me too. I feel like I'm holding back."

But does that mean we're supposed to do something about *this* yet? This thing between us? I've only been back in town for a few days. We've only been doing this—whatever this is—for a few days. No way can I pressure her to go all-in on a romance with me, even if I might think I'm ready.

Wait. Am I? I drift off for a beat. Is that actually what this heaviness in my chest is about? Not just the lying, but the growing awareness that maybe...just maybe...I know what I want.

I return to the here and now, my gaze traveling over the strong, centered, passionate, bold woman who's somehow interested in me too.

And I know—I don't want to give her up, no matter what.

It's a privilege—like touching her—to know your heart's desire. To know the cost.

I think I'd pay that price.

I'm almost certain I'm ready. Ready to face Coach's ire. Ready to handle whatever comes my way. Ready to face the fallout. Because the way I felt when I walked in the door moments ago? It was like the sun rising, illuminating the truth of the past year or so.

With Leighton, I feel like I can slow down. Enjoy the

present. Savor every second without thinking constantly about moving forward. I can just...*be*. But it's more than that—I can be happy, and holy hell am I ever happy with her. Every time I'm with her, I don't want the moments to end, and that feeling's intensified since I met her. I've been falling for her for more than a year. And even when we tried to stay away, I fell more. Even when we tried to be friends, I fell deeper. I look at her, this woman who makes me believe I can handle anything, and I know she needs to hear the truth—even the parts I'm not proud of. "I need to tell you something —when I was with Joanne, she asked me to be more vulnerable, and I said, and I was a dick about it, '*My knee is sliced in half—how much more vulnerable do you want me to be*?'"

Leighton's expression is etched in sympathy. "You were hurting," she says, exonerating me.

Maybe I deserve it. Maybe I don't. But I need her to know I've changed.

"I'm not proud of that moment. I wouldn't do that with you," I say, my voice as raw as my heart feels. "I don't want to do that with you."

"Then don't," she says, her voice steady, certain.

She's young and already so strong. She knows her worth. Knows what she wants. And maybe it is me. "I won't do that," I say, in a bare promise of who I want to be with her.

A better boyfriend.

I haven't said those words exactly. But that's what I want. I want to show her I can be that for her. I have plans for her. If she'll have me.

She cups my cheek. Her hand soothes some of the guilt away. "But it's also okay if you're human. You don't have to be perfect. You don't have to take it all on. I can take things on too."

"I know that, but I want to take things on for you," I say. If she'll let me. If she'll allow me to carry whatever burdens she needs carried.

"I know you will. You're amazing with me." She takes a breath, her eyes searching mine. "And don't let the past eat you up. We all say things we regret—it's what we do next that matters."

Next. I want all the nexts with her.

But I don't want to lose her with the intensity of my emotions. When my dad took off, I stepped up, learned to cook, handled the cleaning, looked out for my siblings, aced every class, helped in every way. I took everything on as I moved forward. But I'm not that kid anymore. I'm an adult, so maybe I can move forward one step at a time. Starting with a simpler next.

"Next," I say, turning the word over, tasting its sweetness, the possibility it holds. "I can't stop thinking about the fact that on Sunday night, you might leave. And I don't want you to leave."

Her lips twitch, and the hint of a smile she gives me feels like hope. "What are you saying, then?"

"I want you here," I say, an admission that sounds as helpless as I feel right now. "So damn much. It's all I think about, Leighton. That's part of why I felt awful earlier. Because when Tyler asked me about you, I said we were friends, and I felt as terrible lying to him as I felt lying to your father."

Something dark passes in her eyes. "I didn't like having to do that earlier today either. I don't know how long I can do it," she says, and that's the crux of the issue.

We're sneaking around. This thing with us is

borrowed time. Soon, we'll have to do what I've always done in life—move forward. Is she ready, though, like I think I am? "I don't like saying we're just friends. Though you are...a friend, and I love that," I say, taking a small step.

I love so much more about her, but I keep that inside.

Leighton challenges me gently, asking, "What are we, then?"

I hold her beautiful gaze, my heart beating so fast as I say, "So much more than friends. And I want you to stay for longer. Can you...can you just...stay?"

Maybe a few more days, weeks, and we can figure it out. Maybe then she'll know what I already know—that she's the one for me.

"No one has to know," she says, almost like a question.

"No one," I confirm, since her yes is all I want.

"Just us," she adds.

"You and me," I say out loud, and in my head I tell myself I'll show her that I can be not just a better boyfriend—but the best one. And maybe then she'll be where I am. Ready too.

"You and me," she says, reaching for my hand.

I squeeze her fingers and it feels like a promise for a future.

Then she nods to the stairs. "Right now, though, there's something I want to do."

I follow her. I'd follow her anywhere.

* * *

"A do-over."

Leighton's words shimmer in the night air as she leads

me into the bedroom. Her camera is perched on the tripod and positioned toward the bed.

A do-over for the day we spent together that started in her studio, and also a do-over for last night.

Except as I glance around the bedroom—*ours*, this is definitely our bedroom—I wonder if she planned a sexy treasure hunt again. I scan for the evidence, but of course she'd hide lacy things better for a geocacher like me. I've got a feeling though—a gut feeling—that she means something else. Something that makes my cells crackle with excitement.

When she meets my searching gaze with mischievous blue eyes, she asks, "Are you ready?"

She has no idea. "I'm always ready for you," I say.

She tugs on my loosened tie. "Do you still like pictures, Miles?" It's a tease of a question.

"If you're in them," I tell her, running the backs of my knuckles down her cheek.

"Do you still like pictures of both of us?"

Heat roars through me, a scorching fire raging in seconds. "I do."

"Do you still get off to them?"

I'm a five-alarm blaze now. This woman has my number. "You know I fucking do, sweetheart."

She nibbles on the corner of her pretty, glossy pink lips. "Then let's take some pictures of you and me."

You and me.

The three words I said earlier. It's like she's reinventing them. She's turning them into something wholly new. Something unbearably sexy. Something that's just for us. And as she unbuttons my shirt, she affirms that, saying, "Just for us."

"You're the photographer. We're the subject," I tell her, giving her all the permission she needs.

She grabs her little trigger remote from the night-stand, the one she used more than a year ago in her studio. Moving behind the camera, she fiddles with some settings. When she comes around the front once more, she says, "Kiss me the way you want to."

I take that filthy invitation and I RSVP. I crush my lips to hers, giving her a hot, deep kiss that goes to my brain. All my synapses are firing, right along with the camera. She must be pressing the trigger, since the Nikon is click-ing. My mind is frying and I'm alive and electric with the desire for her. And...with this pulsing need to see what we look like. I don't know when she'll snap the next ones but I don't want to waste a second.

After I give her one more deep possessive kiss that has her melting in my arms, I make quick work of her clothes. Tugging off her shirt, kissing her neck, fiddling with the hooks on her bra. For a second, I consider the implica-tions. She'll be shirtless on camera. But one look at how fearless she is and I know this is what she wants. I know, too, that she's in control—that remote in her hand, and the camera she owns are the proof.

I unhook the bra, dropping it onto the bed, because you should be nice to lingerie. Cupping her tits, I bury my face between them, kissing between the valley. Drawing the right nipple into my mouth and sucking, biting, grazing my teeth along it until she's panting in my arms, all while taking pictures of us. Talk about a multi-tasker. I give the other one the same treatment since fair's fair when it comes to nipple play.

She clicks, then gasps an "aah." Grabbing my head with one hand, she breathes out hard and yanks my mouth to hers. She kisses me for a few dizzying seconds all while grappling at my shirt again, hastily shoving it off me while still snapping pictures.

For fuck's sake, she's incredible. The way she takes pictures while undressing me is the sexiest thing I've ever experienced.

Now, I'm shirtless. That's nothing new. Nothing that hasn't been seen on social media a thousand times over. But this is different. Because these images are only for us. Knowing that, I break the kiss but pull her against me, wrap my arms around her then urge her, "Put your arms around me."

She loops her bare arms around my neck, then presses the button again. I can hear the click of the camera capturing us skin to skin, holding each other in a moment of unchecked desire, but more so...of total trust.

The sound stops and I meet her gaze. There's so much in her blue eyes—this passion that matches mine, and I hope...the emotions too. But for now, I focus on the physical, asking, "Limits. What are your limits on camera?"

"It's my camera. As much as you want."

She's so fucking fearless. Me too, but I'm also torn. Half of me wants to keep sex itself ephemeral, a memory for our minds only. The other, greedy, dirty part of me wants it all on film. "I want everything till I fuck you. And maybe even that," I say.

"I guess someone wants it all," she teases, then holds up a finger and slips away to the bathroom, likely taking out her hearing aids. I've learned that's how she prefers to fuck.

When she returns to me, she lifts her chin. "Take my clothes off."

That's all she needs to say.

I'm stripping her bare, peeling off her jeans, then standing in front of her where she's wearing only a pair of pale pink panties. I drop to my knees as she pushes the button, capturing me worshipping her like she deserves. I look up at her and I'm keenly aware of the position, what it says, and more so what it means about us. She is a goddess. She is *my* goddess. One hand sifts through my hair, the other takes pictures as my hands circle her waist. I kiss her belly, then lower still and slowly, deliberately peel off those panties.

My engine revs and I groan, need pulsing through me, hot and electric as she steps out of them. I pop up so I can lift her and put her on the edge of the bed. With my back to the camera, and most of her shielded by me, I say, "I want to know how you look when I go down on you."

She shudders, a full body tremble moving through her. She doesn't answer with words. She answers with deeds, grabbing at my slacks and undoing them, then shoving them down my hips. I yank them off, and I'm wearing only my boxer briefs when she pushes my right shoulder down so I can kneel in front of her on the bed.

"Like this," she instructs, the photographer positioning her subject.

She leans back, her chestnut hair spilling down her back, her perky tits pointing up, her lovely legs spread for me. The controller in her hand.

My gorgeous, sexy, daring woman.

She's a gift, and she's unwrapped herself for me. I bury my face between those pretty thighs and I kiss her sweet, hot pussy on camera.

In seconds she's panting and moaning, but the camera's not clicking.

Pride floods me. She's so into this she forgot to trigger

the shot. I stop for a second, squeeze her thigh to get her attention. When she lifts her face and locks eyes with me, I arch a brow. "Take a picture. It lasts longer."

Her eyes widen, flickering with surprise and filthy delight. "Yes, sir."

She raises her hand and makes a show of pushing the button on the remote. Again and again, and the Nikon clicks, recording the back of my head, some of her face— who even knows. Her fingers rope through my hair again as I lick and kiss and suck.

But I don't let her forget her job. "Push the button, baby," I tell her once more when the camera's gone silent.

"If you insist," she says.

"I really fucking do," I say, in a tone that brooks no argument.

She obeys, then rocks against my mouth, wet and slick and needy and almost there. A flick of my tongue, a kiss from my lips, a finger crooked inside her, and she's shaking, shuddering, then dropping the remote, which I'll call a victory. Then she shouts my name as she comes on my lips for no one to see later.

That's okay. The memory's seared on my mind.

I'm more aroused than any man has a right to be. I'm ravenous to look at all these photos right fucking now.

But first I need to live the rest of it. No, I *get* to live the rest of it.

Turbocharged by lust, I stand and I stare at the beauty in front of me, flushed cheeks, pink spreading all over her chest, breasts heaving.

I grab her chin, roughly tug her toward me the way she likes. "I made a decision."

"What do you want, Falcon?" she asks. It's a challenge and I love it.

"I want it all," I tell her roughly.

Her eyes sparkle, and I can tell I gave her the exact right answer. "You want us fucking?"

Thank god she's kinky in all the best ways. The ways that match mine. "You perfect, dirty girl. I want you on all fours. Remote in your hand and you taking pictures when I fuck you good and hard and make you come again and again."

For a second or two, she hesitates, and I try to read what concerns her. But then I don't have to because she points to a standing mirror in the corner of my bedroom. "Move the mirror so I can see your face."

That's it. I'm done. My heart jumps so hard, it's official. I'm so fucking in love with her. I bend down, cup her cheek, and give her a soft, quick kiss before letting go. "You're fucking perfect, and I love that you told me exactly what you need."

Because as I stride over to the mirror, I get the double meaning here too. This way, with me behind her, she can still see my face if she needs to *see* what I'm saying, to *hear* me with her eyes.

Naked and lithe, she stretches out on the bed.

Our bed.

Ours.

Everything feels like ours, and I hope she travels to where I am emotionally. But I can do my part in getting her there—by being the best boyfriend there is. And part of being a good boyfriend is listening. I move the mirror so she can watch us—I can watch us too—then grab a condom and shed my boxer briefs.

On the bed again, I climb over her, kiss her sweet mouth, then pull back. "Do whatever you need to do with your camera. But I need to get inside you and then get off to it tomorrow."

She gasps, wriggling under me, kissing me more.

"Leighton," I warn. "Do it now. Your man is going to make you come so fucking hard again."

"So cocky," she teases, then hustles behind the camera. When she returns to me, she grabs the remote and gives me the most provocative stare. "Make me forget to take pictures."

"I'll make sure you remember," I taunt right back before I grab her, tossing her onto the bed the way she likes being handled.

Rough.

I haul her up by her hips to all fours, position her so she's facing the camera, then yank her pretty body into place. As her tits sway beautifully, the camera clicks, capturing us.

My sexy shutterbug is already taking pics.

As I run a hand down her back, as I slide on a condom, as I notch the head of my cock against her wet pussy, the camera clicks again and again. The sound of it cranks me up. It's the sound of her setting the pace, dictating the rules, recording the filthy, beautiful moments we share. Time for me to move it along, so I sink in, my breath stuttering out of my chest in a rush at the tight, hot feel of her. She's watching me in the mirror. And I know now it's not just so she can see my lips move. She's watching every detail of the way we fuck, studying every reaction of mine as I fill her, cataloguing how the pleasure, the heat, the tightness, makes me shake with lust.

I meet her dirty gaze in the reflection. "Watch me," I tell her in the glass.

"I can't look away," she says breathily, her hand curled around the remote, triggering shot after shot.

I ease out, raise a hand, and smack her ass as I slide back in. She yelps and it's gorgeous. "You like that," I say. It's not a question at all. It's a statement.

Still, she answers with a shuddery, "God yes."

I do it again, lifting the same hand, easing out, sliding in, and swatting her ass.

She moans, her face twisting with pleasure. She's not too far gone though. She presses the button. Another click. I ease out. Lift my other hand.

Smack. Click. Fuck.

Soon we find a filthy rhythm. Of triggers. Clicks. Slaps. Thrusts. Moans. And us, as I say to her in the mirror, my jaw ticking, my bones tight with need, "I love fucking you."

It's simple. It's not sophisticated dirty talk. But it's pure, raw truth.

"I love when you fuck me," she pants out.

I piston my hips, pumping into her, taking her, and listening for all her cues. Watching them, too, like when her grip loosens. Her hand uncurls. The clicks stop as her breath comes faster. I cover her, my chest pressed to her back, then I slide a hand over her tits up to her throat, and I curl my palm around her. The noise she makes is a needy, desperate whimper.

"One more, baby. Give us one more picture," I urge.

"You do it," she says, like she's too drugged out on the pleasure to think.

I reach for the remote by her hand and press the button. Not artfully like her. But bluntly as I fuck my woman. I fuck her on camera. I fuck her in the mirror. I fuck her on the bed. And I record it for us as I give it to her exactly how she wants it because she gives me everything I want—*her*. At some point, I stop clicking and it's just us, two people who can't get enough of each other as I fuck her to another orgasm. And her sounds, and her screams, and her cries wring a powerful one out of me, too, as we fall apart together.

Watching us in the mirror.

* * *

Later, when we're cleaned up, she brings her tablet into bed with us. She's downloaded the pictures to a password protected folder. She shows me every single one. It's the hottest slideshow I've ever seen.

"That's you and me," she says.

I kiss her temple. "You and me."

And it feels like the start of a whole new future.

Only, there's so much I have to figure out. So much I'd have to say to someone—one person I respect immensely.

But most of all what I need to figure out is if she's as all in as I am. Because that's what matters most.

41

THE GREAT SORTING

Leighton

Fine, *fine.* Birdie was right. Miles *is* a chef. He shows off his kitchen skills over the next several secret days and nights at his home, after he returns the four-pack to his mom's.

I miss them fiercely. I kind of wish, too, I could have gone with him to return them. But that might have opened us up to too many questions—questions neither of us wants to face right now.

But his mom and Harvey are traveling to their hometown of Seattle soon to see both Patti LuPone and old friends, so there may be more dog-sitting in my future.

For now, there are nights with him in between an away game here or there.

One night he whips up homemade pizza with artichokes and olives, along with a perfect kale salad drizzled in a delicious olive oil. Another night he crafts a buttery mushroom risotto and asparagus that makes my tastebuds weep in happiness, serving it alongside a salad of spring greens dusted with an olive oil I deem mouth-watering. Then it's arugula and hearts of palm, and after one bite at the counter, I declare the olive oil exquisite.

Miles smirks like he has a secret.

"What's that for?" I ask.

"You."

"I figured as much. But why?"

"You, Shutterbug, have fancy taste in olive oil."

"That so?" I ask, unsure what he's getting at.

"I've been secretly testing out various olive oils for you the last several nights."

My jaw drops. "You're tricking me," I say, but I'm hardly mad.

"Maybe. But now I know your favorite—the most expensive one. That way, I can always make what you like best," he says, and that makes my heart flip. "And make you happy."

"It's working," I say, feeling all kinds of fizzy.

"Good. I'll keep making your favorite things," he says, then pours me some more Riesling, with a nod to the pretty white wine. "And keep them here for you too."

He lifts his tumbler of amber liquid and we toast to my *exquisite taste in olive oil and men*. I clink my Riesling to his vile scotch. But it doesn't taste so vile when I kiss it off his lips.

In fact, the kiss is as exquisite as the sex is hot when he takes me upstairs and bends me over the bed.

I think I like this little arrangement a lot. I like, too, the text message that Melissa sends me that evening.

Melissa: I think I'm ready!!!

. . .

I write back immediately telling her how happy I am to hear that, and that we'll find a time soon.

Everything feels like it's falling into place.

* * *

"Do I *finally* get details now? You've been holding out on me," Maeve says with an over-the-top pout as we step out of Effing Stuff, the cutest little tchotchke shop on Fillmore Street the next day. The shop smells like lavender and lemon, and its shelves are crammed with quirky treasures, fun mugs, and playful decor—including Maeve's love lessons mirrors. They're flying off the shelves; we just dropped off several new boxes. I'm seriously proud of her, and I've told her as such many times.

"Have I been holding out?" I tease, but I know I have since the memory of last night rushes hot and bright through me on this Tuesday morning, along with all the things we've done the last two weeks—movie nights at home, reading together on the couch—him with his thought-provoking sci-fi allegories or books on human behavior, me with photography tomes. Then, our secret dates at Birdie's coffee shop. Maybe someday soon I'll join him with his geocaching club, but not yet.

Maeve stops and stomps her foot. "Yes!" She keeps walking. "You made me do all *this* work stuff first. So, now it's time. Dish."

Gladly. My secret nights and days are too good to keep from a friend. "It's been two weeks, and we've pulled it off —this secretly-living-together thing," I tell Maeve, and I can't strip the giddiness from my tone. Nor do I want to.

"Impressive," she says, her voice warm with approval. "I tripped up so many times in the early days with Asher."

I nod, remembering the chaos of their accidental Vegas marriage. Brunches, dinners—pretending to be a real couple while navigating their very real, very messy feelings. And yet, somewhere along the way, they became everything to each other. "It's easier for me, though, since we're not a public thing like you two were," I say, a little defensively, but not because she's attacking me.

"Right. Sure," she says. "But I'm still impressed you've done it."

It's a compliment from a friend. I know it is. And yet, I feel a little icky. "It just makes sense right now. It's... prudent," I say but my chest tightens at the justification of our secrecy. "My dad's too busy juggling his job and raising my teenage sister solo to keep tabs on me. He's either at the rink or having dinner in Mill Valley with Riley. It's not like he'd even know where I was staying."

That's what I have to tell myself. Because what's the alternative? I'm simply not ready to tell my father about my feelings for one of his star players. I'm still sorting them out. And he doesn't need to be a part of The Great Sorting.

"That's good," Maeve says, but her brow furrows. "We had the opposite problem—everyone expected us to live together."

I glance at my artist friend, her pace slowing as we stroll up Fillmore. The easy rhythm of our conversation falters when she turns to me and asks thoughtfully, "But what happens next?"

My stomach knots. "You mean how long will we keep this up?"

"Yes," she says gently, her concern laced with kindness.

I don't answer right away. My thoughts bump into each other—the way I feel for Miles, but also how sticky the situation is. How long can it go on like this? But then, there are all my own fears too—of the future and what it holds for me. I just don't know what that means for romance, for a partner, or for how I might want to, or more so, *need to* live my life. "I don't know," I admit honestly. "It's a lot to figure out—how to time everything right. I don't want to shock my dad or hurt him, especially this early in the season. Plus, Riley's already looking into where she might want to go to college, so the two of them are trying to squeeze in some college visits when he has a day off here and there. He's ridiculously busy. And there's just...other stuff too," I say since some things you need to sort out for yourself.

Maeve nods thoughtfully, understanding passing in her eyes even if she doesn't know the specifics of my fears. "You don't have to have all the answers right now."

It's a relief to hear that from her—maybe exactly what I needed this morning. "And..." I hesitate, before another truth springs free. "I want to be sure. I'm only twenty-four. Do you really meet *the one* at this age?"

Her smile is a little sly as she says, "I met Asher when I was nineteen."

"But you became friends," I say, pointing out the obvious. "You didn't fall for him till ten years later."

"True," she acknowledges, sighing too. "A lot's at stake. You want to be sure, especially if it's scary."

I do want to be certain. At my age, what are the chances that this is...the big love? Should I upend so many lives for something that might not be? "Exactly. It's good to be practical. To be certain," I say, my fingers drifting to the flower stud earrings Miles gave me more than a year ago—I've never stopped wearing them, but is that the same as being sure he's the one? Questions plague me, and my muscles tighten with worry as my mind whirs. But rather than carry this alone, I turn to Maeve, stopping on the street corner and blurting out, "What if this is the wrong time in my life? There's so much I want to do work-wise—I even have some great ideas about how to expand my business to help with the rent situation at the studio. The job will end soon enough with the Sea Dogs, but I came up with a plan yesterday when I was at the arena, and I've been working out the details in my head." My heart beats faster, but it's the kind of speed that comes from being chased. "Is now even the time in my life to…"

Her smile is soft, full of wisdom as she says, "To fall in love?"

I wince. "Yes, it's kind of awful—falling for someone."

That cracks her up. "Yes, yes it is."

But will it last? Is it the kind of thing that's worth all the upheaval? "I want there to be no question," I say.

"I hear you." She pauses, squeezes my arm briefly. "And what I really hear is you need more time, friend."

And that word—*time*—settles my wild thoughts. She's right. That's exactly what I need. "I do. Thanks. I didn't even realize how much I needed to hear that."

She lets go. "I'm always here to share whatever little wisdom I might happen to have."

"I'd say you have a lot."

"Love you. I'm proud of you. Tell me about your business idea next time I see you."

"I will and I'm proud of you too," I say since you

should always tell your friends they're amazing. "Love you too."

We part ways and I feel more calm, thanks to her. As I head to High Kick to meet Miles, I try to let go of the questions that chase me. The how, the when, the will it work?

A few minutes later, my pulse races in a new way, fluttering with excitement once more. Even though I saw him this morning at home, these secret dates are special—necessary even. I have my trusty camera with me so I'll take the latte and pastry pictures, but the flicker inside me comes from knowing I'll see him in public.

But where it's safe to see him.

Like Maeve said, I do need time. And I also need this kind of *time* with Miles. This almost feels like a real romance—dates, shared moments, a glimpse of what life together could be.

As I push open the door, passing the glittery Dolly, I leave the rest of San Francisco behind. Birdie flashes me a knowing smile from behind the counter, grabs a brownie, and hustles around it. With the treat in hand, she ushers me to the back of the café.

"A table for *Cindy* is ready," she says, and yep, with her use of the dog's names for us, she's definitely earned her admission into The Underground Grandma Matchmaking Society.

Miles is here already with a new mason jar of wildflowers for the table, but they have different colors this time—peaches and plums, and the fact that he's mixed up the assortment every time we've met here is so very him. So is the affection in his dark brown eyes. It's hard not to fling myself at him. To rise up on tiptoes when he stands, to kiss him here, then beyond the doors.

But I dig my nails into my palms, a reminder that we're here as...friends.

It's not the brownie I can't wait for. It's the moment when I'll have no more questions.

Today, though, I'm ready for another step—a smaller one, but an important one nonetheless. "You asked about my rent the other week, if I wanted to talk about it," I tell him after Birdie brings me a tea and him an espresso.

"I did," he says, his eyes sparkling, clearly eager for me to share.

"So I actually had this idea when I was shooting the tunnel picture of you yesterday for the calendar."

He holds up a hand. "If this is about a Miles-only centerfold calendar, I should warn you—it's strictly a one-person distribution."

I laugh, but the laughter softens as I focus on my plans. Nerves flutter in my chest, but I share them anyway. "Speaking of, that's kind of my idea."

His brow arches. "You're saying people would be more interested in buying a calendar of you?"

"In a way," I say, then explain. "I was thinking of offering boudoir sessions for some of the players' wives and girlfriends—like Melissa, maybe Christian's wife, or Freya, Alexei's girlfriend—and making calendars they could gift their partners."

The delight on his face is undeniable, and it tells me I've hit on a good idea. "Is that why you were looking at calendar templates on your tablet the other week?"

I nod, surprised, but delighted he remembers that. "I was brainstorming, and it hit me—it's a perfect extension of what I'm already doing. Melissa wants to do a shoot, so I'm excited to pitch the idea to others too."

He leans closer, his voice warm. "I love the way your brain works. I love that you're sharing this with me."

"Sharing isn't really my forte, but maybe it can be," I say.

"It can," he says, and I know it's true—I just had to get there on my own. "But I do have one suggestion."

"Hit me," I say, emboldened by his support.

"I think you should raise your prices."

My face goes blank for a second. "Really?"

"You're worth it," he says, his voice steady and certain, like it's the most obvious thing in the world. "Your landlord raised the prices, and you're a phenomenal photographer who makes clients feel beautiful and empowered. Maybe just five percent, but it's time. You're worth it."

You know what? He's right.

I am.

Soon, he heads to the rink to work out, and I stop by Hush Hush to make sure I have everything I need for my next set of shoots.

I don't love showing up at the Sea Dogs arena with him—it feels too public, too risky—so arriving separately also makes everything easier.

In the early afternoon the bus drops me off for another calendar shoot. This time, I take playful shots of Little Friends' adoptable mutts causing mayhem in the locker room—chewing on skates, chasing pucks, or sitting triumphantly on the benches.

As the guys shift into pre-game mode, I put my camera in the bag and swing by Melissa's cookie cart near the concession area.

"If you're ready, I am too," I say.

She draws a big, nervous breath but grins. "Sexy and sweet, here I come."

Sexy and sweet. The words spark something—an idea that clicks perfectly into place. Her sweet with my sexy. "Would you ever want to do a collab?"

"I love partnering with smart, savvy businesswomen," she says. "Tell me more."

Within ten minutes, we're brainstorming packages of lingerie-shaped cookies and sexy pics for boudoir-themed bridal showers, bachelorette parties, and other events. We even schedule a time for her session.

Maybe this is part of what I needed with time—time to see that I can keep growing my business. That I can give my work the attention it deserves and I want.

When the game starts, I take my spot in the stands. My good mood flickers momentarily when I see my dad in his suit, game face on, leading his players. I don't want to keep lying to him, but I know I need to be certain before I say anything.

I do my best to push the thought aside, letting the fast pace of the game pull me in, feeling a connection to Miles that's both wonderful and a little painful. I want to cheer louder for him. The loudest, actually. I want to wear his jersey. He's never asked me to but I know he'd love it, especially considering how wild it made him the night I wore it on the dog-cam. I want to wave to him. To wait for him. To be the one who asks how he feels after a win or loss and to listen no matter how he feels. I want to be the safe space for him to open his heart to not just in his home, but out of it. But does that mean I'm ready to take this terrifying step into a future I've tried to meticulously, painstakingly plan for?

I shudder, wishing I had all the answers and trying vainly once more to focus on the ice. It's hard to separate thoughts of him from the game. But by the time intermission starts, I'm ready to focus on my next shot.

Sabrina glides onto the ice with an effortless grace, her skating style both fun and athletic. She tosses T-shirts into the crowd, her spins and axels breathtaking, her energy infectious. It's hard to look away from her, and I'm pretty sure no one does.

When the game ends, I meet Everly near the locker room to snap a shot of Sabrina with some of the guys on the team.

Including Miles's brother, who seems determined to get in the shot. Or at least on saying hello. Maybe he noticed her at the end of intermission, skating off the ice? I bet he did.

"Wow," Tyler says, stepping into the corridor as Sabrina approaches. His tone is casual, but there's a flicker of curiosity in his eyes. Maybe intrigue. "You were amazing."

Whoa. Did Tyler just single out her figure-skating moves?

Sabrina smiles at him. "Thanks. You're not so bad yourself."

"I do my best," he says dryly.

Everly must notice their interaction since her eyes light up. "Why don't we take a picture of you two on the ice?"

Tyler fights off a smile, offering a stoic, "Sure."

She guides them back down the tunnel, and I follow. Once there, I snap their photo, and the way he wraps an arm around Sabrina tells me everything I need to know. The dude has a serious crush.

But the glint of a ring on her finger reminds me that Tyler's crush might be real, but it's going nowhere.

Later, at Miles's house, I show him the photo of the two. "I think your brother has it bad for the taken figure skater."

Miles studies it, a smirk shifting his lips. "Yeah, that's definitely a crush. Better luck next time, little brother," he says with a chuckle.

Then he pulls me in for a kiss—one that's interrupted by my phone buzzing.

I grab it and check the screen. My dad. He's sent a picture of Riley and me—from his digital frame. In it, we're holding mugs at a diner. It's from a couple years ago. *Before* I started lying to him, only he has no idea that's how I'm marking time. My stomach drops as I read his note.

This was fun! We should grab breakfast again soon. I've been slammed with college stuff. What are you up to tonight?

My face burns with guilt as I type back a lie. ***Just editing photos.***

The truth presses at the edges of my thoughts, demanding its release. I wish I didn't have to lie—but I'm not ready for the conversation that comes with the truth.

Not yet. But maybe with a little more time.

42

MORNING TEA

Leighton

"It would be silly to think it would never come up," I say, for what feels like the tenth time the next morning as I rush around Miles's place, grabbing my things so I can get to the arena. Am I supposed to get there before him today? Or after?

"Right, but still, I wish you didn't feel this way," he says, watching me as I yank open my camera bag on the coffee table, checking to make sure I have everything. Do I?

"Me too, but what can you do?" I mumble, my thoughts racing too fast to focus on anything but the job. Today means more calendar shots, which means more Miles and my dad in the same vicinity. My gut churns. I glance at Miles as he sips his coffee, leaning against his kitchen counter. "Am I going first, or are you?" My voice sounds like it's stitched together from pure dread.

He sets the mug down and steps toward me, his hands

coming to rest on my shoulders. "You are. But I can take you if you want."

I shake my head quickly, side to side. "No, I'll catch the bus. It's fine. It's totally fine. We can only really arrive together every now and then. Too much and..."

No point finishing that sentence—*someone will find out.*

The silence spreads for several seconds, and everything feels heavy. "Leighton, we could do something about the way you feel," he offers gently, but his gaze holds mine with clear intent, those deep brown eyes soft but serious.

I could ask, *What do you mean?* but I know exactly what he means—he means come clean. He means admit we're together. But even though I felt ready last night at the game as I pictured all the things I truly want in my heart, admitting them out loud could spiral my life out of control right when so many good things are happening— the collab, the calendars for the players' wives and girlfriends, my boudoir work. Riley's college visits, the team's strong record, Miles's season, my dad's season—everything. Just everything. It could lead to my dad being disappointed in me. To him shunning Miles. To damaging Miles's reputation. Letting the world know the coach's daughter fell for a player—against her father's wishes.

"I need to get to work," I say instead, and my voice wavers in a way I hate. "I'm meeting Melissa too. She has some ideas about our collab." I scoop up my things and head toward the door, but he stops me, his hand firm and steady on my arm.

"Breathe. Let me call you a Lyft," he says.

I realize I'm practically gasping, my chest tight, breaths shallow and uneven. But he's right—a few extra minutes in the car might help. "Okay. Thank you."

"Of course." After he books the ride, he presses a soft

kiss to my forehead, pulling me into his arms. "Have I mentioned I love having you here?"

Warmth spreads through me, chasing away some of the tension. "Maybe."

"Well, I do. I want you here," he says firmly, his arms still around me. When he finally steps back, his expression turns serious. He's not wearing his glasses today, probably because he's heading straight to the rink. "And I meant what I said. We could do something about this."

Yes, we could. But I can't think about what that would mean—not now. I need to get to work.

* * *

Once I'm at the Sea Dogs arena, my mission is singular—set up for the team calendar shoot. This one should be easy enough: players on the bench with some senior pups next to them. I'll head to the ice first, check the lighting, and get ready.

Get ready to act like I'm not falling for Number Twenty-One.

Ugh. I hate this feeling.

I try to slough it off as I pass Ruben at the doors. "Hope you enjoyed the chocolate," he says, waving me in.

My brow furrows. "What?"

"The ones your dad got," he says. "They were amazing."

I have no idea what he's talking about, but I can figure it out later. Except...I'm not sure I can wait. Something pulls me toward my father's office. Maybe my own worries? My need to know what's going on? Yes, that's it.

When I reach his office, my stomach dips, but I knock. Dad looks up, beckoning me closer.

"Come in," he says, lowering the music. Ella Fitzgerald this time.

"What's going on? Ruben mentioned something about —" My gaze lands on a box of chocolates on his desk. From Elodie's. The same place I gave him chocolate from a couple months ago. Relief floods me. He probably picked some up this morning on the way to work. That's all. I was twisted up about nothing.

"Nice chocolate," I say lightly.

He says nothing for a beat. "I walked past the shop last night and saw these—they're made with green tea so I thought of you and grabbed them," he finally admits. "It's not too far from your place. But when I went to drop them off, I discovered you aren't staying there anymore."

Guilt roars through me, hot and shameful. He went to my apartment—the one I supposedly share with Indigo and Ezra. My heart hammers painfully.

"I..." I begin, but this is foreign terrain. I swallow, trying to get a grip on...anything.

"Indigo said you haven't been there in a while. Everything okay?"

It's asked with such fatherly concern that my heart nearly breaks.

I'm a liar.

A shameful, awful liar. And my dad doesn't deserve that—not from me. Not after my mom. Only, I do it again.

"I've...actually been staying at Miles's place. It's just been so much easier to stay there," I ramble. "He has a lot of space. Two floors and all. He has a guest room, you know, and it even has an en suite..."

Then I'm going on about how it's quiet there, how I don't have to deal with the fighting, how I can focus on editing photos, how he and I are friends, and it's easy, so easy, and technically that's all true. I have been staying there. We are friends. He does have a lot of space. The quiet helps me immensely.

But it's still a lie.

Dad relaxes—somewhat. "Good. I'm glad," he says, but his tone is a touch distant.

It cuts deeper than I'd have expected, that small shift in his voice. He's giving me grace I don't deserve, and I hate myself for taking it.

When I leave, I feel like my mother.

43

THE NOW

Leighton

That evening, the feelings haven't dissipated. They've worsened, like this morning was the first cough of a cold, and now it's turned into a full-on fever as I return to Miles's home, punching in the code and stepping inside. He's finishing up a meeting with his agent, so I'm alone.

And I try to breathe in the silence. To enjoy the space. To revel in all the reasons I told my dad I'm here.

But I still feel uncomfortably like my mother.

And I hate it.

I pace, flashing back to this morning, to Miles's words.

Flipping to my chat with Maeve.

Cycling back to all the times I've spent with Birdie.

Then lingering in the memories of how I feel with Miles.

I pace in the quiet, and I weigh them. On one hand, I can't stand the way I feel right now.

On the other hand, I think I—

The door snicks open, and I spin around. He's home.

His brown eyes are soulful. His hair is wild. His gaze, locked on me.

"Leighton," he says, importantly. Like there's something on his mind.

But there's something on mine too. And I need to go first, since he's taken so many steps.

Sometimes you don't get all the time you think you need. But maybe you didn't need it at all. I've spent so much time planning for the future that I don't want to miss the present. Not with him. Not with us. "My mom had an affair with my dad's agent before she left him. Us. It was a mess. I never wanted to be like her. A liar," I say, closing the distance between us, then stepping into *the now*. "I want to do something about the way I feel," I say, borrowing his words from this morning. "I want to tell him."

Miles's eyes sparkle like a thousand stars. "Yeah?"

I laugh, powered by nerves, fear, and hope. "Why are you so excited?"

"Because I'm crazy about you, Shutterbug," he says, then pulls me into his arms. "And I want to be with you."

Emotions tighten around my throat as he hauls me closer, sweeps his lips across mine, then stops, cupping my face. "You want this?"

"I do," I say, breathless. "But what about...are you afraid?"

He shakes his head. "I was. I'm not anymore. You're worth it."

God, his certainty is the sexiest thing I've ever seen because it's the sturdiest. "Let's do it tomorrow," he says.

I laugh. "You have a game. He'll be in game mode."

"He's always in game mode," Miles says.

"I know. But he has meetings with his coaches, and practice, and video review, and the game itself. And I don't want to do it while he's at work. I'll take him to breakfast this weekend—to his favorite diner—and tell him then."

"Good. I fucking can't wait."

"Really? You're not afraid?"

"I want you more than I want the life I had before," he says, and a tear slips down my cheek. From his passion, from his certainty, from his heart. And from that sly smile on his gorgeous lips. "But why don't I show you?"

I arch a curious brow. "What do you mean?"

"Let's go geocaching."

Without a second thought, I take his hand, and we leave.

44

WHAT SHE MEANS

Miles

It's an evening in late November, so it's dark and a little chilly. But that's what jackets and lanterns are for. Sure, there are phone flashlights and real ones, too, but this camping lantern is way cooler—and extremely necessary —as we walk down Tennessee Hollow Trail. We're not taking the same path we did when we came here more than a year ago. There's a shorter route close to the same spot where we went on our very first date. Good thing, too, because there's a geocache we need to find.

"It's close to that other one," I say, eyes on my phone making sure to study it closely so she doesn't realize I'm faking it.

This cache isn't listed on any app.

"Are we almost there?" she asks.

"Right around the bend in the trail," I say, and when we near the footbridge, I grab her hand and point to a rock.

"It's across from the bench where we found the first one?" she asks, her voice laced with disbelief.

Fine by me.

"Looks like it," I say, keeping my poker face on and my tone even, giving nothing away. Inside, though, I can't wait.

We're a minute away, but it feels like forever until we reach a boulder by the creek. She looks around it, then stops. There's another lockbox next to it.

But it doesn't look like the first one. This one is silver, ornate, carved with intricate floral details—like wildflowers. In the middle of the box, there's an engraved L.

She bends closer, staring, her lips parting in amazement. "This is gorgeous," she says.

My heart is bursting, but I keep it together, pretending to read from my phone like it's a clue. "Here's the code to open it," I say.

I read off some clues I came up with quickly. They aren't hard, but they are specific.

"A hat trick. What a win is worth in the standings. A goal counts this much."

"Three, two, one?" she asks, but her blue eyes sparkle with recognition. She's putting it together—these are my clues. But she plays along, opening the box that I left here this morning.

Hoping we'd come back to it soon.

And then she gasps. Her hand flies to her mouth, then to the chest of her jacket.

"It's the heart locket," she says, her voice soft, like it's the last thing she expected. And that's perfect. More perfect than I'd imagined. And I've imagined this a lot.

"Is it the same one?" she whispers, like she doesn't want to dare to believe it.

It's like the sun is shining inside of me. "It's the same one."

She can't speak for several beautiful seconds that make my heart soar. Her reaction is even better than I'd imagined.

"But...how?" she finally asks.

"Let me put it on you, and I'll tell you," I say, my voice bursting with hope.

She shudders, then nods several times. "Yes, put it on me now."

Someone is eager, and I love it. She reaches for the locket, handing it to me before standing. Spinning around, she holds up her hair, revealing her gorgeous neck. I hook it in place, letting the metal fall against her skin, then turn her to face me. It's like the locket has come home.

"How did you do this? How is this possible?" she asks, her voice full of wonder.

"That day Birdie brought the replacement bracelet here for me?" I prompt, reminding her.

"Right. Since you'd retrieved mine already that morning," she supplies, nodding for me to go on.

"After she went, she happened to mention that there was also a locket in the box. Which made me realize you must have put it back that same morning. As soon as I returned from the road trip I was on, I took my chances and came here, hoping no one else had found the cache. The locket was still there, and so was the bracelet from Birdie. So, I left the bracelet, took the locket and held onto it."

Her hands cover her lips before she drops them and whispers, "For a year?"

"More than a year, sweetheart."

Her voice trembles as she asks, "But why?"

The easiest and the hardest reason ever. "I think I always knew I was never going to be able to resist you. No matter how hard I tried. Because I always knew it was you."

She clasps the locket tightly, covering it with her hand, then closes the remaining distance between us, looping her arms around my neck, our chests pressed together. I can feel that peace in the present again—because she feels the exact same way.

"I have something for you too."

I can't wait to see what she means.

* * *

We return home. She shows me a picture of the same locket. "I took it the day I returned it," she says, her voice soft. "So I could always remember that day." She pauses. "Do you want to frame it?"

"I do. For here."

Sometimes you just know when you meet the love of your life.

* * *

The plan is simple. As we walk into High Kick together— on the way to the arena the next afternoon, since really, what's the point in pretending we're not living together now?—Leighton reviews it with me. "I already texted him and asked him to have breakfast at our favorite café on Saturday."

"We'll be back from the road trip," I say, eager to show I remember every detail. We play Dallas at home tonight, then travel to Los Angeles late tonight for a game tomorrow.

"And Riley has the SAT on Saturday morning, so he'll be free," she continues, then adds, "it's a busy week already, with the meeting Melissa booked us on Friday morning with the bridal website about our collab, so the timing works out perfectly." Her voice picks up, like she's relieved the pieces are falling into place. "And...at breakfast, I'll tell him we're dating."

Best plan ever.

But as we approach the counter, I stop her, giving her a playfully stern look. "We're not just dating, sweetheart," I say, my voice low and steady, my gaze locked on hers.

She dips her face, as if she's a little shy. "I know."

We're at the counter, though, so I drop the conversation and say hi to my grandmother. Birdie's eyes are twinkling like she already knows. She doesn't, but in some ways, I think she always has.

Leighton orders her Earl Grey latte, since Birdie has won her over with it, and I opt for a vile coffee today, and we hand Birdie our to-go mugs.

"Coming right up, Boo," she says with a wink, sticking a decal with the name on the mugs before filling them.

When the drinks are ready, she sets them at the edge of the counter and beckons us over, whispering, "I'm earning my stripes, right? I've got a feeling, looking at you two."

Leighton lets out a hopeful breath. "Soon. Really soon. And thank you. You deserve it, Birdie," she says, but there's a touch of nerves in her voice.

"You know what? I do. Underground Grandma Matchmaking Society, you'd better look out! I'm running for president," Birdie quips, flashing a grin.

We leave and slide into my car. But before I turn on the ignition, I try to lighten the moment and give Leighton a mock-serious look. "So if we're not dating, what are we doing?"

"You're my boyfriend," she says, her voice cracking the slightest bit. Nerves again. I wish I could ease those nerves for her, but I know she's the one who has to tell her dad, and it's not going to be easy no matter how well we plan it.

"That's right. I'm finally—fucking finally—in the girlfriend zone with you," I say, not caring if I sound like a besotted fool. I am one with her. She grabs my tie, and I drop my mouth to hers for a hot, quick kiss, then drive to the arena. I swear I'll be counting the seconds until Saturday. I'll be ready, too—for the fallout. Ready to talk to Coach. Ready to let him know that even if he's pissed, even if he's mad, even if he can't stand me, I'm the man for his daughter. Her dad might bench me, freeze me out, or worse, cut me loose entirely. But losing her? That's not an option.

I counted down the days we were apart. Now I'll count the minutes until we're no longer a secret.

When we arrive, we're careful. We don't touch or flirt. I even walk her in through the main door so it doesn't look like she's getting special treatment by using the players' entrance. We're early since she needs to be here before the other players arrive so she can take pics of the guys showing up for work in their suits—myself included. As we walk, heels click sharply behind us, cutting through the Thursday afternoon pre-game hum of the arena. A polished, smooth voice calls out, "Leighton, baby."

Leighton freezes mid-step, the color draining from her

face. I follow her gaze to the well-appointed brunette with a perfect blowout striding toward us, and I know instantly.

That woman can only be Leighton's mom.

45

MOVE IT UP

Leighton

I haven't seen her in more than a year, yet she looks exactly the same. Like she's just stepped out of her latest Botox appointment. Her white teeth gleam, her lasered skin glows, and her perfectly styled hair shines. My mother has always known how to take care of herself, exuding the polished air of someone who runs a handbag empire.

But seeing her now feels like being caught in a spin cycle—she's glossy and chaotic all at once. I brace myself for impact.

"Wh-what are you doing here?" I stammer, my voice uneven and so unlike me.

"Honey, is that any way to greet your mother?" she asks, arching a brow.

There's no right way to greet someone you didn't expect to see today, especially not at work. "How are you?"

I try again, though my voice wavers like I'm the clothes tumbling in that wild washing machine.

"So glad you asked," she chirps, all smiles, clearly pleased I've spoken correctly now. "I'm in town for business—I have a very big retail partner here in San Francisco. But I figured I'd swing by, too, to share the good news. But first..." She turns to Miles, assessing him with interest. "You must be...let me guess...Miles Falcon."

Miles is stoic, game face on. "Yes, ma'am. Pleasure to meet you," he says, extending a hand, his polite smile unshaken despite the awkwardness as he waits for her to supply her last name.

"Grace. Grace Adley," she says with a smirk, taking his hand and shaking it.

"Nice to meet you, Ms. Adley," he says, and this moment feels surreal—like one of those uncomfortable dreams you wish you could wake up from. And yet, here we are as my mother practically bounces like she has a secret she's dying to divulge.

"But—confession: my name's about to change."

And the whiplash continues. I shake my head like she can't have just said that. Like I heard her wrong. "It's about to change?"

She turns directly to me, her tone exaggerated as she repeats, "Yes, it's about to change." She raises her volume unnecessarily and over-pronounces every word. It's condescending, but I don't have the energy to correct her. She's never taken the time to understand that I'm not broken.

But I'm not going to teach her now. Instead, I say, "Why is it about to change?"

I have a feeling though that I already know the answer since she said she's here to share good news. Still, it's best to let her have the spotlight. I already strongly dislike her being in my place of work. It feels unsettling, like I'm walking across a funhouse floor.

She takes her time, assessing me up and down, and even glances at Miles again. He seems to realize that he shouldn't be here for this conversation. Reading the situation perfectly, he decides this isn't his moment as my boyfriend yet. After a brief pause, he says, "I'll excuse myself so you two can have some time to catch up. It was a pleasure meeting you, Ms. Adley. Good luck with everything."

He strides away, heading toward the locker room.

"What's your news, Mom?" I ask, pasting on a smile I don't feel.

She beams at me, her excitement so bright it almost feels blinding. "Baby, I'm getting married!"

My stomach twists as she adds, "And you're never going to believe who I'm marrying. It's Michael! We got back together."

"Michael," I repeat flatly, needing a moment to process. Michael, as in my father's former agent. Michael, the man she had an affair with while she was married to my dad. Michael, whose "romance" with her only lasted about a year after the divorce.

Michael—the reason my family shattered when I was just fourteen.

"Yes! Isn't it wonderful? We ran into each other again, and sparks flew. It was magical. I knew he was the one who got away." She clutches her chest dramatically, like she's describing a scene from a Hallmark movie.

"I'm...so happy for you," I manage to say, forcing my lips to curve into a polite smile.

"And, of course, you'll take the photos for my

wedding," she says breezily, as if it's already a done deal. "I won't take no for an answer."

Her tone is chipper, but we both know it's not a joke. She expects my yes to be handed over on a silver platter.

"When is it?" I ask in my most professional tone possible.

She rattles off a date in two weeks, and my stomach sinks. I already know I have a conflict. "I have the final calendar shoot with the team that day."

Her smile vanishes into smoke. "Can't you just change it this time?"

Change it? Like I'm the one inconveniencing her by having a life?

I exhale, trying to steady myself. "I'll see what I can do."

The words taste bitter as they leave my mouth, and I want to walk them back. To say no. To tell her it's inappropriate to show up at my place of work to demand I take her pictures. But guilt is already clawing at me, forcing its way into every corner of my mind.

"Baby, I just love that you're such a family gal. Working with your dad, working with your mom. You're so loyal." She waves, adding, "I should go find Eleanor—we always make time for each other. I bet she'll love hearing all about the wedding!"

Of course she has friends in high places. It's her style. Always making herself at home.

What's my style though? Sneaking around?

Ugh. But in a couple more days, it won't be. I can simply be the storytelling photographer I want to be—creative, reliable, with an excellent eye.

Yes, that's who I'll be.

But as I walk away, I start to wonder. What am I waiting for?

Maybe I don't need to wait for Saturday. Maybe it doesn't need to be perfect—it just needs to happen.

If I keep looking for the perfect time, I'll keep losing the one thing we can't get back—time.

I check my phone. The guys arrive in fifteen minutes for the "suit walk."

Why wait? It's not going to be any easier no matter how perfectly I plan it.

As my mom disappears in a cloud of Dior J'adore and entitlement, I go the other way.

Straight to my dad's office.

My heart thuds louder with every step. Telling him now—a few hours before a game—feels terrifying.

But the thought of waiting another day feels worse.

46

LIPS READ

Miles

Holy shit.

I'm in the locker room staring at the text message Leighton sent me a couple of minutes ago.

She's supposed to be outside, snapping photos of the guys arriving, but I'm guessing that's the last thing on her mind right now. Because she's marching into the lion's den —right fucking now.

I want to tell her she's got this.

That I'll be there if she needs me.

That I can walk upstairs and explain to her father just how serious I am about his daughter.

But my woman's decided she needs to do this on her own, and this message is the best thing I've heard in a long time.

Leighton: I can't wait. Going to talk to him now. Wish me luck.

As I'm typing a **hell yes** reply, my brother's voice carries across the locker room. "What's that look on your face for?"

Tyler's here early, tugging at his tie. He's clearly not a fan of the suit walk dress code.

"Leave the tie on," I instruct. "Leighton wants a pic of both of us. She might be a few minutes late."

He shoots me a look that says he's had enough. "Dude. You need to deal with—"

I hold up a hand, cutting him off. "It's happening. Right now. The dealing with it."

His brow shoots up. "Yeah?"

"Yep."

He offers me a fist for knocking. "Good on you."

"Thanks," I say, but it feels strange to sit here doing nothing while she's upstairs having what's probably the most intense conversation of her life. I want to be there. To do something. To say something.

Tyler moves closer, sits next to me, lowering his voice. "You're good with whatever happens?"

I scrub a hand over my jaw. "The way I see it, I face off against brutes like you every day on the ice. I can handle this."

"Handle what?"

Fuck.

That's Coach. He's already here.

Tyler's eyes widen like saucers, and with his back to Coach, he mouths to me, *It was nice knowing you.*

I swallow hard, forcing myself to get my act together as I meet the cool blue eyes of Coach McBride. "Handle Dallas, sir," I say, keeping my tone steady.

Coach gives a sharp nod, his expression unreadable. "Good. After you do your promo or whatever it is, I'd like to chat with you."

Tension slams into me. Did she talk to him that quickly? Is he okay with it? She must've moved fast. But maybe...maybe it went okay? He's a good guy, after all. A great one. He's the one who helped turn my career around. And his daughter came to him right away to tell him about us—well, as fast as was reasonably possible. He probably appreciated that.

Hope sparks in my chest. "I'll be there, sir."

Meanwhile, Tyler is very interested in his phone.

Coach nods again, rapping his knuckles against the doorframe before walking off.

When the coast is clear, Tyler drops the act and bursts out, "What the fuck? Are you the luckiest guy in the world or what?"

"I don't even know," I admit, smiling dopily, reeling from surprise. Could it really have gone that well? Maybe it did.

"Did he just find out you're down bad for Mini Mac One and he's cool with it?" Tyler whisper-asks, as gobsmacked as I am.

"Stranger things have happened," I say, trying not to let my hopes get too high, but also letting them.

Seconds later, there are footsteps, and Asher's voice cuts across the room. "Hey, you slackers. Chanda says to get out there and make it look like you just arrived at work. Leighton's taking pics of the suit walk. And Little Falcon isn't wearing his sandals. He can learn," Asher says, gesturing to Tyler's feet and his visible socks with... are those illustrations of cat butts with his wingtips? For fuck's sake. He's always been a troublemaker.

But I guess today trouble is good.

I grab my coffee cup and head down the corridor so I can look like I just arrived. Leighton's already there, camera in hand, snapping shots of us like nothing's out of the ordinary. She's calm. Composed. Cool as ever. Like she always is behind the camera, where she's in control.

Yeah, it all went well with her dad.

Ford's heading down the hall, AirPods in, listening to some audiobook, like he always does before games.

Christian's striding toward the locker room, poised and confident, a true captain.

Max's game face is on, like always.

After the photos are done, I head back to the locker room, ready to text Leighton to ask how the talk went, but I spot her in the stairwell, pacing the narrow space, camera still in hand. She looks up when she sees me, relief and hesitation flickering across her face.

I step closer. "What's going on?"

She stops pacing and exhales. "I was waiting for you. I didn't want to text this."

Something about her tone sinks like a stone in my gut. "Tell me what?"

"I didn't talk to him. He wasn't alone," she says quietly, her fingers tightening on the camera strap. "Clementine was in his office."

My pulse races as my blood chills. "And?"

She swallows hard, locking her eyes on mine like she's bracing herself. "I heard them—well, *saw* them talking. The door was cracked open, but it was enough for me to see their faces. They were talking about a trade."

The word slams into me like a hit I didn't see coming. "Who?"

She's silent for a few seconds too long. "Your name came up, Miles."

Everything stops. My pulse pounds in my ears as I stare at her. I know trades are always a possibility, but distantly. They don't groom someone to be co-captain just to trade them. But also, I don't have a no-trade clause, given that I was picked up on waivers. In a few short years here, I've rebuilt my career into a solid, dependable, reliable one, and now...it's in peril?

"I'm sorry. I didn't want to tell you before the game," she says, her voice small. "But I couldn't...not tell you."

I look at her, forcing calm into my voice that I don't feel. "You did the right thing."

But I'm not calm at all. I'm reeling. Does Coach...know about us? Is that why he's thinking of trading me? Did he put two and two together when Leighton told him yesterday that she was staying with me? Then...I go cold everywhere. He must have figured it out for sure when she scheduled breakfast with him.

"Are you okay?" she asks with so much concern it nearly breaks my heart.

I have no idea how to answer, and when I hear Asher calling distantly—"Get your ass on the ice, Falcon"—it's simply time to go.

"I have to—"

"I know," she says.

Then we leave, heading in opposite directions, and that feels like a harbinger.

47

APPROPRIATE

Leighton

As my mom texts me that she's heading to Eleanor's suite for the game—*what an unexpected treat*—and asks if I want to join, I burst into laughter that feels wholly inappropriate for what just went down. Of course I don't want to join her. That's so *her,* barely caring that I'm here to work.

Fine, I'm not the main game action photographer, but I do have to capture the players tossing more crocheted dogs into the stands at the end of warm-ups, and it feels like the definition of irony. Me doing something sweet and innocent when I was anything but.

I try to stay focused as I snap, but my mind keeps replaying that moment in the office.

Dad stood near his desk, arms crossed, his face tight. Their voices were too low for me to hear, even with my hearing aids. But with my angle right outside the half open door, neither could see me, though their faces were right in my line of sight. I couldn't stop myself from glancing closer.

"Falcon," he'd said—like a question. "They want Falcon?"

I selfishly hoped they meant his brother, then hated myself for thinking that.

"They want points on the board," Clementine had replied, and my heart sank, knowing that meant Miles, on offense, not Tyler, on defense.

"It's a nice offer," she'd added.

There was a shuffle of feet, and I'd spun around, ducking into the stairwell, breathing like I'd run a marathon.

This couldn't be because of me. *Could it?* I had no idea, but even so I texted my dad that Mom was here. I didn't want him blindsided. He replied with a **thanks for the heads-up.**

I try to shove it out of my mind as the warm-ups end, and fans fill the arena. I don't have to stay for the game since I've finished my workload for the day, but what would I do at home? Pace and wait? The two people I need to talk to are here, so when Josie texts that she has an extra seat with Maeve, I join her.

I don't tell them a thing though. The situation is far too messy to let others in on—and too personal too.

Instead, I keep myself busy between texts with Melissa about our meeting tomorrow with the bridal website and Sabrina's message asking about photos for her new skating coach business. Good news, but it feels wrong to have it when I have no idea what's happening with my... boyfriend. But he's not really mine yet. Not till we do the hard thing.

I slump in the chair just as Wesley passes to Miles.

"Go, go, go!" Josie shouts, and when Miles scores, she throws her arms around me.

But I'm not even excited about the goal.

"What's wrong, friend?" she asks.

I wince. "I don't know. That's the issue."

Maeve gives me a sympathetic smile. "Do you want to talk about it?"

It's a good question, but I don't know where to start. "Maybe later," I say, and they both hug me. It helps. For now.

When the game ends—with a win—I make my way out of the stands and toward the hallway leading to the locker room. Maybe I'll grab some post-game photos since I still have my camera. Just to have them. Can't hurt, after all.

As I snap Miles and Wesley high-fiving, Tyler and Rowan heading to the locker room, and Christian and Hugo knocking fists, my mother strides over to me once again, a VIP pass dangling around her neck.

"Good news," she declares, just as I capture the last of the guys.

My stomach dips. "Mom, I'm working."

"And you're so good at it," she says breezily. "But I wanted to let you know I talked to Eleanor, and she said she thinks she can reschedule the calendar shoot. So you can do the wedding."

"Mom. I really wish you hadn't intervened in my work. I could have asked her myself," I say, though truthfully, I wasn't going to. But *fuck her* for taking away my autonomy.

"This way you don't have to worry about it."

"I didn't want you to," I snap, furious. "It's not appropriate."

She snorts a laugh as I lower the camera, letting it rest on the strap around my neck.

"What was that for?" I ask.

"Nothing," she says, rolling her eyes. Then, she adds casually, "Baby, appropriate or not, let's just say it's fine with me if you bring Miles to my wedding as your date."

I freeze. Ice in my veins. Terror in my heart.

"What did you just say?" I whisper.

The players have all gone. It's just us in the hallway now.

"Oh god, I'm so sorry," she says quickly, waving an airy hand my way. "I sometimes forget about your little issue." Then she raises her voice, over-enunciating each word: "Miles. He can be your date. Won't that be nice to go with your guy?"

And that's when my dad emerges from the tunnel at last, stopping dead in his tracks. Tilting his head. Eyes lasered right at me. "Your guy?"

My mom spins around. "Hi, Noah. Good to see you. What a great game."

But I don't care about the game, and neither does my father.

"What did you just say, Grace?" he asks, his voice deadly calm.

"I was telling Leighton to bring Miles to my wedding to Michael," she says, chipper as ever. "You can come too if you want."

Dad's gaze whips to me, eyes etched with shock, his jaw set hard.

"You're in a relationship...with Miles?" he demands, then turns to Mom. "And how did you know before me?"

Mom cackles like it's the funniest thing in the world.

"Oh, Noah, you were never good at anything besides hockey. You just can't catch on. They went to a coffee shop together before they arrived together, and they had the same name on the cups. *Boo.*" She pauses dramatically, then adds, "It's a nickname for a significant other."

I. Die.

"It's his dog's name," I blurt out defensively, too defensively, but it'll do nothing pointing out the name of Miles's mom's pup.

She laughs. "Leighton, baby. Really?"

"Yes," I shout because this isn't how my dad was supposed to find out. This is an epic shit fest.

"We're rooming together," I add, scrambling. "We got coffee on the way to work. That was it."

Oh, fuck. Oh, shit. I'm lying now. I'm *my mother.*

And I can't let that happen. I part my lips to speak, to tell my father the truth I'd planned to tell him before the game when my mother smirks and says, "Is that why you were in the stairwell together too?"

My heart plummets.

She saw us.

"Leighton," my father says heavily.

The ground is opening up beneath me and swallowing me whole. This is so much worse than I'd imagined.

Mom shrugs. "Besides, I saw the way he looks at you. Like you're the one. Really, it doesn't take much to put two and two together. But that was never your forte, was it, Noah?"

She's awful. But I'm worse.

I turn to my dad. "Yes, we're together, Dad," I say just as Miles emerges from the locker room, dressed to board the bus that'll take them to the team jet.

My dad snaps his gaze to the guy he wants to trade, looking at him like he can't believe he ever trusted him. Then he looks at me the same way.

I can't believe how badly I've messed everything up.

48

EXCUSES, EXCUSES

Miles

For several interminable seconds, Coach McBride doesn't move. He doesn't move a single goddamn muscle on his face. And I have no clue what that means because he has the best poker face I've ever seen. Then he says, "Excuse me."

That's it. Just *excuse me*—and he walks away, heading down the hall. Leighton's mom has the decency to look mildly chagrined as she says to her daughter, "I'll check in with you soon about the wedding photos," then disappears the other way.

Leighton doesn't answer her.

I don't know what to say.

My world is cratering. He might be trading me. But the fact that he might be mad at his daughter is what matters most. I look at Leighton. Then I follow him, catching up quickly with her right behind me.

"Sir, I'm sorry, but it's true. I'm crazy about your daughter—"

Coach holds up a stop-sign hand. "I am not interested in hearing about your emotions right now. I am disappointed in you—no, disappointed doesn't even begin to cut it," he says, his voice ice cold, like a knife's steel edge in winter.

Holy shit. I can't believe I'd thought this would be easy. I can't believe I was such a fool, thinking the fact that I've had a good relationship with him means anything. I'd thought him being a good guy would matter. But the problem isn't him—it's me. I pride myself on being a good guy. But I didn't act like one.

I swallow roughly, past the knot of shame in my throat. "I'm sorry, sir," I say, but that hardly cuts it. That doesn't do a damn thing to cover up my grave mistake.

Then he turns to the woman I love. "I am more hurt that you didn't trust me enough to tell me you had fallen for someone. Haven't I taught you that you can come to me for anything?"

Her eyes rim with tears, and she rolls her lips together, trying so hard—vainly—to hold them in. But one falls. "You have, and I'm so sorry," she says, and she sounds like she's breaking. All I want to do is hold her so she doesn't have to fall apart alone.

But he's not done with me either.

He points a finger my way, and it feels like I've been stabbed as he says, "And you—why didn't you have the guts to come to me and say, 'I'm involved with your daughter. Deal with it.'"

I flinch. He's not wrong. "You're right, sir. That's what I should've done."

"Damn right that's what you should've done. And now

you're going to get your ass on the bus. I'm finished with you."

Chastened beyond words, I turn around. Shame crashes over me like a wave, but underneath that is something sharper—a deeper ache. I've always wanted to do right by Coach McBride. I owe him. He turned my career around when I needed it most, and I've spent years trying to prove I deserved that chance.

Now I feel like I've lost his respect, and honestly, I probably have. It shouldn't hurt this much—but it does. It feels like someone I care about is walking away, and it hits me square in the chest, raw and familiar. Because I've felt this before—when my dad walked out and left us behind. When someone you look up to turns away, it doesn't just hurt. It hollows you out.

Behind me, Leighton's voice cuts through the quiet. "I'm so sorry. I came to the office today to tell you, Dad. I wanted you to know. That's why I was there. That's why I texted you. That's why I wanted to have breakfast with you."

"I can't talk about this right now. We'll handle this when I'm home. Good night, Leighton," he says, more stoic than I've ever seen.

Then, he's gone, up the stairs, and I rush back to her. Leighton's hands cover her face, tears streaking her cheeks. My heart shatters.

"Sweetheart," I say, desperate for words. All my schooling, all my talk of learning from my mistakes, and I've come up empty. Only that won't do. I've got to do right by her. I reach for her hands, peel them off her eyes. "We'll figure it out. I promise. Can I call you tonight when we land?"

She sniffs, swiping at her cheeks. "Go. Focus on playing. Don't worry about me."

"But I *do* worry about you."

"I don't deserve it," she chokes out. "I ruined everything. I acted like my mother. This was awful, and it's all my fault."

"Leighton, it's not. This blew up—it's too much for anyone."

"It *is* my fault," she insists, her voice ragged. "I ruined it for you. For him. For us all. And now this talk of a—"

She doesn't say the word *trade,* but it hangs between us like a curse. My chest tightens. I want to tell her we'll figure that out too. But what the hell do my assurances mean anymore? I'm supposed to be the calm, steady hand. Lot of good that did.

And while her words gut me, I don't want to make anything worse. "The whole thing...it just..." I drag a hand through my hair, searching for something to say to make it better.

But I find nothing.

"Go." Her tone softens but still cracks. "You need to play well tomorrow. It's an important game, and I can't ruin things more."

I hesitate, trying again. "I'll fix this, I swear."

She stops crying, staring at me like she's seeing straight through me. "You've got a team to fix. And you should talk to your agent. I can handle myself."

Dread roars through me. Does she want to *cool it*? I'm not sure I can even say those words. "What do you mean?" I ask, and there's horror in my voice.

Her gaze flickers. "Miles, your career was perfect before this. You've worked too hard to let me mess it up. Everything I planned is spiraling out of control, and I won't drag you down with me." She looks at the time on her phone. "And if you're not on the bus going to the airport, they will trade you for sure."

My gut twists. I want to argue, but I can't push her. Not now. And the fact is, she's right. I've got to get my ass on that bus. Plus, she has her meeting with Melissa tomorrow. She has her dad to face. Me? I've got this epic failure of leadership to answer for.

But as I watch her retreat behind her walls, something cracks inside me too.

49

THE BAMBOO BIKE MAKERS
STRIKE AGAIN

Leighton

"I feel we should tell her," Indigo says.

I privately groan as I walk through the doorway of the bedroom and into the living room, the early morning sun spilling through the window.

"I feel it's a mistake," Ezra says.

They must be really used to not having me around if they're speaking like this with me here. But they both turn at the same time as I trudge to the kitchen in my old apartment turned temporary refuge from my own bad decisions. From the mess I made of my life. I didn't have the heart to go to Miles's home last night. It felt wrong. Presumptuous, even. So I came here. Much to their surprise. And clearly, they're not really accustomed to me being here anymore. It makes sense. It's been close to a month since I've stayed, and I've only returned a few times to grab clothes.

Indigo meets my gaze and gasps, her braid whipping

around as she turns and faces me. "Oh. I didn't realize you were up."

Ezra winces, dips his head, his man bun bobbing with him. "Oops." When he looks up again, he turns to her and says, "I told you so."

These two haven't changed one bit. "So tell me what?"

Indigo twists her fingers together, looks at Ezra with *I'm sorry* written in her eyes, and says to me, "I feel you should know we've been performing fellatio and cunnilingus in your bedroom."

My eyes don't even pop in surprise. This is super on brand for them.

"I feel you should know I didn't want to tell you," Ezra adds.

I should be annoyed by them. I have been in the past. But I'm not—I'm jealous for the first time. Because the thing is—they're making it work better than I ever could. These two talk about everything. And what do I do? I keep secrets and push people away. Instead of being with the guy I fell for, I'm further apart from him than the miles between us.

I just shrug. I am a shell of whatever this morning. "It's fine," I say, not caring they've been getting it on in my room. I walk through the kitchen to the cramped bathroom, shutting the door with a loud rap.

I shower quickly, get dressed, and get out of there as fast as I can. I have my meeting with Melissa in a couple hours, but I'll use this free time to walk, think, and strategize over how to fix all of the relationships I've wrecked. Starting with my father.

But how? I have no clue what to do next. His words won't stop repeating in my mind—*I am more hurt that you didn't trust me enough to tell me you had fallen for someone.*

They cut deeper each time I play them in my head. I need my friends. Need to discuss what to do next, to figure out how to fix this.

But just as I'm tapping out a mayday text to the crew, a new text from Riley lands on my screen.

> Riley: School has a late start today. Guess who's wandering around Japantown at nine in the morning with nothing to do? Come whisk me away for a boba. 😊

My thumb hovers over the mayday text. I'll want that later, but right now, sister time is exactly what I need.

* * *

After I order a green tea boba and a mango bubble tea for Riley, she tells me she's all set for the SAT and refuses to study again for the next twenty-four hours. So once our drinks are ready, we grab them and wander around Japantown.

"Tell me something, anything not related to college or the SAT," she says.

I scoff as we pass a cute little shop peddling all manner of Hello Kitty merch.

Perhaps intrigued by my scoff, she arches a brow. "What have you got?"

In the past, I might have held back. She's sixteen, after all. But she's the only other person in the world who knows exactly what makes our dad tick. Besides, I've never treated her with kid gloves, and I don't want her to treat me that way either. I tell her everything because I don't have a clue how to fix this mess but I know I need to start with my father.

Riley's eyes widen until she stops mid-sip, dropping her metal straw in the cup. "Wow. You're kind of the bad child now."

"As if you were ever in consideration. You've always been good."

She flicks her hair but then turns serious. "This is actually a big deal," she says, heavily.

I sigh and take a sip. "Yeah, I know. What do I do, Riley?" I ask, hoping. Imploring.

She hums then stops outside a sticker store and says, "Look, I'm not always the good child. Dad and I have fought plenty. But when I've really screwed up, I always write him a letter. It's just easier to say everything on paper—and he listens better that way too."

Riley's words sink in. I've let this guilt fester. I've fed it, watered it, grown it. It's time to let it go.

With the truth.

* * *

I have a free hour before my meeting with Melissa, and I feel the pull of High Kick. It's our place—Miles's and mine. And right now, I don't feel at home anywhere else. Not with Indigo and Ezra, and not at Miles's place. Birdie's café has always been where I figure myself out, and maybe it's where I'll start fixing things with Dad too.

While I'm there, I finish a photo collage on my iPad. There are pictures of all the things my father has taught me over the years.

How to ride a bike.

How to read.

How to cook.

How to balance a budget. How to save money. And how to apologize from the heart.

He took pictures of me doing all of those things over the years, and the story they tell—it's the story of a girl who learned how to be a strong woman from her dad. He's not the only one who keeps photos of special moments and memories. I guess that's something else I learned from him.

In the middle of all those moments is a letter.

Dear Dad,

I can't say I'm sorry enough. Truly, I can't. I am very sorry that I hurt you. You taught me better. You've always listened to me.

But you also taught me to be independent. To handle the world. To make it on my own. And to trust myself. Part of trusting myself is choosing who I want to love. Part of choosing that also means knowing when it's time to share that love with others. I wasn't honest with you. For that I am sorry. But I am not sorry I fell in love with Miles Falcon. I'm not sorry that I'm going to pursue this relationship with him. I'm not sorry I want to be with him at all. He's kind, caring, and strong. He makes artichoke pasta, orders the tea I love, brings me wildflowers in a mason jar, and makes sure I have everything I need.

Best of all? He listens to me.

That means everything. As you know.

I also know you think no one is worthy of your daughters, but I'm here to tell you—he is worthy. Believe me. Trust me. I chose well, Dad. And I chose well in part because you taught me what I'm worth—the world. And he gives me that.

I hope you'll forgive me for lying, and I also hope you'll have dinner with my boyfriend and me sometime soon. Because I love you, and I love him.

Love,

Leighton

I email it to him and let out a sigh that's full of hope and wistfulness. Hope for the future. Wistfulness for the past. And a new faith in the present. When I'm done, I take a photo of the locket around my neck and I send it to Miles.

It's the story of us—our beginning and the rest of our story, waiting to be told in photos, in words, and in days and nights together.

After my meeting with Melissa and the bridal web site, I tug my hair into a ponytail and go to pole class early, repeating *you can do it* in my head as I ask Jewel to lower the volume of the music. "I can hear you better if you do that," I add, and I don't feel like I'm drawing attention to myself. I'm asking for what I need.

She doesn't bat an eye. "Of course. Thanks for letting me know," she says.

And this time, I can hear her above the beat as I spin. Turns out she's a pretty good instructor after all.

50

I'VE BEEN BUSY

Miles

A little earlier

Morning skate is brutal.

Coach works us harder than usual—sprints, extended drills, endless shots on goal. It's punishing, especially for an out-of-town practice. And I can't help but feel like it's my fault.

When it's over, Coach blows his whistle and sends us to the locker room. He paces as he reviews this afternoon's game plan, cool and methodical as ever, not once looking at me. When he finishes, he gives a curt nod and walks out.

I don't know if this is the start of a "you're dead to me" relationship or if he's treating me like someone he's about to trade. I called my agent this morning, and I'm waiting to hear back. But honestly? The trade isn't what I care about. The captaincy isn't either.

It's her. Just her.

But before I can figure out what to say to Coach, Rowan and Tyler pull me aside as we leave the locker room, their faces grim.

"Dude," Tyler begins.

"What the fuck?" Rowan seconds.

We understand each other perfectly with very few words. I scratch my jaw, blow out a breath. "Yeah. It's all kinds of fucked up."

And I'm no closer to knowing how to handle it than I was last night.

"I've never seen him like this," Rowan says, dead serious. "In all my years playing for him." Then he winces. "I heard some of what went down in the hall."

Ah, shit. That sucks, but of course, that's the price to pay. "Well, at least I don't have to tell you what's going on then."

"Right, but if he's pissed, you need to get this straightened out," Rowan says, all business. "No one likes an angry Coach."

"You gotta man up," Tyler adds.

They couldn't be more right. "But how? He already knows. I tried to say I'm sorry. What do I do? What would you do if this happened to one of your daughters?"

Tyler cringes. "I don't even want to think about my nine-year-old dating."

"Yeah, dude. Mia's seven, for fuck's sake," Rowan chimes in.

"You get my point though."

Tyler curls his nose. Rowan growls. They both sigh.

Then Tyler says, "First off, no man is good enough for my daughter."

"What he said," Rowan adds.

"But if anyone ever is, all I'd need to know is that she's his first priority. Always."

And all at once, I don't know why I didn't think of this sooner. But I've thought of it now.

"That's perfect. Thanks," I say, then head to find Coach right away. It's not hard. He's fifty or so feet away, down the corridor right outside the visitors' coaches' room, head bent over his phone.

I jog toward him. But as I get closer, I notice he's swallowing, rolling his lips together, then swiping at his cheek.

I slow my pace, studying him as he reads something on the screen. Is now a bad time? I really don't know, but still, I go for it. "Sir, could I please talk to you?"

He draws a big breath. "Not now."

Then he turns and walks the other way.

Fuck.

This man is not making it easy. I lean against the wall, scrubbing a hand across the back of my neck, regrouping.

I'll have to find another chance, even though I'm already so tired of waiting.

Good thing we have an afternoon game, though there's no time to nap—and I couldn't nap if I tried. Especially since my agent calls just as I'm wrapping up a light workout.

"All right, man. I called Clementine, but she hasn't called back yet. You have to remember there are always trade talks," Garrett says.

"You think it's just talks?"

"I hope so, Miles," he says, his tone careful, making no

promises. "But try to put it out of your mind and play the game. You've always been good at focusing."

A knot tightens in my chest. He's right on both counts, but I also know better than to trust reassurances. This game is all about leverage—and right now, I don't have much.

But I think about the word he just used—*focus*. I think about the future. I think about Leighton. And the thing is —maybe I don't have leverage. But I have options. I have choices. I have agency. I can always...*quit.*

I blink, my mind wrapping around an idea I've barely dared to entertain. And yet...here I am, entertaining it.

It's not my favorite choice, but it's one I could make. I don't have to accept a trade. I can also walk away and walk into something else entirely. Something different.

The knot loosens. I have choices and that is a damn good feeling. I can choose how to move forward. The thought of walking away is both terrifying and oddly freeing.

I thank Garrett and get ready to play, choosing to leave these career fears behind.

As I lace up, I know exactly what to say to Coach. I rehearse the words in my head. I'm a planner, a learner, an achiever. And that's a damn good thing. I also know how to focus on a goal. I hit the ice an hour later, putting the trade talks out of my mind.

Yes, I want to stay, but the only way to control that is by playing the best hockey I can. The rest is out of my hands, and that's fine by me. Because I know what I want and what I'll do to get it. I know what I've done too, on and off the ice.

And soon, Coach will as well.

* * *

He can't avoid me on the plane that evening. Well, maybe he can. But I won't let him. Even though he's talking to the assistant coach as we hit our cruising altitude, I push up and out of my seat and make my way to the second row. "Hey. I need a word, please."

"Sure," the assistant coach says, and that's that.

I grab his seat before Coach can give me the cold shoulder. I turn to him, and I don't ask—I tell. "I've been keeping secrets."

He barks out a humorless laugh. "I'm well aware of that, Falcon."

The hum of the plane and the chatter of conversations behind us make this moment private enough.

But I've got a hell of a lot more to say. "Sir, what I mean—"

He snaps his gaze to me, his blue eyes sharp and assessing. "I suspected you two had a thing once you finished up that dog-sitting situation," he says in a low, cool voice, and I'm momentarily surprised. But then I shouldn't be. He's a strategic man. He traffics in strategy. It's literally his job to read other teams and respond. "I thought you'd talk to me. I thought she respected me enough to trust me with this."

His words twist like a knife, but it's okay. I can handle it. And clearly, he needs to say this. "I saw there was some...flicker between you two. And I didn't hate it, but I figured you'd both come to me."

He takes a beat, and I seize the chance to wrestle back some of the conversation. "I wanted to, sir. But I also wanted to be patient with Leighton. To make sure she was ready on her own and not simply because I was ready," I say, and I'm not throwing Leighton under the bus but making sure he knows I prioritize her. Then I add, "But I had to take care of something first."

He blinks, perhaps confused, but barrels on. "I was waiting for you to realize you're the man for my daughter. To show me why you're worthy. Because I want someone who's willing to fight for her."

He has no idea. But he's about to find out.

"About that," I say, and I take a deep breath. Holy shit. This is hard, and I practiced. I practiced with others. I practiced in class. But now it's real. My hands feel clumsy already. What if I mess this up? What if he doesn't understand what I'm trying to say? But this is how I'll fight for her. I don't speak the words. I sign them.

I am serious about her. I will fight for her.

His jaw slackens, his hand hovering in the air like he's about to gesture but doesn't know what to do. It's like I've knocked his world off its axis. He's quiet for a long, long time, his gaze switching between my hands and my face, like he's seeing me in a whole new way. We might even be nearing San Francisco when he finally answers me in the same language.

When did you learn?

No more lies. No more secrets. I don't have to tell him what we did on our first date. But I can tell him I signed up for an American Sign Language class a year ago, right after I found out Leighton knew it.

I can hear her voice telling me during our first stairwell encounter: *Just in case.*

I'm not fast at making words. I'm not perfect. I'm sure I'm getting some things wrong, but I do it anyway. *A year ago.*

His lips part, but he says nothing, just shakes his head.

It's not like he's saying no though. It's like...he's astonished.

Well, there's more where that came from.

I keep going, signing what I practiced before I hit the ice today so I could get it right. *I want to communicate with her for the rest of her life.*

She doesn't need to use ASL now. She may not need it ever. But I want a future with her for all time. I can almost hear her teasing me, sharing her opinion, telling me I didn't have to go this far. But I do. She's worth it, and I want her to know I'll show up for her every day.

Coach covers his mouth, sighs heavily, then mutters, "Goddammit, Falcon."

I'm not sure what that means, and all the uncertainty rushes through my veins, but so, too, does the certainty of what's next—the future with Leighton.

His head hangs.

Disappointment reverberates through me. He's still pissed off? What can I ever do to win back his respect?

But then he turns to me again, speaking in a lower voice. "I'm mad at you, Falcon. But you are the right man for her."

And I'm a firework. I'm a ticker-tape parade. I'm hoisting Lord Stanley's Cup.

"Thank you, sir," I say, all the emotion and thrill coursing through me.

I'm about to pop out of my seat when he pushes down with his hand, telling me to stay. He lifts a finger to make a point. "But I don't know if a man who keeps this a secret is the right man for a captain," he says, and that's fair.

That's so fucking fair.

I sign back, *That's fine.* Then I say, "If that means I get Leighton, that's what I want."

"And the reason why is you kept secrets from me. I need to trust you if you're captain. Don't do that with her. Don't lie to her," he says, sterner than he's ever been.

"I won't. I promise," I say, so sincerely, meaning it to the depths of my soul.

He nods, accepting my word. "You better go fix what you fucked up."

I will, I sign, and I try to wipe the smile off my face, but it's useless. I can't stop grinning.

I pop up, but then one more question hits me before I reach the aisle. "Are you trading me?" I ask.

He tilts his head. "Why would you ask?"

"I heard a rumor," I say, and I'm not lying to him, but I'm not revealing my sources. "I hope the answer is no, but don't think you can get rid of me that easily. I'll make it work with your daughter no matter what," I say, smiling once again. Then signing, *She's worth it.*

"You fucking pain in the ass," he mutters. Then he sighs and says, "Chicago called about you. They floated a number. A good number."

I hold my breath. "And?"

He shrugs and smiles wickedly, a man with the upper hand again. "I said you're too valuable. Now don't make me regret it."

I could kiss the sky. "I won't, sir."

Then I head to my seat and fire off a text to Birdie, hoping she'll get it when we land. I really need her to earn her Underground Grandma Matchmaking Society stripes tonight.

51

FIRST KISS

Leighton

High Kick isn't even open this late. It's past nine in the evening, but Birdie called, desperate, begging me to come in to take some pictures.

"I need them tonight, darling. It's completely my fault. My baker made the most incredible cinnamon rolls and I'll be offering them tomorrow. But I need a decent picture for social. I can't take photos to save my life," she'd said. "Do this for me and I'll leave the shop to you in my last will and testament."

"You'll do no such thing and I'll be there in an hour," I'd told her.

"Perfect. Can't wait," she'd said.

So here I am, answering the SOS. Even by Birdie standards, it's unusual. But I love all her eccentricities. I love, too, the way she relies on me. Fact is, I rely on her as well, and I really should let her know that. But also, being here will keep me busy till I can see Miles again. He returns sometime tonight and he texted me after I sent that photo saying, *I can't wait to see you.*

No idea when that'll be, but I know it'll be soon. I know, too, even if I've messed things up, I have the power to fix them. By talking, writing, speaking, photographing, communicating. My father wrote back to my email with six simple words: I love you and thank you.

And that was enough. Now, I rap on the locked door to High Kick and Birdie hustles over, unlocks it, and yanks it open. "Hi, darling! Thank you for coming, you're simply the best," she says, then shuts the door in a flurry, and adds, "would you look at the time."

Then she's off with a wink, rushing to the back of the shop and I'm...bewildered.

Until I turn to the counter where twinkle lights are set up behind it, flickering softly. Where mason jars of wildflowers line the coffee bar. And where the man I love stands behind the counter. Waiting. His hands parked on the Formica.

Like he's ready to take coffee orders.

It's just him and me here in the shop, and my heart sprints toward him. It's been too long—the last twenty-four hours. Absently, I lift my hand and touch my heart locket as I walk toward him, like I'm in a trance.

"Hi," I say.

"Hey," he says, then smiles like he has a secret and adds, "what would you like to drink?"

Okaaaay. We're really role-playing here at this barista-and-customer thing. I look at the chalkboard menu and play along. "An Earl Grey latte."

But he tilts his head in confusion, then points to his ears.

Oh. He's wearing AirPods. "I can't hear you. I have AirPods in," he says.

I furrow my brow. Um, he can just take them out. But I say again, "An Earl Grey latte."

And he shakes his head, then raises his hand and signs, *Do you want steamed milk and I love you on top?*

I. Have. Chills. From the confession, but also the way he's made it. I start with that. "You...know...ASL?"

His smile is wider than the city. More satisfied than all the cats in the world. And all for me as he signs, *I started learning last year.*

The words echo through my body, settling deep in my heart. I answer him in the same language. *You did? Why?*

I believe my eyes but I also can't quite believe he's done this.

Yes. Because I love you.

And my heart flies as joy floods every cell in my body. "I love you too."

Then, he hops over the counter. Hops! Cups my cheeks, drops his mouth to mine and kisses me soft and tender, like he's been counting down the seconds till he saw me again.

I feel the same way. When he breaks the kiss, I wobble. My knees are weak and I'm melting but he steadies me, looping an arm around me.

"On the plane, I told your dad I learned it. I told him I'll fight for you. And then he told me to fix everything with you," he says, then grins. "Did it work?"

I laugh, then grab his face and pull him closer. "It worked, Miles. It definitely worked. Everything worked." I feel like I'm floating as I kiss him again, but I still have so many questions. Like this one. "Are you being traded? Because I'll stay with you even if you're traded. We can make it work. Long distance. Anything. I'll make it work with you." And that's the most vulnerable thing I've ever said in my whole life, but I mean it completely. It feels good and right to say those words to him.

He shakes his head, that grin never leaving his face. "Nope. Chicago called but Coach said I was too valuable. I don't think I'll be captain, but I don't care. Want to know why?"

"Why?" I ask, and I should be sad but I can't be when he's so happy.

"Because I got you," he says, then he kisses me once again, making my head swim with happiness. When he lets go, he takes a step back and signs—not fast, not perfectly, but clear nonetheless—*Come home with me.* Then he says, "Move in for real. Tonight. And don't ever leave."

This man. This love. This night. "You had me at 'I've got this,'" I say. Those were the first words he ever said to me when he held open the door to this shop.

He takes my hand and we go, the twinkling lights illuminating the way.

But we make a pit stop at the apartment and toss the rest of my things in grocery bags first. I won't miss this place one bit. As we slide back into his car, my belongings in tow, I feel like it's the getaway vehicle and we've made our great escape into our happily ever after. As we go, I have so many questions about him learning ASL. Where? How? Who was the teacher? He tells me he took a class through a local university from a funny, sarcastic deaf teacher named Daya, who promised she'd keep the secret that he was learning it.

"You should meet her someday. And the other students—they're mostly deaf. They had to keep it a secret too," he tells me. "Which means that's one of the first words I learned to sign."

I laugh, then laugh again when he takes his right hand off the wheel to tap his thumb twice against his lips, right as I'm doing the same.

But we're no longer a secret, and that feels so good.

We cruise through the city, the lights of the Golden Gate Bridge calling us home. Soon, we're pulling into his garage and heading inside.

Home, I sign, feeling it deep in my soul.

You're home, he signs, then he scoops me up, tosses me over his shoulder, and carries me up the stairs.

And he shows me how much he's missed me in those twenty-four hours, kissing every inch of my body, touching me everywhere, driving me wild, then fucking me like I'm the love of his life.

When we're naked and sated, lying there in bed, he traces the locket with his finger.

"Open it," I say, and now I'm the one with the secret.

His eyes glint as he flicks it open. A wicked smile crosses his face as he gazes at the photo I've put in it. A shot of our first kiss.

The start of our story.

EPILOGUE: YOU AND ME

Miles

As Leighton comes down the stairs, I finish making her Jasmine Downy Pearls and set a steaming mug on the counter. She's still on the phone, wrapping up her call.

"I'll have the calendar proofs to you later this morning." A pause. "Yes, it looks incredible. I think you'll be thrilled." Another pause. "We can look at them together. And Melissa has her sweet and sexy cookies for you."

With a laugh, she says goodbye and heads over to the counter, eyeing the mug. "Well, aren't you the perfect man?"

"Fact," I say.

She smiles, takes a sip, and sighs happily. "There's only one thing that would make this better."

"I know," I say, "but you'll have to wait till tomorrow. He's coming then."

She pouts. "I can't wait."

"Yes, you can," I reply, handing her a canvas bag. "In the meantime, here's something for tonight's game."

With a curious smile, she dips her hand into the bag and pulls out a jersey with my last name and number on it. Her fingers run over the stitching, and her face lights up. I love seeing her in my jersey. It doesn't have a captain's "C," but that's okay. Coach explained that even though he does trust me now, he didn't want anyone thinking he's playing favorites. I get it. Funny how you can work so hard for something only to realize it wasn't what you really wanted after all.

"I love showing everyone that Twenty-One is mine," she says, taking another sip before glancing at the clock. "I need to meet with some of the Renegades' wives today."

The wives of some of the football players have started doing boudoir calendars too, and they've been a huge hit —no surprise there. So has her collaboration with Hugo's wife, Melissa. Between the cookies and bridal packages, her business is thriving, and I couldn't be prouder. Her boudoir photography is booming as well and more profitable than ever, thanks to her decision to raise her rates. She's busier than ever.

Good thing she wrapped up her assignment with the Sea Dogs so she can focus more on her passion—shooting boudoir and empowering women. And she's damn good at it.

Another thing she rocks at? Taking glamour shots of adoptable dogs for Little Friends. She volunteers for the rescue, lending her shutterbug services to snap pictures of pups in snazzy bandanas posing for the camera. The pics have helped the shelter find even more homes.

But here's what she doesn't take pictures of—her mother's handbags. She didn't take photos of her wedding either. I'm so damn proud of her for cutting that kind of toxicity out of her life.

Tonight, though, she's not working. And I get to see her at a game in my jersey. That's something I've always wanted. And now I have it. She's worn mine before but they're big and baggy on her. I had one custom-made to fit her and seeing her in it feels like a dream. A dream that's become real.

Like all these days and nights with her in our home.

Before she leaves, I tell her I'll see her later at the game.

"I'll blow a kiss from the stands."

"You better," I say.

A little later, as morning skate comes to an end, Coach calls me over and I join him by the boards, my stick in hand, my breath coming fast from the workout.

"Winters is stepping down at the end of the season. I'll need you to be captain then," he says.

There's only one answer. "Yes, sir."

Pride suffuses me, along with the feeling that I've earned it this second time around.

When I head into the locker room, Rowan is grumbling about some date Hugo's trying to set him up on with a friend of a friend of Melissa's. "Dating is hell," he says.

"He's at it again?" I ask.

Tyler smirks. "We're going to have to babysit him at every team function at this rate," he says, having quickly learned that the anti-romantic Rowan is the king of grumps, especially when it comes to all things dating.

"That is not true. You don't have to babysit me," Rowan says, scowling.

"Denial will get you nowhere," I say, laughing. Then, out of nowhere, I flash back to something my mom once said. About a matchmaker. An idea clicks into place—a potential solution for Rowan. One I'll have to mention to Tyler later.

For now though, I turn to my brother, asking, "Is Agatha still on vacation?"

He sighs heavily, probably still bummed that his kid's nanny has been so homesick for her own family, that she's been returning to Los Angeles as often as she can. "Don't remind me. At this rate, I'll need to find a new nanny soon."

"Good luck, man," Rowan puts in. "That is never easy."

That night, though, I put all thoughts of them aside and play for my girlfriend, who's in the stands with her friends, wearing my jersey.

Ah, who am I kidding? She's not my girlfriend. She's my future wife.

* * *

Leighton

As I'm heading toward the arena for tonight's game, I'm chatting on the phone with Isla Marlowe. "Sure, I can talk about the ideas of grandma as a matchmaker on your podcast."

"Great," says the upbeat woman who's become a friend recently. "I've been wanting to explore all manners of matchmaking. How singles are moving away from apps and trying more tried and true ways. And your story fits."

"Birdie is the ultimate matchmaker, that's for sure," I say, then pause. I don't know why I didn't think of this before. "Do you want to come to a hockey game soon? With Sabrina and me?"

"That sounds fun," she says.

And I smile, grateful to keep making new friends. To give back in a way. Once upon a time, Everly took me under her friendship wing and introduced me to some amazing women who are now my besties. I'd love to do the same.

We finish the call and I head inside.

A little later, as Tyler blocks a shot on goal, Sabrina cheers. "Go, Falcon!"

She's here with me tonight, along with Josie, Maeve, and Fable. Josie lifts a curious brow at the cheer, but says nothing.

I invited Sabrina since we've been getting closer since I took photos for her new figure-skating coaching business.

For a moment, Sabrina's cheer feels personal. But when Max blocks the next one, her voice rings out, clear and confident, "Nice block, Lambert."

Even so when Tyler skates off for a line change, he glances in our direction. Or really, hers.

I glance at Sabrina and smirk. "I think he has a crush on you."

She laughs it off, lifting her hand with the shiny diamond on it. "I'm taken."

"And he still has a crush on you," I tease.

"Pretty sure Leighton is right," Josie chimes in.

Sabrina smiles again, but she won't touch that topic, it seems. Instead, she says to me, "Speaking of being taken, maybe you can take my wedding photos?"

"I'd love to," I say. The conversation shifts from Tyler to her upcoming wedding plans, and soon the game ends with a loss.

Shame. But you win some and lose some. After I say goodnight to my friends, I wait for Miles in the corridor, but my dad finds me first. He walks up, his gaze landing on my jersey. "Nice jersey," he says dryly.

"Thanks, Dad."

"But McBride would be better," he teases, squeezing my shoulder. "It's nice seeing you at games."

"I've been to games before," I point out.

"I know. And I like it," he says. His voice is quieter than usual, like he's letting me know this matters to him. We make plans to grab breakfast at our favorite café this weekend, and all feels well. I'm glad too that he started seeing someone. A kind, funny woman who Birdie—of course—set him up with.

What feels best though is when Miles and I head home together. It feels like Christmas Eve. In the morning, we pick up a grumpy little Beagle mix named Oliver. He's ten years old and needs a foster home until he finds a forever family. We dog-sit for Miles's mom sometimes, and we've talked about fostering for months. When we heard Little Friends needed fosters for senior pups, we knew. We just knew it was time.

He's our first foster, and we already have a hot tub for him. Once he's home, he explores every inch of the place before settling into his warm bed with a contented sigh.

This too—fostering dogs together—feels like home.

And it feels like our future. Wide open and wonderful. Full of the great unknown. I'm ready to step into it with Miles, growing and changing together. But right now, I focus on the present as he slides a hand through my hair, the other touching my locket. I close my eyes as he kisses me once again.

* * *

Binge the entire Love and Hockey series today!

Want to see how generous, filthy-mouthed hockey star Wesley falls hard for his teammate's little sister? **Grab The Boyfriend Goal Here!**

Max and Everly's enemies-to-lovers, player and the publicist, forbidden romance is told in **The Romance Line!**

Asher and Maeve's brother's marriage of convenience hockey romance with an absolutely obsessed hero is here in **The Proposal Play!**

Rowan's romance is coming soon in Merry Little Kissmas and be sure to turn the page for a sneak peek of Tyler and Sabrina's single dad/nanny romance in The Overtime Kiss!

For more Miles and Leighton, click here for an extended epilogue or scan the QR code!

EXCERPT - THE OVERTIME KISS

Tyler

Ah, there's nothing quite like a night off from the kids. Don't get me wrong—I love those two little stinkers more than I love playing hockey. But an evening without a request for mac and cheese? Without complaints about who got more or whose turn it is to do the dishes? I'll happily take it.

It's been so long since I've had a free night that I'm barely even sure what to do with my time. After finishing dinner with my agent at a restaurant here in Cozy Valley —a productive meeting where we agreed to focus on making the next season better, both on the ice and with sponsorships—I head to the hotel bar. I'm staying overnight in this small town about forty minutes outside San Francisco, since I'm playing golf tomorrow in a local tournament some friends here roped me into joining. But until tomorrow morning, no one needs me.

When I catch sight of the baseball game on the big screen, I know this is exactly what a perfect night off looks like. The bar has a warm, relaxed vibe, with wood-paneled walls, a long polished counter, and a vintage record player playing a pop tune I won't admit to my teammates that I know by heart. A row of wooden stools lines the bar, and there's a faint hum of chatter from a handful of patrons. A woodcut sign boasts brews crafted locally.

I grab a seat, say hello to the bartender, a weathered old dude in a vintage concert T-shirt whose name tag reads Ike. Fitting. He slaps down a coaster and asks, "What'll it be?"

"Whatever you've got on tap," I say, since I'm not picky, and I bet he thrives on being trusted to pick a beer.

With a quick nod, he says, "You look like a lager type."

"Works for me." I settle in, letting the pressure of the past season—a tough one with a new team—melt away as I focus on the game on TV and the cold glass of beer Ike brings me. Trouble is, the game isn't exactly relaxing. By the second inning, it's clear the umpire needs to be tossed out.

"Are you kidding me? That was such a strike," I mutter.

"Nope. It dipped by the outside corner, Tyler. Hanging curve that hung too long," a confident, feminine voice says. Someone who clearly knows me.

I turn toward the sound, and my brain fractures for a second. It's like running into your doctor in the cereal aisle—that is, if you have a wildly inappropriate crush on your gorgeous, sassy doctor.

Or your ten-year-old's ice skating teacher, who's incomprehensibly here in a small town hotel bar instead of the city where I see her every seven days, but who's counting.

Sabrina Snow flops down onto the seat next to mine in a cloud of white poof and a lopsided tiara. But she doesn't look like the polished, pink-cheeked, ponytailed woman who teaches Luna how to execute toe loops every Wednesday afternoon. With her wind-whipped blonde hair, tiara askew, and a wedding dress that seems completely out of character, Sabrina looks like she's seen better days. Especially since she's kicking a foot back and forth—and I can't help but notice she's wearing mismatched shower slides. One pink, one orange.

"Sabrina?" I blurt out, the cognitive dissonance choking me.

"That's me," she says, dryly. Too dryly. Then, she seems to force out a laugh. "Fancy meeting you here."

"Sure is," I say since running into this woman on her wedding day was not on my bingo card. Especially since – call it a gut feeling – I'm not sure the groom is around.

"How's Luna? What's she up to since I saw you all the other day? Are you having a fun little family getaway?" she asks, but her voice is full of manufactured cheer.

I shake my head. "Nope. The kids are with my mom and her husband." I'm about to say *and you*, but I think the better of it. Read the room and all.

But with a level of hope that honestly shames me, my gaze dips to her left hand. That massive rock that's been mocking me since I met her is still shining brightly, but her smile isn't. Doesn't take a genius to know she hasn't removed the ring yet, but I can make an educated guess — the bling's on a goodbye tour. I shouldn't like the fact that she's single so much. But whether her status is self-induced or not, I make the only offer I can. "Let me buy you a drink."

She sighs heavily, like the weight of the world escapes her with that one breath. "I guess it's obvious I need one."

I don't say, *Yeah, it seems like your wedding day went sideways,* or, *What the hell happened?* She'll tell me when she's ready. Instead, I keep it light. "You are in a bar, so I figured you might want one—context clues and all."

She gives me the smallest smile that seems to say thanks for that softball answer. With a glance down at her skirt, she gathers some material in her hands, then flicks it dismissively. "I was heading for the local rink, but it was closed. So yeah, it really feels like a tequila kind of day now."

I'm guessing I've got a jilted bride on my hands rather than a runaway one, but I've seen enough movies to know the two usually go hand in hand.

Preorder The Overtime Kiss here!

Want to be the first to know of sales, new releases, special deals and giveaways? Sign up for my newsletter today!

A NOTE FROM THE AUTHOR

Dear Reader,

Leighton's experience with hearing loss, the type she has, the hearing aids she uses and the way she interacts with the world is based on extensive research into hearing loss, interviews with people living with hearing loss, and my own personal experience. As someone with the same type of hearing loss Leighton has—moderate sensorineural hearing loss—some of Leighton's experiences interacting with people, places, sound, music and noise come directly from my own lived experiences, and others come from insight and interviews with people living their best lives with hearing loss. I am deeply grateful to Sophia Soames and Zach Perez for taking the time to share their experiences with hearing loss and hearing aids with me. Their insight and stories about work, family and navigating today's world informed Leighton's backstory and her present day experiences, as did my own. I am also deeply appreciative of Dayamarali Espinosa, who shared her expertise in ASL with me to help inform Miles's efforts to learn the language. Thank you to Grace Wynter for her sensitivity read as well. I am so grateful for all of you. Any mistakes are entirely my own. And, ultimately, everyone's experience of hearing loss is unique to the individual.

My best,

Lauren

ACKNOWLEDGMENTS

Thanks to so many amazing people! I am grateful for Rae, Lo, Kim, KP, Lauren, Rosemary, Sharon, KP and many others!

Thank you to Lo for you guidance on the story and your insight. Thank you Kayti for brainstorming. Thank you KP for seeing the whole thing through.

I am so appreciative of Sharon for checking all the hockey and guiding me through the sport. Thank you to Rae and Kim for helping me fine tune details.

With deep gratitude to my editors Lauren and Rosemary who make stories shine!

Big love to my author friends who I rely on daily — Corinne, Laura, AL, Natasha, Lili, Laurelin, CD, K, Helena, and Nadia, among others.

Thank you to my family for making it all worthwhile.

Most of all, I am so amazingly grateful to you — the readers — for picking this up! I hope you love Miles and Leighton like I do!

BE A LOVELY

Want to be the first to know of sales, new releases, special deals and giveaways? Sign up for my newsletter today!

Want to be part of a fun, feel-good place to talk about books and romance, and get sneak peeks of covers and advance copies of my books? Be a Lovely!

MORE BOOKS BY LAUREN

Double Pucked

A sexy, outrageous MFM hockey romantic comedy!

Puck Yes

A fake marriage, spicy MFM hockey rom com!

Thoroughly Pucked!

A brother's best friends +runaway bride, spicy MFM hockey
rom com!

Well and Truly Pucked

A friends-to-lovers forced proximity why-choose hockey
rom com!

The Virgin Society Series

Meet the Virgin Society – great friends who'd do anything for
each other. Indulge in these forbidden, emotionally-charged,
and wildly sexy age-gap romances!

The RSVP

The Tryst

The Tease

The Dating Games Series

A fun, sexy romantic comedy series about friends in the city and
their dating mishaps!

The Virgin Next Door

Two A Day

The Good Guy Challenge

How To Date Series (New and ongoing)

Friends who are like family. Chances to learn how to date again.
Standalone romantic comedies full of love, sex and meet-cute
shenanigans.

Shut Up and Kiss Me

Kismet

My Single-Versary

Ballers And Babes

Sexy sports romance standalones guaranteed to make you hot!

Most Valuable Playboy

Most Likely to Score

A Wild Card Kiss

Rules of Love Series

Athlete, virgins and weddings!

The Virgin Rule Book

The Virgin Game Plan

The Virgin Replay

The Virgin Scorecard

The Extravagant Series

Bodyguards, billionaires and hoteliers in this sexy, high-stakes series of standalones!

One Night Only

One Exquisite Touch

My One-Week Husband

The Guys Who Got Away Series

Friends in New York City and California fall in love in this fun and hot rom-com series!

Birthday Suit

Dear Sexy Ex-Boyfriend

The What If Guy

Thanks for Last Night

The Dream Guy Next Door

Always Satisfied Series

A group of friends in New York City find love and laughter in this series of sexy standalones!

Satisfaction Guaranteed

Never Have I Ever

Instant Gratification

PS It's Always Been You

The Gift Series

An after dark series of standalones! Explore your fantasies!

The Engagement Gift

The Virgin Gift

The Decadent Gift

The Heartbreakers Series

Three brothers. Three rockers. Three standalone sexy romantic comedies.

Once Upon a Real Good Time

Once Upon a Sure Thing

Once Upon a Wild Fling

Sinful Men

A high-stakes, high-octane, sexy-as-sin romantic suspense series!

My Sinful Nights

My Sinful Desire

My Sinful Longing

My Sinful Love

My Sinful Temptation

From Paris With Love

Swoony, sweeping romances set in Paris!

Wanderlust

Part-Time Lover

One Love Series

A group of friends in New York falls in love one by one in this
sexy rom-com series!

The Sexy One

The Hot One

The Knocked Up Plan

Come As You Are

Lucky In Love Series

A small town romance full of heat and blue collar heroes and
sexy heroines!

Best Laid Plans

The Feel Good Factor

Nobody Does It Better

Unzipped

No Regrets

An angsty, sexy, emotional, new adult trilogy about one young
couple fighting to break free of their pasts!

The Start of Us

The Thrill of It

Every Second With You

The Caught Up in Love Series

A group of friends finds love!

The Pretending Plot

The Dating Proposal

The Second Chance Plan

The Private Rehearsal

Seductive Nights Series

A high heat series full of danger and spice!

Night After Night

After This Night

One More Night

A Wildly Seductive Night

Joy Delivered Duet

A high-heat, wickedly sexy series of standalones that will set
your sheets on fire!

Nights With Him

Forbidden Nights

Unbreak My Heart

A standalone second chance emotional roller coaster of a
romance

The Muse

A magical realism romance set in Paris

**Good Love Series of sexy rom-coms co-written with Lili
Valente!**

I also write MM romance under the name L. Blakely!

Hopelessly Bromantic Duet (MM)

Roomies to lovers to enemies to fake boyfriends

Hopelessly Bromantic

Here Comes My Man

Men of Summer Series (MM)

Two baseball players on the same team fall in love in a
forbidden romance spanning five epic years

Scoring With Him

Winning With Him

All In With Him

MM Standalone Novels

A Guy Walks Into My Bar

The Bromance Zone

One Time Only

The Best Men (Co-written with Sarina Bowen)

Winner Takes All Series (MM)

A series of emotionally-charged and irresistibly sexy standalone
MM sports romances!

The Boyfriend Comeback

Turn Me On

A Very Filthy Game

Limited Edition Husband

Manhandled

If you want a personalized recommendation, email me at
laurenblakelybooks@gmail.com!

CONTACT

I love hearing from readers! You can sign up for my newsletter today! Find me on Instagram at LaurenBlakely-Books, Facebook at LaurenBlakelyBooks, or online at LaurenBlakely.com. You can also email me at lauren blakelybooks@gmail.com